The
SECRETS
WOMEN
KEEP

Also by Fanny Blake

What Women Want
Women of a Dangerous Age

The
SECRETS
WOMEN
KEEP

Fanny Blake

First published in Great Britain in 2013 by Orion Books,
an imprint of The Orion Publishing Group Ltd
Orion House, 5 Upper Saint Martin's Lane
London WC2H 9EA

An Hachette UK Company

1 3 5 7 9 10 8 6 4 2

A CIP catalogue record for this book is
available from the British Library.

ISBN (Hardback) 978 1 4091 2845 8
ISBN (Trade Paperback) 978 1 4091 2847 2
ISBN (Ebook) 978 1 4091 2846 5

Typeset at The Spartan Press Ltd,
Lymington, Hants

Printed and bound by CPI Group (UK) Ltd,
Croydon, CRO 4YY

The Orion Publishing Group's policy is to use papers that are natural,
renewable and recyclable products and made from wood grown in sustainable
forests. The logging and manufacturing processes are expected to
conform to the environmental regulations of the country of origin.

www.orionbooks.co.uk

For my mother and sister, with love

We never knows wot's hidden in each other's hearts; and if we had glass winders up there, we'd need to keep the shutters up, some on us, I do assure you!

Martin Chuzzlewit by Charles Dickens

September

I

The dark outline of the doorway framed a section of the sun-drenched garden beyond, the brilliance of the outdoor colours such a contrast to the house's shady interior. From where she was standing, Rose could see the vivid splashes of roses, geraniums and bougainvillea, the silver green of the olive trees in the distance, the startling blue of the sky. But she was enjoying being indoors. Even here she could feel the heat, despite having pulled the shutters to against the sun, aware of how much the temperature outside had risen since breakfast time.

Eve and Terry had announced they'd be arriving at Pisa around midday, then driving down, so a simple late lunch would be perfect. Rose pulled the strings of her apron around her so that they tied in front of her stomach, not quite the washboard of years ago, but could be worse given two children and a healthy appetite. Choosing a couple of onions and some garlic from the hanging mesh basket and the plumpest tomatoes from the dish, she laid them by the small bunches of oregano and thyme that she'd snipped from the garden. As she began to chop, she hummed an indecipherable tune under her breath. Just another day in paradise.

'What's for lunch?' Daniel had snuck up behind her, putting his arms around her and planting a kiss on the back of her neck.

Smiling, Rose turned to him, her face lifted to his. 'Wait and see.'

'Spoilsport!' But he put a hand to her cheek then kissed her again, this time on the lips. Slow and caring. She leaned into him, her eyes closing.

When they finally separated, Rose glanced at the station clock over the oven. 'Look at the time! I've got to get on.' She removed his hands from the curve of her back. 'I'll never be ready otherwise.'

Turning down the corners of his mouth in exaggerated disappointment, Daniel picked up the beach towel from the back of the chair where he'd left it. 'If there's really nothing I can do, I'm off for a swim.'

She stretched up to kiss his cheek. 'Don't worry. It's all under control. Just be ready for when they get here.'

He strolled out of the house and down the slope, eventually disappearing through the gate to the pool. Only then did Rose return her attention to lunch.

Pottering about the kitchen was one of her great pleasures, especially here in Casa Rosa, the renovated farmhouse that they had bought so many years ago. Back then it was a dilapidated shell, but they'd been seduced by its hillside position. They tracked down the local farmer, then endured the time-consuming process of unearthing the family members who owned the house, securing agreements one by one until finally it was theirs. She smiled. Daniel had been a more patient man then. These days, he would never tolerate the wait. Slowly, together, they had brought the place back to life, bringing the family here every summer for more years than she could remember; all good memories.

Rose thought of her daughters with a fond sigh. Anna, the elder, should be arriving later that afternoon, no doubt in a typical whirlwind of plans and problems. As for Jess . . . there was a question mark hanging over her visit after the recent clash with her father. Out of sheer pique, she had announced that she wouldn't come this year after all. She would be staying at home with Adam and their toddler, Dylan.

'Dylan! Ridiculous name! We're not Welsh!' Rose remembered Daniel's immediate verdict when their grandson was named after Bob Dylan, a musical giant in Adam's eyes. Whatever Adam liked, guaranteed Daniel wouldn't.

She comforted herself with the knowledge that Jess and Daniel always made up in the end. She couldn't bear to think that their younger daughter would miss the traditional fortnight-long family holiday; a sacrosanct annual event still, even now the girls were grown up and had their own lives. Apart from Christmas, this was the one time when they all got together and relaxed. Rose refused to contemplate any alternative to her usual family gathering. She'd made up Jess and Adam's bed anyway, with a small mattress on the floor for Dylan beside it. The child's stool that Daniel had made for Jess's fourth birthday and that Rose had painted with characters from *Alice in Wonderland* was waiting there too. She eased the problem from her mind. She would tackle Daniel about it later, when the moment was right. For now, she pictured her young grandson, anticipating the intense pleasure of seeing him again.

Reaching for the tin can that sat on the chipped tile at the back of the worktop, she poured a ribbon of olive oil into the frying pan, and turned up the gas. A moment later she tipped in the onions and garlic, stirring them as they sizzled, the smell taking over the kitchen. She was tossing in the chopped tomatoes when her iPhone buzzed, announcing a text. That would probably be Eve to say they'd been delayed. Her hands wet with tomato juice, Rose wiped them on the skirt of her apron, then reached for the phone, which was hidden between the bowls of fruit and vegetables on the table. Sticky with heat, she pushed her fringe off her face with the back of her arm and read the message displayed on the screen.

She frowned, and read it again. This certainly wasn't Eve.

Miss you. Love you. Come back soon. S

In fact, nobody she knew would write to her like this.

A misdial, no doubt. She replaced the phone on the long oak kitchen table, nudging it until it lay between the two earthenware bowls, one with its cargo of beef tomatoes, aubergines and courgettes, the other crowded with the figs she'd picked from the tree that morning and a few misshapen pears and apples from yesterday's market. She turned down the heat under the tomato sauce, leaving it to simmer while she tidied and wiped the work surface, putting what she could into the dishwasher, washing up the rest. She removed her apron and hung it on the back of the door, all the while imagining the person the message was for and wondering what the repercussions might be when they didn't receive it. She pushed her rolled sleeves above her elbows. Perhaps she should

5

change this shirt for something cooler before the others arrived. But the message nagged at her, drawing her back to the table. She picked up the mobile again and turned it over in her hand.

On its shiny black back were the familiar scratch and the gold star sticker that distinguished it from hers. This was Daniel's phone. With a thudding heart, she realised the message was for him.

Shaking her head in disbelief, she looked again. The words ricocheted round her brain as she struggled to catch her breath. She turned the fruit bowl slightly, replaced the phone. If it weren't for the regular tick of the clock, she would have believed time had stopped dead.

She rushed to the sink, retching over the coffee mugs that she'd left there after they'd sat together just half an hour earlier, discussing what the following week would bring. She reran their conversation. Had there been any awkwardness, anything unusual, any clue at all that something was wrong between them? Nothing that she remembered. Not then, not during the last few weeks. She ran the cold tap and splashed her burning face and neck.

Drying her face with the dish towel, she realised the absurdity of her reaction. Daniel have an affair? He couldn't. He wouldn't. The message must be from a colleague. Of course. There must be a problem at one of the hotels that only he could solve. How quick she'd been to leap to conclusions. They trusted one another implicitly. Didn't they? She hesitated. But *Love you*. Who would say that to him?

She reached for the phone again.

The words were still there: *Miss. Love. Come back*. Whoever had written them must have realised that someone other than Daniel might see them. So there had to be an innocent explanation. But if not a colleague, then who? She rubbed her thumb along the length of her middle finger, studying her square, capable hands, her neatly rounded fingernails. Perhaps the message was a joke of some kind. The initial S: sign-off and single clue to the sender's identity that simultaneously preserved their anonymity. She must have misinterpreted the desire she first read into the text. Every bit of her refused to accept that her husband would betray her. And yet . . . Wasn't this the sort of thing that happened in marriages? Wronged wife finds giveaway receipt, note, text. Frantic, she ran through the possible explanations again. A colleague? A joker? A wrong number? Another woman? Her breath caught as the last one hooked itself into her mind . . .

The monastery bell tolled the hour. Eve and Terry would be here at any minute. She should sort this out first, just to put her mind at rest. A band of tension tightened around her head, as her puzzlement gave way to panic. She sat with her head in her hands. What if?

Outside, a dog barked, then a splash as Daniel dived into the pool for his obligatory one hundred body-conditioning lengths.

Women loved Daniel. Rose had always known that. He only had to enter a room and heads turned. His energy and charisma made him friends easily. If he had enemies, she didn't know them. If he had lovers . . . She didn't believe he had. She had always been there for him, always would be. As he had been for her.

She poured herself a glass of water and drank quickly. Whatever she was going through, nothing must spoil their family holiday. Trying to gather her fragmenting thoughts, she filled the large pasta pan and put it on the hob, ready for later. Then she picked up the knife and stabbed it into the last tomato, catching the point of the blade in the board, and drew it down through the skin. There had to be an innocent explanation. All she had to do was ask.

She slid the tomatoes into the frying pan, then switched off the gas. Picking up the phone again, she walked outside, every step an effort. A green and black lizard skittered out of her path into the shadow of the pot of pink geraniums. The intense summer heat enveloped her like a blanket, but did nothing to warm her or to slow her racing thoughts. Pausing on the vine-sheltered terrace to put on her straw hat, she looked past the spreading walnut tree that shaded the table where they'd have lunch, through the olive trees and down to the pool, where the sounds of Daniel swimming a determined crawl rose to meet her. A couple of orange butterflies danced past as she made her way over the grass, feeling its spring

7

against her instep until she reached the path descending to the pool. She watched as Daniel flip-turned at the far end, his iron-grey hair disappearing under the water in a surge of bubbles. He looked in his element, cutting cleanly through the water, the sun glinting on the ripples and throwing faint shadows through the blueness around him. Her eyes stung with tears.

She crossed the paving and stood right on the edge of the shallow end for a second before moving on to the top step, the chill of the water jolting her into the moment. She flicked at a fly that landed on her shoulder. Only another couple of strokes and Daniel was beside her. She stepped out of the water back on to the side. He grasped the edge of the pool and looked up, shaking his head, tipping it one way then the other, tapping his lower ear each time, then removed his goggles and dropped them on the ground by her feet. He squinted into the sun as he looked up at her.

'Everything all right?'

Even his smile hurt her. She noticed a splash of tomato on the hem of her pink linen shorts and scratched at it, distracted.

The neighbours' hunting dogs, caged under an oak tree by the track, began barking again.

'Perfectly.' She heard the catch in her voice but he appeared not to notice. 'You've got a text.'

He looked surprised.

The pulse in her throat beat faster as she held out the mobile, the sun glancing off its face.

'Really? I'm not expecting anything. I'm sure whoever it is can wait. You didn't have to come out.' He hoisted himself up to sit on the edge of the pool. She registered his slight paunch, which he controlled with determined exercise, his chest covered with grey curls. Water ran down his face and plastered his hair to his head until he rubbed it with one hand so it stuck up on end. Even so, she couldn't help thinking that there was still something absurdly Greek god-like about him. And tanned, he looked his best. There was no doubt, her husband was still . . . well, better than lukewarm for a man of his age. Perhaps she wasn't the only one who thought so. Her stomach turned. She studied his face for signs of guilt, but there was nothing there.

'Well, you never know. Perhaps it's more important than you think.' She laid the phone next to his towel, briefly touched that it wouldn't occur to him that she might have looked at it, shocked by the fact that she had. 'Eve and Terry will be here soon and I thought you'd want to be ready for them.'

He groaned. 'It's so perfect when we're here on our own.'

Yes, it had been. Until ten minutes ago.

Just ask him, her inner voice insisted. Ask him.

But as much as she wanted his quick reassurance that the message meant nothing, she was terrified of being told the opposite. She remained silent, steadying herself. Confronting him now, moments before the others arrived, was a bad idea. As she ran her finger along the chain around her neck, catching it on the delicate gold heart that he'd bought her on their anniversary, she said, 'You know you love it when there are people staying. And Anna should be here by this evening.'

The thought of their daughter brought another smile to his face. 'Wonder what hare-brained scheme she'll have dreamed up this time.'

Rose looked skywards, shaking her head in mock despair. She couldn't speak.

Daniel laughed and ran a finger up her calf. 'Come on, she's not that bad.'

She froze at his touch, then stepped to the side, resisting a sudden urge to kick him. How did he have the power to make her feel like this? 'I hoped that she was settling down at last. Doing those horticultural courses.'

'Our Anna? Dream on, old thing.' He angled his face to the sun, eyes shut, propping himself up on his arms.

'Less of the old.' Her response was automatic. 'At least I act my age.' Wishing she hadn't said that, she tried to swallow the lump in her throat as she prepared to back-pedal.

'What's that supposed to mean?' But his eyes remained shut, and if anything, he sounded amused.

'Nothing.' She corralled the words that were crowding on to the tip of her tongue and dug her nails into her palm, the pain focusing her. Self-control: that was the key. She had to hold on to herself, delaying the conversation until the two of them had some uninterrupted time together. Until there was an admission of guilt, nothing had changed. 'I'm going back to do lunch. At least one of us should be ready for them.'

Daniel got to his feet. 'Looks like it's too late for that.' He wrapped the red towel around his waist and they both turned towards the house at the sound of a car bumping over the uneven drive.

'Time and again I've told Marco to shut the bloody gate. Doesn't he ever listen? What's the point of having security if we don't use it?'

Languages were not Daniel's strong suit, but he insisted on speaking them loudly even when English would have been better understood. Marco had once lived in Cricklewood for three years and still talked as if it was the centre of the universe. Now loyal gardener, pool boy and general odd-job man to a number of English-owned houses in the area, his English was fluent, but Daniel persisted in dragging out his very rusty A-level Italian at every conversation. Everyone who heard him was impressed in equal measure by his efforts and his cloth ear. Rose was used to having to explain for him later.

As she followed him up the garden, she watched the way he held himself, confident, easy and unconcerned. Despite her efforts to control it, anxiety was knotting itself tight in her stomach, making her almost oblivious to anything else. All she wanted to do was lie down and pull a sheet over her head, shutting out the world while she tried to digest the awful nagging suspicions that wouldn't leave her alone. But she couldn't. She had to go through the motions of normal behaviour, however desperate she felt. They rounded the corner of the house as a small black car reversed into the space beside theirs. An arm emerged from the window to wave a greeting, sun glinting off a gold bangle. The car had barely stopped when the passenger door was flung open and Eve burst out of it.

'At last! I thought we'd never get here. Terry wouldn't rent anything faster or bigger than this. But you know what he's like about saving the planet!' She embraced Rose warmly, and Rose responded, inhaling her friend's familiar floral scent. The cavalry had arrived.

Eve turned to Daniel. 'Come here, you gorgeous man.'

As she hugged him, Rose watched for a second, amused to see how unprepared Eve seemed for the simplicity of villa life. There was no compromise in her wardrobe. A fashion guru would never be disappointed walking through her door. 'If I'm run over by a bus tomorrow, at least they'll know I had taste,' she once said to the accompaniment of her friends' laughter. 'Teaming and toning' was her watchword, demonstrated in her tan sandals, cream Capri pants, voluminous swirly top in various shades of brown and coral, and gold jewellery. Rose wished that she herself had changed into something more chic than shorts and shirt. She ran a hand through her cropped hair, tucking it behind her ear, aware how dull it must look beside Eve's expensive streaks. But those hours in a hairdresser's chair weren't for her.

'Rose. You're looking great,' said Eve. Daniel's arm lay loosely round her shoulder.

Terry stood in front of Rose, arms held wide, expectant. Un-usually unshaven, his face looked thinner, emphasising the narrow-ness of his nose and the set of his ears. She was immediately ashamed of her uncharitable thought that her brother was not at his best in shorts. He'd never quite grown out of the lanky stage that had disqualified him from the sports pitch at an early age, despite his enthusiasm for it. Perhaps it was just that she was more used to seeing him in a suit and tie: the uniform of accountancy. She smiled her welcome before being caught up in an awkward embrace, her face rasped by his stubble. Even as brother and sister they didn't do closeness well. She extricated herself as swiftly as she could and took a step back. She ordered herself to make an effort.

'Good to see you both,' she said. 'Shall we take your luggage in now?' Terry had already lifted the boot of the car and was hauling out a single small case.

'Just the one? You're usually much less restrained.'

Terry looked sheepish. 'They've lost one of them. But—'

'Not just one of them, Terry,' interrupted Eve. '*My* one!'

'They've said it'll be with us by nine o'clock tonight,' he explained, obviously in the wake of a major row. He spoke carefully. 'They're putting it on the last flight out of Stansted.'

'We'll see,' muttered Eve. 'Bloody disorganised hellhole. And in the meantime, I've nothing but what I'm standing up in.'

Rose made sympathetic noises, aware of the amount of clutter that would be airborne in their direction that night.

Eve saw her expression and slipped an arm through hers. 'You know I can't travel anywhere without my straighteners, my hairdryer and all my creams and lotions, plus a change of clothes for every occasion. Got to keep up the good fight, and I'm not giving in yet. They take up so much space, that's the problem.'

'I'll say,' said Rose. She felt some relief now that Eve was here. Perhaps she would talk to her about the text. Eve would know what she should do, would reassure her that she'd got the wrong end of the stick. 'Lost bags almost always turn up. Don't let it spoil things. You can always borrow something of mine.'

Eve snorted. 'Of yours? Kind offer, dearest sister-in-law, but one of your dresses would just about fit round my thigh.'

Rose laughed. 'Nonsense. Come in and I'll see what I can dig out.' She took the case and carried it towards the house. 'Good journey otherwise?'

'Bloody awful.' Eve was right behind her. 'I vowed last year that I'd never fly budget airline again, but you know what Terry's like if he sniffs a bargain. So it was the usual being herded on to the plane like cattle and then we had to sit on the bloody runway for an hour and a half because of heavy air traffic at Pisa. Then when we arrived we had to bank for another half an hour, flying so low we were practically scraping the tiles off the roofs. Terrifying. Haven't they heard of timetables in Italy?'

'Oh, you know what it's like here,' Rose said vaguely, as she led the way round the main building to the outhouses. 'You're in the old stable this time. OK?'

'Provided there's mosquito netting at the windows and the horses have been moved out, anywhere's perfect.'

'I hadn't forgotten, so I've put in every deterrent I could find in the Co-op, plus some calamine just in case.' She opened the door of the old stable, now a sparely furnished but comfortable sitting room, bedroom and bathroom. 'Why don't you unpack what you've got and then come over to the terrace for a drink?' Suddenly she had an overwhelming desire to be on her own as she admitted what must be the truth to herself for the first time. Eve wouldn't be able to reassure her, because Daniel must be having an affair. That could be the only explanation.

'A drink sounds like a fine plan. I'll be two minutes.' Eve sized up the extremely narrow double bed, the only size that would fit in the space. 'No twin beds then?'

Rose shook her head, pretending not to notice Eve's small despairing sigh. Her brother and sister-in-law's sex life was not something she wanted to go into. 'Anything you want, just give me a yell.'

'Are you OK?' Eve put her hand on Rose's arm.

'Yeah, of course. Why?' To her horror, Rose felt tears pricking at her eyes.

'I don't know, you just seem a bit . . . I don't know . . . off.' She pulled Rose towards her. 'Look at me.'

'Don't be silly.' Rose turned her head away, blinking. 'I'll just go and rescue lunch, and look out some clothes for you.' She manoeuvred her way around Terry, who was blocking the doorway. She didn't look up, just in case he noticed something was wrong. 'See you in a minute,' she called, her voice as steady as she could manage.

Eve said something in reply, but Rose didn't hear what. Her head felt as if someone had poured a ton of setting cement into her skull. Her limbs were leaden as she made her way into the kitchen. Daniel. An affair. The words thumped inside her head. That text, so passionate, so needy, had driven home what until that moment she had always been able to ignore. Other women still wanted him. And this time he must have responded. She shivered, suddenly as cold as if a sharp wind was blowing around the back of her heart. What on earth was she to do?

2

Impatient for lunch to be over, Rose dipped in and out of the conversation, only responding to the remarks addressed to her then drifting off again, wondering what would happen to their family gatherings if she and Daniel split up. She picked at her pasta and salad, nausea having taken away her appetite. The others tossed around suggestions about what they might do over the following week like juggling balls, all of them possibilities but no one catching them: days of rest, country walks, visits to Arezzo, Cortona, San Gimignano, Siena or Lucca and its Festival of Lights. Eventually the talk turned where it always did: towards their families.

Eve had already extolled the virtues and despaired of the vicissitudes of her own four children, Charlie, Tom, Luke and – at last, a girl – Millie. Charlie at least had a job, whereas the twins, Tom and Luke, had sailed through school and university and emerged without a single idea of what they wanted to do in life. They depended on unpaid work experience, contacts they hadn't yet made and parental handouts. Millie was still at college doing a degree in media studies, whatever they were, and with as much clue about her future as her brothers had about theirs. But she was having a good time, and that was what it was all about, wasn't it?

The cotton kaftan that Eve was wearing, bought for Daniel on a Moroccan holiday, was far from cool – in any sense. Eve fanned herself with a frantic hand. 'What about Jess and Anna? What are they up to?'

'Anna should be here soon,' answered Daniel, glancing at his watch. 'When's her flight land, darling?'

'Six thirtyish, I think,' said Rose, picking up a knife to cut a sliver of taleggio, then changing her mind. She couldn't look him in the eye. 'She should be here for supper.' Anna's presence would provide another welcome distraction. Her elder daughter could be relied on to assume the focus of any gathering, although often for the wrong reasons. She could be funny, and full of ideas, like her father, but opinionated, difficult and self-centred were qualities she could assume with equal brilliance.

'What's she up to now?' Eve reached across the table for the wine bottle and poured herself another glass. They all pretended not to notice the pointed way in which Terry cleared his throat.

'The café closed down about eighteen months ago and she's been on a horticultural course ever since. Living in some sort of commune. At thirty!' Rose closed her eyes for a second. Her headache was getting worse. 'I'd so hoped she'd be settled down with a proper job by now.'

'Charlie mentioned that he'd seen her.' Eve always talked about her eldest son with a dash of reverence, as if surprised that he could possibly be theirs. 'Said she was cooking up some scheme.' She raised her glass to her lips, narrowing her eyes as she sipped.

Daniel groaned. 'Now what? We've had the teaching, the stall, importing rugs, the café, tutoring . . .' He counted them off on his fingers. 'She's got the sticking power of a used stamp. How's Charlie's teaching going?'

'Oh, no worries there,' Terry assured him quickly. 'He loves Gresham Hall and they love him. Not what I was expecting him to do at all – rather hoped he'd follow in my footsteps – but it's going well.' His paternal pride was expressed in a narrow smile that transformed his rather nondescript features, creasing his eyes into slits.

Rose understood exactly how proud her brother must be of his eldest son, her nephew. She wanted success for her own children too. There was at least some sort of security to be found there. Though not always happiness, she reminded herself. Charlie had broken away from family expectation and pressure. Not for him the family hotel business, now run by Daniel, nor his father's sound accountancy profession. No, he wanted something of his own, and teaching seemed to be his thing. She had hoped once that Anna would go down that path too. After dropping out of her university course, her elder daughter had embraced the teacher-training course that Rose had found for her with barely expressed gratitude. As soon as she'd completed it, with minimum accolades all round, she had decided to run a market stall selling paste jewellery. Nothing that came close to a career as far as Daniel and Rose were concerned. Not, of course, that the stall lasted long. Just as with everything else, Anna soon got bored.

'And Jess?' Eve's question broke into Rose's thoughts, but she was too slow to prevent Daniel replying.

'Just great. Doing a wonderful job managing Trevarrick – well, deputy managing in fact, but it's only a question of time. If only it weren't for—'

'Anyone for more fruit or cheese?' interrupted Rose, fanning herself with a napkin, feeling sweat begin to prick at her forehead. She wondered how the girls would react when they heard their parents were separating, then stopped herself. Perhaps the affair (if that was what it was) wasn't as solid as the fragment of text implied.

'Are you all right? You look pale.' Eve's words seemed to come from a distance.

'Fine. It's probably just the heat.' Rose waved a hand, dismissing any thought of illness. All she wanted to do was remove herself to lie down and think. Alone.

'I thought you said it was cooler here than last week,' Eve accused Daniel. 'It's like a bloody furnace.' She picked up her BlackBerry, which had been lying silent on the table, and began accessing her emails.

Terry glared across the table at his wife and coughed that cough again: short but disapproving. 'Do you have to?'

'What?' she complained, scrolling down a list. 'They're not responsible for the weather, Terry. I'm not being rude about the house. You all know I love it here. I just like to be able to breathe, that's all.' She held up her arms to both sides, as if the non-existent wind would blow into her armpits, then lifted her hair from the back of her neck.

'You know that's not what I mean. Can't you leave your

17

BlackBerry alone while we're on holiday? Or at least when we're all together.'

'You are silly, darling.' Eve smiled a taut little smile, putting all the stress on the last word. 'They don't mind. They know I need to keep in touch. An agent's on duty twenty-four seven. And I'm expecting to hear from Rufus.' Her attention returned to the phone.

Terry shook his head but said nothing. His mouth was drawn into a thin, irritated line.

To Rose's relief, their spat had distracted Daniel from what he'd been about to say. She couldn't bear another rant about Adam: unreconstructed hippie, ten years older than Jess, with no career prospects, and on and on. Instead, he smiled, the genial host once again. 'This *is* much cooler,' he insisted. 'You'll just have to get up early and sleep through the middle of the day.'

'Too late for that now.' Eve smiled. 'It's nearly four. Time for a bit of pool work, I'd say. I couldn't eat another thing.' Satisfied there was nothing urgent demanding her attention back home, she stood up and began helping Rose clear the table.

'Nor me.' Terry got to his feet, flapping away an inquisitive wasp. 'I'm taking my book into the shade somewhere.'

The others studiously but obviously avoided catching each other's eye. Terry's dedication to *The Global Effect of Micro-Economic Management Techniques*, a tome that had lain on his chest while he snoozed, always apparently open at the same page, had been the family joke of last year.

'Don't say it,' he warned, as Rose raised an eyebrow. 'I've brought a Harlan Coben with me this time.'

'Only because I made you swap it for that economics textbook you'd laid out.' Eve threw the words back over her shoulder at him. 'He was livid,' she whispered to Rose.

'I'm interested in the subject, OK? Nothing wrong in that.' Having had the last word in his own defence, he left the table.

Rose gave a weak smile. They'd made Terry the butt of their family jokes for years. As his sister, she sometimes wondered whether she ought to be more protective of him, but he rose to the bait so readily, and anyway, he usually sniffed out the funny side of things in the end. He was too easy to tease.

The two women crossed the terrace into the kitchen, the relative cool of the room a welcome contrast with outside.

'I'll make coffee.' Still on autopilot, Rose picked up the stained espresso maker. 'Dan won't have any, though. Mustn't pollute the temple that is his body.' She unscrewed the gadget and dropped the top half on to the worktop with a crash.

Eve looked up, unable to ignore either the irony or the noise. 'What's going on between you two? Something's up, I can tell.'

'Sorry to disappoint, Miss Marple.' The words were almost lost under the noise of the water running into the sink before she filled the base.

As Rose ground the coffee beans, Eve held her hands under the tap, then splashed her face and her neck, soaking the top of the kaftan. She seemed oblivious. 'Have it your way. But if you do want to talk, you know you can trust me.'

'I know. Thanks, I appreciate it.' The coffee on the hob, Rose set about the washing up, Eve alongside her, crumpled tea towel in her hand. 'But it's nothing. Nothing I want to talk about at the moment anyway.' She banged a saucepan down on the draining board.

Eve looked at her quizzically but obviously thought better of saying anything.

Rose trusted Eve not to leak a secret outside the family, but . . . to keep it from Terry? Would she? Eve and Terry's marriage had always been a mystery to Rose. She had been delighted when Eve accepted Terry's proposal. Eve had been her closest friend since Edinburgh days, when she and Daniel had studied at the university and Rose was at the art school. At the same time, she'd worried that Eve was still on the rebound from her marriage to Will: a marriage that had only lasted a couple of years since their hasty wedding that first summer after they'd left university. On the face of it, Eve and Terry seemed to have so little in common. Eve was expansive, outrageous, fun. With the best will in the world, none of those adjectives could be applied to her brother. Yet despite Rose's doubts, Eve and Terry had stuck together over the years, presumably happy with one another despite their habitual public bickering. She had never been able to fathom the mechanics of her brother's relationships. He wasn't an intimate talker or sharer, never had been. Eve must find that frustrating. Or perhaps when they were together he became a completely different person and the two of them did hold those conversations that made so many marriages. Rose would never know.

She and Daniel told each other everything. Always had. Always. Or so she'd thought. *S*: the letter hissed through her thoughts, winding round the Sarahs, the Susans, the Samantha and Sally they knew, but never wrapping itself round any of them for long.

What would this mean for their marriage? Everything she thought she knew, on which her life had been dependent, had been thrown into doubt. If Daniel had kept this woman secret, what other secrets did he have? How much had he said that he didn't really mean? She stopped the questions there. If she confided in Eve, there was no guarantee Terry wouldn't get to hear, and he, soul of indiscretion and insensitivity that he could occasionally be, was perfectly capable of blurting out something to Daniel without thinking.

'OK. Let's not talk about you.' Eve put the dried pan in its place, and adopted a tone that invited gossip. 'Anna told Charlie that there's been an almighty row between Jess and Daniel. True or false?'

Rose tutted. Family and secrets – the two words didn't compute in *this* family. One or other of them was always succumbing to the temptation of showing off whatever nugget of knowledge they had that the others didn't. Not that she was blameless either. She had never been allowed to forget the time she'd let slip at a family dinner that Eve was pregnant with twins. How hurt her brother had been that he wasn't the first to know. Reasonably so, Rose admitted, not for the first time.

If Eve suspected something, then it was Rose's duty to do a bit of damage limitation before her sister-in-law's vivid imagination and love of pot-stirring made the situation worse than it already was.

'It's Adam, isn't it?' Eve had abandoned the drying up and was perched on the edge of the table. Her face was redder than ever and circles of sweat decorated the underarms of the kaftan. 'You don't have to pretend. Daniel's never made any secret of his feelings. He nearly said something at lunch. Just because Adam's not the sort of husband that he would like for Jess. Why should he be the same age as her or have a conventional "career"?' She air-punctuated the word. 'After all, people have earned their living doing carpentry or woodturning or whatever he likes to call it for much longer than they have doing hotel management. And it's not as if Jess hasn't got a decent job. What's the big deal?'

Rose welcomed the chance to talk about something else. 'It's all so stupid. Bloody men and their pride. Dan asked if Adam would do some joinery work, odd-jobbing at Trevarrick. He thought Adam needed the work, and proposed to pay him at the going rate, of course. He was trying to help,' she protested on his behalf. 'In return Adam called him patronising and turned the offer down, explaining why being a woodturner was quite different.'

'Doesn't he need the work?' Eve picked at one of her nails where the canteloupe-coloured varnish had started to flake. 'Dammit! I knew this manicure wouldn't last.'

'I would have thought so. But he's proud and doesn't want favours, least of all from Jess's dad.'

Eve pulled out the chair beside her and patted the green-striped cushion. Rose removed the coffee from the hob, took out a couple of red and orange espresso cups and saucers and sat down with a sigh.

'You shouldn't do that. You sound about a hundred years old.' Eve took the coffee and began to pour the thick black liquid into the cups.

'I *feel* about a hundred years old.' Rose leaned back, feeling her body start to relax at last. 'Families! Who'd have 'em?' She straightened up and took a sip. 'Christ, that's strong.' She replaced the cup in the saucer. 'Sorry. The trouble is, it doesn't matter what Adam does. One, Dan doesn't like him, doesn't think he's good enough for Jess – God knows why – and two, he thinks Adam ought to be out there supporting Jess and Dylan, not the other way round. On the other hand, Adam knows what he wants from life. He won't be told what to do by anyone – least of all his father-in-law.'

'Can you blame him? Anyway, Jess loves the hotel, always has. I can't imagine her working anywhere else, or indeed not working at all.'

'But Dan has this antediluvian idea that his daughters should be kept in the way . . . oh, you know.' Rose gave up in despair. They all knew how devoted Daniel was to his daughters and how he wanted only the best for them. The best as he saw it, that was. Did the best involve their father having a mistress? she wondered with a pang. And they also knew his obstinacy, the obstinacy that Jess had inherited. 'Anyway, the long and the short of it is that Jess stuck up for Adam, as you'd expect. She and Dan had words – understatement of the day – and she's said that they're not coming this year.'

'But they must. I haven't seen Dylan for months.'

'I've got to speak to Dan, but as usual, it's a question of finding the right moment. He's going to have to back down. You know what Jess's like when it comes to her family. And we all know exactly where she gets it from.' The knot in Rose's stomach tightened. 'When will he realise that the girls are grown up and can lead their own lives without his interference? It's always me who has to pick up the pieces.' To her horror, one of the tears she had been holding back since the morning trickled down her cheek.

A lizard scurried up the wall by the door, then stopped motionless about halfway up.

'Hey, hey.' Eve put her arm around Rose's shoulders. 'This isn't like you. If you won't tell me what's really wrong now, you've got a few days to change your mind.'

'About what?' Daniel stood in the doorway, his shadow slanting into the room. 'What trouble are you two concocting?'

'Nothing.' Eve moved away from Rose. 'You've got such a suspicious mind, Dan. I was only asking when we were expecting Jess.'

Rose didn't miss the almost imperceptible flicker of irritation in

Daniel's face, the one-fingered scratch behind his left ear; both sure signs he was exercising extreme self-restraint. She began to put away the pans.

'Jess?' he said. Perhaps Eve didn't notice the tension in his voice. 'Any day, I think. Rose knows all the details.' He crossed the kitchen towards the corridor.

The anger she'd felt earlier returned. His not facing up to the situation he'd created was absurd. 'I think she's waiting to hear from you,' she said pointedly to his retreating back. 'Before she makes up her mind.' Rose knew full well that Jess and Adam's tickets were booked for a flight in three days' time, but also that Jess was perfectly capable of writing off the cost if her father didn't make peace.

'Really?' He sounded surprised. 'I didn't think she and I had anything more to say to each other.'

'Oh, Daniel.' Rose stopped, aware of Eve's beady eyes watching them, alert for every nuance. She wouldn't give her sister-in-law the satisfaction of seeing them argue, thus confirming her suspicions. Especially not when she was afraid that any loss of temper could evolve too easily into something else. But however much she might want to avoid any kind of confrontation on holiday, they would have to discuss Jess and Adam before it was too late.

'Well, we can talk about her later. I'm off for a quick nap.' He ended any possibility of discussion by disappearing towards their bedroom.

He rarely took a siesta so late in the day. She looked after him, infuriated, frustrated and sad.

'Now tell me there's nothing going on between you,' said Eve, adjusting her top across her shoulders.

'Eve, please.' Rose got up to cover the cheese board with a muslin dome, brushing away a couple of persistent flies. 'I said I'll talk to you when I'm ready. And I will.'

'You're just as stubborn yourself, you know. But OK. In that case, I'm going to give in to the tyranny of the pool, and find myself a parasol. If there's one big enough to provide the amount of shade I need.'

Rose allowed herself a brief smile. 'Don't be an idiot. You're looking great.'

'Just what I meant! But once I've got Jess's old maternity cozzie on, things may change. You wait.'

The costume Jess had left behind a year ago was the only one with a cat's whiskers' chance of fitting Eve.

'I'll see you down there later. I'm going to try to catch Dan before he nods off.'

'Bad move, sister. I'm warning you.' Eve shook her head as she left the room.

She was probably right, thought Rose, but sorting out Jess's visit was vital. Otherwise the moment would be gone, and she wouldn't come at all. Once that was done, she would concentrate on how she was going to deal with that text, the words of which still resonated in her memory. *Miss. Love. Come back.* With a heavy heart, she walked slowly towards the dimly lit staircase that led to their room.

3

Eve angled the lounger, straightened the beach towel and moved the parasol to give her enough shade. She glanced up towards the sound of snoring. There, slung between two olive trees, was a hammock containing the slumbering Terry, on his back, mouth open. His paperback lay on the ground beside him. Not even Harlan Coben had the page-turning power to keep him awake.

Above them the sky was an uninterrupted cornflower blue. She organised all the essentials – her suntan cream, Kindle, BlackBerry and dark glasses – on the table, then went to dip her hand in the water. She pulled it back sharply. She'd expected the temperature to be much more inviting. Then she recalled the spartan thread that ran through Daniel. Anything sporty must push you to your limit. Not for him the heated pool. She had a sudden memory of him coming into the refectory of their student halls in Edinburgh, having run round Arthur's Seat before breakfast. In those days, running was for the few, and at that time of the day, certainly not for the student. How different things had been then. The two of them had never made the mistake of believing they were in love with one another, but their relationship had certainly been satisfyingly intense and, if she thought about it, pleasantly fulfilling during the short time it lasted. Then Will came along. Then Rose. But that was all a long time ago.

Reproaching herself for being so feeble, she walked to the end of the pool, relishing the sun on her pale skin, feeling the modesty frill on the maternity costume tickle the tops of her thighs. She paused for a moment, then swung her arms in front of her and pushed off with her toes. The dive was executed perfectly. As she entered the water, the first shock of the cold paralysed the nerve endings the length of her body. By the time she was halfway down the pool, that sudden numbness had begun to wear off. She surfaced with a gasp, treading water as she took in her surroundings: the olive grove below the pool, the sloping stretch of garden between her and the old farmhouse itself. They'd all thought Rose and Dan were crazy when they'd bought such a wreck of a place. But the pair of them had lavished such care and attention on it over the years that it had become a haven for all of them.

She concentrated on pushing herself through the water. Dan had given her her first lesson in crawl in the sea off Musselburgh that summer after she'd confessed that the only stroke she'd mastered at school was a stately, head-held-out-of-the-water breaststroke. In those days she hadn't been put off by the cold. He'd laughed and showed her how to propel herself through the water, to time her breathing, to turn her head every third stroke, to use her arms and kick. After a few lengths, she slowed down and rolled on to her back, keeping herself afloat with gentle movements of her arms and feet. The vast blue bowl above her was marked by the vapour trail from an aircraft, high, high up, moving like a rigid faraway bird.

She shut her eyes, tried to empty her mind, to concentrate on the heat on her face, the sensation of weightlessness. But it was useless. One by one her children – though strictly speaking they were too old to be called that – came marching into her mind, besieging her with one trivial kind of worry or another. She didn't want to have to think about the squalid flat where the twins were living, whether they were ever going to earn enough to cover their living expenses, whether it was going to work out at Gresham Hall for Charlie or whether Millie would get her meaningless degree and what she would do with it if she did. Beyond that, there was her own future. The small literary agency for children's authors and illustrators that she'd dared to set up years ago was facing a tough time in the current economic climate.

She kept her eyes shut against the sun, aware of dogs barking in the distance, the buzz of an insect flying by her face. Weightless, suspended, alone.

Eyes closed, she ran through her client list. As far as she was concerned, there wasn't a dud among them, not really. She had left the large London literary agency where she'd trained when she was pregnant with Charlie and they'd moved to a village outside Cambridge. Not long after his birth, she had started her own business, not taking on more clients than she could responsibly handle, running it from the kitchen table. As the children got older, she had rented an office and slowly expanded her client list, until three years ago she had taken on Amy Fraser as her assistant. Only three months ago she had rewarded Amy's dedication by agreeing she should become an agent in her own right.

Amy Fraser: well educated, well tailored, well spoken, well versed in the business of the agency. What the hell was she playing at? She had failed to return any of Eve's emails since she had left the office the previous Friday. Eve couldn't fault Amy's dedication to her work, yet sometimes she suspected the young woman had another agenda that she wasn't sharing.

The sound of a splash made her start. Her eyes flew open just as a wave of water washed over her, unbalancing her. As she surfaced, coughing as she righted herself, she heard laughter. Wiping her eyes, she saw Terry on the edge of the pool.

'Couldn't resist. You looked so peaceful.'

'Most people would see that as a reason to leave me alone.' Just a few strokes to the end, where she walked up the steps and shook out her hair. 'Only you would think that was funny.'

'I'm sorry, but all that splashing woke me up.' As he walked towards her, she couldn't help thinking, not for the first time, that the way his hair grew forward and the prominent set of his ears made it look as if the breeze was blowing him in her direction, as if they were destined for each other. The sun bounced off either side of his temples where his hairline had receded beyond the point of disguise. He ran his fingers down her spine. 'Relax. We're on holiday.'

Instead of responding, she concentrated on re-angling the parasol against the sun, before arranging herself on the lounger.

'Mmm. God, I'm exhausted.' She took a long, deep breath as she felt the sun warming her limbs, and an overwhelming desire to sleep took her over.

He sat on the next lounger before helping himself to the pricey sun cream that she'd bought for herself in the departure lounge. She watched him with one eye, cross that he wasn't using the Nivea they'd bought for him.

'I'm not surprised,' he said, slathering the stuff on to his ashen calves.

Immediately she was on the alert. 'What's that supposed to mean?'

'As if you didn't know.' He lay back with an audible oomph of satisfaction, hands behind his head, legs splayed.

Budgie smugglers not a good look on an older man, she couldn't help remarking. On Tom Daley they were one thing, but add a few years . . . She'd meant to buy Terry some more discreet trunks for holidaying in company, but what with one thing and another, they'd been forgotten.

'Do you have to drink so much? It was only lunchtime, for God's sake.' His voice was low, as if someone might overhear.

'Is that why you've come over? Just to tell me that?' Eve propped herself up as she recalled their lunch. The wine had been the ideal accompaniment to the meal. Light and dry and white, chosen with typical care by Daniel. Perhaps I did have one glass too many, she thought, remembering with slight embarrassment the way she had continued to help herself long after the others had slowed down and how inappropriately loud her laugh had been at one of Daniel's jokes. She knew Terry had been watching her, had been aware of the occasional pressure of his foot under the table, but if anything, that had only encouraged her. A sort of reckless defiance had taken her over, even if it was 'only lunchtime'.

'It's not good for you and I don't want you making a fool of yourself.'

'Why not?' Eve protested. 'It's only your sister and her husband, both old friends of mine who know me better than . . . anyone.' She stopped herself in time from saying 'than you'. That would be too hurtful. But it was true.

'Maybe, but you should take it easy all the same. Give your liver a breather.' He laid his hand on hers to reassure her that he was only thinking of her own good.

She snatched her hand away. 'If my liver needed help, I'd know about it. Drink oils the wheels sometimes, that's all. And anyway, I enjoy it.' She was uncomfortably aware that this was beginning to sound like the self-justifying rant of an alcoholic. 'You may not, but other people do know the difference between being a drunk and having fun.' There. She waited for his reply.

But Terry was already on his feet, heading back to the hammock. She punched the cushion. He could be so maddening sometimes. Making his point was always enough. Her thoughts on the subject were irrelevant. The pleasant drowsiness brought on by the combination of sun, exercise, good food and drink had all but evaporated in her irritation. She watched his familiar bouncing gait, his slim physique. She reached for the sun cream and began massaging it into her cleavage. As she did, she was reminded once again of the cruel truth that while her body showed the evidence of time and the rigours of childbirth, his had remained comparatively untouched by the passing years. Even so, the Speedos were still a mistake, bought as a joke when they'd gone together to the South of France a couple of years ago. But if he was the same as ever, why didn't she find him as attractive as she once had? Pondering the matter, she picked up her BlackBerry and checked her emails. Still nothing from Amy.

She brought up Amy's address and quickly typed:

Any problems? Eve

She hesitated. That rather suggested she expected there might be, which was unfair. If you didn't count the weekend, she'd only been out of the office for less than a day. Perhaps she was being too abrupt. She added an x after her name – the kiss that took the sting out of any email. Then she deleted it for not being sufficiently businesslike and added:

Do get back to me re Rufus's contract. And have you had time to look at the new Alasdair King illustrations yet?

She reread the message. Too authoritarian? But what if it was? It was important to establish which of them was in charge and what was still expected of Amy, whatever her job title. All the same . . . She reinstated the x, then sent the email without more ado and moved on to the most pressing incoming messages, reading a few of them, replying, then stopping. There was nothing more here that couldn't wait a couple of hours for an answer. She slid the phone into the shade beneath the lounger, closed her eyes and abandoned herself to the moment.

Halfway down the corridor to the stairs, Rose had second thoughts. She was so confused and upset, so unsure of the right way to handle her discovery. If she was right, if Daniel was having an affair, she didn't trust herself to be alone with him just yet. Not even to discuss Jess. She was frightened of what she might blurt out in the heat of the moment, and worse, of what he might say in reply.

Instead she turned in to the small studio room where she kept all her painting materials. She stripped off, hung her shift on the back of the door and put on the smock and skirt that hung beside it. She found a talismanic comfort in their familiarity and would draw or paint in nothing else. She picked up a large sketchpad and her bag, put on her hat and left the house.

She heard the sound of voices by the pool. Terry and Eve. Bickering probably. Their relationship seemed to flourish on their differences, a way of relating that Rose couldn't imagine for herself. From the outside, their marriage couldn't be more different from hers and Daniel's. But now she wasn't sure any more. An undertow of sadness tugged at her, that and fear of the future. Nothing would be the same now.

The path took her along the track that ran between fields of dying sunflowers, their large blackened heads turned away from the sun, hanging dejected towards the ground, their leaves pale and wilting. But she was oblivious to her surroundings until she passed the field containing rows of glittering black solar panels. Just beyond them she turned up the hill, past a narrow vineyard, to the edge of a small oak wood. There the track became a narrow path, less stony underfoot, that she followed up and round the edge of the trees till she reached a clearing where the treeline drew back behind a patch of rocks. This was where she always came when she needed time out, rediscovering it with every change of season.

From this vantage point she could see down the valley to vineyards like perfect corduroy, and two old farmhouses basking in the heat. In the distance, a small medieval hilltop village, its church spire marking the summit. The sound of children shouting carried up to her on the air, then the solemn tolling of the monastery bell – every hour on the hour. She settled herself on her favourite rock, the one that dipped against a taller one to make a natural seat, and took out her sketchbook, watercolours and paint-brushes.

Within ten minutes she was absorbed in capturing the landscape, the trees and the light and shade of the valley around her, as the sun began its slow descent. Daniel, their marriage, gradually retreated to the back of her mind as she concentrated on her painting. When the bell tolled the hour again, she came to, almost surprised at having cleared her mind so successfully. Six o'clock. Immediately her focus switched to home. Anna would be arriving soon, and she must be there to greet her. Daniel would be awake and wondering where she was. Then: *Miss. Love. Come back.* Each word a knife thrust to her heart.

She laid her pad on the ground beside her, her thoughts turning around her marriage again. But as she cleaned her brush, then threw out the coloured water from the jar, she identified an additional emotion to the disbelief, pain and confusion she'd experienced since the morning. The first stirrings of anger were adding themselves to the cocktail. After all these years, how dare he? After everything they'd been through together, Daniel was prepared to toss the whole lot away.

If she knew him at all, he'd be finding confession difficult. How long had it taken him to admit that he and Eve had been lovers, albeit briefly? He didn't tell her that for one whole year. A year in which her friendship with Eve had been built on her ignorance. Eve had kept her silence too. By the time Daniel had finally admitted the truth of their relationship, all three of them and Will had become so close that Rose hadn't wanted to unpick things. She loved Daniel and was confident he loved her. Eve was her closest friend by then and deep into her relationship with Will. If anything, sharing Daniel had brought them closer together. The deceit had only been for her benefit and their affair was in the past. Unlike this one. Well, so be it. She would wait until he had no option but to confess. And then she would be ready.

Slinging her bag over her shoulder, she started for home with a heavy heart. By the time she arrived, the others were on the terrace. She heard the click of dominoes, Eve's voice and then Daniel's laughter before she slipped into the house, dropped off her stuff in the studio and went up to their bedroom. Leaving her painting clothes on the bed, she went into the bathroom and turned on the shower. While the water warmed up, she brushed her teeth, staring at her reflection. A middle-aged woman stared back, although something of the tomboy that she had once been was still close to the surface: hair cut short to frame her face, skin freckled, and the beginnings of a few fine lines.

What did 'S' look like? she wondered, shivering slightly despite the heat. What sort of woman would have succeeded where she suspected many had failed? Her polar opposite? She ran through the sex goddess clichés: large, bosomy, fleshy arms and legs, big hair, large-featured, smoky eyes, bee-stung lips. Her breath caught as she pressed her own less generous ones together, watching her eyes well up. She looked away quickly and stepped into the shower, where the jets of water beat on her head, then her face, until she felt nothing but a deep, angry despair.

From the shower she went through to the wardrobe and ripped a choice of clothes off the hangers. What was appropriate for a wronged woman? Having chosen a pair of white linen trousers and an aquamarine T-shirt (as inappropriate as anything else she had), she replaced the rest, slid her feet into her sandals and returned to the bathroom, hand-drying her hair on the way. Just as she was putting on the merest hint of make-up – might as well remind him what he'd be missing – she heard the sound of the door opening. She braced herself.

'Mum!'

Anna. She rushed through to the bedroom, and hugged her older daughter to her. 'I didn't hear the car.' Then she pushed her away so she could see her. 'You look so well.'

Anna's dress sense was nothing if not idiosyncratic. Taller than her mother, she was wearing a long flounced flowery skirt, a skimpy top that emphasised her skinniness, and countless necklaces, and bracelets that clashed together every time she moved her arms. Her long dark hair was pulled back and fastened behind her head with a hibiscus flower clasp. Her face was pale, elfin-like in its sharp lines. A pink sapphire nose stud drew attention to the curve of her nostril.

'And you look, well . . . I don't know. The same as usual, I guess.'

Rose laughed. 'Have you seen the others?'

'Of course not. I wanted to see you first and I guessed you might be here. Pre-drinks shower and all that.' She hadn't forgotten the family routines that had ingrained themselves over the years.

'You know me too well.' Rose took her hand. 'Let's join them. Oh!' She lifted Anna's once pretty hand to the light, now with nails bitten down to the quick. 'I'm not sure about that one. Dad'll hate it.'

'Too bad.' Anna twisted her wrist to admire the large silver ring in the shape of a skull that covered the whole of the lowest section of her middle finger. 'I'm thirty, for God's sake. My life. Remember?'

'I know.' Rose pretended resignation. 'Come on then. I've so much to ask you.'

'Uncle Terry here? And Eve?' Anna sat on the edge of the bed, rattling her bangles up and down her wrist.

'Of course. I'm sure I told you they were getting here before you. Eve's in a state because her case hasn't arrived.'

Anna smiled, knowing too well the hoo-ha that would involve. 'You probably did, but I forgot. I was hoping to catch Dad on his own before they got here.' She looked up at her mother, lifting a

33

hand to her mouth and scraping the top of her thumbnail on a front tooth – a nervous habit.

Rose resisted saying anything. She's not a child any more. She's a grown woman.

'Still, I'll find my moment.'

There was something in Anna's eyes that worried Rose. She must want to wheedle something out of Daniel that she knew he wouldn't easily give. Again. Rose put a hand out to still the clatter of the bangles. She wouldn't ask. Easier to deal with the request when it came, rather than anticipate the worst. Her thumb traced the faint but unmistakable white scars that marked Anna's forearm.

Anna snatched her arm away, strategically rearranging the bangles. 'Have they started arguing yet?'

'Anna, really!' Rose tried to sound disapproving. 'They're not that bad.'

'Yes they are. They're always bickering. At least you and Dad have never been like that.'

'Some people get on best when they're arguing. The bad times make the good times better.' She wasn't sure that was what she really believed. 'Who knows what makes a marriage tick? Not even the people involved . . .' She left the sentence unfinished.

'Mum!'

Anna's voice brought her back to her senses, reminding her that she mustn't let her guard slip. 'What?' she said quickly. Her daughters must know nothing until she and Daniel had sorted things out.

'That's very philosophical for a Monday night.' Anna looked perplexed, as if wondering what had come over her mother.

'You know me, darling. Full of surprises.' Rose stood up, fighting a pressing desire to run away. 'Come on, they'll be wondering what's happened to me. And you must say hello.'

'Make my entrance, you mean?' Anna laughed. 'If you insist.' And she followed her mother from the room.

4

'You're being so obstructive, Dad.' Anna put down her glass and swept her hair back over her shoulder, shaking her head so it fell straight. The hibiscus clasp lay discarded on the table. 'You know you want Jess here as much as we do. It's not going to be the same without them. Just call her.'

Daniel looked up from his fig tart, putting down his spoon. His eyes widened slightly under the frown, surprised at someone disagreeing with a decision he'd made. 'Anna, you don't know what you're talking about. Adam refused the work I offered him.' His voice was quiet but firm as he leaned back in his chair, crossing his arms over his chest. 'If Jess chooses not to come here as a result of what was said, that's her business.' His foot tapped on the floor. Just once. Then again. He scratched behind his ear.

The five of them sat at one end of the large farmhouse table on the terrace, sheltered by the vine-clad pergola. A shaft of light beamed through the open kitchen door, but too far away to il-luminate the table. Instead, the outdoor light over the sitting room door added to the light of the candles. Rose and Anna had made a chestnut and butternut risotto, followed by saltimbocca alla Romana, delicate veal *scaloppini* with prosciutto and sage, all pro-nounced excellent by the others. Until now, the atmosphere had been convivial, relaxed.

Rose recognised the warning signs and stepped in swiftly. 'I'll talk to her,' she said. 'I'll explain and then they'll be on that plane as planned.'

Eve yawned. 'Well one of you should do something, or you'll miss the boat altogether.' She laughed at her rather feeble joke, apparently heedless of the stony silence into which she'd dropped it. 'Or the plane – just like my wretched case!' she added.

Sometime before dinner, Terry had spent an hour on the phone trying to trace the missing luggage. For some reason, it had been rerouted to Rome. The airline had promised to deliver it the next day. In the meantime, Eve was making do with what she could borrow. At the moment she was sporting a generously cut dress of Rose's in fine blue-and-green striped jersey; a much more casual look than she was used to.

Beyond the terrace, down past the pool, the land fell away into the valley towards the inky silhouettes of distant hills pricked with orange and white lights marking out villages or lone farmhouses. The candle flames flickered in the breeze sending shadows slipping across their faces. Rose pulled her pashmina tighter around her shoulders.

Daniel pushed his chair back, noisy on the stone. 'I've got a couple of emails to deal with, if you'll all excuse me. See you in the morning.'

As he disappeared inside, the four of them looked at one another. It was unlike him to leave a gathering early. Rose speculated miserably on the reasons why, but said nothing. Instead, she took a deep breath, hoping to suppress the anxiety that had formed like a marble in her throat. The family had been together for less than twenty-four hours, and nothing was as she'd imagined it.

At least Daniel's absence meant that any row over Adam had been averted before the red light blazed and the rest of them were forced to run for cover. The worst of Daniel's rages were reserved exclusively for his family. Outsiders were rarely exposed to them.

Rose pushed away her half-eaten pudding.

'Go after him, Mum. Now's your moment.'

That spell in therapy had led Anna to believe that she knew what made other people tick, and that gave her the authority to tell them what to do. But Rose, Eve and Terry knew better than anyone how mercurial Daniel's moods could be. Quick to come and quick to go, but best avoided.

'I don't think that's a good idea. You know what he's like. If I go now, he'll only get more entrenched. We'll leave it till the morning.'

'Adam might not be the husband Dad would have chosen for Jess, but he ought to at least give him a chance.' Anna took a small blue tobacco pouch out of her bag. 'I'm never going to get married, if this is what he's going to be like.'

'Anyone on the scene?' Eve leaped at a change of subject.

Rose gave silent thanks for her sister-in-law's insatiable curiosity.

'Hardly.' Anna grinned as she unfolded a Rizla. 'I've been seeing a guy who works in the City, but it was never going to work. He's well into his suits, his cars and owning property. He's even in a choir, and he's not even thirty-five. And I'm . . . well, I'm not like that. He hated the way I dress and we had different opinions on everything.' She looked thoughtful. 'In fact it's a bit of a mystery how we got together in the first place. The sex was pretty good, I guess.' She shredded some tobacco on to the paper and rolled herself the meanest cigarette Rose had ever seen. She'd prefer Anna not to share quite so much of her personal life at the supper table.

Eve laughed. 'Sounds like just the sort of guy that Dan would love for his daughters.'

'Oh, please.' Anna took her lighter from her bag. 'A lifetime of missed opportunity, chained to a kitchen sink, clearing up after our snotty kids and hanging on to his arm at office dos. No thank you.' She pretended to make herself vomit.

Rose was painfully aware how closely the description fitted her own married life, a life about which, until this morning, she had had no complaints. 'Anna, don't.' She grasped her daughter's wrist and pulled her hand away from her mouth, then clasped it in her own. 'That's disgusting.'

'Only to you, mother dear.' Anna wiped her hand on her skirt and lit her cigarette, the loose shreds of tobacco glowing before they flew into the night.

Rose didn't need to remind everyone why she'd reacted as she had. Those days when Anna's departure from the table at the end of a meal was immediately followed by the slam of the bathroom door, then the distant flushing of the toilet, were – thank God – a thing of the past. But Rose remembered them clearly, them and the crushing anxiety and sense of powerlessness that used to be her daily companions. Was there anything worse than your child's life being under threat from an illness you had no power to heal? If there was, she couldn't imagine it. Nothing Dan could do would hurt her as badly as that.

Terry coughed.

'And to you then, Uncle Terry. Sorry. But Eve doesn't mind, do you, best aunt?'

'*Only* aunt,' Eve corrected proudly. 'But if that's how you feel, how's the rest of your life going to pan out?'

Anna filled her glass with water. 'Oh, I've got plans. Men are on hold at the moment while I get things off the ground.' A secretive look crossed her face, swiftly replaced by a worrying (to those who knew her) beam.

'Really? Need any help?' Terry could be relied on to join in when the conversation took a business turn. He wasn't an easy conversationalist in company, never had been. He preferred things one to one. That was something that he and Rose did have in common, although she had learned to be more gregarious.

'Maybe eventually, but not yet. First I've got to convince Dad of their brilliance. And no . . .' She looked towards her mother; Rose was bristling with alarmed interest, aware that if she expressed it, Anna would just clam up. 'I'm not going to tell you anything until they're more definite. You mustn't mention anything to Dad just yet. I'm going to grab him tomorrow when he's in a more receptive mood.'

Rose felt Eve squeeze her thigh under the table. Eve knew Daniel as well as anyone, and like Rose, she knew what sort of response Anna was likely to provoke if she asked for money again. Rose groped for her sister-in-law's hand and squeezed back, grateful to have an ally who understood.

'But it's Eve's birthday,' she said, grasping at the excuse. 'And we're going to Arezzo.'

'That's in the morning.' Nothing would stop Anna when her heart was set on something. 'I'll find a time and then we can celebrate doubly in the evening.' She clapped her hands. 'You're going to be so excited.'

'I hope so.' Another squeeze from Eve. The list of other great ideas that had so rapidly transformed into disasters was already running through Rose's mind. Every time Daniel had supported Anna in one of her ventures – the market stall, importing carpets from Morocco, the café – he was the one who came out the loser. Whatever the reason – bad timing, or Anna's loss of interest – every foolproof project designed to make father and daughter so much money hit the buffers one after another. After the café, Daniel had sworn he'd helped her out for the last time, and that was when she'd taken up gardening, tutoring children in English, maths and French to finance the horticulture course.

'Tell you what,' Eve suggested. 'If you're not going to tell us, why don't you find the Scrabble while we clear the table? In fact, why don't *I* do that, Rose, while you call Jess?' Eve followed Rose into the kitchen, the baking tray containing the remains of the fig tart in her hands. 'At least you can head off one drama at the pass before the next one comes along. And I'd say it was only a matter of hours.' Then, in an undertone so Anna wouldn't hear, 'This looks like it's going to be an extremely interesting couple of weeks.'

'Oh God. Must I call her now? It's late. All I want is a hassle-free fortnight and for everyone to enjoy themselves. Is that really too much to ask?' They both put what they were carrying on the kitchen table.

'Far too much.' Facing her, Eve put a hand on each of Rose's shoulders. 'You've got a conveniently selective memory. A family holiday wouldn't be the same without an argument or two. Don't you remember last year, when Anna almost burned down the garage? Just relax and go with it.'

'If it weren't for you . . .'

'I know. But it cuts both ways. You've supported me when Terry and I have had our bad patches.'

'Because my brother can be such a twit. Sometimes I wonder how you've put up with him for so long.' She darted a look at Eve. Had she gone too far?

But Eve was smiling. 'Don't let's go there. We may regret it.'

Rose thought she detected a hint of sadness. Not Eve and Terry too.

'Go on. Go and phone Jess. I'll take your turn if you're too long.'

Eve's enthusiasm for Scrabble provided the annual proof of Rose's complete ineptitude at the game. Resigned to being soundly thrashed yet again, but delaying the moment, she left Eve to the clearing up and went into the sitting room. Plumping herself on the red sofa, she looked about her, finding comfort in her surroundings. One day she would read all the Italian-related novels and travel literature, memoirs and history books that she'd collected over the years. Time, that was all she needed. Or would she? If Daniel left her, what would happen to Casa Rosa? She couldn't bear to think of the possibilities.

She glanced at the botanical illustrations that she'd completed after the course she'd taken at the Chelsea Physic Garden years ago, inspired by those in the books her father collected. Her progression from the first shaky single hellebore through to the increasingly confident tulips, irises and roses was striking. As she lifted the phone, she wondered briefly whether she should try her hand at them again. Such a precise skill and surprisingly time-consuming, but the satisfaction she'd got from doing them had been exhilarating.

She checked the clock over the fireplace. Nine thirty. It would be an hour earlier in England. Dylan should be in bed by now, upstairs in his tiny blue bedroom, mobile churning out a tinkling version of 'Greensleeves'. Adam and Jess would be downstairs in the cottage, Jess exhausted after a long day at the hotel, sitting down to a dinner cooked by Adam. Daniel should cut him some slack. Adam struck her as an attentive and loving husband. What more could a parent want for their daughter? According to Daniel, plenty more. Could he be right about Adam having an ulterior motive for marrying their daughter? People didn't really marry for money these days, did they? Wasn't that the stuff of Jane Austen? Beside, three modest hotels hardly represented a fortune. But Daniel was so sure . . .

She dialled the number, listened to it ringing. As she straightened the dog-eared editions of the magazines in the basket beside her, she noticed one of Dylan's board books at the bottom. Jess must have left it behind when they'd stayed in the spring. She held it on her lap, tracing the outline of the large green caterpillar with her finger, waiting for them to pick up. Eventually the answerphone kicked in. Adam's voice invited her to leave a message. The fact that they must be deliberately not answering the phone made her uncomfortable.

'Jess, it's Mum.' She hesitated, not sure what to say next, not wanting to make things worse, aware they might be listening. 'Do call and let me know when you're expecting to get here. Love you . . .' She hung up. That was enough. Better to pretend nothing was wrong and then everything might just fall back into place by itself. A coward's way out, but, she reminded herself, sometimes the way things worked best.

She lay back against the cushions. The effort required to get up and rejoin the others seemed suddenly overwhelming. Keeping up the pretence that nothing was wrong was already taking its toll. But if she didn't, Eve's suspicions would grow and she'd have to admit what was wrong before she was certain. With that thought, Rose pushed herself to the edge of the seat and stood up, despite her weariness.

On her way to join the others, she was passing the door of Daniel's study when she heard his voice. There was something she didn't recognise in the way he was speaking, quietly, confidentially, but with an undertow of something else. Anxiety? Nervousness? *Miss. Love. Come back.* She found herself straining to make out what he was saying. 'Never,' she heard, then, after a moment, 'We can't.' Her stomach lurched. *We?* If she hadn't read the text, she would have thought nothing of such a conversation. Now she was looking for another meaning in everything he said.

The feelings she had been trying to ignore roared to the front of her mind, fury taking the lead. Wasn't this her moment? Wasn't their marriage more important than anything else? All she had to do was throw open the door and challenge him. Caught in the act of talking to 'S', Daniel would have to admit the truth. Then the affair would be in the open and they'd have to deal with it – together. She rested her hand on the solid wooden door and prepared herself.

'Mu-um! Are you coming?' Anna's shout stopped her. Her arm dropped to her side. No. However much she was hurting and wanted everything in the open (though she dreaded it too), she would hold to her original plan. She was frightened of a confrontation, because . . . then what?

As she bent to pick up the board book, which had slipped from her hand, the door flew open. Daniel watched as she straightened up to face him. Was that a flicker of guilt in his eyes as he stared at her in surprise?

'I thought I heard something. What on earth are you doing there?'

'I'm just going out again, but I dropped this.' She passed him the book and saw his face soften. 'I called Jess, but there was no reply.'

The tenderness in his expression disappeared as he handed the book back. 'I've got a few other things I need to do before I go to bed. I'll see you up there.' He turned back into the study. 'Wouldn't mind a cup of tea, if there's one on the go.'

'I'll make you one.' Her routine response; even through gritted teeth, it was one of the many familiar patterns of behaviour that made up the tracks on which their marriage had run so smoothly.

'Thanks, darling.' And the door shut between them.

Had he been talking on the phone to *her*? Were the words that she'd heard significant? In all the years they'd been together, she had never imagined there was a duplicitous bone in his body. As far as she was aware, he had always insisted on fair dealing in both his personal and professional lives.

Rose marched through the kitchen, ignoring the kettle and the ceramic jar of tea bags, the coloured mugs hanging from the hooks on the dresser, and went out to join the others where the Scrabble board was set up with a couple of words already on the board: LIES criss-crossed with RELATE. Terry was puzzling over his letters, Eve clucking with impatience for her turn. Anna was staring out towards the mountains, smoking, no doubt dreaming about her latest scheme and how best to worm the support she needed out of her father. Someone had poured Rose another glass of wine. She sat down and took a gulp. Daniel could make his own bloody tea.

5

The back of Daniel's ears had deepened to a dark red and his fists were white-knuckled on the steering wheel. 'Bloody tourists,' he muttered. 'We should have known.' He pulled into yet another side street crowded with parked cars, not a space in sight, reversed into an opening, gears crashing, and turned around to go back the way they'd come.

They'd left home early that morning to take the scenic route to Arezzo through vineyards, fields of overripe sweetcorn, dying sunflowers and rows of tomatoes ripe for the picking. Finally they joined the spaghetti of arterial roads close to the city. Following the signs, they'd driven towards the centre, only to discover their usual car park full. Roadblocks and diversion signs had sent them into a confusion of residential streets where they were now lost. Daniel stopped the car, ignoring the shout of a man guiding a van out of a gateway beside them.

'Look, why don't you get out here? I'll try the station and then meet you in the square in a couple of hours.' He gave an impatient gesture at the man in the street, indicating that he should wait a second, and was rewarded with a string of expressive but incomprehensible Italian expletives.

'I'll keep you company, Dad. I've seen the frescoes often enough to last a lifetime. We can have a wander and a coffee together.' Anna climbed out with the others to take Eve's place in the front seat, ignoring Daniel's insistence that he'd be all right on his own. She waved as they drove off, giving Rose and Eve a thumbs-up.

'Trust her to find her moment.' Rose began to cross the road, with Eve behind her.

'Poor old Dan. Doesn't know what's about to hit him.'

'Oh, I think he'll have a fair idea.' When she reached the

44

pavement, Rose turned to wait. 'After all, it's not the first time it's happened. This way.'

Eve followed Rose along Via Francesco Crispi, turning into the Corso Italia and up the hill, past the shiny modern shops, diving into the shadow where she could, feeling the sun burning her skin when she couldn't. She hesitated in front of a couple of clothes shops – there was something about Italian style – then caught sight of herself, hot and bothered in Daniel's walking trousers. She'd zipped off the bottom half of the legs, turning them into the most unflattering of shorts. The belted waistband was hidden, but its bunched outline was obvious under the slightly too tight sleeveless black T-shirt she'd plundered from Jess's maternity wardrobe. She pulled it away from her midriff then let it spring back. In contrast, on the other side of the glass, staring back through her reflection, were pin-thin mannequins dressed in winter grey wools and suedes, plum faux furs, high black boots. No, now was definitely not the moment for shopping. Turning away, she saw smiling customers leaving a shop licking multicoloured ice creams that overflowed their cornets, or spooning mouthfuls from tubs. She peered into the shop's cool interior, where rows of gaudy ice creams called out for her to try them, but Rose was too far ahead to be stopped, pressing on through the shoppers, not wanting to be late.

Keeping her sister-in-law's red sundress in sight, Eve followed her round a corner and up some steps to the rough stone facade of the Basilica San Francesco. By now her hair was sticking to her forehead and the back of her neck, her back running with sweat. By contrast, Rose was looking almost as cool as when they'd started out.

'A quick drink at that café?' Eve suggested, picturing a glass of iced tea packed with ice and lemon, so cold that condensation ran down its sides.

'They're timed tickets, so we'd better not.' Rose looked apologetic. 'But as soon as we're done we will. You do still want to see the frescoes?'

'Of course. I just hadn't imagined that it would be this hot this early.' Eve fanned herself with the guidebook that she'd picked up on the way out of Casa Rosa.

'That's why we're here now. We'll be back home by the time it really heats up.'

Eve nodded, resigned to feeling like a wrung-out old dishrag for the day. 'I just haven't got used to it yet, that's all.'

Inside the barn-like Capella Baci, there was at least immediate respite from the sun. The sound of music from somewhere outside broke the reverential hush. Knots of people whispered to one another in front of the shadowy paintings along the walls. Incense scented the air. Eyeing the rows of chairs with longing, Eve was aware that a blister was forming on the sole of her foot. If she'd only had her comfortable but oh-so-stylish sandals, which were still in her case. At the chancel, Rose presented their tickets to the attendant, who held back the red rope.

In the small area behind the altar, Eve gazed in awe at Piero della Francesca's frescoes of the Legend of the True Cross. Rose had told her how magnificent they were, but she had not been prepared for this. Rose spoke softly, explaining the cycle of paintings, but after ten minutes Eve's concentration was wavering and she could no longer ignore her stinging foot and the crick in her neck from looking upwards. The heat in the small space was overwhelming, thanks to the vast uplighter illuminating the walls. She opened her camera case with a loud Velcro rip that made heads turn. A man wagged a disapproving finger at her. Rose shook her head. Eve shut the case again, even though other people were snapping away regardless. With her back against the altar wall, she sank to a sitting position and pulled out her BlackBerry. Her attention having waned, this seemed as good a moment as any to check whether Amy had emailed her yet. She hadn't.

'Was I boring you?' Rose whispered, crouching beside her. 'I got a bit carried away.'

'No. It's not that. I thought I'd check whether Amy had been in touch.'

'What's the point in having an assistant if you can't trust them to hold the fort without you?' Rose stood, obviously upset by Eve's lack of interest.

'Don't be like that.' Eve shoved the BlackBerry back in her bag as she got to her feet. 'I think they're marvellous. Really, I do.'

'I know I go on.'

'I promise you I do.' Eve winced as her blister stung. 'I just had to sit down for a moment. Now, tell me about the last two. I want to know,' she protested to Rose's look of scepticism.

Beside them a family of three English boys stood to attention as their father pointed out the artist's use of perspective, just as Rose was explaining it to her. Eve tried to concentrate on what she was being told but instead found herself imagining Terry and her bringing Charlie, Tom, Luke and Millie here. They'd have lasted two seconds before boredom morphed into mayhem. But of course she'd have had to drag Terry in, in the first place. Renaissance art was not on his list of must-sees. For him, Italy was for hedonism only. He was happiest by the pool or in the hammock, relaxing until the next meal or drink came along. And if she was honest, Eve was more than glad to follow suit most of the time.

'Oh come on.' Rose smiled. 'I know when I'm beaten. Let's go and get that coffee.'

Almost crying out loud with relief, Eve limped beside her towards the exit and into the small piazza outside, where they took a table in the shade at the café opposite.

'Whatever you think, I love all this and having you as my guide.' The truth. But just not in this temperature.

'It's fine. Really.' Rose called the waiter over. '*Un te freddo e un caffe macchiato, per favore*. It was hot in there.'

After a while, she asked for the bill. 'We'd better get going. I want to show you the one della Francesca in the cathedral before we meet the others.'

'Don't you ever let up!' Eve groaned, her foot pleading for release.

'If you'd rather not . . .' Rose pulled her purse out of her bag and put it on the table.

'I was only joking,' Eve hastened to reassure her. 'Where's your sense of humour? This isn't like you.'

'Feeling a bit sensitive, I suppose. No reason.' Rose twisted her wedding ring round and round her finger. 'Sorry.'

'Thinking of the others, what's up with Dan?' Eve couldn't resist asking. If Rose wouldn't talk about herself, then perhaps she would about her husband.

'Nothing, as far as I know. Why?' Rose counted out her euros. They chinked as they hit the saucer.

'He's normally so relaxed here, but this time . . . I don't know.' Eve watched Rose put away her purse. She could see from her friend's closed expression that she'd touched a nerve. Once she'd done that, she didn't like to give up until she'd unearthed the problem. Rose didn't always confide easily, preferring to mull over her troubles, hoping they'd resolve themselves without having to involve anyone else. However, there had been the time when, over a couple of bottles of wine, Rose had finally told her about Anna's eating disorder and then her self-harming. Since then, she'd admitted that being able to talk about her worries had helped her get through that difficult period, when she and Daniel were at odds over what to do. Afterwards, though, she'd retreated back into the shell of her marriage, where she and Daniel were most comfortable.

If there was anything disturbing the status quo, Eve wanted to be able to help fix it. Rose and Daniel's relationship usually struck her as the perfect balance of independence from and dependence upon each other. They never seemed to have had any doubts about their rightness for one another. They may have had the odd difference of opinion, but where was the harm in that? Having the downs made you appreciate the ups so much more. And she should know. And despite Dan's love of company, Eve suspected they had no real need for anyone else. Rose's confidence in her marriage and her unshakeable belief that it was for keeps were enviable. She had never voiced the kind of doubts about the partnership that nagged away at Eve about hers.

'Evie. Stop fishing. There's nothing to catch.'

Eve wasn't convinced, but they were on their feet, arms linked as they walked up through the narrow streets to the top of the hill. Inside the main doors of the cathedral there was an air of expectancy. People were milling about, dressed up to the nines.

'A wedding,' Rose said. 'Let's look quickly at La Magdalena and then we can come back.'

'Look' and 'quickly' – two words that Eve would never have put together when it came to Rose's love of art. However, she followed her towards the altar.

By the time they'd seen the small fresco – 'Hands like a prize-fighter' was Eve's response, which earned her a quick glare then a resigned shrug – a crowd was hovering around the brightly lit vaulted side chapel. The guests trooped down the red carpet to the sound of organ music, stopping and chattering, finding their seats. The clamour at the cathedral door increased as the bystanders separated to reveal the groom, a slight young man drowned in a shiny blue suit ('Bought for him to grow into,' whispered Rose), his hair greased into place and a look of terror in his eyes. Beside him walked a beaming older woman ('His mother?' wondered Eve), who nodded greetings at those she recognised. She led him down the red carpet to the altar, where he stood waiting.

'Just like a lamb to the slaughter,' whispered Eve.

'Here comes the lucky woman.' Rose nodded in the direction of the bride, who stepped into the cathedral on the arm of her father. Unlike her groom, the buxom young woman was like a well-plumped white satin cushion, a picture of glowing expectation.

'Look at her shoes,' muttered Eve as the bride swept past. The hem of the bridal gown was lifted enough to show off a pair of towering heels that raised the bride to a full five foot two or thereabouts. The organ music paused as a medieval-uniformed herald trumpeted her approach. When the fanfare died away, the familiar notes of Handel's Wedding March struck up. The groom turned, a nervous smile lighting up his face.

'Little do they know what lies ahead.' Eve was already heading for the door.

'Cynic! Where's your spirit of romance?' Rose tore herself reluctantly away from the ceremony.

'Lost in a reality check years ago.' So many of those early expectations that came with her marriage to Terry had tarnished with age or rubbed away altogether. 'Don't tell me yours has survived unscathed. I won't believe you!'

Outside, despite the shade offered by the narrow old streets, it was hotter than ever. They stuck close to the tall buildings until they entered the loggia at the top of the Piazza Grande. Passing through one busy café after another, they finally spotted Daniel staring across the sloping square where another bride and groom were posing for photos on the steps of the old tribunal palace. Opposite him, Anna was gesticulating wildly as she made a point, minuscule roll-up in one hand, smoke pluming from her mouth. His face was as solemn as hers was excited.

When she stopped, Daniel shrugged, apparently unmoved. He looked around as Rose touched his shoulder, a small complicit smile crossing his face. The speed at which Rose removed her hand struck Eve as unusual.

'You'll never guess what,' he said. 'Anna's asked me to support her in her latest plan. She's going to open a nursery.'

Eve heard Rose's gasp, although Daniel showed no sign that he thought the idea was in any way preposterous.

'Really?' she said weakly.

'Isn't it brilliant?' Anna rounded on them. 'But I need some financial help to get me going.'

'*Some* help?' Dan interrupted. 'You're asking me to finance you to the tune of thousands of pounds.'

'But Anna,' Rose protested, alarmed. 'Have you had enough experience of teaching?'

'What?' Her daughter turned on her, her face pinched with irritation. 'What are you talking about?'

'Opening a school means . . .' Rose stopped as Daniel smiled broadly, Anna wound like a spring beside him, both their eyes on her.

'She's talking about a garden centre,' Daniel explained. 'Not a school, darling.' He sounded as if he was talking to a three-year-old. 'She wants me to back her . . . again.'

Eve stifled a laugh. This was obviously not the moment.

'And you won't? I should have known.' The ten-year-old Anna revealed herself in the pout, the crossing of her arms and the angry toss of her head.

'Did I say that?' Daniel finished his coffee. 'No. What I said was that I would need to see some proper financial projections that would convince me the project was viable. I need to meet this Rick, if he's going to be your partner, and listen to what he has to say too.'

'Exactly. You won't.' She reached into her tobacco pouch for her cigarette papers.

'Anna, listen to me,' insisted Daniel. 'No one with half a business brain would lend you the money without them. I'm surprised that you thought I might. You're asking for a considerable investment, not a packet of sweets. Besides, what about Jess? I'd need to square things with her. No, this has to be a proper business arrangement between us.'

'That's just an excuse. You're against it on principal because I've had some bad luck in the past. This time I've got the ideas and the support. I'm older and I've learned from my mistakes. It can't go wrong. You'll see.' She began to roll another cigarette, her mouth set, her shoulders tense. 'We might as well go now.'

'Perhaps we should,' agreed Rose, wondering when Rick had come into the picture. She would find out later, no doubt. 'I need to pick up a few bits and pieces for tonight on the way home.'

While Daniel went inside to find the waiter, Anna stood up. 'I think I'll go on ahead. He can be so bloody unreasonable.' She put the shoulder strap of her bag over her head, bangles rattling, and walked off.

'Can't you try to talk some sense into her?' Rose begged. 'She won't listen to me. I need to go to the deli; I'll meet you all back at the car.'

'I'll do my best.' Eve promised, even though Anna was no more likely to listen to her than she was to Rose.

Anna was heading across the sloping square towards the church in the far corner. By the time Eve had elbowed her way through a bunch of Lycra-clad cyclists who'd dropped their cycles where they'd got off them and were showering bottles of water over each other, her quarry had disappeared between the buildings. Wondering whether she wouldn't be better removing her sandals, which were now rubbing on her other foot too, Eve limped after her, biting the corner of her lip to displace the pain.

She eventually caught up at a row of canvas-covered street stalls. Anna was talking to one of the stallholders who was surrounded by cages of small birds. Eve approached just as her niece handed over cash in exchange for a cage containing two zebra finches.

'What *are* you doing, Anna? You're not taking them back in the car? You can't. The poor things.' Having been sent ahead to put matters right, Eve realised that the situation had already slipped right out of her grasp.

Bar a long-suffering glance, Anna ignored her. Not entirely surprised by the lack of reaction (four children of her own meant she knew what to expect), Eve watched as Anna put the cage on the ground, opened the door and reached inside for one of the birds. She held it cupped in her hands. A few passers-by had stopped to see what she was doing, but she ignored them. She held the bird up, looking into its beady frightened eyes, kissed its orange beak then tossed it into the air.

A knot of people gathered round her, cheering. There was a click of a camera as she reached down for the second bird. Playing to her growing audience, she stood, showed it around, then repeated the performance. The second bird flew upwards to join the other where it sat on a tree branch. For a moment they looked down at the crowd before disappearing together through the branches above them into the sky.

'Freedom, Eve. We're all entitled to that.' Anna handed the cage back to the open-mouthed stallholder and wiped her hands on her skirt, looking satisfied with what she had just done.

Eve said nothing. Perhaps this was not the best moment to remind Anna of birds of prey, of nature red in tooth and claw, of the fact that freedom often came at a price.

6

Rose's harmonious family holiday was in free fall. Experience should have taught her, but she had successfully blanked all those nightmare holiday moments from the past, which now rushed unbidden into her mind – trapped in a freezing Welsh cottage, rain battering at the windows, with only one jigsaw that was missing the vital pieces; losing Anna on a crowded beach; Jess burning her hand on a Calor gas light that had been left on the floor during a power cut; the hire boat capsizing when Dan insisted on diving off it – each one a cause for upset or reproach. Back then, an argument could be resolved, a mood transformed, a doctor called, a game begun, the TV switched on. But now . . . now things were very different.

She sat slumped at the kitchen table. How had they ended up with two daughters who, so many years later, could still cause them so much heartache? Was it the way she and Daniel had brought them up? As for Daniel . . . the sick feeling in the pit of her stomach that had been lodged there since the previous day gave another roll. If only everyone would disappear so they could talk. Perhaps it wasn't too late. Perhaps she had overreacted and things hadn't gone as far as she feared.

Jess had still not returned her phone call. Not even a message. Of course, she was busy managing Trevarrick all day, but was that also a convenient excuse not to contact her? Had Daniel finally driven a permanent wedge between them? But surely Jess realised that her father would come round in the end.

Meanwhile Anna, who had endured the drive back from Arezzo without another word to any of them before refusing lunch, was now sulking by the pool. Rose had gone down to try to persuade her to eat something, but Anna's head was turned away, her eyes firmly shut, her earphones in. The message was clear.

Daniel had been unusually quiet since they'd returned. As soon as he could, he had shut himself in the study under pretext of work that needed to be done. *Miss. Love. Come back*. The words tormented Rose.

She had noticed Terry's surprised reaction to Daniel's departure. When her brother holidayed, he didn't muddle pleasure with work. Never. His life was organised within an inch of itself with each of its compartments distinct from the rest. However, since they'd been back, Terry and Eve had clearly had some kind of tiff and were now barely speaking. He had retired to the sitting room, where he was glued to Sky Sports, the sound of the excited commentary just audible in the kitchen. Eve had disappeared to their room to sleep off the couple of large glasses of white wine she'd downed at lunch in the face of Terry's obvious disapproval – again.

Rose picked up her mobile and stared at Jess's number. She could put herself out of her misery by simply making the call. Her finger hovered, then pressed the home button. Nothing worse than a nagging mother. Nothing. Not that she had had one to compare herself to. Her mother had lived a life at one remove from her children, often retiring to bed 'tired and emotional' after too much refreshment or when she was feeling under par. Nonetheless, when Jess got married, Rose had made herself a shortlist of don'ts as a reminder.

Don't nag.

Don't worry.

Don't interfere.

Don't moan.

Don't compare.

Don't be wise after the event.

Don't treat them like children.

She suspected that she'd failed on all counts already.

She tucked the phone into her apron pocket, and turned her attention to weighing out the flour to make Eve's birthday brownies for that evening's celebration. Every year Eve asked her not to make a fuss, and every year Rose took no notice. Eve would be so let down if there weren't a party, however low key. Besides, having something to do occupied her. Cooking was a great soother of the soul. Breaking the eggs into the sugar, she balanced the bowl on a damp cloth to steady it and began to beat them with strong, regular strokes. Comforted by the rhythm, her thoughts wandered back to Daniel and Terry.

During all the years he'd looked after the hotel's finances, nothing of Terry's pragmatic attitude towards business had rubbed off on Daniel. Her husband's work–life balance was non-existent and always had been. Where Terry could delegate, Daniel hated handing over responsibility for anything, even to his brother-in-law or daughter, the two people he probably trusted the most. As a result, he was on call twenty-four/seven. Rose was used to him disappearing to take care of whatever needed his attention and re-appearing when things were sorted. Her own involvement in the business had ended years ago, when she chose to be a full-time mum, and she was grateful that Daniel had embraced so whole-heartedly what her parents had left them. But her recent discovery had thrown his absences into question. For the first time, her trust in him had been rocked.

Rose's only company was a tiny lizard poised motionless halfway up the wall by the door. She wrapped a couple of handfuls of walnuts in a tea towel and crushed them with the end of a rolling pin. It was hot in the kitchen, despite the sun never penetrating the furthest reaches of the room. The shaft that did enter the doorway acted as a sundial. As it narrowed and slanted more obliquely towards the dresser, she knew it must be nearing five o'clock. She wiped her face with the edge of her apron.

Humming 'I Vow to Thee My Country' – one of her old school hymns – she eventually put the brownie mixture into the oven and began to clear up. She wasn't religious, despite her haphazard C of E upbringing, but there was something soothing about the music of her childhood that she returned to without thinking when she needed a little balm in her life.

'What is this? A funeral or something?'

Rose looked up at the sound of Anna's voice. 'Just singing to myself.'

'I'm sorry, Mum.' Anna came over to put her arm round Rose's shoulders, licking the middle finger of her other hand and wiping her mother's cheek. 'You've got flour all over your face!'

Her gesture revived times past when, to cries of protest, Rose would spit on the corner of a hankie to clean up the girls' faces. She lifted a hand to her other cheek and gave it a swift rub.

'Look, I brought these. Will they make up for my being such a sulky bitch?' Anna handed over a small candy-striped paper bag.

As Rose opened the bag, she began to laugh. 'They're heaven! Where did you get them?' In her hand lay ten cake candles: ten plump little pink wax bodies on sticks, five of them buxom in salmon-pink basques, white stockings and suspenders and five of them in posing pouches, bow ties and cuffs.

'One of those gift shops that are full of crap no one needs – except for these.'

'Eve's going to love them.' Rose slipped them back into the bag and put them next to the cooling rack.

'Can I do anything?' This was Anna's way of making up.

Rose could feel her own relief at the return of Anna's good humour. 'Not really. But you could dig out the Happy Birthday banner and pin it up.'

'Are you sure? Isn't she a bit old for that sort of thing?' Realising how scathing she sounded, Anna modified her tone. 'Wouldn't something a bit more sophisticated be better?'

'If you can think of something, then by all means.' But Rose knew that Anna, like the rest of them, relied on these totems from the past. These familiar and well-loved traditions saw them through every year.

Anna had already opened the cupboard at the far end of the room and was rootling about. 'Oh my God. I can't believe you kept this.' She pulled out a broken piñata – a donkey made out of frills of green, yellow and pink paper, one ear hanging off, a useless remnant of her twenty-first party that Rose hadn't been able to bring herself to throw away, for silly sentimental reasons. As she tried to unearth the banner, Anna spoke again, this time more tentatively. 'You don't think the idea of a garden centre's mad, do you?'

The need for reassurance was a touching reminder of the child Anna had been.

Rose chose her words carefully. 'No, not mad exactly.'

'Well if not mad, then what?' Immediately Anna was on the defensive. 'It's exactly what our area needs. Lots of gardens, nowhere to buy plants. It's just a question of finding the right property.'

'Really?' Rose said vaguely as she tried to smooth out the crushed Happy Birthday banner, wishing she'd had the forethought to buy a new one. 'I'm sure you could make it work. It's just that—'

But Anna didn't let her finish. 'Well then, Dad's just got to help us. You'll talk to him, won't you?'

So that was the reason for her apology. Good old Anna, always to be relied on to think of number one.

'Darling, there's no need for me to talk to him. All you have to do is produce the paperwork he's asked for.'

'I might have known you'd be on his side.' Anna got up, the heel of her espadrille catching in the hem of her skirt. She righted it with a frustrated tug that ripped the stitching. 'Shit!' The bangles rattled.

'I'm not on anyone's side,' protested Rose, but her words were wasted on her daughter, who was already disappearing down the corridor.

Rose sat back on her knees and sighed, closing her eyes and, with her thumbs pressing against her cheekbones, massaged her temples in slow, soothing circles while waiting for Anna to return. Her daughter never gave up that easily. If only she could be more like Jess instead of constantly swimming against the current. They had always been so different. While Jess worked in the hotel bar or as a chambermaid during the school holidays, Anna would be mucking out at the local riding school or working as a track hand at the nearby go-kart circuit. When Jess was at home playing or reading, Anna would escape for hours with their Border terrier, Button, down to the beach or the long wooded valley that stretched inland near the hotel. They had no need of the company of anyone else. Those days were easy in comparison with this.

She didn't have to wait for long. The smell of the brownies was filling the kitchen when her daughter returned, obviously having composed herself to try again.

'If it's being fair to Jess that's worrying you both, I really don't think you should.'

'I suspect that's not Dad's main concern.' Leaving the banner on the table, Rose took the brownies from the oven, plunging a skewer into the nearest.

'She has got the hotel, after all.'

Rose studied the chocolate goo on the skewer, satisfied. Then, 'Hardly "got",' she corrected.

'Maybe not, technically. But it's only a matter of time. She's managing Trevarrick now. I know she's answerable about every-thing to Dad, but even so.'

'But you never wanted to have anything to do with the place,' Rose objected. 'Jess has worked every holiday there since she was a teenager and took her hospitality business management degree exactly so that she could make her career there. She loves Cornwall, whereas you flew off to the other side of the world as soon as you could.' She decided not to remind Anna that the trip was some-thing else largely funded by Daniel.

'Exactly. My point. I didn't want to work there, true, but Dad has supported her all the way. Now that I've found something I really want to do, that I believe in, it's my turn. It's only fair.'

Rose's heart sank. So that was it. Jess's focus and stability had always rankled with her sister, despite all her airy reassurances to the contrary. As parents, she and Daniel had tried to ensure that everything they gave their daughters was divided equally. However, as they grew older, that became more difficult. Toys were one thing, easy to share, but what was given in terms of time, love, support and so on was unquantifiable. It had been too easy to dismiss Anna as wilful, headstrong, while praising Jess for her single-minded dedication and pleasure taken in her work. Rose was beginning to realise that supporting Anna in her madcap schemes set against Jess's involvement with the hotel had not been perceived as equality. But did Dan?

'I don't want to get involved in whatever you're discussing with Dad. It'll only muddle things.'

'But you could talk to him?' Anna gnawed at her thumbnail.

'I could. But I must sort out this nonsense between Jess and him first. It won't be the same if they don't come.'

All she got in reply was an irritated 'Pah!'

'We can talk to Dad after they're arrived. One thing at a time. Be patient.' As if Anna could ever be that. *And our marriage has to come at the very bottom of that list, when it should be at the top.* Rose's stomach twisted again. She poured herself a glass of water.

'And if she doesn't come? We'd all get by.' Anna sounded so matter-of-fact as she studied her thumbnail.

I wouldn't, whispered a small voice inside Rose's head. *I know I shouldn't mind so much, but it wouldn't be the same.*

'Anyway, she's got Adam and Dylan. They . . .' Anna was obviously about to say something dismissive but thought better of it and changed the subject. 'Where shall we hang this banner?' She'd lost interest in what didn't immediately concern her.

Rose's desperate hope that, with time, Anna's youthful solipsism would give way to altruism had yet to be fulfilled. How she missed Jess's straightforward down-to-earth approach to life that generally made her so much easier to deal with than her older sister. Everything she did was considered, the pros and cons weighed up, the risks assessed before she acted. Her only blind spot was where Adam was concerned. Her loyalty and support for him was unswerving. Just as Rose's had always been for Daniel. How ironic that it should be that quality, inherited from her mother, that was causing ructions in the family.

Rose followed Anna outside, each of them carrying an end of the banner. A bank of cloud was gathering in the west. The walnut tree creaked in the breeze, its leaves rustling. There'd been talk of storms since they arrived the previous week, but as yet no sign. Was the weather about to break at last?

Rose climbed on to a chair and fastened the ends of the banner on the two nails on the pergola that had supported more birthday banners over the years than she cared to count. Hung high enough for the creases to be unnoticeable as it fluttered in the wind, it gave a certain festive feeling to the terrace. The tired melted stumps in the lanterns needed to be replaced. She wondered where she'd put the new candles. With them and the red paper napkins, a good meal and the stack of brownies with their wax strippers, the atmosphere would be suitably celebratory.

'And I'm going to do the cocktails,' Anna announced. 'Prosecco and brandy. That should warm the old man up.'

'Oh Anna, no. Can't you leave well alone for one night? For Eve's sake, if no one else's. It's her birthday and you've got the next ten days to talk to Daniel. Why does everything have to be done in such a rush?'

Anna stood still for a moment, as Rose's words sank in. Eve was her aunt and godmother. She loved her. She screwed up her face as she considered. 'OK. But I'm still going to make some killer cocktails – you know Eve'll love them – and I will ask him again once this stupid Jess business is sorted.'

So she *had* taken on board what her mother had said. Not quite a first, but a pleasant surprise nonetheless. The two of them went indoors and began to get everything ready that was needed for the table that night. As Rose tried to find enough matching knives and forks in the dresser drawer, her mobile rang. She took it from her apron pocket. Jess, at last.

'Jess! I hoped you'd call.' Don't sound as desperate as you feel.

'But you left a message, didn't you?' Jess sounded puzzled.

'Of course. But I know how busy you are.' And don't be too craven either. She could hear Dylan burbling in the background. The sound of him made real how badly she wanted them to be at the villa. She waited for Jess to speak.

'The thing is, Mum . . . Sorry.' She stopped to shout, 'Adam, can you take Dylan? He's trying to eat the cat food.'

Rose waited, picturing the scene in the tiny kitchen where Jess would be edging to one side as her burly husband swept Dylan up into his arms, tickling him with his beard. She could hear her grandson's squeals of laughter receding as Adam removed him into another room.

'Mum, the thing is . . .' Jess was back, her voice hesitant but serious.

'Yes.' Rose dreaded what she was about to hear, but was aware of Anna watching her and tried to compose herself.

'Well, Adam and I have been talking . . .'

For God's sake spit it out. Put me out of my misery. Just say you're not coming and I'll have to get on with it.

Anna took a can of Coke from the fridge and opened it so it sprayed over the table. Rose, reaching for a cloth, barely caught Jess's words.

'We've agreed that it's better if he doesn't come to Italy this summer.'

'But you always come.' The words burst out of her. 'You must.' She felt Anna's hand on her shoulder.

'Mum! You're not listening.' Jess sounded impatient. 'I'm coming with Dylan but we're leaving Adam behind. He's going to prepare some pieces for an exhibition and this is a heaven-sent opportunity for him. He's had some wood he's been waiting to turn for ages.'

Rose grabbed a kitchen chair and sat down, all her strength deserting her. 'You are? Really?' The tears that never seemed far away since the previous morning threatened. She wiped her eyes with a tea towel as Anna's grip on her shoulder tightened.

'Yes, really.' Jess laughed. 'I'd miss it, and I know how much you want to see Dylan.'

'And Adam too,' she insisted.

'But Dad can't go on treating Adam the way he does. He's my husband whether he likes it or not. And I'm happy that he's a woodturner. Money isn't everything. Dad's got to realise that.'

'I'll talk to him. I promise.' How many times had she said that over the years?

'No.' Jess was firm. 'I want to be the one to make him understand that he can't run our lives. Is he there?'

'He's catching up on some work.' Familiar family shorthand for 'he mustn't be disturbed'. He could be doing anything. Rose didn't want to think about the calls he could be making.

'OK, but I definitely want to speak to him myself and get a few things straight between us before we fly.' For once, Jess wasn't going to take no for an answer. 'I'm working this evening so I'll call him tomorrow. You'll tell him, won't you?'

'Wouldn't it be better to wait until you can talk face to face?' Rose asked, despite knowing that Jess had already made up her mind.

'We will. But there are a couple of things I want to say to him before I get there. Sorry, Mum, but that's the way it is. I've got to – for Adam's sake. Try to understand.'

Rose reluctantly conceded, and they finished the conversation shortly afterwards. As she returned to the party preparations, she realised that the joy that she'd expected to feel with the knowledge that her family would be complete as they gathered around her had been superseded by a feeling of dread.

7

That afternoon, sleep had eluded Eve. Lying on her bed, loosely covered with a sheet, she had lain gently sweating, wishing her case would arrive. If Terry had booked them in with a scheduled airline, this would never have happened. Another tiny strike against him. She could see her one and only pair of knickers drying on the back of the chair outside. Jess's maternity pair that she'd been lent were humongous and uncomfortable, baggy even, but at least she could get them on, unlike Rose's.

Before they'd left for Arezzo, Rose had knocked on their door.

'I just thought you might need these,' she said, holding out a froth of fabric. 'They're new. Bought for the holiday.'

Eve had taken and separated the offering into three ridiculously exotic pairs of women's briefs – pink satin adorned with black lace; gold and black polka dot; coffee-coloured lace. And brief was the word. She stared at them and gulped, remembering the plain black cotton knickers she'd stuffed into her case. 'They're, er . . .' She struggled to find the right word. 'Perfect. Perhaps just a touch on the small side.'

'Nonsense. They'll stretch. Anyway, have them as an extra birthday present.' Rose was completely serious, apparently not seeing that there was as much chance of Eve fitting into them as her flying to the moon. She left her staring at them. But their size wasn't what had upset Eve. Instead, it was what they said to her about her sex life. She was more of an M&S girl herself – safe, neat but not sexy. Whereas these spelled out raunch, seduction, action. Maybe the difference symbolised her and Terry's dwindling bedroom activity. Dwindling . . . hmm. She thought about it. They'd definitely reached some sort of hiatus over the last few months. Except that the word hiatus suggested that business was to be resumed as usual. There was no evidence to suggest that this was the case. Perhaps if she sported underwear like this, Terry's interest would be reignited.

But what about her own interest? If she was honest with herself, she couldn't remember when she had last wanted Terry. Maybe when they needed to replace one of the irritatingly fiddly ceiling downlighters, to fix a jammed lock or something to do with the car or a computer. But beyond that . . . not really wanted him. Not in that way. It was all very well blaming his lack of interest, but she was no better. Those early flames of passion had been doused long ago. The children and their respective jobs had driven them apart. Exhaustion had been fanned into flat-out lack of interest. What was it they said? Use it or lose it. Quite. And over their long marriage, they'd more or less lost it. But why them? She'd bet Daniel and Rose didn't have that trouble. They were probably at it right now – after all, what else was a siesta for?

Not for sleeping. At least not in this heat. She threw the sheet back, wandered to the terrace door where the muslin curtain billowed in the breeze and stepped outside. She guessed that Rose would be busy preparing a birthday dinner, despite Eve having told her a hundred times not to bother making a fuss – after all, it was only another birthday. But she knew how much Rose liked a family celebration. Eve hadn't the heart to insist she *really* didn't want one. The birthdays seemed to arrive with greater and greater frequency as the years rolled by with gathering speed. She felt as if she'd only just had the last one. That was one of the reasons for coming away – being out of the country meant that the children didn't have to bother making a fuss that only made her feel even older than she was. That was the trouble with having children in their twenties. She could no longer kid herself she was young any more. In that awkward stage between children and grandchildren – that was where she was now. Not young, definitely not that, but not old either. Not really.

She eased herself on to the lounger, comfortable in the shade, dislodging her knickers as she laid her head back, but leaving them where they fell on the terrace. A loud miaow made her start. She opened her eyes to see the ginger cat from the neighbouring farm winding itself around the legs of the lounger, tail up, back arched, demanding to be stroked. Eve absent-mindedly obliged.

She picked up her trusty BlackBerry. Checking her emails, she was surprised by the continuing silence from Amy. What the hell was the woman playing at? If only Eve were more like Terry, able to leave the business to his two partners while he was away, but she was used to holding the reins and she didn't feel totally confident in Amy's ability, however confident her co-agent seemed. That was one of the unnerving things about her – she flew by the seat of her pants, shored up by an innate ability to bluff without even a flicker of guilt. A modern young woman.

Just as odd was the lack of an email from Rufus for the fourth day running. Normally a day didn't go by when they didn't communicate. Rufus Hegarty had been her first client, and his illustrated books had gone from strength to strength, building into steady best-sellers whose success was largely responsible for keeping her business afloat. She had met him through Will, her then shiny new husband, when the two men worked in lowly positions at the same ad agency, before Will upped sticks to try his luck at his real passion of wildlife photography. When Will had left both the agency and then her without a word of warning, Rufus had taken her side at the expense of Will's friendship. He had always credited Eve with his success and became like a brother to her, probably knowing far more than was good for him about the workings of both the agency and her heart.

Eve busied herself answering a publisher's query about the delayed delivery of some picture book illustrations, an author's plea for help over the publicity of her book, another author in despair at the lack of publishers' interest in her work. This was Eve's lifeblood. Now the children were grown up, with lives of their own, her authors had stepped into the space they once occupied. She cared about them and their futures almost (but not quite) as much as she cared about her children's. The difference was that she could be instrumental in helping her authors along, whereas her children had long ago lost interest in her opinion. Besides, she felt it was her duty as a parent to separate from them, to make sure they could stand on their own two feet. Wasn't that a parent's role? To set them up so they could fly without help? Her authors and illustrators weren't like that. They needed her. Her responsibility for their livelihoods was a constant preoccupation; a preoccupation that Terry simply didn't understand. When his office door shut, he left everything behind it. Her work wasn't like that. But the more time she spent dealing with the unstoppable flow of queries and problems and pleasure, the less time she spent with him, and the more irritated he became. Perhaps, over recent years, she should have made more effort to carve out some time for them to spend together.

The silence was broken by the sound of a car on the gravel. Could it be? She leaped from her chair, grabbed a cotton dressing gown from the end of the bed and almost ran out to the drive, where a white van was pulling up, fumes of acrid exhaust overwhelming everything else. The driver sprang out, went to the back of the vehicle and flung open the doors. And there, all on its own, scratched but safe, was Eve's distinctive shiny red suitcase. Never had she been so glad to see it.

At that moment, Rose emerged from the front door. 'It is! Thank God. When I answered the buzzer, I thought it must be.'

The driver heaved the enormous case on to the ground, where it stood with its sides winking in the sun. Eve signed the receipt with a flourish.

'Let me take you to my lair,' she murmured as she started to wheel the thing in the direction of their room. She couldn't wait to unpack, to strip off the pregnancy gear and get back to normal. 'I'll be back to help in a minute.'

Rose laughed. 'A minute? There's nothing to do, honestly, and anyway, I know you'll be much longer than that. Enjoy your reunion!'

She was absolutely right. An hour later, Eve was ready. The wardrobe was full of her clothes. The top of the chest of drawers was cluttered with her hair products, hairdryer and straighteners; the bathroom was littered with every beauty accessory she possessed. And she was feeling good. Oh yes. She gave a twirl in front of the mirror. The long grey linen shift she'd bought especially was cut to flatter, the bright pink beads went well. She'd straightened the kinks in her hair and had added a tiny layering of make-up that made her look younger. She was ready to party after all.

As she left the room, Terry appeared on the path that had taken him walking to the nearest hamlet, a few ancient houses and a bar with a TV that seemed always to be showing sport. He looked hot and tired, his old cricket hat tipped back on his head. He raised a hand, a gesture of appeasement she guessed, and she waved back. He wasn't really so bad. They just approached their maturing marriage in different ways – like a couple high-fiving but just missing.

When she reached the living room, the other three were already there, having changed for the evening ahead. Daniel and Rose looked fresh from the shower, their damp hair brushed flat. Eve was relieved to see that the situation seemed harmonious, although there was something tense about Rose's bearing and she was definitely paler than usual.

'Drink, Eve? Or should we wait for Terry?' asked Daniel.

'We should wait,' said Anna firmly, cutting off Eve's acceptance. 'We can't start without him, that wouldn't be fair. Come on to the terrace. The sunset's going to be beautiful.'

Together they went out on to the west-facing terrace, where five canvas chairs were arranged round a low table that held bowls of pistachios, salted almonds and fat garlicky black olives. The sky looked like a child's painting, with long, low streaks of cloud coloured the brashest red and bronze that Eve could remember seeing. If one of her illustrators replicated this, she would have asked them to tone it down for reality's sake.

'Have you cleared the air with Daniel?' she asked Anna, quietly enough to prevent anyone inside from hearing.

'Not exactly. I'm waiting for him to sort out this crap with Jess and Adam, then I'm going in for the kill. Only joking,' she reassured, on seeing Eve's despairing expression. 'In fact, Mum's in a better mood since Jess called.'

'And?'

'She's coming with the gorgeous Dylan, but they're leaving the OAP in Cornwall. But he *is* older,' she added, seeing that Eve was about to object to her poking fun at Adam's age. 'And she's insisted that she talk to Dad about it tomorrow morning. So once that's all sorted out and they're on their way here, it'll be my turn.' She concentrated on tucking her T-shirt into her waistband before tightening the wide woven belt by a notch.

How Eve suddenly sympathised with Rose. Her niece had to be one of the most selfish young women she'd ever met. Delightful, but selfish. But before she had time to remonstrate, they heard Terry's voice. At the cue, Anna rushed back inside, where Eve could see her mixing the cocktails. She turned away, leaning on the balustrade to admire the magnificent view.

'Happy birthday.' Rose was beside her, handing her a glass. 'Cheers. Now – presents.' From under one of the chairs, she pulled a parcel so beautifully wrapped and beribboned that it was almost a shame to open it. When Eve said as much, Anna stepped forward.

'Open this first, then.' She handed over a small package wrapped in newspaper.

Eve tussled with the Sellotape until the paper fell away to reveal a small box, inside which she found a dark pink resin ring with a squared-off top, one that would look wonderful on Anna, but on Eve? The words mutton and lamb chimed loudly.

'I love it.' She slipped it on to her finger, where it sat uncomfortably beside her more traditional jewellery. Out of the corner of her eye she noted Terry's shake of the head, while the others made polite admiring noises. Anna looked pleased.

Eve turned to Rose and Daniel's gift. Inside was a pair of pyjamas. 'Perfect.' She kissed Rose's cheek, then Daniel's. 'Thank you.'

'Hard to get my hand all the way up those legs,' Terry murmured as he passed over his own gifts, apparently unaware of the embarrassed silence that followed his remark.

'Uncalled for, darling,' said Eve tightly as she accepted his offerings. If she could have kicked his ankle with no one noticing, she would have. Why did he feel he had to make out he was some kind of rutting stallion when nothing could have been further from the truth? The answer's in the question, she pointed out to herself.

'Just a joke. Didn't mean to offend anyone.' He sat down, sheepish, as Eve slid the wrapping paper off the larger of the two.

She opened the box inside to find the sort of complicated corkscrew that resembled a miniature instrument of torture, the enclosed birthday card carrying a picture of the Houses of Parliament. Looking up at him, she understood precisely the intended message. A subtle reminder of the government guidelines on drinking. She refused to rise to the bait, but instead said, 'Thanks. Just what we need.' And the moment had gone.

Inside the other package was a pair of aquamarine stud earrings. Terry had always had an eye for earrings. On special occasions over the years he never failed to find something stylish to add to her collection. This had become so much of a ritual between them that she would have been disappointed if it didn't happen. She turned them in her hand before getting up and kissing his cheek. 'They're beautiful, darling. Thank you.'

Terry reached up to touch her face, but missed as Eve turned away to the glass door, using her reflection to guide in the earrings. Instead, he scratched his head as if that was what he'd meant to do all along.

Shortly afterwards, Rose and Anna disappeared inside to put the finishing touches to the meal, accepting Terry's offer to lay the table. Left with Daniel, Eve began to relax. It wasn't often the two of them found themselves alone together, but when they did, she was aware of the ease that still existed between them. She wondered if he felt it too.

'You don't need to be so harsh on him,' Daniel said, sipping his drink. 'He's not a bad man.'

The reprimand made Eve more guilty than ever. 'I know that. I do. My husband, your brother-in-law. How did we end up here?' She got up and went to the edge of the terrace.

'You married him, remember? For better, for worse.'

As if she needed reminding.

'Of course. But when I think back to when you and I . . .' She stopped as he shook his head.

'No,' he said firmly. 'It's a long time ago. You went off with Will and I met Rose and . . .'

'And you haven't looked back.' She finished the sentence for him, a game they used to play when they were young.

'And you have?'

'Not really.' If she wasn't careful, this conversation could take them into dangerous waters. 'But Will made it so hard.' Despite everything that had happened since, she would never forget the evening she came back from work to find her first husband outside their flat, his car bursting with his belongings, his face more serious than she could remember seeing it before. 'I'm leaving you.' That was all he had said. Later she discovered that he had tossed two years of marriage into the air because at a school reunion he had met the girlfriend he'd had before her. They'd slept together that same night, while Eve was visiting an author in Manchester with her then boss. At the time she had watched in disbelief as he had driven off. She remembered exactly the numbness she had felt as she went indoors, the grief she had endured when she saw the space where his pillow belonged. His taking that seemed so final. And the pain she had suffered until, a year or so later, Rose had introduced her to her brother, Terry.

'Do you know what he's doing now?'

'No idea. Once we'd divorced, there was no need. And I didn't want to, once I'd started seeing Terry. And you two were so supportive.' Rose and Dan had sided with her and, as far as she knew, had never contacted Will again. 'Is Rose OK?'

'Mmm.' He sounded distracted as he concentrated on spearing an olive. 'I think so. Why?'

'She's not herself.'

'It'll be the girls. Rose worries too much about them – they're grown up now, for God's sake.' He passed across the bowl of olives.

'These are from our own trees. They're not bad at all.' He waited while she took a couple.

'You fathers find it easier to step back.' Not that Eve was one to talk. She was moving forward into another stage of life at the same time as her children did, even if it occasionally made her look as if she didn't care. If only Rose could do something of the same. 'Ouch!' She slapped at her bare calf and scratched at the skin. 'Bastard mosquito. I'm drowning in Deet and it doesn't make any difference.'

'That's fathers for you.' Daniel smiled that smile that would melt an ice floe, the one that registered in his dark eyes as well. He stretched out his legs, crossing them at the ankle. 'Awful Neanderthal beasts without a grain of sensitivity in their souls.' He threw back his head and laughed – a short sharp bark. 'Oh Evie. If only you knew.'

There was an immediate one hundred per cent shift in her attention from the bite to Daniel. 'Knew what?'

But after a fleeting look of sadness, his face had closed up. 'Let me get you something for that. Rose's got a cupboard full of first-aid stuff.'

'Don't worry.' She was anxious to get him sitting again, to get him talking. She'd *known* there was something wrong. 'It's not that bad. Really.'

'Well, another drink anyway. I know I could do with one.' He took her glass.

'Oh, good timing.' Rose appeared in the doorway, undoing her apron and seeing their empty glasses. 'Your dinner is served.' She gave a mock curtsey. 'Come through.'

Frustrated by having such a promising conversation curtailed, Eve rallied and followed them inside, checking that her BlackBerry was in her dress pocket. She'd never be able to eat without the reassurance of knowing that she would be aware of the moment Amy and Rufus broke their separate silences. Whenever that might be.

8

The night had closed in around them. Now they were cocooned in the glow from the candle lanterns on the table. At one of the outside lights over the doors, an angry hornet buzzed. What had been a pleasant breeze during the day was stronger now, wilder, as if a storm might be in the offing at last. Rose was grateful that the meal had gone as well as it had, given the undercurrents swirling between them, and relieved that no one had commented on her lack of appetite. Every mouthful had been an effort. But everyone had put aside selfish concerns to give Eve a special birthday supper. The mood was relaxed, the conversation as easy as it could be between old friends. The ravioli and sage was followed by grilled pork served Italian style with a slice of lemon, then salad and cheese. Daniel kept their glasses topped up with a regular stream of crisp Soave or smoky Chianti. The candle-studded brownies were the hit of the evening.

'What the . . .' Eve leaned forward to examine the candles, fumbling for her glasses, then laughed until there were tears in her eyes.

Anna sat beaming with satisfaction.

'I've got to blow them out before they melt completely. They're too good to let go.'

'A blow job – how appropriate.' There was a moment of silence before Terry laughed just a little too loudly at his own joke. Anna and Daniel echoed him in a half-hearted and dutiful way, while Rose managed a thin smile to cover her habitual despair at her brother's schoolboy humour. None of them wanted to spoil the atmosphere.

Eve said nothing, but her face said everything.

Rose saw the danger signals, the tilt of the head, the flash of the eye, the reaching for the glass, and tried to step in. 'I thought we might go to Lucca for the Festival of Lights.'

But too late.

'Why do you always have to lower the tone?' Eve's voice was flat, cold.

'It was a joke among friends.' Terry looked around for support, his face reddening. 'That's all.'

'Look at them, Terry. They're not laughing. That's the sort of remark that might go down well in your office, but not here.'

Suddenly the wind blew colder. Rose buttoned up her cardigan. How could she defuse this?

'Easy, Eve. It's fine. It's us.' Dan picked up the empty white wine bottle. 'Shall we have coffee now as well?'

'It's not fine, Dan. We all put up with it, have done for years, but sometimes I get sick of it.'

Terry was looking embarrassed, his eyes fixed on the red paper napkin that he was twisting under the table. 'Don't make a scene,' he muttered.

Their marital spats were familiar enough, but as Rose watched her brother's embarrassment and his wife's icy fury, she felt hopelessly divided between the two of them. When she'd introduced them, Eve on the rebound from Will, she'd never intended to play Cupid. Back then, as his big sister, she'd viewed Terry's taste in women with despair. The few of his girlfriends she'd met had always been of a type: dolly birds who were pretty, giggly and monosyllabic. But to her and Daniel's amazement, he and Eve had hit it off immediately. The slightly older woman. They always had something to talk about, and if they weren't deep in conversation, they hadn't been able to keep their hands off each other. David Bowie, the Rolling Stones, Jim Callaghan, cricket and pear drops provided a little of the obvious cement that bound them together at first. She had to hand it to Terry: he had never been a stereotypical accountant, although his occasional social gaffes had sometimes made her cringe. She'd sometimes wondered whether he fell somewhere on the autistic spectrum. If he did, it wasn't enough of a somewhere for their parents to have noticed or to have tried to do anything about it. People tended not to so much then. Not that they had noticed much where their two children were concerned. Instead, Terry blundered through life without ever offending anyone enough to cause him serious trouble. Except, of course, Eve.

'I'll do that, Dan. You get another bottle.' Rose pushed back her chair. 'Anna, could you help?' If they all left Eve and Terry alone for a moment, things might simmer down. That was the usual nature of their disputes – quick to blow and quick to go.

'Sure.' With a rattle of bangles, Anna stood and reached out for the wooden pepper grinder and the bowl of sea salt that were still centre table. Her hair fell across her face, hiding her expression.

In the midst of this flurry of activity, Terry and Eve sat frozen. Neither of them could speak without embarrassing themselves further. Then, breaking the silence, came the shrill ring of Eve's phone. Thankful for the distraction, she answered the call despite Terry's despairing shake of his head.

She held up a hand to excuse herself as she turned away from the table to have the conversation. 'What? What did she say?' Her voice grew louder, her forehead creased into a frown. 'Hang on just a moment.' She looked at Rose, just returned with the coffee cups, and made a gesture to say she couldn't understand what was being said to her. 'I'm sorry, but I have to take this.' She crossed to the end of the terrace to stand in the shadows, where she could talk more privately. At the table, the others sat down again, Terry apologising, the others reassuring him. Snatches of Eve's conversation blew their way and they pretended not to hear.

'What do you mean, retire? . . . That's absurd . . . What? Say that again . . . Of course I'm not . . .'

As time went on, the others gave up any pretence and sat transfixed, trying to follow the threads of Eve's conversation. 'She's doing what? . . . But I can't, I'm here . . . You're breaking up . . . Of course she knows that . . .'

Eventually they heard clearly, 'Oh shit! The bloody signal's gone.'

She returned to the table, sat down heavily, put her elbows on the table and her head in her hands.

Rose was the first to speak. 'Something wrong?' she asked, aware that that was likely to be the understatement of the evening.

Eve let out a dramatic groan. 'Only everything.'

'For God's sake,' muttered Terry.

Rose's heart sank as Eve rounded on him. 'For God's sake what? This could be very difficult for me. Apparently Amy's been telling my clients that I'm retiring.'

'Retiring?' Rose repeated. The thought of her sister-in-law giving up her agency before she was carried out of the office in a box was inconceivable. 'You never said.'

'No! Because I'm not. As if. Why would she do that?'

Terry sat and stared up at the stars, as if he couldn't begin to imagine and wasn't much interested.

Hearing Eve's irate intake of breath and fearing another outburst at her brother, Rose went inside to get the coffee.

'There must be a misunderstanding.' Daniel was standing behind Eve. He put a consoling hand on her back as he refilled her glass. 'No one would mistake you for an almost-pensioner. That's ridiculous.'

'I should bloody hope not.' Eve sat upright, eyes blazing. 'Apparently Mary Mackenzie's pissed off because I haven't got her the sort of deal she thinks she deserves. She told Belinda, another of my clients, that Amy told her I was signing off on the agency. Belinda's just phoned me to see if it's true. In fact, I asked Amy to look after Mary – big mistake, probably – but that was as far it goes. Oh God. I should be there to sort this out. I should never have trusted her.'

'Then why don't you go home? You might as well be there anyway, the amount of time you spend on that thing.' Terry gestured at her BlackBerry.

'Thanks for your unwavering support, Terry.' She spun the phone in slow circles on the tabletop as she thought. 'Actually, you know what? If that's how much you want me to be here, I think I bloody well will.'

'Will what?' Rose returned, pot of coffee in hand, and took her place at the table.

'Get a flight back tomorrow. I ought to be able to change my ticket.'

'Eve, you can't.' Rose couldn't keep the alarm out of her voice. 'You'll miss Jess and Dylan.'

Daniel turned to look at her, an eyebrow raised in question, just as the first roll of thunder sounded in the distance.

'And you've only just got here,' added Anna, without breaking her concentration on rolling a cigarette. She glanced at them all as she licked down the length of the Rizla, stuck the paper together then put the roll-up on the table by her tobacco pouch.

'Let's all calm down.' Daniel pushed his specs back up the bridge of his nose. 'Aren't you being a bit hasty? Decisions should be slept on. In the morning you can use my study and the landline to sort out whatever's going on.'

'I can't sort out anything if the wretched woman won't answer my emails.'

'Haven't you tried calling her?' Anna took her pashmina from where it had slipped off the back of her chair and wrapped it round her bony shoulders before lighting her cigarette.

'Of course not.' Eve was incensed by the suggestion. 'Until now we've always emailed when I've been away. We only ever talk if there's an emergency.'

'What do you call this then?' Anna looked mystified as she blew a long stream of smoke into the night. 'Sounds like one to me. I'd call her.'

'I think you should stay out of this, Anna.' The clink of the jug against the coffee cups betrayed Rose's shaking hand.

'Don't talk to me as if I'm ten! I've as much a right to an opinion as anyone else around this table.' Self-expression and assertiveness: sometimes alarming qualities that had been drilled into her during those expensive therapy sessions. Rose wished she hadn't spoken. But as the whole edifice of the happy family holiday finally crumbled, she'd reacted without thinking.

'Easy, you two.'

The feel of Daniel's soothing hand on her thigh was like a burn. Rose twisted her legs away from his touch, knocking one of the cups and saucers on to the floor, where they smashed, rivulets of black coffee running into dark gullies between the tiles. As she turned from him, she caught the bewilderment in his eyes. For a second, she wished she'd controlled her reaction, then she remembered. *Miss. Love. Come back.* 'We can sort this out without you interfering,' she said sharply.

His puzzlement deepened, then he shrugged. 'All right. I'll get something to clear this up with, then.'

Eve was on her feet, having missed their brief exchange, making her way round the table. 'Anna's quite right. I should call her. If she thinks she can put her feet under my desk while I'm away, she's got another think coming. Ouch!' She sat down heavily beside Rose, lifting up her bare foot with one hand and examining it. A thin stream of blood ran between her toes.

'Oh Eve, I'm so sorry.' Rose bent over to see the injury. 'Don't move – I'll get you a plaster.'

Squatting beside them, Daniel was picking up the scattered pieces of pottery. The way he moved told Rose how hurt he was by her dismissal. The knowledge gave her a shaming stab of pleasure.

'I'll get it,' he volunteered. 'I'm going in for a cloth anyway.'

While he disappeared inside, Rose looked closely at Eve's foot. 'It's only a tiny cut.'

Eve scratched crossly at a new mosquito bite on her ankle. 'Don't worry about it, really. But I must talk to Amy.' She pulled her injured foot from Rose's grip. Making the call, she jiggled her right leg, impatient for Amy to answer. After a few seconds she returned her BlackBerry to the table. 'She's not picking up. She must be deliberately fielding my calls.'

'She's more likely to be out.' Rose was desperate to restore the earlier atmosphere of the evening.

'Mmm. More likely she's up to something. Plotting.' Eve reached across the table for her drink as Daniel re-emerged with a bowl of water with a whiff of disinfectant, a flannel and a packet of sticking plasters.

'Don't be so suspicious,' Rose countered. 'There's probably a perfectly simple explanation.'

But she could see that Eve's thought process was speeding down its own track. Nothing was going to stop it. 'She couldn't be planning to set up on her own, could she? Taking some of my clients with her?' She spoke slowly, as if she was thinking out loud as the idea took root.

'She wouldn't.' Rose was shocked that Eve would even consider her close colleague capable of such a thing.

'You always see the best in people. That's one of your great gifts.' Eve cleaned the cut, took a plaster from the packet and stuck it between her big toe and the next one.

'Not always.' They'd forgotten about Anna, who had been silent till now. The candlelight danced on her face, exaggerating its angles and planes, making her look thinner than ever. She sat with her coffee, picking at the remains of her brownie, covering her plate with crumbs, smoking. In a gesture of defiance, she stubbed her cigarette out on her plate.

Rose decided to ignore the remark and the cigarette, both calculated to enrage her. Rising to either would only make the evening even worse.

Beside Anna, Terry was stretched out in his chair, arms behind his head, eyes shut, as if waiting for the evening to resume as normal. She felt like strangling both of them. Why couldn't they help pull what was left of the party back into shape instead of leaving it to her?

'Whatever she's doing, you're not going to be able to sort it out now. It's too late. So why don't you give up and enjoy the rest of the evening?' Daniel suggested as he sat down again.

'I can't enjoy it now. The bloody woman's ruined it.' Eve poured herself another glass of wine. 'I'm going to have to work out some sort of damage limitation exercise the moment I get back.'

'Please don't go,' Rose urged. 'The holiday won't be the same without you.'

'Surely you can deal with this from here.' Dan emptied the Soave into his glass. 'A few judicious phone calls and a message letting her know that you know what's been going on.'

'But I don't,' insisted Eve. 'I've no idea.' She pressed a few brownie crumbs on to her finger and licked them off. 'That's the trouble with being in contact every hour God sends. I know too much but not enough.' She closed her eyes with pleasure at the taste of chocolate.

That makes two of us, reflected Rose, darting an angry glance at Daniel. He was sitting at an angle to the table, legs crossed. Immune to the mosquitoes, he always wore shorts in the evening. Tonight they were paired with a deep blue linen shirt, his chest hair visible in the opening. He was quite still, eyes on her, obviously puzzling over the reason for her shutting him out.

'Well . . . looks like the party's over.' Terry stretched his arms into the air so that his striped polo shirt rode up to expose his sunburned stomach. 'Think I'll turn in.'

'Just like that? Don't you have an opinion about Amy or what she's up to?' Rose's impulse to protect her friend finally took over.

'I'm with Daniel.' He slipped his feet back into his sandals. 'Things will look different in the morning. They always do.'

Rose heard Eve's frustrated tsk and tried again. 'What about Eve going home early? You don't really want that, do you?' Surely he'd come on side to stop her carrying out her threat.

Terry gave a languid smile, tucking his polo shirt into his trousers. 'Dear sister, you should know by now that when it comes to the agency, Eve will do exactly as she pleases. That's one of the reasons it's been so successful. She doesn't always do what's expected.'

The way he looked at Eve told Rose more than she'd previously appreciated about her brother's marriage. Whatever their apparent differences, he obviously admired Eve's business methods and the success she'd achieved.

'Not true, my love,' interjected Eve bitterly. 'I play by the rules. And that's why it's worked so well. I'm not going to sit back and watch Amy destroy it.'

'*If* that's what she's trying to do.' Anna took a walking stick that was leaning against the balustrade and walked off the terrace to the nearest fig tree. Raising her arm, she took aim with the stick and hit the nearest branch. She aimed again. Gathering up the fallen figs, she dropped the stick where she stood. 'Night, all.'

'Think I'll do the same. Read my book for a bit.' Terry kissed both Eve and Rose's cheeks, and took himself off. 'Sleep on it,' he advised. 'I would.'

An hour later, Rose followed suit. She had stayed up to try to persuade Eve to take Terry and Daniel's advice, but her sister-in-law was too anxious to listen. In the end, she had given up and left her to look for an available flight home.

Rose opened the bedroom door quietly, hoping to find Daniel asleep. Instead, the light was on and he was sitting propped up against the antique wooden bedhead. As she came in, the curtains billowed and the window slammed shut in the wind. She went over to secure it as, in the far distance, lightning flashed over the mountains.

Daniel put down his book and looked over the top of his reading glasses. 'Well?'

'Well what?' Rose took off her trousers and hung them up before going to the bathroom. She could hear his voice over the sound of her overly brisk teeth-brushing and the running tap.

'Have I done something to upset you, sweetheart?' He sounded genuinely perplexed.

She threw the rest of her clothes into the laundry basket. As she reached for her nightdress on the back of the bathroom door, she noticed a tiny chip of flaking blue paint and picked at it, trying to control the uncontrollable rage that swept through her. *Miss. Love. Come back.*

'No.' She bit her lip till her eyes watered as she brushed her hair, then cleaned her face and smoothed in the night cream that cost the equivalent of the national debt and had yet to make any noticeable difference. She was trying to put off for as long as possible the moment when she would have to join him.

'Rose. I know there's something wrong. I'm not going to sleep until you come out and talk about it.' Daniel was placating, confident he could talk her round from whatever it was that was upsetting her. He was so good at that.

She half opened the door, wishing she could vanish from the face of the earth. Or that he would.

Daniel patted her side of the bed. 'Come on. You must be as exhausted as I am. All this entertaining. But let's sort this out.'

Throughout their years together, Rose had followed to the letter the one piece of parental advice given to her the night before their modest registry office wedding. 'Never go to bed on an argument if you want a happy marriage,' her mother had advised from the hardly exemplary bedrock of her own. Well, thought Rose, not this time, Mum. This isn't something that can be mended that easily.

'Sort it out?' She heard her voice rising. 'How can we sort this out?'

Daniel looked alarmed. This was not what he was expecting – or used to. He ran a hand through his curls, his brow furrowed. 'What? What are you talking about?'

'I read that text. I read it.' No! That was not what she had meant to say. But too late.

'What text? What are you talking about?' But as his hand dropped from his head to the bed, she could see that he knew.

'You know bloody well which one. The one I brought out to you at the pool yesterday. "Miss you. Love you. Come back soon."' Her voice was a shrill imitation of another woman's. 'That one.'

She took a breath, feeling her heart pounding in her chest, watching his face change, the light fade in his eyes. He seemed to deflate in front of her. But it was too late to take back her words, however much she didn't want to have this out now. She didn't want another shadow cast over everyone's holiday, over their marriage. If only the clocks would wind back to the time before she'd picked up his phone in mistake for hers. But it was too late. The words were out.

Despite his tan, his face had paled. He sat alone in their bed, looking as if he'd been turned to stone. 'You did?' He spoke so softly that she could barely hear him.

'By mistake,' she justified herself. Perhaps this was all a misunderstanding after all. 'I thought it was my phone.'

He gave a short rueful laugh. 'I should have taken it with me.' He swung his legs out of bed and picked up his glasses.

'Where are you going?' Rose watched, astonished, as he made towards the door. He took his dressing gown from the row of heart-shaped coat hooks. 'You can't just walk out.' She ran across the room, and grabbed a handful of his pyjama lapel. 'We've got to talk.' His reaction could mean only one thing: the realisation of her worst fears.

'I can't right now. I'm sorry.' He yanked the fabric out of her hands.

Changing tactics, she dodged behind him and stood with her back pressed against the door, one hand on the latch, refusing to let him by. 'You can't,' she insisted. 'Who is she? Who is "S"?' To her fury, she realised she was crying, the tears blurring her vision, though not enough to prevent her seeing him flinch at the mention of the letter.

'Shh.' He reached out a hand to her, tentative. 'Please don't cry.'

'Don't shh me.' Her fist banged against the door to emphasise each word. 'Just tell me. You owe me that.'

'I can't talk to you when you're so upset.'

She had never seen Daniel look so old. Even through her tears, his face was drawn, the bags under his eyes looked fuller, his jaw less defined, the lines deeper. Despite his height, he seemed to have shrunk to half the man he had been only minutes before.

'I'm not upset,' she insisted, wiping her nose with the back of her hand. 'I'm angry. Really angry. I wasn't going to say anything until the others had gone, but now I have, and I wish I hadn't. But I do want to know the truth. I want to know that it's not too late.'

'It's complicated.' His voice was level, but she didn't recognise it. 'But you must believe me, it doesn't change what I feel about you.'

'But it might change how I feel about you,' she gulped, with tears streaming down her cheeks.

'Rose, trust me, please.' He removed her hand from the latch. 'I'm going to sleep next door tonight. We will talk, but not now. Not with everyone here. Not when you're like this and it's so late. I never meant to hurt you. You know I wouldn't do that. I'm not proud of what's happened, but I will make it up to you somehow. I promise. It's not what you think.'

'What do you mean, it's not what I think? What is it then? Daniel, you can't . . .' Stunned by his refusal to talk to her, she hesitated as he opened the door.

From downstairs, the unmistakable click of the latch on the study door echoed through the stillness of the house. Eve. She was the only one of them still up. Could she have overheard? Horrified by the idea of their private argument being shared, Rose took a step back into the room, giving Daniel the opportunity to leave it. He turned, one finger on his lips, and tiptoed next door.

This couldn't be happening. The shock of his walking away from her was as much of a blow as his betrayal. There was no question in her mind now that that was what this was. The temptation to go after him was almost irresistible, but trying to make him talk when he didn't want to would only make him dig in his heels. Having been overheard by Eve was humiliating enough. She didn't want to make matters worse by enraging him.

Sitting on their bed, she mopped her eyes with a corner of the sheet and blew her nose on a bit of old tissue she found under her pillow. Her head was spinning, making coherent thought impossible. What had just happened between them? What had she missed? They only ever slept apart if one of them was ill. 'It's not what you think.' What could that mean? As the rain began to beat against the windows, she fell back, eyes wide open, staring at the old-fashioned ceiling fan, trying to make sense of things.

During what seemed one of the longest nights of her life, Rose lay alternately weeping into her pillow then trying to work out what Daniel could have meant, why he hadn't held up his hands and confessed. But 'never apologise, never explain' was one of his guiding rules in life. And until now, he had never needed to. She had always trusted him completely. In fact, they'd even joked together after parties where women had flirted with him. In her eyes, he had been the perfect husband.

How could this have happened? She went through the previous months, looking for clues, but finding nothing. Dan's behaviour hadn't changed. He'd been busy, spent time in the Arthur, the hotel he had just opened in Edinburgh, with occasional visits to Trevarrick when he wasn't in his London office at the Canonford. When he'd spoken to her, at least twice a day, there had been no hint that anything unusual had happened. If it had, she would have known. She would have heard a change in his voice. She knew him too well. They had been looking forward to Italy together . . . as always. She imagined Daniel lying awake on the other side of the wall, and could only hope that he was as tormented as her, and that sleep wouldn't come easy for him either. He would have to talk to her the next day. She would make sure they found a moment.

9

Eve was up early the next morning, planning her last day in the sun. An early-morning swim would banish the slight headache that hovered behind her right eye. She shifted her weight from one foot to the other as she wrestled on her 'comfy control' swimsuit. 'Eight pounds lighter in eight seconds' boasted the ad. How anyone got the damn thing on that quick was beyond her. With a final tug she got it over her bust and slipped her left arm through the one armhole.

Throwing open the doors of the stables, she stood there disappointed. Instead of the blue sky and the heat that they banked on at this time of year – goddammit – she was confronted by a sky thick with grey cloud that obscured the sun completely. Drops of rain shimmered on the pale blue flowers of the plumbago that grew up by the doorway and on the scorching red geraniums in the pots beside her. Broken twigs and windfalls from the fig tree were strewn across the path where puddles had gathered between the stones. She shivered in the breeze and pulled down the bottom of the suit; despite its body-firming and controlling properties, it did little for her bum. She returned inside to cover-up.

Terry snuffled and turned in the bed when she tiptoed into the bedroom. To her huge relief, he had been sound asleep by the time she'd finally gone to bed, so they hadn't had to speak. She had stayed up, determined to change her flight home. Having succeeded, the adrenalin flooding her system meant she was wide awake, so she fired off a few emails to her most precious clients, assuring them that any rumours about her impending retirement were no more than that. She had never been more in the saddle than she was now.

In the cold light of day, she was annoyed with herself for reacting so precipitously and taking too seriously what were probably only Chinese whispers. She began to wonder whether she had been too hasty in changing her ticket. Belinda had probably got her wires crossed in that other-worldly way she had. But Terry had wound her up, making her overreact. Too late now.

As she took a change of clothes from the wardrobe, the metal hangers rattled, waking Terry, who rolled on to his back. His arm emerged from under the sheet, then fell across her side of the bed. 'C'm 'ere.'

Eve stopped dead. What was he suggesting? Sex? In the morning? In his dreams.

In the beginning, they hadn't been able to keep their hands off each other, but that early passion had given way to babies, years of broken nights, then the morning frenzy of getting children off to school. Once the kids could look after themselves, the two of them had taken to sleeping as long as they could, then leaping out of bed in a rush, anxious about being late for work. The pleasures of early-morning sex had vanished along with their youth. But wasn't reviving the flagging libido what holidays were for? She took a step towards the bed, quite tempted for once. As she moved, the constricting powers of her swimsuit reminded her of its presence. Its removal would take for ever, killing the moment completely. Suddenly self-conscious, she stopped in her tracks. Instead, she bent over to add her flip-flops to the armful of clothes she was holding.

His eyes half opened and he lifted his head, then dropped it back on to the pillow. 'What're you doing?' His voice was muzzy with sleep.

'Going to the house to make some coffee. Want one?' The moment, such as it was, had definitely passed.

'Nah,' he muttered, rolling back on to his side with a contented groan. 'I'll be up in a minute.'

For minute, read hour, she thought as she went to the bathroom to get dressed. But what matter? Switching on the light, she caught sight of herself in the mirror. Trim in the swimsuit, true, but just below her right shoulder blade was a blazing brace of mosquito bites. Immediately she spotted them, they began to itch. Cursing herself for not having unknotted the mosquito net over the bed the previous night, she wrapped her left arm round her body in a vain attempt to scratch them. Bending her right arm up her back didn't reach either, so she resorted to using her hairbrush. As a result, the bites itched until she was frantic. She hid the resulting welts under a loose patterned cotton kameez and pulled on the linen trousers with an elasticated waistband (a design detail that she'd once sworn she'd never wear but that now she wouldn't be without).

When she put her head around the kitchen door, the house was quiet. But the coffee pot when she reached for it was hot. So someone else was up. Then she remembered the raised voices she'd heard last night, the bangs as if someone was hitting something. Daniel and Rose. In however many years she'd known them, she'd never seen them argue. And this had sounded like a ding-dong of an argument from what she'd been able to make out.

To her slight chagrin, she recalled how, when she'd heard voices, she had put her head out of the study door, then stood at the bottom of the stairs to find out what was wrong. She justified her behaviour as born from concern not curiosity. The sound of their bedroom door opening had sent her scurrying back to the study without having made out a word. Had she heard two doors shut after that? The idea of her dearest friends rowing, spending the night apart, made her profoundly uneasy. But her first instincts had been right. Something was very wrong indeed.

Just then Rose appeared. Her face was drawn, her eyes puffy. 'Morning.' She didn't wait for a reply. 'Weather's rotten, but the forecast says it'll clear by mid morning. Orange juice?' She took several oranges from the hanging mesh baskets in the corner of the room, laid them on the counter and pulled the juicer out from the back.

'Bad night?' Eve asked tentatively.

'No more than usual.' Rose was clipped, uncommunicative.

'Daniel up?' She tried again.

'Think so. He's probably working.'

Right on cue, Daniel appeared at the door to the garden. 'Just been out seeing what damage the storm's done. Doesn't look too bad. Few branches and a couple of tiles off the garage roof.'

His last words were drowned out by the sudden noise of the juicer.

He sounded as if it was just another day, but he looked as if he was suffering from as sleepless a night as Rose. He was unshaven, with purple smudges of shadow under his eyes, shoulders tense as if they were carrying the cares of the world. 'Can I help?' he offered.

Rose ignored him and carried on with what she was doing. Daniel made a face at Eve and shrugged his shoulders. 'Coffee?' he asked, and took over the corner of the kitchen where he could make a fresh pot. Rose's displeasure at his interference was unspoken but clear from the slight shake of her head and the brief irritated sigh.

It was too chilly to eat outside, so she was laying breakfast at the table at the end of the room. Not that the atmosphere indoors was much warmer. Cutlery and plates were being clattered and banged into place. A cereal packet went flying, sending cornflakes crackling on to the floor. Eve dived behind the curtain dividing the utility room from the kitchen and emerged with a dustpan and brush. As she knelt to her task, she wondered whether she should retire until hostilities were dropped.

'I think I'll take some coffee to Terry,' she said, making her excuses.

Rose said nothing.

Dan shook his head. 'No need. I've just seen him. He'll be here in a minute.'

'Who will be?' Anna appeared in jeans, her T-shirt covered by a cardigan. She had pinned up her hair with a couple of chopsticks that stuck out at angles. In her hand was a bag containing two loaves of fresh bread. She dropped the car keys on the table.

'Terry,' answered Eve, simultaneously making an alternative getaway to the sitting room, taking Terry's coffee for herself and leaving them to it. She reflected how her own spats with Terry always blew over quickly. They were habit. No one took them seriously, not even them. This was not the same at all. She fingered her ever-present BlackBerry, checking the time. Five past eight. Too early to call Amy. She didn't function until she got into the office at ten. Perhaps she wouldn't call her at all. Perhaps best to surprise her by returning without warning. Eve smiled as she pictured Amy walking into the office the following morning. She would be sure to have got in first and would be sitting at her desk, waiting. Surprise. The best form of attack. A fine plan, but she had to phone her . . . had to.

Making herself comfortable on the sofa, she picked up one of Rose's art magazines, contenting herself with the pictures in an article about an exhibition devoted to the early works of Caravaggio. Absorbed in the faces of adolescent boys who stared out of the shadows, she only looked up at the sound of footsteps. Rose.

'Breakfast – if you want it.'

'Of course. Thought I'd be better off out of the way. Has something happened?'

Rose took a step into the room, shutting the door behind her. 'Eve! For God's sake stop asking me if something's wrong. If I wanted you to know, I'd tell you.'

They stared at each other, equally shocked by her outburst.

'Sorry.' Eve automatically took a sip of the coffee, then spat it back into the cup. 'No sugar.'

'Oh God, it's me that should be sorry.' Rose lifted both hands to her face.

'No, I shouldn't have said anything.' Thinking for a moment that Rose was about to cry, Eve wasn't sure what to say.

Rose ignored her. When her hands dropped, her face was tight with emotion.

'Daniel's having an affair.' The words dropped into the silence between them like pebbles into water, the ripples spreading outwards.

Eve's first impulse was to laugh, but then she saw the confusion and perhaps fear in her friend's eyes. 'No! Are you sure?'

'As sure as I can be.' Rose stared at the floor, shaking her head. 'I wasn't going to tell you, but . . . I've got to talk to someone. I can't keep it to myself.' And she began to tell Eve everything that had happened.

After a night deliberating, Rose had decided not to make things easy for Daniel. She would go along with him – up to a point. If he didn't want to explain, then she wouldn't press him, however desperate she was to get to the bottom of things and however frustrated by the presence of the others. She would avoid him when she could and let him sweat, let him wonder what she was thinking, what she might be planning.

But when she'd arrived in the kitchen, appearing normal had been harder than she had imagined. Everyone must be able to see how awful she looked. Every time she blinked, she felt as if her eyelids were scraping her eyeballs clean. Her nose was sore from where she'd blown it so often. Whenever she thought about what Dan had said, tears immediately came to her eyes. Convinced she could get through by focusing on the daily routine, one thing at a time, she had set about making breakfast.

Dan's entrance was torture to her. But however difficult it was being in the same space as him, concentrating on breakfast helped. Had Anna noticed anything wrong? Unlikely, since Anna's world revolved around the one still centre that was Anna herself.

She hadn't meant to say anything. Not to Eve. Not to anyone. But when Eve asked her for the nth time what was wrong, it was as if a cork had been taken out of a bottle. She hadn't been able to stop herself.

As she related the previous evening's row – if that was what it had been – between her and Daniel, Eve was visibly shocked. She shifted along the sofa until she could put her hand on Rose's knee, saying nothing, letting Rose explain. Even that small gesture was a comfort.

'Mu-um! Are you two coming?' Anna's shout broke the spell. 'We're all having breakfast.'

'Just coming.' Rose stood up. 'You won't say a word, will you? Not to Terry. No one. I do feel better now I've told you, but

Daniel and I must sort this out our own way before anyone else knows. Promise?'

'You've my word.' Eve pressed two fingers against her shut lips before following her out. 'This is between you and me.'

10

Apart from Terry, who, like Anna, seemed not to notice any tension in the air, everyone spent the morning avoiding one another. Eve took herself into the study, where she could use the landline to call Amy. She didn't want to leave Rose, but business was business. What Rose had told her had stunned her. The idea of Dan having an affair contradicted everything she knew about him. She wanted to find out more from Rose, but first she had to silence the rumour put about by Amy. She left Rose going to pick flowers for Jess's room.

After several rings, all Eve heard was her own voice parroting the answerphone message. 'One of us will get back to you as soon as possible.' Huh.

She looked at her watch. Where was the bloody woman? At the very least she should be in the office, manning the phones, keeping the business going. Despite Rose's pleas for Eve to stay on after all, the right decision had to be to go home, however difficult it was to leave Rose and Daniel like this. She punched the number into the phone again. Just as she was about to hang up, Amy answered.

'Hello. Rutherford and Fraser Literary Agents.'

A sliver of steel penetrated Eve's soul. Her co-agent sounded out of breath, as if she'd just run up the stairs from the estate agent's on the ground floor.

Eve imagined Amy dropping her bag on her chair, putting down her Starbucks and then sitting on the edge of the desk, one leg straight, one bent, studying the nails on her free hand. She must have adopted the pose from those TV shows about which she was so knowledgeable. Her hair would be in place, her palest pink nail varnish freshly applied, her make-up immaculate: the picture of self-confidence and efficiency. And now Eve was going to puncture all that.

'Amy?'

She heard a tiny surprised gasp. 'Eve?'

'The last time I looked at the agency name, there was no Fraser in it. As far as I can remember.' Her voice was at its most chilly.

'No.' Amy sounded almost calm again as she staged a speedy recovery. 'But I thought if they believed you'd made me a partner the clients would have more confidence in me while you were away.'

The girl had balls. No question. However. 'I think the clients know me well enough to know that there's no reason for them to doubt the agency. Unless of course they were led to believe I was ill or might be retiring . . .'

'Ah.' Shaken again. But only for a moment. 'I can explain that.'

So it was true. 'Please do. I was hoping you would.'

'When I last saw Mary Mackenzie, she was complaining about the agency. She said that you hadn't got her the deal she wanted last time round and was interested to hear if I had any new ideas.'

Eve tapped her pencil on the desk. She had done everything she could for Mary, an author who couldn't accept her flagging popularity. In Eve's view, she would never find new success as a children's novelist without a large injection of imagination. 'Yes?' she snapped. 'And?'

'I thought when she threatened to find another agency that if I told her you were retiring soon, she might stay on.' She paused. 'And she does seem happier with me looking after her.'

The doodles of stars and diamonds with which Eve was covering the sheet of paper in front of her had become boxes inside boxes, the lines getting thicker, darker with the increased pressure.

'We agreed, if you remember, that all decisions about *our* . . .' the word stuck in her throat, 'authors and illustrators would be taken together.'

'But you weren't—'

Eve spoke over her protest, slowly, calmly. 'So perhaps you could contact her, explain that you've made a mistake and that I have no intention of retiring. If she still decides she wants to leave, then we'll decide what to do – together. If we're going to work as a team, then we need to be open with each other. At all times.' She put down her pencil and smoothed the legs of her linen trousers.

The brief silence between them contained something moment-ous, something that Eve couldn't quite identify. Then Amy spoke, quietly conveying exactly how much she disliked being told what to do. 'All right. Is that all?'

'Not quite.' Eve was going to have the last word. 'I'd be grateful if you would go through the emails I've sent you and reply to each of them, this morning if possible.'

'Everything's under control, if that's what you're worried about.'

'Amy, all I'm asking is for you to let me know where we are on a couple of things. Do you think you can do that? If you're unhappy about the way things are run, we can have a chat about that when I'm back.'

Which will be sooner than you think!

They exchanged goodbyes and Eve hung up, exhilarated by the way she'd handled things. Whatever tricks Amy had up her sleeve, she was equipped to deal with them. Sitting at Dan's desk, she leaned back in the chair and swivelled it idly from side to side, planning her return to the office. Stilling herself, she smacked both hands on the arms, pleased with her decision, imagining the look of surprise on Amy's face. Now she could get back to Rose.

Leaning forward as she got up, she glanced at the paperwork Dan had left on his desk. Perhaps a clue to the identity of this mystery woman might be hidden somewhere? Turning to check the door was closed, she started leafing through, careful to make sure she left things looking undisturbed. Everything appeared to relate to the hotels. Three piles of business dealings, each one associated with the different boutique hotels in the family business: Trevarrick in Cornwall, the Arthur in Edinburgh and the Canonford in London. The spreadsheets meant little to her. She always left her own for Terry to deal with, although she was intelligent enough to know when the figures were good or bad, and these were definitely good. She moved the heavy Murano glass paperweight, hefting it in her hand, feeling its weight.

A click of the door. She spun round. Daniel.

'Beautiful, isn't it? I just wanted to make sure you had everything you need.'

Having been so nearly caught snooping, her heart was racing. However, she held her nerve. 'Yes, everything thanks. In fact I'm done now.'

'Just one of my collection.' He indicated a glass-topped table by the window. Inside were about thirty millefiori paperweights of different sizes and shapes and a riot of colours: baby blues and pinks, rich yellows, greens and maroons, deep blues and whites.

'They're gorgeous.'

'Aren't they?' He reached out for the one she held. 'I found this one in Cortona.'

Their hands touched as he took it. Eve's breath caught at what felt like an infinitesimal sexual tug between them. She'd felt the same when, on their arrival, he put his arm round her. Had he felt anything? He'd never given her the remotest reason to think so. For her, those rare, brief moments of contact were enough to remind her how different her life might have been. Her fate had been settled that night on Arthur's Seat, when Will and she had taken a drunken student bet that they wouldn't be able to get to the top and back before dawn. Despite his being a friend of Daniel's, she hadn't known him well. By the time the dare was over, she knew him much, much better. After that, they were rarely out of each other's company and Daniel, a highly satisfactory fling while it lasted, had been unceremoniously discarded. Only when art student Rose had come on the scene had they mended the fences, frequently becoming a foursome. That was when her friendship with Rose had been forged.

He seemed to have aged in the two days since they'd been there. Lines she'd never noticed framed his mouth and eyes. He straightened a pile of papers then returned the paperweight to its correct place.

'I'm sorry you're leaving,' he said. 'We really can't persuade you?' He paused. 'I know Rose would love you to stay. We both would.'

'She's told me, Dan.' Outside the window, the sky was clearing. It was going to be a glorious last day after all. She'd promised Rose not to say anything to him, but perhaps she could help.

'Of course. I thought she must have.' He took the worn leather armchair in the corner of the room, moving one of Rose's tapestry cushions to one side so he could lean back. He looked more beaten than Eve had ever seen in the long years she'd known him. He hadn't looked as bad as this even when he and Rose were beside themselves with worry over Anna's eating disorder and self-harming.

'You've got to explain, Dan. That's the very least you can do. She's going mad with not knowing.'

'It's difficult. I . . .' He covered his mouth with his hand, rubbing his upper lip.

'I don't care how difficult it is,' she insisted. 'And I don't want to hear any self-justification. Tell it to the person you should be talking to – Rose. This is something between the two of you.'

'You're right. I know.' His face was strained as he pulled the cushion from behind his left elbow and held it on his lap, one finger tracing the richly coloured flowers in the design over which Rose had taken such care.

'Well, do it then, Dan. What's stopping you? You've never been someone afraid to express themselves. Why not now?'

He didn't look up from the cushion. 'The thing is, I've met . . .' He hesitated. 'Someone who . . . Oh God, this is so hard . . . so difficult to know how to . . .'

A sound of impatience escaped Eve; enough to stop Dan from continuing. He looked out of the window into the distance, lost in thought.

The ringing of the phone interrupted the awkward silence that had fallen between them.

'Eve, could you get that?'

She leaned forward to hear him better. His voice was little more than a murmur.

'I can't speak to anyone right now. Tell them I'm not here.' He buried his head in his hands.

Eve turned back to the desk. 'Hello.'

'Auntie Eve? Is that you?' Jess's cheerful voice was a welcome distraction. 'How long have you been there?'

'Jess! Great to hear you. We arrived on Monday.' She swung the office chair round to face Daniel, who was shaking his head, zippering his mouth. 'When are we expecting you?'

'That's what I'm phoning about. I need to speak to Dad about it all. Is he there?'

It took a nanosecond for Eve to decide to ignore Daniel's gestures. 'Yes. He's right here.'

Daniel's eyes widened at her flagrant disregard of his request. He wasn't used to non-compliance by anyone, least of all his family. And Eve knew that. He shook his head again, trying to impress on her that she was doing the wrong thing.

Amused by his reaction, and enjoying being the one in control, Eve held out the phone and said loudly enough for Jess to hear, 'It's Jess, Daniel. She wants to speak to you.'

He clenched his jaw, gripped the cushion then flung it on the floor in anger.

Eve raised her eyebrows, cocking her head to show she was not impressed. As he snatched the phone from her, she reached for the cushion and got up to tuck it behind him.

'Jess?'

If she couldn't see for herself how grim he looked, Eve wouldn't have guessed anything was wrong. He made a dismissive gesture with his hand, asking her to go. This time she respected his wishes and slipped out, leaving him to it.

She found Rose sweeping the floor in Jess's room. Like the other bedrooms, it contained the minimum of furniture. Beside the bed was a small nursing chair holding two more of Rose's tapestry cushions, and a single mattress on the floor with a knitted Peter Rabbit and a Paddington Bear on its pillow. Above it hung a mobile made up of brightly coloured hot-air balloons that swayed in the breeze blowing through the open window. Beside it was the

Alice in Wonderland chair that Rose and Daniel had made together. Eve leaned against the door jamb and waited while Rose brushed the dust into the long-handled dustpan.

Only when the job was done did she look up. 'Did you get hold of Amy?'

As Eve relayed their conversation, Rose was totally engaged. 'Yes, I can see why you've got to go home,' she concluded when Eve finished. 'I wish you could stay, for my sake, but you need to sort this out.'

'You'll be all right. Anna and Jess will get you through.'

Rose looked horrified. 'I'm not going to talk to them about Daniel. You don't think I should, do you?'

'Not until you know what's really going on. Then you can decide how much they need to know. By the way, Jess just called.'

'She did?' Rose face lit up with pleasure at the news.

'I left Daniel talking to her. He didn't exactly leap at the opportunity but I didn't give him a choice.'

Together the two women returned to the kitchen. Rose began to empty the dishwasher, putting things away, while Eve went out to the terrace, where she sat at the table, picking up a copy of the previous day's paper. She found a crossword and began to fill it in.

Suddenly there was a shout. 'Bloody, bloody girl.' As she got up, through the doorway Eve saw Daniel come into the kitchen. Rose swung round.

'What's happened?' she asked, but not in a way that suggested she much wanted to hear the answer.

Daniel looked as if he was going to go to her, but he caught sight of Eve coming through the doorway and stopped. 'Jess has seen fit to lecture me about my shortcomings as a father. She said she had to make sure we all know where we stand before she arrives tomorrow.'

'She is coming then?' Rose's relief was all too evident.

'Yes, she is. And without that wastrel Adam, thank God. But I'm not going to be spoken to like that by my own daughter.'

'Like what?' Anna had been drawn to the kitchen by the sound of raised voices. 'She's nearly twenty-nine, Dad. We are adults, you know, whether you like it or not.'

'Not you too!' Daniel spun round to face her. 'I've had enough from the women in this family. I'm going out.'

'Where to?' Anna, a pad of paper in her hand, had obviously come in search of him.

'For a run.'

That was always the answer, Eve recollected. Face down emotional trouble with physical exercise. When Daniel couldn't cope with a problem, there was always the squash court, the swimming pool, the gym.

'Isn't it too hot to go running now?' Rose was putting the cutlery back in the table drawer and spoke as if she was barely interested. 'Why don't you go for a swim instead?'

'Because I don't want to be told what to do, where to go, or how to behave. I've had enough of that for one morning.'

From where she stood, Eve could see that the Daniel she'd been talking to earlier had vanished. Now he was pulled up to his full height, his face set as if he was controlling himself.

'But Dad, I wanted to talk to you.' Anna ignored Rose's slight shake of the head in her direction and held out the exercise book towards him. 'I've sketched out what everything will look like.'

He took it as if it was the last thing in the world he wanted. 'Later.' Exasperated, he slapped it on the dresser with such force that a couple of plates wobbled. Eve reached out to rescue them.

Rose's measured 'Daniel, please' was only just audible under Anna's furious 'Dad! For God's sake. I only want to show you my—'

'Well I don't want to see them. Not now.' He strode out past Eve towards the washing line, where, sending pegs flying, he ripped down his running kit. The three women gaped after him as he marched back into the house to change, saying nothing as he clipped his thigh on the corner of the table. Rubbing his leg as he exited the room, he left them pinned to the spot, not quite knowing how to react. Eve was the first to crack. She hadn't seen such a petulant display of temper since her teenage sons' performances. Reminded of them, a short laugh escaped her that she quickly turned into a cough.

But not quickly enough. Anna, who by this time was rescuing her book, couldn't disguise her shaking shoulders and the splutters that she was having difficulty controlling. The two of them, infected by each other, burst into uncontrolled laughter. Rose stared at them both. Eve was bent double in the doorway while Anna had picked up the book and was sitting on the floor, equally hysterical. As soon as one of them stopped, the other started them off again. After a minute, during which she looked as if she might burst into tears, Rose pulled out one of the kitchen chairs and sat down as if she had no energy left in her body. Gradually a smile crept across her face, until she could no longer hold back and even she had no choice but to join in.

II

Perhaps laughter really is the best medicine, reflected Rose. She had felt better since the hysteria that had taken them over as Dan left the kitchen. More than that, Eve had been a great listener. She knew the right things to say, but also managed to keep her peace when they weren't wanted. Rose wouldn't consider confiding in anyone else. Giving away her most private anxieties didn't come easy.

Now they lay side by side in the shade of two parasols by the pool. Terry had retired to his favourite hammock above them, leaving them to it. Daniel had yet to return. He'd probably thought better of running in the heat of the day and had stopped off in the tiny roadside restaurant on the Siena road. Most likely he'd cool down over one of the house specialities and a cold beer. He sometimes went there when he wanted to think or to while away time with Ignazio, the laid-back owner of the place, before walking on. They were probably playing cards. Anna was in the pool, treading water in the deep end, only her head and the sharp bony crest of her shoulders showing.

'Do be careful, darling,' Rose advised. 'Your shoulders are burning.'

'Mum, I'm a pro tanner and know what I'm doing.' That don't-mess-with-me tone was back.

Glancing at the tube of factor 10 sun cream, Rose doubted that she did, but she couldn't be bothered to argue.

'You OK?' Eve looked round the edge of her Kindle. Her big black sunglasses covered half her face. They reminded Rose of a giant bluebottle, but she was too polite to say so.

'Actually, more fine than I was expecting,' she replied. 'I'm keeping calm and carrying on now. What else can I do? I might feel differently when Dan gets back, but right now I want to enjoy having you all here, and look forward to Jess and Dylan arriving tomorrow.'

'Good. That's more like it.' Eve put down her reading and removed her sunglasses before rolling over on to her front. She adjusted the top of her swimsuit, less secure now that she had managed, with great difficulty, to engineer her left arm out of the one and only arm hole. 'I bet there'll be a perfectly good explanation.'

'Thanks for listening.' Rose didn't look at her, but lay on her back, eyes closed, doubting.

Eve half turned her head. 'Don't be daft. Any time. You know you only have to say. And no, I won't say anything to Terry. I know what he's like!' Smiling, she reached for the straw fedora that she'd borrowed from the sunhat collection hanging on the hall wall, and jammed it on the back of her head. 'This sun'll turn my hair to straw.' She shut her eyes, letting one hand drop to the ground. 'Better make the most of my last day,' she murmured.

Rose didn't move, enjoying the sensation of the heat on her body. As her eyes closed, the years rolled away, taking her back to the time when the three of them first met: Daniel, Eve and her. How different life had been, packed with dreams and expectations. Enrolled at the Edinburgh College of Art, she and her fellow students had had little to do with those at the university. That at least had been the case for her until the evening she attended a black-tie dinner-dance celebrating her flatmate Morag's twenty-first. When Morag had first told her of her parents' plans, to say Rose was apprehensive was an understatement. She had never been invited to anything so grand in the Cornish backwater where she'd been brought up. But as the occasion approached, she began to share the excitement, despite the nagging anxiety over what she would wear.

'Oh, I've got something you can have,' Morag offered when Rose confided her worry, a little bit of her hoping that that would be the excuse she needed not to go. Her friend rummaged on the hanging rail she used as a wardrobe until she produced a deep green satin evening dress.

'I'm going shopping, so this old one's yours. I've only worn it a couple of times and it's beautiful,' she added, seeing Rose's dubious expression. 'You'll look great in it.'

She was right. The dress fitted as if it had been cut for her and made Rose feel like another person: confident, attractive, as good as the rest. She remembered how she had wished her parents had been there to see her. There had never been an occasion at Trevarrick when she had needed to wear something so classy.

She and Morag had arrived at the function room together, excited and a bit tipsy from the gin and tonic they'd sunk for Dutch courage. Rose immediately lost Morag to the party and found herself talking to a young man she had never seen before. He had torn himself away from a group where he was the centre of amused attention and come to her rescue as she had stood uncertain on the edge of the gathering.

'You obviously know everyone,' she'd said, impressed by the way he kept smiling and nodding at people who passed.

'Not a soul,' he said, beaming at her. 'I'll tell you a secret. I haven't been invited. If I hear there's a black-tie do on somewhere, I sometimes gatecrash.' He laughed at her astonishment. 'If you look the part, no one stops you getting in. They always assume someone else must know you. I usually meet someone I like and there's always free food and drink – good food and drink at that.'

Before she had time to express her outrage on Morag's behalf, he asked her to dance. Then, when the music stopped, he asked her again. Then again. When, during supper, Morag came across to find out who this handsome interloper was, Rose introduced Daniel as though she'd known him for years. Before Morag could object, he had engaged her in conversation. Rose had long forgotten what about. Any objections Morag might have had melted away as she was drawn in, laughing at his jokes as he focused on her as if she were the only girl in the room – apart from Rose, whose hand he did not let go.

As for Rose, she was smitten. She went home in a daze, unsure what had just happened to her. She couldn't forget the irrepressible chancer who had rescued her evening. When he phoned the next day, she accepted his invitation to the cinema without a moment's thought. Before long, they were going everywhere together. It was during that term that she met Eve.

They had left Daniel's flat in Inverleith Terrace to go to Paddy's Bar. The Rose Street pub was already overflowing with customers. As soon as they pushed their way in, Dan froze. Rose immediately sensed that something was wrong, even though the smile hadn't left his face.

'Dan!' A young woman, flamboyant in a ra-ra skirt that matched the scarlet slides in her hair, elbowed her way through, exotic-coloured drink held high. A reluctant-looking man followed in her wake. Daniel's grip tightened on Rose's hand. Just as the woman reached them, someone gave her a shove so her drink slopped over Rose's white broderie anglaise blouse.

'Oh God, I'm sorry.' She flapped her hand at the spreading stain as if to magic it away. 'Cinzano and orange.'

Rose stood motionless, aware of the eyes of the pub on her, waiting to see her reaction. But the shock of the icy liquid had taken her breath away.

'Rose.' Dan heaved a despairing sigh. 'Meet Eve . . . and Will.'

'I know, I know,' fussed Eve, ignoring Dan's glare. 'Come to the Ladies' with me. You can take off your blouse and borrow my cardigan. I don't need it.' The cardigan in question was red cashmere that had obviously shrunk in the wash so it looked like felt rather than wool. The sleeves hardly reached Eve's wrists.

As Rose discovered later, Eve had no need of it because the crowded pub was sweltering. But by the time she realised this, the two women were well on the way to becoming friends, the rinsed-out blouse crumpled up on the bench between them. Later, Dan told Rose that that was the evening when he and Will had been forced to mend fences. He hadn't spoken to either Will or Eve since they had hooked up together. At the time, Rose was blissfully ignorant of what was going on. Thanks to an unspoken pact between the others, she remained unaware of the tangle of their lives for months.

'What are you smiling at?' Anna dripped some water over her mother as she bent over beside her, arranging the towel on the third lounger.

'Just memories.' Rose propped herself up. 'Actually I was thinking about when we all met.'

'When Eve threw her drink at you?' The story had become part of family folklore.

'Not threw, Anna,' Eve interrupted, removing her sunglasses to squint at her, her eyes screwed up against the sun. 'Someone pushed me. It couldn't be helped.'

'Was Terry there too?'

Rose was pleasantly surprised by Anna expressing interest in their past, however idle.

'God, no!' Eve propped herself up on her elbows. 'Your mother didn't introduce me to him for years. I had to get married and divorced and move south before then.'

'So on the rebound then?'

'Anna!'

Had all that therapy taught her daughter to be so tactless, or did it just come naturally?

There was a crack of a twig as Terry got out of the hammock. The sound of him clearing his throat.

Having straightened the towel, Anna angled the lounger to get an even exposure and lay on her back, her ribs and hip bones prominent in the sun.

Eve just laughed. 'Hardly. Once I set eyes on Terry, I knew he was the man for me.'

She really sounded as if she meant it, thought Rose, grateful that her brother's feelings had been spared and briefly curious again about the dynamic of their marriage. If she hadn't known, she would never have guessed at the hostilities of the previous night. Of course their courtship took place so long ago that Anna's remark shouldn't affect them. All their relationships had changed so much since then, shifting like sand. What had once seemed so certain had in fact been transient.

'Good to hear it.' Terry's voice floated down from above them. 'Oughtn't you to be getting ready? It's four thirty. We'll have to leave at seven to get you to the plane.'

Eve rolled on to her side, clutching the top of her swimsuit. 'Oh God, is it really? Thanks, darling. I'll be right up.' She began collecting her belongings and stuffing them in her metallic-weave beach bag. 'Bloody Amy Fraser. I really don't want to go now.'

'And we don't want you to. Do stay.' But Rose knew that Eve's mind was made up really.

Her friend reached across and squeezed her hand. 'I can't. You'll get on fine without me.' The look she gave her reminded Rose of all they'd discussed.

Anna lifted her head, the sinews in her long neck standing out like ropes. 'Where's Dad? He went out hours ago.'

'He probably spent the afternoon with Ignazio. But he'll want to say goodbye to Eve. He'll be back soon.' The sinking feeling Rose had, as she foresaw an evening of awkward negotiation at best or confrontation at worst, was tempered by the knowledge that at least Jess would be with them the next day. Eve was right. The affair must be symptomatic of some unaccountable mid-life crisis, not something that would last. They'd got carried away last night. She'd taken the whole thing too seriously and let the situation get out of hand. But: *Miss. Love. Come back.* The words echoed in her head like the tolling of a funeral bell.

'I'm going for a walk. Anybody want to come?' Terry leaned over the rustic fence.

'I will.' Anna sat up and gathered her still damp hair, twisting it into a knot on the top of her head. She rammed her biro through it to secure it in place. 'We might meet him on his way back. I won't be a minute.' She left all her belongings exactly where they were, scattered about her lounger.

Rose swung her legs round and bent forward to pick them up, glad of something to do.

'Leave them,' advised Eve. 'She can get them later. You don't have to clear up after them any more.'

Rose straightened up. 'You're right. Just habit. Why don't you get yourself ready and then there'll be time for a farewell Prosecco before you go. We'll toast the downfall of Amy.'

An hour and a half later, Rose and Eve were on the terrace. The cork had just been popped from the bottle and two chilled glasses were being filled. Next door's ginger cat had made itself at home on one of the chairs. Beside them, Eve's red case stood to attention, ready for the journey home.

'To the Rutherford Agency and down with its detractors.' Rose raised her glass and clinked it with Eve's.

'To you and Dan. May you work it out.' They clinked again.

'We will,' said Rose, as confidently as she could manage. 'We'll get through this. We may need a bit of time to sort things. That's all. I only wish I hadn't said anything now. If I hadn't, he would almost certainly have seen sense and realised what was important in his own good time.'

'Well, you did.' Eve could be relied on for down-to-earth pragmatism. 'So you'll have to deal with it. But I know you will.' She glanced at her watch. 'Terry's cutting it a bit fine. I wonder where they've got to.'

As if on cue, the sound of rapid footsteps on the path made them turn. It was Anna, alone, half running, her feet slipping out of her espadrilles. There was no sign of Terry or Daniel.

Afterwards, Rose would remember how she had first noticed the bloody scrapes on Anna's knees, her legs covered in grey dust from the track, the stricken expression on her face as she kicked off her shoes and raced towards them over the grass. Her hair had come untied and was streaming out behind her.

'Whatever's happened?' But Rose didn't expect Eve to answer.

Both women were already on their feet. They had only taken a few steps forward when Anna reached her mother, flinging herself at her, almost bowling her over. Instinctively Rose put her arms round her daughter and led her, sobbing and incoherent, to a chair. As she pulled one out, Eve's case was knocked over, forgotten.

'Anna! What is it? What's happened?' She tried to make out what Anna was saying, but the words weren't making sense. They were lost among the frenzied sobbing and gasps for air.

'Where's Terry? What the hell's happened?' Eve sounded terrified.

'It's Dad . . .' was all Anna could choke out. Then, 'Terry's stayed with him. You've got to come. He . . .'

As her daughter tried to go on, Rose felt herself disconnecting from the scene. Something terrible had happened to Daniel. Something worse than terrible. The sun still shone, the trees moved in the breeze, a black beetle scuttled past her foot, but she was locked off from it all, at one remove from everything. There was a rushing in her ears as if she was being swept underwater. She could see Anna's mouth moving, her face wet with tears, her hair wild. Only the noise of her daughter's crying anchored her to reality.

Rose felt Eve's arm round her shoulder. She shook her off, trying to move away from Anna, not wanting to hear whatever she was struggling to say. But Anna was clinging to her, wiping her nose on the back of her arm, crying, crying as if she would never stop.

'You've got to come . . .' Anna stumbled to her feet, pulling at Rose's hand. 'We . . .'

Rose stared at her, felt her hands rising to cover her ears. She didn't want to hear. She didn't want any of this to be real.

For a moment Anna looked as though she wasn't going to be able to go on, but somehow she regained sufficient control. 'We found him.' She paused, aware that two pairs of terrified eyes were on her, waiting. 'He's about a mile back down the track.'

'But he's on his way home?' Rose said, desperately seeking assurance as she extricated her hand from her daughter's grasp. She needed to talk to Daniel. They had so much to say to one another, to sort out. So much unfinished business.

'Terry's called the police.'

'Police? Why? What's happened? Is he OK?' But she knew. She knew.

Anna gazed at Rose. Rose saw the fear and the pity in her

daughter's eyes. She saw how reluctant she was to be the one to break the news. She watched her bite her bottom lip, how it slid away from under her teeth. She could see the white mark of an old chickenpox scar above her mouth. She watched how Anna closed her eyes and took another breath. She saw the fine blue veins on her eyelids. Then:

'He's collapsed. We couldn't find a pulse. Terry's trying . . .' She stopped again, as Rose and Eve waited, silent. 'Mum . . . I think he might be dead.'

Eve gasped. Then, silence. Even Anna was quiet. It was as if they were waiting for Rose to react, so say something, to make it all right.

A bird trilled in the walnut tree. A butterfly flew past, then another.

Rose felt something give way inside her. She felt herself being cradled in someone's arms. A glass of water. A rug around her shivering shoulders. She heard a murmur of voices so far away. She needed to see Dan. She had to speak to him. He couldn't leave her now, not when they had so much left to say. She heard a long-drawn-out wail, the sound of someone suffering terrible grief. It was never-ending. Never-ever-ending. Would they never stop? Then she realised. That keening was coming from her. And nothing she could do would silence it.

January

12

Rose was late. Eve was standing in the theatre foyer, just beginning to wonder whether she should leave the ticket with the box office and go in alone. She checked the time. Five minutes till curtain-up. The other theatregoers were filing past both sides of the small bar into the auditorium. The unpromisingly titled *Rubbish* had been written by the husband of one of Eve's authors. Billed as 'a climate-change comedy', the concept had made her heart plummet. However, presented with two complimentary tickets from said proud author, she'd accepted gracefully, while wondering which of her friends she could strong-arm into accompanying her.

She hadn't asked Rose. A comedy, however politically incorrect, didn't seem the appropriate invitation when Dan's memorial was taking place two days later. But when on the phone she moaned about having to go, Rose had volunteered to keep her company. 'Everybody's still treating me like a piece of cut glass, only inviting me to the dullest events in case I crack up at the sight of someone enjoying themselves. I'd like to.'

She had insisted, and now she wasn't going to make it. Eve was almost the last person in the foyer when Rose materialised in the doorway, long brown and tan zigzag-patterned coat blowing out behind her as she stuffed her gloves into her bag. As she removed her fur hat, Eve noticed that her face had filled out a little. Rose had lost so much weight after Dan's death, it was a relief to see the terrible gauntness less pronounced and some life back in her eyes.

'I'm so sorry,' she panted. 'Roadworks. Anyway, I'm here now.'

They embraced with a kiss, and followed the stragglers into the auditorium. Forcing an entire row to stand up, the two of them shuffled gratefully along to their seats. They were still removing their coats as the lights went down. As Eve wrestled her bag under her seat, she was aware of Rose glancing around her, then stiffening, her gaze fixed on someone in the scaffold of the circle.

'Who is it?' Eve scanned the couple of rows of faces, almost indistinguishable in the gloom.

Rose whispered something and gripped Eve's wrist as if she was trying to break it, then, remembering where she was, let go. At that moment, the stage lights went up and a dustbin lid crashed. Further talk was impossible as the cast hurled themselves into what turned out to be a sharp, fast-paced script that was far more entertaining than the title had suggested. Relieved that she would not have to pretend her appreciation to the playwright's wife, but concerned about Rose, Eve occasionally cast a brief sideways glance at her friend to check she was enjoying it too. Although Rose's gaze was directed at the stage, she looked as if she were a million miles away.

When the interval arrived, Rose stared up to her left again as the house lights came on. Then she shook her head. 'How stupid of me,' she muttered.

'Someone you know?' Eve had her bag on her lap and was standing ready to go to the bar. 'I already ordered interval drinks. Merlot OK?'

'Perfect,' Rose replied, leading the way out. As they reached the aisle, she looked upwards again. 'I thought I saw Dan. Him.' She gestured towards a man reading his programme. 'It isn't, of course, but don't you think they're alike?'

Eve stared at the man in question, trying to spot a resemblance. Perhaps the shape of the nose in profile. A bit. Perhaps the chin at a certain angle. Dan with a haircut, maybe. But swarthier, greyer, older. Perhaps. 'No, not really,' she concluded.

'When we come back, and the lights go down, take another look.' And Rose started up the stairs. 'I often see him.'

Startled, Eve watched her back, her shoulder blades visible under her lavender jumper. Was Rose deluded with grief? Still? Four months after Dan's death and Eve had hoped that she was coping a little better now the first wave of terrible debilitating sorrow had broken.

They stood squashed together as the crowd swelled around them. Rose, seeming untroubled, looked about her. 'I didn't notice that,' she said in reply to Eve's criticism of one of the actors. 'I still can't concentrate on anything, but at the same time, I do want to get back to normal. Well, the new normal. Seeing Dan threw me. It shouldn't, though,' she went on without giving Eve a chance to interrupt. 'I've seen him before.'

'You have?' For once, Eve didn't know how to react. What she wanted to do was sweep Rose, who still looked so fragile, into a hug, but even had there been room, she would not have welcomed the gesture. Publicly demonstrative Rose was not.

'Mmm, yes. It's funny. I don't find it upsetting, not any more. At first it was, well . . . odd, I suppose. I'd see him walking down the street, in a passing car or waiting for me. But then I'd get up close and realise it wasn't him at all. In a funny way, it's rather comforting.'

'Comforting? It'd scare the bejaysus out of me.' Eve took a sip of her very welcome wine.

'It's the same when I'm at home,' Rose went on. 'But different, because of course no one's there. But I keep expecting him to appear, just like he used to. I imagine a door opening and him standing there.'

'Are you all right living on your own?' Eve was feeling slightly out of her depth. 'I rather thought you'd go and stay with Jess.'

'She offered. So sweet of her.' Their shared but unspoken thought was of Anna, who had done no such thing. 'But I wouldn't want to get in their way. She's got so much on her plate now Dan's not here to oversee everything. And to be honest, it's hard spending too long with her or Anna when my decision about what to do with the hotels is hanging over us. Obviously they know that Dan left me his share in the business, so I own two thirds of it now. And they know that Madison Gadding have increased their offer for all three, thanks to Terry. I should make a decision before they withdraw their interest, but equally I don't want to rush into anything. I want to be sure I do what's right.'

'People say you're not meant to do anything for a year,' Eve advised, then added as an afterthought, 'I hope Terry hasn't been pressurising you?'

Rose shook her head. 'How is he?'

'Unmanned might be one way of describing it,' Eve suggested. 'I know redundancy is always a terrible shock, but he's taken it so badly. And on top of Daniel's death.'

'I'm sorry I haven't done more.' Rose ran the tip of her finger around the rim of her glass.

'For heaven's sake, woman, you've had enough on your plate without this. He'll get through in the end.' But remembering the Terry she'd left at home, Eve was less sure than she sounded. 'He didn't see it coming at all. He needs to work, for his own self-esteem more than anything, but there are no jobs around. And he's hardly in the first flush.'

Before she could say any more, the bell cut their conversation short. Back in their seats, Eve followed Rose's gaze to the man in the circle.

'How funny,' Rose said wistfully. 'He's not like Dan at all.' She wrapped her arms around her body as if comforting herself.

Afterwards they emerged into the freezing night and trudged through the frozen slush, the last bleak reminder of the snowstorms that a week earlier had thrown the country into chaos. They headed towards the French restaurant Eve had chosen.

Tucked into a side booth, they got the ordering out of the way – two steak and chips and two glasses of house red – before Eve asked, 'How are you, Rose? Really.'

Rose leaned back against the seat, her bony left hand flat on the table, the other playing with her engagement and wedding rings that slid up and down her finger as easily as they twisted round, much looser now. 'I don't know,' she replied. 'I was so shocked, so bewildered at first. My life seemed to have stopped dead while everyone else's was going on without me. Now I feel as if I'm slowly coming to my senses. I've got to keep putting one foot in front of the other; it's all I can do.'

'Will you be all right for the memorial on Wednesday?'

'I think so. I've had so many lovely letters, some from people I've never met, who are all coming. The weird thing is they all talk about another Dan rather than the one I knew.' She stopped playing with her rings and waited while the waiter poured their drinks. 'No one says a bad word about him! Of course they wouldn't, but they all conjure up some kind of saint. And that he wasn't! It's as if there were two of him. In fact, sometimes I think I like their Dan more than the one I had.'

'You're not still worrying about that affair? If that's what it was.' Over the intervening months, Eve had wondered whether the whole text message thing hadn't been blown out of all proportion.

There was a pause as the waiter put their food in front of them.

'Not worrying, no. It's over. But sometimes I feel so angry with him for screwing everything up just before he died. How could he do that?' Rose gripped her knife so her knuckles turned white.

'He was trying to tell you,' Eve reminded her, remembering her own final conversation with him. 'Us all being there made it impossible. We've talked about this.' And they had, time and time again. In the confusion of the days following Dan's death, Rose didn't remember their conversations. She forgot them in the same way she forgot arrangements she had made, or went to keep appointments at the wrong time, or left the iron on, or forgot to leave the money for the cleaner. Then she'd make Eve laugh by confessing her latest slip-up, unable to believe she could have been so stupid, smiling at her own incompetence.

Afterwards they would return to the ghastly business of registering the death, repatriating the body and telling friends and family back home. Eve hadn't flown back to England as planned but had left Amy to manage the agency after all. Somehow the four of them – Rose, Eve, Terry and Anna – had negotiated that ghastly evening together: the visit to the hospital, the nightmare of not being able to understand clearly what they were being told, of waiting for someone who could translate for them, the sight of Daniel lying alone, cold. None of them knowing what to do.

'Was he?' asked Rose, sawing at her steak. 'Wasn't he just a man with a thirty-one-year itch who thought he could get away with it?'

This was new. During the couple of weeks since they had last seen each other, the old Rose had apparently lifted a corner of her shroud of despair and begun to peep out. During the immediate aftermath of Dan's death – a brain haemorrhage, they'd said once a doctor who spoke fluent English had been found, which translated as a massive stroke – Rose had shut down. In those first terrible days, Eve had found it hard to control her own grief while she tried to support her friend. Meanwhile Rose herself remained stony-faced, concentrating on all the necessary administration as if that would stop her from going under.

'I'm not sure that's the attitude you should have just before his memorial service!'

'True,' Rose agreed with a smile. 'But they'll all be there celebrating the life of the man I thought I knew when I obviously didn't really and now I never will. That's quite a thing to come to terms with.' She paused as a thought struck her. 'You don't think she'll be there, do you?'

'Who? "S"? She wouldn't have the nerve.'

'But we wouldn't necessarily know. It happens in films all the time.' Rose mused. 'She'll be wearing a black suit and a tiny black hat with a veil . . .' She picked up a French fry in her fingers and stared at it.

'And looking deranged,' added Eve, warming to the theme. 'She'll be peering out from behind a gravestone, or standing almost hidden by a yew tree, watching us all file into the church . . .'

They laughed, then Eve raised her glass. 'To Dan. Whoever he was.'

'To Dan,' Rose echoed. 'And the fine mess he's got us into.'

'You don't mean Jess and Anna? Can't they see there's a world where they're not at its centre?'

'That's not fair. You know that Jess blames herself for his death, thinks that if they hadn't argued he'd still be here.' Rose moved the remains of her food to one side of her plate and placed her knife and fork together beside it, perfectly aligned.

'That's crazy. Finished with these?' Eve stretched across and helped herself to a couple of Rose's discarded chips.

'I know, I know. And she's devastated that she wasn't there. But whatever I say doesn't make a difference. So she's working incredibly hard to make herself worthy of him. She wants me to keep the hotels so she can run them for him, eventually.'

'And Anna?'

'With immaculate timing, she's found the "ideal" property for her garden centre and is desperate for me to sell and release some cash to her.' She paused as she sipped her wine. 'I honestly haven't a clue what to do.'

'Do nothing,' said Eve firmly. 'One day you'll wake up and you'll know what's right.'

'At the moment I feel as if I'm being blown about by the wind. So I hope you're right.'

Some time later, Eve having dashed off to catch the train back home to Cambridge, Rose let herself into a silent house. Her only welcome was the hall light that she'd left on. Hanging up her coat, she shivered in the bitter draught of air that had entered the house with her. The corridor and stairs were shrouded in shadow that disappeared as she twisted the dimmer switch. She rubbed her hands together, then opened the kitchen door, half expecting Daniel to be waiting for her.

Alone, she had no one with whom to discuss the mildy amusing play she had insisted on going to. Friends had rallied round excessively in the months after the funeral, but now they had backed off, as if they felt she should be back leading an ordinary life. Such a thing felt impossible, but she had to try. Would she ever get used to Daniel's absence?

She went through the motions of making a mug of tea before realising that she didn't really want one. That was something they did together when Dan was alive. They would take their tea to bed sometimes, last thing at night, or just sit here and talk about their evening until one of them made the first move upstairs. That was never going to happen again.

She tore off a bit of kitchen roll and blew her nose, then sat at the table. Exhausted. Alone. Burying her head in her hands, she sobbed.

When she had finally run out of tears, she looked up. Everything was so familiar and yet curiously unfamiliar at the same time; different without Daniel to give it meaning. She pulled a brown ceramic vase towards her and removed the dead roses. The buds had never opened; just flopped over in the warmth and hung forlornly. It cost her all the energy she had to cross the kitchen and bin them. Returning to the table, she picked up the vase, turning it in her hand, letting the light catch the richness of the glaze. She remembered how, years ago, towards the end of a trip around Morocco, she and Dan had caught the bus from Marrakesh to Safi. Somehow this vase had made it back home with them intact. The small shop where they'd found it was thick with cooking smells wafting through from the back. When they'd commented on them, they'd been invited to stay to eat. Buying the vase was their thanks. Life had been so simple then. They could go where they wanted, when they wanted. But then they'd had Anna, their much-wanted first child, and shortly afterwards inherited Trevarrick. Rose and Terry's parents had died in quick succession only months apart, surprisingly, as if her mother couldn't live without her father. And then Jess came along.

She returned the vase to its place in the centre of the table. The digital clock on the oven flicked to 12.30. Getting late. But she didn't want to go to bed. Lying awake in the middle of the night, waiting for the hours to pass, was when everything became unbearable. Then, Daniel's death and its consequences seemed insurmountable. Lying on her back, as if in her own coffin, next to the cold space beside her that Dan had once filled, her nights were long and sleepless. But what was the alternative? The doctor had given her sleeping pills immediately after she'd eventually returned to England with Dan's body, but after a couple of months she had stopped taking them. They did their job, knocking her out at night, but every morning she had woken unable to function properly until almost midday. In those early days of grieving, she had found a certain comfort in their shared bed.

Beside her were the shelves filled with books and a row of family photos. His was in the centre, one he'd once had taken for a hotel brochure, and surrounded by photos of Anna, Jess and Dylan. He'd brought it home to her, pleased with how distinguished he looked.

'Oh Dan, I need you to tell me what to do,' she whispered.

He looked back at her, his enigmatic half-smile undercutting the gravity of his gaze. He was dressed in a grey suit, hair short and smart. But this wasn't the man she wanted to remember. She took the photo and laid it face down on the shelf, then brought to the front an old photo of the two of them skiing. They stood, arms around one another, sun goggles pushed back on their heads, laughing at a joke. Then she remembered those words. *Miss. Love. Come back.*

'Bastard.' She slipped the photo to the back of the collection after all. *Who was she? What would have happened to us if you'd lived?* This time she didn't speak the words aloud, but they were as loud in her head as if she had.

Those were the questions that she'd asked herself over and over again since that day. She was no nearer finding an answer than she had been then. She had tried to follow Eve's repeated advice to put the existence of this other woman out of her mind. Of course she was right. There was no point in dwelling on her. Whatever Daniel and 'S' had had together was over. When his life ended, Daniel had been where he belonged – with Rose and his family. But even when she did succeed in blocking this woman from her thoughts, it was never for long. Within hours she was back, with her perfect body, her sultry eyes and lips, her scarlet nails, the letter S hissing from her mouth before she threw her head back and laughed at Rose. She hated this stereotyped cinematic image that she'd manufactured, but with nothing to go on, this was the siren who haunted her. Knowing that she still existed somewhere was like a slow water torture – a constant drip drip drip that wouldn't go away. She had been through every one of Dan's suits, his wallet, his briefcase, the forgotten contents of drawers, everything. There was no note, no hotel receipt, no clue of any kind. Even his diary, kept in the most peremptory way, full of hieroglyphic-like scribbles, held nothing. She had kept it on her desk, occasionally trying to decipher his writing and cancelling arrangements when she could. To begin with, it was as though she was keeping him alive, in her own and other people's minds, but now his notes had almost run out.

'Don't torture yourself,' Eve had insisted, when Rose had asked her what she thought an entry said. 'Whatever it was is over. You've got to concentrate on the here and now.'

But she couldn't obliterate the last moments they'd had together, regretting the row, wondering how she could have handled it differently, persuaded him to explain.

Forcing herself to face the inevitable, she went upstairs, taking each step as slowly as if it was her last. She must try to get some sleep, ready for the arrival of the girls the next day. Opening the bedroom door, she experienced that same sense of expectation that she had felt going into the kitchen. But the room was empty, the bed smoothly made, her chair draped with a couple of jumpers. She had left one of his where he had last put it, unused. She ran her hand over the rough Aran wool, remembering. These feelings were her companions now, and she almost welcomed them. She undressed, then opened the wardrobe, where she hung her clothes next to his. His familiar smell still lingered there. She took the sleeve of one of his favourite jackets, deep blue wool, and put it to her face, then dropped it.

Preparing for bed was one of those small daily routines that had kept her going through the darkest times; done on autopilot but, nonetheless, keeping her grounded. In the bathroom, his shaving kit and toothbrush had been left untouched. Getting rid of his things seemed so irredeemably final. Perhaps once the memorial was over, she would be able to begin to let go.

13

Surrounded by friends, family and well-wishers, Rose looked up to the wooden-timbered roof of the church. Were churches built deliberately to make you feel like a speck in God's eye? She certainly felt very insignificant and alone right now, despite the fantastic turnout. Beside her sat a portly and asthmatic cousin of Daniel's with his family. When he had squeezed the five of them into one of the four family pews, wheezing his sympathies to Rose, nobody had the heart to ask him to move in order for Anna and Jess to take their rightful place beside her. Instead, her ousted daughters were across the aisle. Whenever she glanced over to see how they were faring, Rose caught the basilisk glares Anna was shooting in his direction.

Her daughters barely looked like sisters. One so waif-like, her hair falling from a messy bun; the other attractive in a more classic way, her face and figure fuller thanks to the baby weight she had yet to lose, her hair neatly pulled back in a chignon. Rose tried not to compare her daughters, but it was impossible not to notice the difference between them. Anna had made no concession to the occasion, despite Jess's loud objections that morning, but remained true to herself, dressing the way her dad would have expected. In wild contrast to Jess's formal grey suit, black tights and heels, Anna wore thick leopardskin-patterned tights, her biker boots, and a short turquoise dress with strings of tiny coloured beads round her neck. Rose could imagine Dan's objections to her get-up being thoroughly ignored. That was indeed what he would have expected.

What he would have been more surprised by were the flowers. Rose had asked Anna to do them, while Jess looked after the catering. Anna had done her dad proud. In two large black urns at the front of the church and one at the entrance were stunning loose arrangements of early spring flowers: catkins, budding magnolia, purple irises, daffodils, mimosa and Dan's favourite scented white narcissi. They were perfect.

As the vicar asked them to stand, Rose gazed down at the order of service. On the front was a photo taken by her at Casa Rosa. Dan was sitting at the table under the walnut tree, tanned and smiling, raising his glass in a toast, a plate of cheese in front of him. That was how she wanted everyone to remember him: as a man who loved company and the good things in life, and as the man who loved her. She remembered the anniversary they were celebrating when the photo was taken, and could hear him saying as clearly as if he were sitting beside her, 'To my dearest Rose, and to our next twenty-nine years. May they be as happy.' They had just returned to Casa Rosa in time for supper, having spent a wonderful couple of days in the Val d'Orcia, mooching around Pienza and Montalcino. He had opened one of the bottles of fruity red Brunello they had bought, while she had cut them thin slices from a wheel of pecorino.

If only she could travel back in time. How she longed to exchange her memories for Daniel himself. The music came to an end. She looked up, and at a gesture from the vicar, left the pew to light a candle in Dan's memory before the service began.

As the service progressed, she couldn't help reflecting how much Dan would have approved. To remember him, she had chosen some of his favourite music, including Mahalia Jackson's 'Come Sunday'. Ella Fitzgerald's 'Every Time We Say Goodbye' produced the first flutter of handkerchiefs. That was followed by the asthmatic cousin squeezing out to read a snippet from Joyce Grenfell: 'Weep if you must; Parting is hell. But life goes on, so sing as well.' Then the recording of Dan playing his guitar and singing 'Blowin' in the Wind', laughing when he got the words muddled. Rose had heard it so many times that she remained quite calm, separating herself from the sniffs and sobs she could hear behind her, remembering.

The smell of roasting chicken brought her back to the service. At first almost undetectable, it was getting stronger all the time. The vicar had warned her that on Wednesdays, the crypt of the church was used as a kitchen for the homeless. She hadn't considered that the consequence would be the smells wafting up into every corner of the church. Occasionally the clash of kitchen pans punctuated the music. She smiled. Daniel would have seen the funny side.

The second reading was Betjeman's 'Trebetherick', chosen especially to evoke Cornwall and the happy years they had bringing up the children there. She had asked for the tributes to be kept short. A childhood friend spoke about Dan's mile-wide competitive streak and his popularity at school. The manager of the Canonford recalled his skills as an hotelier and colleague, while Terry recollected their long friendship and business partnership, coming close to breaking down as he neared the end. As he returned to his seat behind her, Rose turned to see Eve's hand reach for his as he sat down, her other on his arm.

Finally it was the turn of Jess and Anna. Rose had a lump in her throat as she watched her two daughters, so proud of them as they took it in turns to remember their father. As they talked, Daniel the loving father and family man emerged. Anna recalled his dangerous love of DIY that meant little was thrown away – 'Might be useful one day,' he'd say; Jess – the patience with which he taught her to play a few chords on the guitar; Anna – the swimming lessons in the sea in the rain; Jess – the lover of jazz; Anna – the lover of the outdoors. At that point there was an unscripted pause. Jess looked panic-stricken. Rose froze, praying they would reach the end. Anna picked up the baton to tell a story about Daniel's renowned lack of skill in the kitchen, while Jess gave her a tear-stricken glare before she took her turn again. They didn't look at each other once as they returned to their seats.

At last it was over. As the congregation filed out to Alan Price's 'Don't Stop the Carnival', Rose found herself unable to shake off the memory of their last terrible evening together. Her only consolation was that whoever 'S' was, she had failed to separate them, and now she never would. Even though Rose was left behind to deal with the fallout from his death, she and Daniel would always be united in everyone's eyes. No one but her and Eve needed to know what might have happened if he'd lived. She closed her eyes briefly.

Outside, as the guests streamed from the church into the drizzle, Anna and Jess stood on either side of her, shouldering the outpouring of good wishes. After a few minutes, the three of them drove to the Canonford, where they greeted people again and welcomed them in. As the girls separated from her and melted into the throng, Rose looked around her. The room was full, some familiar faces and some less so, but despite them all being there for her family, she felt on the edge, an outsider, unable to throw herself in. In the past, she would have relied on Daniel being if not at her side, at least in the same room when rescue was needed.

But this was her future now, and she was going to have to learn to cope. Anna and Jess weren't always going to be there for her. Perhaps that was as well, given the way they'd been behaving since they'd arrived the night before. They'd clearly had words at some point after Adam and Jess had unpacked: Anna had excused herself without supper because of her early start the following morning, while Jess involved Rose in putting Dylan to bed. She guessed something had been said about the future of the hotels, but they were obviously trying to keep their squabble from her. And something had certainly happened during their tribute, although they hadn't said what. Rose wasn't fooled. The tension between them was palpable. She was only grateful they hadn't let it spoil the service.

She looked down at the glass of champagne in her hand, the bubbles pricking the surface. Was *she* here? S? The question came unbidden. There were so many women who might fit the bill. They came up to her with lipsticked smiles, eyes creased in sympathy, shaking her hand, kissing her cheek, touching her arm. She shook her head. Thinking like this would get her nowhere. Everyone had come to share their memories of Daniel and to give her and the girls their support. That was what she must focus on. Taking a deep breath, she joined the nearest knot of people, a group of staff from the Trevarrick, who welcomed her into their midst.

*

Terry parked the car. He and Eve had driven to the hotel in silence, each deep in their own memories of Dan. The kids had gone ahead, piling into Charlie's old banger. Eve pulled down the sun visor and flicked open its mirror before taking off her dark glasses. Her eyes were pink and circled with smudged mascara. She licked a finger and tried to repair the damage.

'I can't go in like this. I look awful,' she complained, feeling the tears coming again.

'No you don't.' Terry passed her a Kleenex. 'You look terrific. And the worst's over now.'

'Look at my eyes! That "Blowin' in the Wind" was my undoing. Hearing Dan laugh again . . .' She blew her nose, then took out her tinted moisturiser and, leaning forward to see what she was doing, dabbed it on the worst-affected areas. She added a slash of lipstick to her mouth. 'That's the best I can do.'

'And it's a great best.' Terry reached round behind him and took her flat shoes from the back seat. 'Do you need these?'

'Thanks.' She removed her heels and dropped them into her tote.

Terry smiled at her. 'Women and shoes. What's the point in having them if you can't walk in them?'

Though intended as a joke, Terry's words misfired.

'Just because you never spend more than fifty pounds on yours.' Eve slammed the door of his precious fuel-saving hybrid car that must have made more of a dent in their bank account than it had contributed to saving the planet. 'And it shows.'

He winced at the sound of the door, laying his hand on the car's roof as if comforting it, at the same time containing his complaint at its treatment. 'How much *were* those?'

Yes, an argument was hurrying their way.

'Only one hundred and seventy-five pounds.' If you didn't count the bag that she'd bought to match and the leather spray that seemed so essential at the time.

She could have heard his gasp from three blocks away. 'For heaven's sake, Eve. We're meant to be economising.'

'No, darling. *You're* meant to be economising. I'm still earning.'

That was a low blow that stemmed from the smidgeon of guilt he'd provoked. Catching the haunted expression in his eyes, she immediately wished she could take it back. 'I'm sorry, I shouldn't have said that.'

'No, you shouldn't. Today's hard enough without us falling out over something as trivial as a pair of shoes.' He started off, walking so fast she had to run to keep up.

'Then let's not,' she appealed, grabbing hold of his sleeve. 'Please.' He was right. The memorial had been their final goodbye to Dan. All those memories that brought him alive again for a few minutes, then the bleak reminders that they would never see him again. Even if her grief had made her lash out, she should remember that she wasn't the only one feeling bereft.

He slowed down, letting her slip her arm through his. 'Agreed,' he said. 'Let's do what we can to support Rose, poor thing. Today's about her, not us.'

They walked the rest of the short way in silence, turning into the familiar Victorian cul-de-sac. At the end stood the Canonford: three London terraced town houses that had been reconfigured into one oasis of luxury. This had been the most ambitious of Daniel's hotel makeovers; the flagship of his business. He had taken ideas that had worked at Trevarrick, transposing those he could to the town-house hotel, then adding to and adapting them. To begin with, the family had worried that the project was going to be nothing but a money pit. But with hard work bordering on obsession, Daniel had proved them wrong. The hotel was fifteen years old now, and had achieved the reputation for excellence that he'd hoped for.

Eve leaned against one of the pillars at the bottom of the steps to exchange her shoes while Terry sprinted up between the two bay trees clipped like lollipops, their pots chained to the railings, then waited with exaggerated patience by the open door.

'Nice shoes,' he muttered as they entered the reception area together.

'Thanks,' she whispered as he pecked her on the cheek. Turning on her expensive heel, she crossed to the concierge's desk. The young concierge could have passed for an Armani model, with his regular features, bee-stung lips and fine bone structure. Daniel had always believed in the importance of creating good first impressions. Choosing someone like this as the face of the operation was all part of that.

'Do you know where I can find Rose, John?' She adjusted her necklace.

'Last seen in the lounge.' That even-toothed smile was enough to make any woman go weak at the knees.

Eve allowed herself a smile back. To her left was the lounge, its rich green walls complemented by the yellows, reds and turquoises in the furnishings. The room was now crowded with guests. She nodded at Terry and they entered together, arm in arm.

Rose felt too hot in her suit, but couldn't take off the jacket because Dylan had smeared jam across the shoulder of her pale blue blouse just as she was about to leave for the church. A business associate of Dan's had cornered her to offer his sympathies. Behind him she could see Anna and Terry, standing by the bay window, talking earnestly. They made an odd couple: Terry in a dark lounge suit, serious, nodding in response to whatever Anna was saying. Her bangles slid up and down her arms as she gesticulated to make a point, in her hand an unlit cigarette. When Terry finally spoke, Anna concentrated on what he was saying, intently chewing the side of a nail as she listened. Then they both laughed, their heads leaning together as though they were sharing something intimate.

She felt a tug at her skirt and looked down. Dylan, chocolate biscuit in hand! Adam was right behind him, looking uncomfortable in a suit, protecting his son as he toddled through a forest of legs.

'Excuse me.' She interrupted her companion to pick up her grandson. With a final word, the man tactfully withdrew.

'Ganna. Mwah.' A chocolatey kiss on Rose's cheek, then two small chocolatey hands on either side of her mouth that pursed her lips together.

She laughed, took one of them and began to suck it clean. 'What have you been doing?'

Adam put his arm around Rose and for a second she leaned into his reassuring warmth. 'You looked as if you needed rescuing.' His face was just close enough for her to feel the faint tickle of his beard. His wrists, scattered with reddy-gold hairs, spread into large workmanlike hands, patterned with thin scars. There was toothpaste on his breath.

'Thanks. But I shouldn't have been rude.' She adjusted Dylan's position on her hip.

'You weren't. Don't worry. He'd had his moment.' She liked that about Adam. He was always calm, always fair.

'You're so wise.' As she kissed her grandson, Dylan blew a loud raspberry against her cheek, making her laugh before Adam disengaged his boy and took him off to find Jess.

'They do look happy.' Eve had found Rose at last. She had been scanning the crowd for her, wanting to make sure she wasn't overwhelmed, knowing how being the centre of attention didn't come easy. She was watching Jess and Adam, whose joint attention was focused on Dylan.

'Don't they? If only Daniel . . .' Rose stopped.

'Don't. Not now, anyway. We've got to keep it together. Who else is here?' Eve adjusted the wrapover front of her dress, which had slipped to expose more cleavage than was strictly suitable for the gathering. Rose didn't notice.

'So many people I don't really know who knew Daniel through the business. I'm glad your boys and Millie could make it.' Rose paused to shake hands and exchange a few words with an elderly couple come to thank her for such a wonderful service. Eve looked about her, taking in everyone there. Old family friends and acquaintances, even a couple of people they'd known from university. She stopped. Double-took. She thought she had spotted everyone she knew in the church, but clearly not. She would have recognised him anywhere, despite the passing years. Rose returned to her side.

'What is it?' She followed Eve's gaze.

'You didn't mention Will was coming.' There was an infinitesimal shake in her voice.

Rose clasped her arm. 'I'm sure I did. He wrote after the memorial announcement was in the paper.'

A prickling glow was rising from Eve's chest into her face. 'You definitely didn't. I'd have remembered.' She could feel the sweat beading at her hairline. She took a tissue from her bag and blotted her forehead, but not so hard that she wiped off her make-up. She breathed deeply, willing herself to normal.

'You don't have to talk to him.'

'Don't worry, I'm not going to.' Her heart was thumping now. Still slowing her breath, she studied her ex-husband. He hadn't changed so much over the years – apart from the hair. Not only greyer and thinner; it was cut so close to his scalp that from a distance he could be mistaken for bald. He still had that rangy, loose-limbed look that she remembered so well, but on his nose was a pair of rectangular dark-rimmed glasses. Despite the changes wrought by age, he was unmistakably Will.

As another couple claimed Rose's attention, Eve looked around for Terry. He was talking to Daniel's lawyer, an earnest middle-aged man with a firm sense-of-humour bypass whom she had been glad to avoid. Perhaps they should leave now, except she didn't want to abandon Rose to deal with all this. She was being silly. Years had gone by, and the ground floor of the hotel was quite big enough for both her and Will. She would simply avoid him.

She made her way across the reception to the bar, helping herself to a couple of roast beef and horseradish canapés en route. Line the stomach – always wise. As she requested a second glass of wine, she felt a hand on her shoulder. She spun round, but her sixth sense told her who to expect.

'Evie. I thought it was you.' Same voice, same slight Scottish burr. Memories that she had long ago buried knocked at the inside of their coffin.

'Will!' She heard her voice shoot up at least two octaves higher than normal and cleared her throat.

As she said his name, the perfectly rare roast beef and horseradish slipped from the crostini that she had halfway to her mouth. Her other hand rose to catch it, but too late. As she stood nose to nose with her ex-husband for the first time in years, the raw curls of red meat dropped straight down into the depths of her cleavage, one rogue piece draping itself neatly over the front of her bosom, leaving a playful smear of horseradish on the black pattern of her dress.

'Long time,' he managed, then, clearly trying to compose himself, he took her wine from the barman and asked for one for himself. He stood holding both glasses while she fished out the beef from between her breasts. Boiling under his scrutiny, she returned her catch to the crostini, then took a knife from the table and scraped at the horseradish. The result would have been considerably more successful without the serrated edge. With one stroke she removed some of the sauce, simultaneously hooking out several threads of fabric so that the neck of the dress lifted up as she moved the knife away.

'Oh, shit!' A drop of sweat ran down the side of her face.

Freeing the threads, she straightened the irretrievably frayed neckline. Then, with the little dignity she had left, she put the knife down and took her glass. As she raised it to her lips, she caught the twinkle in his eye and couldn't help herself. Instead of all the things that she'd thought she might say if she ever saw him again, that she had rehearsed so tirelessly in those first months after he'd left, she started to laugh.

'What's Eve doing? Who's that?'

Rose turned from Anna to see Eve delving into her dress, then throwing her head back and laughing.

'That's Will, her first husband.' She was so sure she'd warned Eve he was coming, but perhaps she hadn't in the flurry of organisation. In any event, this was the last reaction she would have expected. Fireworks, perhaps. Greeting, chilly. Conciliation, unlikely.

'You're joking. He looks pretty OK for his age. Does Terry know?' Anna glanced over at her uncle.

'Anna, honestly! Looks aren't everything. I don't think Terry's ever met him.' Rose was experiencing a profound sense of unease as she watched the exchange. She looked over at Terry, whose attention, despite being mid conversation, was also firmly fixed on what was happening on the other side of the room. She didn't think of him as a jealous man, but perhaps he had never had reason. But none of them missed the loud laughter and the way in which Eve and Will moved away from the bar together, his hand possessive at the small of her back, his other arm extended to guide the way.

14

Eve and Will had not seen each other from the day she'd found him driving out of her life for good. Any communication they'd had since was via angry phone calls or solicitors. Eve had never had the chance to tell him how much he'd hurt her. Her desire for payback had diminished over time, until she rarely thought of him. Yet to her secret shame, her subconscious had refused to let him go completely.

At night, he still very occasionally came to her in dreams. There, they made rough, passionate love: the sort of lovemaking that she and Terry had long forgotten. She had read numerous articles about how couples should be honest with each other about what gave them greatest satisfaction, but the years had made them either too inhibited or too indifferent to bother. Perhaps neither of them even knew any more. But in her dreams, she and Will had romped in silk-sheeted circular beds, on shag-pile carpets, in moss-floored beech woods or on white-sanded beaches. In the morning, she would wake, confused, riddled with guilt about something over which she had no control, wondering what it all meant.

And now here he was. Anything she had once meant to say was driven from her mind. Time had dropped away to bypass their last encounter and take her right back to their first year at Edinburgh, when they had met in the canteen. Back then, Will was a showman (some might, indeed some did, call him an attention-seeking idiot) wearing a kilt, a cape, his long glossy hair in a ponytail. She was immediately attracted to his eccentricities and his principles. He didn't give a damn about what anyone thought. He wore, he said, and he did what he wanted. Authority was there to be flouted, rules to be broken.

'Coming?' he'd said, offering her his hand. It wasn't his smile that persuaded her but his eyes, intense and inviting.

Her friends had stared at him, then at her, wondering how she would react. She'd looked at him again, then, driven by a sudden unexpected urge to shock, she had taken his hand and left with him. That night they'd climbed Arthur's Seat.

His voice broke into her thoughts as he suggested they go through to the buffet. Just as she had all those years ago, intrigued but aware of the danger . . . she followed him.

As they crossed reception, Eve heard Anna's voice: 'For Christ's sake, Jess! This is completely unnecessary.'

'You did it on purpose. That's so typical.' Jess was squaring up to her sister by one of the mahogany console tables. Adam was making a timely exit, Dylan on his hip, changing bag over his shoulder.

'Look, I know you feel bad about not being there when Dad died and you want to do your best by him now, but messing up your lines isn't important.' Anna flicked her hair back over her shoulder. There might be some truth in what she was saying, but this was not the moment to say it. Jess looked stricken. Eve wished she could help her. They all knew how much she regretted her last words with Daniel, and the fact that she would never be able to make up with him.

'I didn't mess up anything.' Jess's voice rose in fury. 'You went right on and said what we agreed I'd say. The story about him using icing sugar in the gravy was mine to tell.'

'Oh, rubbish! We were both there when it happened. That story belongs to both of us. OK, I know we agreed you'd tell it, but you blanked, so I just carried on. I thought I was doing the right thing.'

Jess was holding on to the marble-topped table as if it was the only thing keeping her upright. A tissue poked out of one hand. 'Well you weren't. You completely threw me. So you said nearly everything. And I said nothing.'

'Oh, grow up.' Anna was dismissive. 'Nobody noticed. And even if they did, it doesn't matter. It's not a competition to prove who loved him the most.'

The guests standing nearby were beginning to stare, quietly

identifying the girls to each other. As word went round that they were Daniel's two daughters, the attention on them grew. Both of them were so engrossed in their argument that neither of them noticed.

'Girls, girls!' Eve detached herself from Will, leaving him looking amused on the sidelines. 'What *are* you doing?' She gripped them both hard by the arm.

Jess looked embarrassed and mumbled something about it not mattering, shaking her arm free.

'Well you thought it did a minute ago,' accused Anna, spitting the words out. 'When you were blaming me for ruining Dad's memorial.'

'Anna, that's enough!' Eve interrupted, tightening her hold on her arm, feeling the bone. 'Stop this immediately. Both of you. Today's about Daniel and Rose, not about you. Your job's to support your mother, not spoil things by fighting like children.'

'I'm sorry.' Anna and Jess spoke at once. Jess couldn't look at Eve, clearly ashamed of the scene they'd been making. Anna held her head high, a defiant glint in her eye.

'Until now, we've all been admiring how well you both did. Don't spoil it. It must have been difficult to speak about him in front of so many people, but you gave a wonderful warm and funny tribute. And it really doesn't matter which of you said what. Dan would have been touched.'

Anna grunted as if to say *I told you so*. Jess blew her nose, hard.

But Eve hadn't finished. 'You said it together and that's all that mattered.'

'You're right, of course. I'm truly am sorry. I'm just upset.' Jess put the tissue away, blinking quickly.

'We all are. And grief can make you behave out of character sometimes.' In fact, nothing seemed to be much out of character here, but calming the storm before Rose got wind of it was what was important.

The level of surrounding interest in the conversation had waned and the chatter had resumed. Only one or two people still bothered to sneak the odd look.

'What's up, Mum? A'right?' Charlie, Eve's eldest son, came up behind her. Curly-haired, attractive in his rarely seen suit, he looked as if he couldn't get out of the hotel soon enough. The red trainers sticking out from under his sober black trousers gave away his rebellious streak.

'We're fine.' Eve dismissed the incident airily, although Anna and Jess's pinched expressions said different. 'Where are the others?'

'In there somewhere, I think.' He gestured at the dining room. 'Coming for a snout, Anna?' He pulled a packet of cigarettes from his jacket pocket. If he noticed the frosty atmosphere, he ignored it.

Eve refrained from comment but she wanted to snatch the pack from him, delivering the usual lecture in a few sharp words: filthy habit, filthy smell and it kills you.

'Dying for one.' Anna reached into her bag for her tobacco pouch and, without saying any more, followed Charlie outside.

'Dan would have hated this,' Rose whispered to Terry. The guests had moved from the lounge into the dining room, where the splendid and generous buffet organised by Jess was laid out on a long table, decorated with flowers from Anna. Proof of a rare moment when the sisters had worked in harmony. 'Buffets belong in his Room 101. We always disagreed, but if I had the choice, I'd get rid of those awful drawn-out meals where you're stuck beside someone you barely know and don't want to know better. That's my idea of hell.'

'Well, you should be thinking of yourself as well as of him.' Terry worried at a pattern on the carpet with the toe of his shoe.

'Better to be able to move around and talk to everyone who's come. They've all got something to say about him.' She was feeling much better now the service was over and so many people had shared their memories of Dan and what he meant to them. She felt an unexpected wave of affection for her brother.

He looked startled as, with a rush of emotion, she clutched his hand. Then he cleared his throat. 'Sis, do you think we could talk?' The scuffing of his foot intensified.

'What? Now? Hardly the ideal moment for a heart-to-heart.' She could feel his hand pulling away from hers, but she held on. Eve had said he hadn't been himself since the redundancy, and Rose now saw that for herself. Terry had diminished in every way; not just in confidence, but physically too. His suit hung loosely from his shoulders.

'Well, perhaps when all this is over.' He freed his hand with a sudden pull.

'All this?' Rose wrapped her arms around herself instead. 'For God's sake, Terry. *This* is Daniel. I'm trying to come to terms with what's happened. I know it's a difficult time for you too, but you can't expect me to behave as if he's just popped out to get a sandwich.'

He ran a finger between his collar and his neck, as if it would help him breathe. 'Of course not. You know I didn't mean that. I'm sorry. But we do need to talk about the hotels. About what's going to happen.' A note of something like desperation had crept into his voice.

'We do. We will,' she reassured him, sympathetic but firm. 'Just not during Dan's memorial.'

He sighed as if all the cares of the world had been piled on to his shoulders.

'Terry, is something wrong?' Those years when her little brother depended on her came rolling back. With four years between them, if he fell, she'd be there to find the Elastoplast; if he wanted a sandwich, she'd make it. Once he had tripped down the stairs and badly gashed his head. Their parents, notorious locally for their hands-off approach to parenting, couldn't be found. By the time the two children arrived at the doctor's, a half-hour walk away, they were both bloody and hysterical. Not long afterwards, thanks to a rich and generous godfather, Terry had been sent away to boarding school. 'Make a man of him,' they'd said. But it wasn't a man who came back, just an introverted, gauche teenager with whom she had little in common. She had gone to university and they'd rarely seen each other until he was in his twenties. 'You can talk to me,' she added, ashamed of the little bit of her that hoped he wouldn't.

He shook his head, still concentrating on the carpet. 'I can't,' he muttered.

'Are you in some kind of trouble?' She leaned towards him.

His Adam's apple moved as he swallowed. 'No. Nothing to worry about. We'll talk another time.' He stepped away from her. Before she had time to say anything more, two old friends came up to offer their condolences, and her concentration was focused on them.

After a few more quiet words with her, Eve left Jess to find Adam, knowing that she would find the comfort she wanted with him. Will was still behind her, waiting.

'I'm impressed,' he said, pushing his glasses up his nose. 'You averted a full-scale international incident.'

'I feel so sorry for them. Especially Jess. She was very close to Dan.' Will didn't need to know the full story of what had happened.

They followed the line through to the buffet, filling their plates then returning to the lounge, where they found an empty sofa and began to talk. Half an hour later, their food remained largely uneaten, knives and forks still wrapped in their red napkins. However, Eve was beginning to wish that she hadn't followed his suggestion to accompany him to the buffet so impulsively. The emotion of the occasion itself, the wine, the shock of seeing Will had all combined to fling her at him before she'd had time to think. He was giving her a heart-rending account of his personal life. His relationship with Martha, the woman he'd left her for, had bitten the dust years earlier and he was now widowed, his wife, Lindsay, having died of ovarian cancer a couple of years ago. His children, Jamie and Tess, were in their teens and mostly lived with their aunt because Will was away travelling so much on photographic assignments. Eve was torn between listening to his story and walking off to find Rose and to check that Terry was all right. But attraction (she couldn't deny it) and a reckless excitement kept her there. If anyone had told her that, meeting him again, she'd have succumbed like this, she'd have laughed.

As she raised her glass, Charlie and Anna walked past. Even though she had no reason to feel guilty, she didn't want to give anyone the wrong idea. After all, it wasn't as if she'd be seeing Will again. This was just an unexpected but superficial catch-up. However, her son and her niece didn't even give them a second look. Of course they didn't. Middle-aged and invisible, that was all they were to the younger generation. On second thoughts, perhaps that was a good thing: invisibility could be liberating. She held on to that thought.

'He's one of mine.' She gestured towards Charlie's back: a wiry figure with an unmistakable limp from an old football injury. The packet of American cigarettes was still in his hand. Beside him, Anna had paused to roll another of those hideous-smelling things she insisted on smoking. Eve could never understand why Rose didn't make a fuss.

'Yours?' Will sounded surprised. 'Somehow I'd never imagined you with children.'

'You probably thought I'd stay single, devoted to your memory for the rest of my life. If you thought at all.' She'd heard enough. He was the one person who had ever really hurt her. After everything that had once gone on between them, she didn't have to put up with anything he said any more. She took her plate and began to stand.

'That's not what I meant.' He grasped her wrist to stop her leaving. 'I don't even know why I said that. Sit down, Evie. Don't go yet.'

His touch sent a shockwave through her. She saw the appeal in his eyes.

'Please.' That familiar twist of the mouth into a half-smile, the right eyebrow raised. Those small things that had made her unable to resist him in the past.

Aware that whatever she did next, leaving or staying, was likely to be something she might regret, she hesitated. Without warning, an impetuous desire to ginger up the routine of her life took over. She looked around. Terry must be in the dining room. He'd be all right. She unrolled her knife and fork from the napkin, smiled and sat down again.

'Have you met Simon Connelly?'

Jess was introducing Rose to someone she didn't immediately recognise. Tall, in his forties perhaps, he looked newly scrubbed, his face smooth, his hair gelled back. His suit was obviously expensive and worn with ease. He offered her his right hand.

'No, I don't think so.' He had a good firm handshake, but despite going through the motions, Rose's attention remained on Jess. She was upset, although doing her best to hide it, but Rose could hear the effort it was costing her daughter to keep her voice steady, and saw her fiddling nervously with the buttons on her jacket. She longed to reach out and comfort her.

'I'm sorry for your loss.' There was something soothing about his northern accent.

She inclined her head. 'Thank you. How did you know Daniel?' How many of these conversations could she bear? None of them would bring him back.

'Simon's just moved down from Edinburgh. He was behind the renovation of the Arthur,' Jess interrupted. 'He's an architect.'

'Really? You did a good job.' Rose's sudden consuming thought was how overwhelmed she was with fatigue.

'Are you all right, Mrs Charnock?' He leaned forward, concern in his eyes. 'Perhaps you should sit down.'

'Yes, I think I will. Thanks.' Jess on one side of her, and Simon on the other, the three of them walked into the lounge, where they found a group of empty chairs. Rose sank into one, feeling relief zing through her body.

'Can I get you some tea?' Simon's voice was warm, concerned.

'Let me,' interrupted Jess, jumping to her feet. 'Mum, I wanted you to talk to Simon, because we're hatching some great plans for Trevarrick.'

'Plans?' Had Jess spoken about them before? Rose couldn't remember. And the last thing she wanted right now was to hear about them. Her mind was as far from Trevarrick as it could be.

Today was about family, about Daniel, nothing else. As much as she loved the place, she couldn't contemplate a conversation about renovating it, or whatever else Jess had in mind. Across the room she noticed Eve and Will deep in conversation. What on earth was Eve up to? She hadn't noticed before how remarkably low-cut her dress was. Quite daring for a woman their age. But that was one of the things that made Eve such fun: she wore what she wanted. Rose looked down at her own neatly buttoned shirt, her tailored suit. She must look ten years older than Eve at least. Eve's legs were crossed, a definitely fuck-me shoe hanging off the foot that she flexed and pointed in the air. Rose glanced at her own boots, smart but dull by comparison. Will leaned towards Eve, said something, and they both laughed. How animated Eve looked, as if life was as good as it had been when she was young. Rose hadn't seen her look like this for years.

'Don't worry.' Simon had stood up and was bending over her. 'We can talk about all that another time. This isn't the moment. I'll leave you to recover.'

She didn't have the energy even to object politely as he turned away, pausing to have a word with Jess as she returned with the tea.

'Sorry, Mum. I'm so excited about our ideas, but stupid of me to think you'd want to hear about them now. I'll fix something else. Here.' She put the cup and saucer on the table and sat down. She'd put a couple of chocolate bourbons in the saucer: Rose's favourites. 'These'll help. I bet you haven't eaten a thing.'

Grateful, Rose took one, biting off a bit of the top layer: old childhood habit. 'Thanks. But have you had anything? You're looking terribly pale.' As she drank the tea, she listened to Jess's reassurances that of course she was fine – not really hungry and just a silly argument with Anna – nothing, really. Despite her very real concern for her daughters and her awareness that the day was as much of a trial for them as it was for her, Rose couldn't give Jess her full concentration now that she had the opportunity. Everything she said, she heard with half an ear. All the time her eyes were fixed on Eve and Will.

15

Eve's head throbbed as she opened the cupboard in the corner of her office that did as a kitchen. She pressed a couple of headache pills out of the blister pack she kept there for emergencies. She filled up the kettle, flicked it on, then washed up two mugs that had been sitting in the sink for the last couple of days. Habit had her spooning instant coffee into both mugs, sugar in one, milk in the other, before she realised what she'd done. Amy was no longer part of the Rutherford Literary Agency. She poured the water into both anyway. That extra caffeine would get her through the morning.

First knocking back the pills with a glass of water, she took her coffee over to her desk. Across the room was her new non-caffeine-drinking assistant's. She blessed the day she'd heard of May Flynn, a promising editorial assistant who had been made redundant in a swingeing round of corporate cuts at Customhouse Books. What a difference May had made to her life, although she had yet to make much of an impression in the office itself. Eve couldn't help but still notice Amy's absence. Amy had cleared out, taking all her file copies, all the small gifts from grateful authors. Her pinboard, to the left of the desk was denuded of the funny postcards, bits of paper, photos of Amy with clients at this occasion and that. May had stuck up a few things of her own, but without the familiar chaos from before. The low bookcase that ran by the wall had been left like a mouthful of rotting teeth, full of gaps where Amy had removed the books she wanted. May had swiftly reorganised them, ordering the replacements they needed, but it remained far from full.

Eve cradled her head in her hands. God, she felt awful. She should have gone easier on the wine once they got home after

Daniel's do, but Terry had shut himself in with the TV to watch whatever horse racing he had recorded and she had been left in the kitchen with her whirling thoughts. Will! After all these years, and how easily she'd let herself be swept along by the moment. Perhaps that was what came from being caught at a particularly low ebb. For four miserable months she'd been dealing with her grief privately, guilt-ridden for feeling Daniel's loss so keenly when such deep-seated grief for him belonged to Rose, her dearest friend and his wife, not to her. She could not get out of her head the image of Rose bent over Daniel's body where they had found him on the stony track, his face scarlet from having lain unprotected in the sun for what they were later told must have been almost three hours. Rose had cradled his head, brushing away the insistent flies. The only sound they heard from her was a second terrible animal-like howl that seemed to go on for ever. The three of them stood around her, shocked into immobility, waiting for the ambulance, until Anna's racking sobs made Eve aware that she had to do something.

The loss of such an old and dear friend before his time had hit Eve hard. Not just because she missed him, but because his death had brought home to her the brevity of life and the imperative not to waste it. Will's unexpected appearance had rocketed her back to those heady student days in Edinburgh when all things were possible and none of them had a care in the world. Being with him, even for that short time, had made her feel like that again, despite the thickening waistline and the other all-too-obvious signs of age.

Taking a sip of the scalding coffee, she thought about the day ahead. May wouldn't be in. Her working part-time suited both of them, leaving May free to pursue her writing career on her days off and Eve to make some useful economies.

Amy had finally declared her hand when Eve had been back from Italy for about a week. Obviously, in Amy's eyes at least, seven days was long enough for her boss to recover from the death of one of her closest friends. Eve had dragged herself into the office when a day under the duvet would have been infinitely preferable. Amy was already slotted in behind an unusually tidy desk.

She waited while Eve removed her coat and put her Tall Cappuccino and a skinny muffin – a comfort habit she'd since broken on the back of a briefly held New Year's resolution – on her desk, before coming to stand in the middle of the room, centre stage.

Even now, Eve remembered looking round the edge of her computer screen, as Amy cleared her throat. 'Something up?' she'd asked, hoping that whatever it was wouldn't take long. However much she didn't feel like working, there was plenty to get through thanks to her protracted absence in Italy.

'There is, actually.' Amy shifted from one sheer-black-stockinged leg to the other, while Eve made a mental note to mention the unsuitability of the length of her skirt – it barely skimmed her buttocks – or was that too old-womanish for words? Probably. Did she care? No. Good impressions were important in business. She was adding it to the mounting list of must-dos that had already begun to crowd her mind, claiming her attention, when Amy began to speak.

'The thing is, Eve. Well . . .' She paused. 'There's no easy way to say this. I've decided to leave the agency.'

Eve took in the sharp but determined face, the discreetly applied make-up, the hair perfectly in place, the whitened teeth, the wide mouth, and felt . . . precisely nothing. Perhaps Amy's leaving wouldn't be such a bad thing. A nuisance, yes, but they weren't working well together any more, and no one was irreplaceable. *Except Dan.* The words echoed in her head.

'What's brought this on? I thought you were happy here.'

'I was. But I want to develop my career and I think I've got as far as I can get here.'

Eve raised her eyebrows, surprised by the young woman's direct-ness. 'Are you joining another agency? Moving from Cambridge to London?' That would be a natural progression for someone with her ambition. One of the big boys would hoover up Amy without a second thought and reward her with the freedom she wanted.

'I've had a couple of expressions of interest, but I'm not sure. I'll stay until you find someone else.' She returned to her desk, subject

145

closed, and didn't address another remark to Eve for the rest of the morning.

Over the following weeks, Amy worked out an awkward period of notice filled with frequent and mysterious absences that she never attempted to explain. An editor Eve knew had mentioned May's name, and within a short time their arrangement was sealed and her terms of employment settled. By the time Amy left they were barely communicating at all. May joining the agency just before Chistmas came as a huge relief. She was bright and willing, was picking things up quickly and would soon be fulfilling exactly the role Eve had imagined for her. The clients liked her and Eve was back holding the reins of the agency.

Then a week ago, the trade press carried the announcement of a new London-based agency for children's authors: AFA – the Amy Fraser Agency – running out of a Wandsworth address. Among Amy's much-heralded initial client list were four authors who until that moment Eve had believed were represented by her.

The cutting was still on her desk. With a red pen she underlined the authors' names: the first in what might be a haemorrhage if she didn't react. At least these were four Eve could afford to lose if she absolutely had to. They were slow writers, and as far as she knew, they had nothing immediate in the pipeline. She was rather surprised that Amy wanted them, but the girl clearly had more cunning than Eve had credited her with. While Eve had mourned, functioning more on autopilot than anything else, Amy had gone behind her back, exploiting Eve's state of mind, working the retirement story no doubt, insinuating her way into the clients' trust until the first agreed to join her new venture. And unless Eve was careful, they might not be the last.

As Eve reached for the phone, she knocked her mug off the desk so that it bounced off a pile of papers by the side of her chair, then smashed against its leg. A tide of greyish lukewarm coffee washed everywhere. Mopping one of the rough (thank God!) illustrations for Rufus's new book with a bit of kitchen roll, Eve felt a cosmic gloom threatening. Her agency was under siege, one of her oldest friends was dead, her children had left home, her marriage was far from fulfilling, and Will had reappeared. Could things get any worse?

She looked around the office at the photos of her award-winning authors, of her children armed with body boards on a Cornish beach, of Terry at a local point-to-point, grinning after winning on a race. These were the people who cared about her and towards whom she had a huge responsibility, especially now that Terry was unemployed. A recent addition was the framed LP sleeve of the Rolling Stones' 'Sticky Fingers'. Rose had asked Daniel's closest friends to pick something that belonged to him as a memento. His extensive vinyl collection was irresistible, and Eve had chosen the album that she remembered him obsessing over at Edinburgh when everyone else's tastes had moved on. She tossed the kitchen roll in the bin. Sod it! Where was the old Eve Rutherford who didn't give a damn, and who never let anyone or anything get the better of her? What was she doing with her life?

She took the other mug and went to the sink, where she poured the undrinkable coffee away, gripped by a new resolve. She would fight the gloom to show everyone, and most importantly herself, what she was still made of.

Two hours later, a rug had been pulled over the coffee stain, the random paperwork sorted and put in May's filing tray, and a bunch of yellow tulips stood on her desk. She still had a couple of hours before Rufus was due to arrive for lunch: plenty of time to open the post and get some admin out of the way. There might even be time for her to read more of that promising paranormal teen romance that had arrived unsolicited a couple of days ago. For the first time in ages, she felt braced and ready to go.

As she settled to deal with her emails, the phone rang.

'Mum!' The sound of Millie's voice always lifted Eve. Immediately a picture of her daughter flashed up in her mind: long, slim legs poured into skinny-fit jeans, ankle boots, cheap black leather bomber jacket, hands in fingerless mittens, a big scarf, and a tumble of unruly hair tied in a ponytail on top of her head.

'Millie, my love. Where are you?' She checked her watch. Eleven thirty. Most likely still in bed, surrounded by the contents of her wardrobe, that she was happier keeping within easy reach on the floor. Why her beloved daughter had turned out to be by far the untidiest of her four children she didn't know. In fact, her attempts to drum the basic principles of housekeeping into all of them had met with abject and frustrating failure.

'I'm dashing out to an exhibition with Flo, but I wanted to be sure that you'd paid that cheque into my account.'

As she spoke, Eve pictured the cheque deliberately propped up on top of the key cupboard by the front door, where they wouldn't forget it. 'Sorry, darling, we completely forgot.'

The despairing sigh that followed told Eve all she needed to know about what Millie thought of them. 'I need it for my rent. I told you.'

'It's not too late,' she protested. 'I'll call Dad and get him to do it this morning.'

'How is he?'

'He's fine,' said Eve breezily, not wanting their children ever to be worried about either of them. That was not their job. 'This'll give him something to do.'

'That sounds a bit patronising.'

'Did it? Wasn't meant to be.' She thought of Terry, still in his pyjamas and dressing gown when she'd left home, and showing no sign that he was thinking of changing out of them. She rammed her memory stick into the side of her keyboard with satisfying force.

'Well,' Millie sounded unsure, 'if you're positive.'

'Of course I am. You get on and I'll call him right now.'

After they'd said their goodbyes, Eve dialled Terry while Millie was still in her mind. The phone rang for so long that, thinking he must have gone out, she was beginning to retract her predictions about the way he was spending his morning. Finally he answered. Her heart sank as she heard his sleep-heavy voice stumble over their number. She explained her reason for calling.

'But I can't.' He sounded almost panicked by this simplest of requests.

'How do you mean, you can't? All you have to do is get dressed and bring the cheque into town. What else have you got on?'

'Well, nothing. Not exactly, but . . .'

She heard the whisper of turning newspaper pages. She didn't need to be told. The sports section, no doubt. For heaven's sake!

'Terry, I don't ask much of you.' She spoke patiently, as if coaxing an intransigent horse into its box. 'But I have a day of meetings and catching up ahead. It would mean a lot if you could just get off your backside and help me for once!'

Not really fair, but with one final shove the horse bolted up the ramp.

'All right. I'll do it this afternoon.' But he made no effort to hide his reluctance.

'Why not this morning?' And she made no effort to keep the annoyance out of her voice.

'Eve! I've said I'll do it. Now leave me alone.'

She took the phone from her ear and stared at it. He'd hung up! Furious, she pressed redial, but this time her call went unanswered. Short of going home and having it out with him face to face, there was nothing more she could do. She banged the phone down on her desk. Immediately it rang. She considered not answering, then cautioned herself. She had a business to run, and if this wasn't Terry apologising – which it bloody well should be – she needed to take the call. She couldn't afford to lose any more of her clients. In fact they were in for a spot of timely love-bombing, did they but know it. She checked the number. Not one she knew. But she recognised the voice immediately.

'It was so good to see you again yesterday, Evie. I wondered whether you'd meet me for lunch. There's so much we didn't talk about.'

'There is?' She had an urgent desire to make this difficult for him. Who the hell did he think he was, exiting then re-entering her life at will? She managed a grim little smile at the pun. The fact was, she didn't want to see him again. Yesterday had been an aberration, and she had more important things to attend to right now.

'Please, Evie.'

She felt herself give a little.

'I'd like to see you again.'

As Will carried on speaking, Eve's gaze travelled to Rose's Tuscan watercolour hanging on the wall over the mantelpiece. If only they could all be whisked back there, to when Daniel was alive. In four short months, how much everything had changed. If he hadn't died, she wouldn't have this potential problem with the agency; Rose's girls wouldn't be arguing; Dan would be shoring up Terry in the way he needed; and as a result, she and Terry might not be at each other's throats at every opportunity. And of course, Will wouldn't have reappeared.

'So why don't we?'

She had missed nearly everything he'd said. 'I'm sorry, why don't we what?'

'Christ, Evie.' She had forgotten that flash of impatience that came to him so easily, and hearing it again reminded her of at least one reason why meeting him was a bad idea. 'I don't know what else to say. It was so good to see you yesterday. You haven't changed.'

Not that corny old line! She expected better of him than that.

'What do you say?'

She hesitated. She remembered his car crammed with his belongings, his sheepish expression as he explained where he was going, struggling for self-justification. Worse, she remembered the pain and turmoil she'd suffered for months afterwards. But now that she'd met him again, all that harboured emotion seemed so long ago. She was curious. And she wanted to experience, just one more time, the feeling she'd had when she was with him yesterday. He'd lifted her out of the doldrums, and made her feel alive again. What was a lunch after all? A couple of hours of catching up, of having her morale boosted, and then they would run out of things to say to one another. That would be that.

He heard her indecision. 'So can I take that as a yes? The Murano at one? Tuesday?'

Despite being tempted by an invitation to the latest 'in' restaurant in town, Eve was brought up sharp by Will's assumption that she would fall in with his plans just as she once used to. Those days were over. Her life was different now. She glanced at her diary. Unimpressively empty the following week.

'I'm sorry, Will. It's not a good idea. I'm tied up next week and I've no plans to come to London.'

He sighed. 'Evie. Come on.' She could hear that he was still a man used to getting his own way. But she could be strong-willed too.

'No. I enjoyed seeing you yesterday, but we should leave it there.' A fleeting feeling of something akin to regret, or even longing, coursed through her.

'Well, if you change your mind, here's my number.' Obviously disappointed, but he wasn't giving up.

She scribbled down the number, resisting the overpowering temptation to change her mind. As they ended the conversation, she glanced at her notepad. It was covered in her absent-minded doodles – hearts and stars. Leaving the phone number intact, she ripped off the bottom part of the sheet, scrumpled it up and tossed it in the bin.

Distracted from her work, she crossed to the mirror and stared at herself. Her face was flushed, her eyes bright. She messed up her hair with both hands so it looked wind-blown, youthful – sort of. Who was she kidding? She stood sideways and studied her profile. Shoulders back and down, stomach in. Not bad. More overweight than she'd like, but passable in a good light. She looked exactly what she was: a middle-aged woman with a family and a demanding job who had been far too easily flattered. That was what they said about first love: it was the one you never forgot. In this case with good reason, she reminded herself. She turned her memory from that time they went skinny-dipping on Gullane beach, then made love hidden in the dunes, and forced herself to remember the way in which he'd left her.

Back at her desk, she took a couple of contracts that had arrived in the post and began to go through them, making herself concentrate. Half an hour before Rufus was due to arrive, she brought out the copies of the rough illustrations for his latest book and laid them out on the meeting table so they could go through them before seeing the artist on Friday. She looked around the office to make sure that it was the sort of place that you would expect from your agent. She pulled down the blue, white and yellow striped blinds so they were exactly level a little less than halfway down the window. At precisely twelve forty-five, the bell rang.

Rufus pounded up the stairs two at a time. He was a man in a hurry with a mind that was always rushing ahead of itself, keeping everyone else on their toes. When she heard him reach the top, she opened the door. Every time she saw him, she was still surprised by how little he ever changed. A Peter Pan of a man who had yet to take his responsibilities in life seriously. Eve was the one rock in his life, as opposed to the tide of women and children he left trailing adoring or angry in his wake. His hair showed no signs of going grey or thinning, and stood out on end where he'd last run his fingers through it. Wearing jeans, trainers and a loose jacket over a checked shirt, he was still slim and relatively unlined, with the energy of a much younger man.

She imagined a momentary reticence in his hug, but dismissed the idea. They had been friends for so long, she would know immediately if anything was troubling him. 'Come in. I've got something to show you.' She gestured towards the illustrations.

Rufus looked awkward as his eyes darted around the room, refusing to meet hers. They finally settled on his shoes. 'Actually, I've seen them.'

'But I've only had them since Tuesday,' she protested, surprised. 'I couldn't show you before because of Dan's memorial yesterday. Did you go to Marie's?' Marie, the illustrator, had worked on all the books in his Animal Planet series, so it wouldn't have been unusual for Rufus to visit her, although unusual of him not to mention it.

'No. Errm.' He cleared his throat. 'In fact Amy showed them to me. Marie sent copies to her too.'

'To Amy?' She was barely keeping up with this conversation.

'Yes.' He studied the nails on his left hand, moving his thumb along his fingertips before looking up. Even then he was unable to meet her shocked stare. 'Look, Eve. We need to talk.'

Not Rufus. Not the one client who had been with her since the beginning. They had been through so much together. Amy couldn't have succeeded in turning him along with the others. Could she?

Eve had an awful feeling that her day had just taken a U-turn for the worse.

16

Rose sat at the table with her untouched breakfast – a bowl of porridge and a pot of tea – with one hand on the condolences book. It had been Jess's idea to have one at both church and hotel to make sure everyone present had the chance to contribute. She sighed. The poor child was doing all she could to alleviate her guilt over Dan's death. No amount of reassurance was enough to make her believe that their argument wasn't a major contributing factor. Rose opened the book at the photo of them all, another of her favourites, bringing with it memories of those happy family holidays when the girls were small. Dan was standing, tall and windblown, by a stone cairn in Scotland. His laughter was directed at Rose, the photographer, while toddler Jess sat on his shoulders, arms around his head, with an eager Anna looking up at him, holding his hand. Rose ran a finger over the picture as she remembered. Then she turned the page.

Had *she* been at the memorial? S? That thought had tormented Rose since her conversation with Eve after the theatre. If she had, would she have signed the book? She looked at the writing on the first page – a warm memory illustrated with a smiley sun from Benny, an old friend from the days when they'd spent six months after Edinburgh crewing together on a luxury yacht in the Caribbean. As she slowly turned the pages, the tributes came from every part of Dan's life. But was one of them from *her*? Occasionally a Sophie, a Suzanne, a Sarah – but these were all women whom Rose knew, admittedly some less well than others. She couldn't imagine Daniel having an affair with any of them. But perhaps that was the point. Even the most evil people didn't present themselves to the world with a tail and horns. More often than not they resembled the man or woman next door. Appearances were irrelevant. He

154

might have fallen for any of these women. And any of them might have fallen for him.

'What are you doing?' Jess came into the room with Dylan fixed to her hip, his attention on a small wooden train engine in his hand. Rose was relieved to see her daughter looking much more relaxed today. Over her nightie, she was wearing a baggy jumper that disguised her shape.

'Just looking through this.' Rose pushed the book across the table towards her. 'Such a lovely thing to have.'

Jess looked relieved. 'I'm glad. I thought having all those memories of Dad might help.' She went to the corner of the counter and took a small carton from a stash of baby food. Emptying the milk into a bottle that she handed to Dylan, she then sat opposite Rose with him on her knee.

'It feels so peculiar now the memorial's over. So final.' She sniffed and dug around in her sleeve for a tissue.

'Oh Jess, don't.' Rose got up to hug them both. Dylan reached up to try to remove her reading glasses. She took them off and slipped them in her pocket before kissing his forehead. 'Dad wouldn't want you to be like this.'

Jess blew her nose. 'I know. But I still feel it was my fault. If only we hadn't had that stupid argument.'

'Darling, you mustn't. The post-mortem said it could have happened any time. I believe that and so must you.'

'I know, I know, but all the same . . . I should have let it go. I'd already made the point by agreeing that Adam would stay behind. I shouldn't have insisted on talking to him. He was so angry.' She let Dylan slide gradually to the floor, where he sank on to all fours and started pushing the train, his teeth clamped on the teat of the bottle so it swung from his mouth.

'There was a lot of other stuff preoccupying him too. That's life, Jess. We mustn't keep going over it. It was nobody's fault.'

'It all seemed so important. I had to make my point. And now I'll never be able to straighten things out with him. It's too late.' She poured herself some tea, looking utterly miserable. 'Were there really other things worrying him?'

Rose knew what she needed to hear. 'He always had a lot on his plate. That's how he liked life. You know as well as I do that you'd have made it up within moments of your arriving. He loved you.' She was relieved that Jess seemed to take some comfort from that without needing to know what else was preoccupying him. 'Look, why don't you get dressed while I do an egg and soldiers for Dylan, and then we can go to the park.'

When breakfast and the endless rigmarole of getting one small child and three adults ready for a winter walk was complete, they set off. At the playground, Dylan was impatient to be out of the buggy, pulling at the straps while Jess was still unclipping him. He made an uneven beeline for the swings, with Adam and Jess in his wake.

Rose chose a bench with a view of her grandson, who was shouting and giggling as his parents manhandled him into a toddler's swing. As they began to push him between them, his screams of delight grew louder, mingling in her memory with those of Anna, a few years older, always wanting to go higher, struggling to stand, knees bent and straightening to push herself higher still. Then her attention would be snagged by something going on elsewhere in the park, and she'd slow the swing and jump . . . Rose's heart would be in her mouth as her daughter sailed through the air, landed safely and ran off. Only once was she clipped on the back of the head by the swing and needed stitches. Jess, on the other hand, would wait to be lifted. Once there, she would sit sedately on the swing, a stolid child, her hands tight on the chains, eyes shining but lips tight shut, content not to fly too high.

Memories.

'Are you all right, Rose?' Adam settled on the seat beside her as Jess took Dylan over to the baby slides. The little boy reached up to hold his mother's hand.

'I was miles away,' she admitted. ' Remembering when the girls were tiny.'

'Hard to imagine.' He frowned as he took a packet of wine gums from the pocket of his overcoat and offered her one. She shook her head. He took out a green and a yellow gum, removed a black one, popped it into his mouth and put the first two back in the wrapper. 'Have they always got on so badly?' His eyes were concerned.

She tucked in her scarf and wrapped her arms round herself against the cold. 'Not as bad as this. I don't know what's going on between them at the moment, but I guess it's to do with the hotels and whether or not I decide to sell them. But it's so soon.'

Adam gazed down at his clasped hands, tapping his thumbs together.

Rose didn't ask him how much he knew. She had long ago learned the truth of 'nature abhors a vacuum'. If she said nothing, he would almost certainly be drawn to fill the silence between them. And sure enough, after a minute or two . . .

'Anna's being completely unreasonable about the business,' he said. 'She's not seeing this from anyone's point of view but her own.'

'Why? What's been going on?' She would expect him to take Jess's side, although this was not a conversation the two of them should be having.

'They both overstepped the mark.' He stroked his beard, unable to look her in the eye. 'Jess really regrets what she said.'

'Which was what?' At that moment, she could see Jess sitting at the top of the slide, arms around Dylan, who was trapped in the V of her legs. As they took off, he raised his arms in the air and shrieked with excitement.

'Something about Anna being selfish, single and a terrible daughter. In a nutshell.' He looked embarrassed at having said as much.

'Oh God.' Rose scuffed at the stones under her feet. Being charged with those qualities would really hurt Anna. She would recognise the grains of truth in there.

She felt Adam's hand on her arm.

'I know this might not be the best moment . . .' He hesitated.

'Go on,' she said. Despite feeling that he'd already said more than enough, she knew that what he said often made sense.

But before he had a chance to say any more, a small girl tripped over in front of them, her hands and knees taking the brunt of the fall. After a second's silence, she let out a high-pitched shriek. Adam was on his feet immediately, picking her up, comforting, looking around for her mother. A woman was running from the other side of the sandpit, a baby under her arm, a wooden scooter in her free hand, calling her name. 'Ellie! It's all right. I'm coming.'

'Look, here's Mummy.' Adam tried to calm the child, but she was too frightened by this large bearded stranger and by the blood oozing from the heels of both her hands.

Reaching them, the mother dropped the scooter and squatted down, scooping her daughter into her free arm, thanking Adam, calming her child. As the tears subsided, he returned to the bench, brushing the dust from the worn knees of his corduroy trousers as he sat down.

'Go on,' Rose invited him. 'Finish what you were going to say.'

'Well, I know it's not my business, but I can't help thinking that if you and Terry were to settle this hotel business one way or the other, life would be easier for all of us. I know it's hard,' he pre-empted Rose, 'but it's tearing them apart.'

''We shouldn't discuss this without the girls being here,' she warned him. 'And Terry, of course. But I wasn't even thinking of selling until Madison Gadding made their offer. I can't pretend I'm not tempted, but it's a huge step. I don't want to throw away everything Dan worked so hard for without thought.'

'Then don't.' He made it sound so simple. 'Jess deserves to have the chance that Daniel promised her. Whatever he thought of me.' He gave a rueful laugh. 'She loves Trevarrick, we're happy there. It makes no sense to sell it. None. I don't know what we'd do without the place.'

Rose sat motionless. Wasn't this what Daniel had feared, what had infuriated him? She had always believed that Adam's first concern was for Jess and Dylan's well-being, not for the convenient roof over their head and the income that came with it. But Daniel had planted that seed of doubt long ago, and despite her resistance, it had lain there waiting to germinate. Could this gentle giant of a man really only be looking out for himself?

'I understand that, of course,' she said eventually. 'But I've got to think about what's good for the rest of us. Anna too.'

'But why doesn't she just get a mortgage or a loan?' he objected. 'It's crazy to sell the entire business to fund another one of her schemes. I understand she's found the ideal property that she doesn't want to miss out on, but there must be other ways.'

For a second Rose was amused by the irony of hearing Adam parrot Daniel's views, then her maternal instincts made her rush to defend her daughter. 'But Adam, no one in their right mind would give her a mortgage or a small business loan – one. And two, she has no money to pay that kind of rent and the overheads it would involve. Think of all the stock she'll have to buy. She only just gets by as it is.' She fielded a stray football with her foot and sent it back to its young owner. 'And she wants something that's her own, just as she sees Jess having Trevarrick. She thinks of this as her chance. I can understand that. Can't you?'

She could see his embarrassment at having spoken out of turn. His eyes, blue as forget-me-nots, gave him away as they shifted towards his wife and son. Dylan had found a digger in the sandpit and was riding it like a horse, Jess standing with hands on hips, watching over him. 'I'm sorry,' he said. 'It's none of my business. I hate seeing Jess so upset, that's all.'

'I know.' Guilty for having thought the worst of him, she patted his hand, just as he was pulling the tube of wine gums from his jacket pocket. The gums spilled everywhere, falling like dull jewels into the grass. The two of them bent forward simultaneously to pick them up and cracked their heads together.

They both sat up, half laughing and apologising to one another. Rose rubbed the side of her cheekbone as tears automatically stung her eyes. She rummaged in her pocket for a tissue, pulled out a scrappy bit of loo roll and blew her nose.

'What are you two doing?' Jess arrived in time for Dylan to fall on to all fours and help his father, his chubby fingers scrabbling at the earth as he tried to pick up a sweet. As Adam took the grimy yellow gum from him, Dylan's bottom lip began to quiver.

'Come on, boy. How about an ice cream instead?' Adam stood and swung the uncertain Dylan on to his hip in one movement.

'An ice cream?' Jess protested. 'It's the middle of winter!'

'An ice cream's an ice cream whatever the time of year, isn't that right?' Adam kissed his son's cheek and tickled his tummy so that the child squirmed in pleasure, his tears forgotten. 'We'll be right back.' He swung the boy on to his shoulders and trotted towards the exit, Dylan bouncing about on his steed and giggling.

'We're not freezing to death while you two disappear,' Jess yelled after them. 'Come and find us in the café.'

Adam raised a hand in brief acknowledgement before grabbing Dylan's leg again.

Not much more than a large wooden shack with a few basic heaters and junk-shop pine tables and chairs, the café provided a welcome respite from the winter weather. Behind the rudimentary counter with its display of home-made cakes and biscuits, a couple of young women in coats, scarves and fingerless gloves served hot drinks.

Jess chose a table close to a heater and left Rose to thaw out there while she bought two hot chocolates with whipped cream and chocolate sprinkles.

'You look tired,' she said as she returned with them to the table. 'Why don't you come down to Trevarrick, Mum? We'd love to have you and the change would be so good for you. All that sea air.' She took off her woollen hat and unwound the deep blue and green home-knitted scarf from around her neck and strung it on the back of her chair.

Rose removed her gloves and began to spoon part of the topping into her mouth. How could she explain to Jess that Trevarrick was the last place she wanted to visit at the moment? Adjusting to life with her memories of Daniel at home was difficult enough. Going to Cornwall would only stir up so many more. She wasn't ready for them yet. Just thinking of the place brought back those days when the two of them and Terry were doing everything they could to turn the hotel into a viable enterprise. Daniel had been exploding with ideas, leaving the two of them in his wake as he worked with the builders, hammering, plastering, painting. Nothing was too difficult, no problem too big to overcome. His passion to turn the place into somewhere special was tireless. He attended to every detail, from the positioning of the sinks in the kitchen to the hot-water bottles in every room. 'Every guest should be more comfortable here than they are in their own home,' he'd say. 'We mustn't forget anything.'

'I don't know,' she said, tasting the rich sweetness of the chocolate.

'I know you're afraid of coming back, but I so want to show you those plans I've got for the place. Simon's been down and he's got some great ideas.' Jess lifted her mug to her mouth. The electricity from removing her hat had sent wisps of hair flying around her face. Her cheeks glowed from being out in the cold.

It was hard for Rose to imagine the hotel changed. But the renovations Dan, Terry and she had overseen were old-fashioned now, and, she chided herself, so was her attitude. What would Dan have wanted? She knew the answer immediately. He'd have embraced the changes, modifying or elaborating them as he saw fit. Nothing pleased him more than a project he could get his teeth into.

'Perhaps in a month or so,' she said, prevaricating, conscious that Jess's keenness for her to see everything was only so that she'd be persuaded not to sell.

'There's so much potential.' Jess could barely contain her excitement. 'I tell you what. I'll ask Simon to show you the plans he's prepared for me. Working with him has really helped me get through the last few months. He's so sympathetic and knows instinctively what's needed. His father died recently too, so we had that in common. When you see them, you won't want to sell up.'

Rose could hear the plea in her voice. Their daughter's enthusiasm reminded her so much of Daniel's all those years ago. Hers was almost as impossible to resist as his had been.

'You see, we could extend the dining room and add an outside deck. And beside it we could build out into a snug, though it won't be as small as that makes it sound; the whole thing will be much lighter and brighter than what we have now. Much more twenty-first century. He's even done a plan for a small swimming pool. You'll see. I know you'll love it all.'

'Stop,' said Rose, laughing. 'You don't need a swimming pool when you're right on the beach.'

'Oh, but we do. Some people prefer a pool. It's not so cold, for a start.' Jess grasped Rose's hand. 'Let him come and show you. Please.' The 'please' was as drawn out as if she was ten again, wheedling a favour from her parents.

The door opened and a cold blast of air circulated round the shed, nipping at fingers and noses. Adam led in a grinning Dylan, whose face and cornet-carrying hand were plastered with vanilla ice cream. He ran over to Jess, who, laughing, grabbed a tissue and began to repair the damage while Adam got himself a drink. She looked over her son's brown curls at her mother. 'Will you?'

'All right,' agreed Rose. 'I give in.' Perhaps seeing the plans would help clear her mind so she could come to a decision.

17

The train into London was held up at signals. Beside Eve, a girl about Millie's age was listening to music so loud that it leaked from her earphones into Eve's head, where the bass thumped and the vocals shrilled interminably. She tried sitting with a hand over her ear, but it made little difference. Opposite her, an earnest young man with a rash of spots around the top of his collar was leafing through a red-top. His hair was gelled into sharp points, his complexion uneven. He was scratching his nose then let his little finger excavate one nostril. As he was examining whatever he'd speared on the end of his nail, Eve cleared her throat. He looked up, their eyes met and he coloured a satisfying shade of beetroot and stuffed his hand in his pocket. Beside him, a ruddy-faced City type was lying back, eyes shut. Everything about him was redolent of a hard night's playing away, including the miasma of alcohol that oozed from his pores and could be smelled as far away as Eve was sitting. She wanted to lean her head against the window in despair, but was put off by a slick of grease from the head of a previous occupant of the seat.

These weren't the ideal conditions for work, but that wasn't an excuse. Eve opened her briefcase and retrieved her client list. She had two: the old list, for her eyes only, marked with angry crosses through clients who had moved to Amy and remarks to indicate her various action plans for those remaining; and the new list, for the eyes of others, that was shorter and mark free. It was the older one she turned to now. Sixty-one clients in all, five of whom had been picked off by Amy, another fifteen of whom she had worked with closely and would be obvious targets. Rationalisation. That was key. Eve had decided that if her business was to survive the onslaught of Amy's attention, she needed to refocus it, to bring on some new writers, attend to the backlist of others and cull the one or two authors she was carrying who took up her time but weren't paying their way. But what she needed most of all was to pull off a couple of big deals that would put her firmly on the map again and show the world that losing her clients, most particularly Rufus, to Amy had not affected her.

Her lunch with him two days earlier had been hasty and difficult. She would rather have stayed in her office to talk, but Rufus insisted on going through with their original arrangement. He must have thought that in public he'd be protected from her reaction. So wrong. In the local Thai, over a couple of Tiger beers, an indifferent green curry and a smartingly hot green papaya and squid salad, he had imparted his most shocking piece of news.

'I don't know how to tell you this.' He concentrated on his finger as he traced a shape on the tablecloth.

Staring at him, waiting for whatever bombshell he was about to drop, trying not to show that a piece of chilli had just taken out the back of her throat, she couldn't help noticing that his hair was beginning to recede at last. She grabbed her glass of water and drank. So age and its attendant insecurities touched even him. That must be hard for a man who had passed as much younger for so long.

'Just spit it out, for God's sake, Rufus. You know I'm unshock-able.' That was far from the truth, but she would put on a good show. She took another drink, swallowing her urgent desire to cough.

He shrugged his shoulders, screwed his eyes tight, then said very fast, 'I've asked Amy to marry me and she's said yes.' He opened them and looked nervously to see her reaction.

Even now, Eve remembered how her stomach had dropped away. If her chin hadn't been resting on her hand, her mouth would have fallen open in astonishment. Except she should have suspected. Put a superannuated but successful Peter Pan with a ruthless young go-getter anxious to make her mark and turn your back – what do you expect?

As she struggled to get to grips with this momentous piece of news, she couldn't find a way to react. Distress? Scorn? Neither of those adequately represented what she was feeling. Then, from somewhere deep inside her, rolling through her body, came laughter: not a nervous, disbelieving little titter but a full-throated, long-lasting belly laugh. She watched Rufus's expression change from anxious to surprised, to hurt, to alarmed, and with each one her laughter grew louder. Tears ran down her cheeks as she tried to control herself. Amy must think she'd had the last laugh, walking away with the star prize. Eve tried hiding her face behind one blue paper napkin after another, but if anything that made it worse. One by one she screwed them up and discarded them on the table. As the paper mountain grew, Rufus tried to speak to her, hushing her. 'Eve, please. I didn't know how you'd take it. Shhhh.' She'd attempt to adopt a serious face and to have the conversation he wanted, but each time she'd collapse again. The other two tables of diners looked on, one or two of them beginning to laugh along with her.

Eventually they'd left the restaurant. By this point her hysteria had waned and all Eve felt like doing was crying, but she was damned if she'd give Rufus (or Amy) the satisfaction. She could picture the two of them together, curled up on the vast studded chesterfield in his medieval timbered home, bought with the profits that she had made for him. Don't be petty, she warned herself, then immediately succumbed to temptation.

Amy would be sleek in her favourite pink bandage dress, earrings dangling by the edge of her angular jawbone, curled cat-like against Rufus, avid to know Eve's reaction. 'What did she say? How did she take it?'

When she heard about Eve's laughter, she'd be perplexed, angry even that she hadn't scored the perfect goal.

However, the loss of Rufus was a massive blow to the agency. Not just because of the income Eve would lose from future books, but because of the message that it sent out to the world. Publishers and clients would wonder whether losing her authors to Amy, especially her most prestigious one, meant she was on the skids. She could imagine them gossiping about her, speculating on the phone, over lunch. But she wasn't going to go down without a fight.

The day ahead of her consisted of back-to-back meetings and an early-evening drinks appointment. As soon as Rufus had left, taking his profuse apologies with him, Eve had fixed three such days during which she would start to rebuild the confidence in her agency. Her other priority was to find a new client or two who would help lift its profile and hers. But where to start?

At King's Cross, she was swept along on a wave of commuters, pressing to get through the ticket barriers and on to the tube. What a horrendous way to begin a day.

After her first meeting, she was ready for lunch. She had spent the morning reassuring Nan French, one of her most talented illustrators, that the agency had been in a period of brief transition as May found her feet, but that now it was business as usual. When she revealed her plan for submitting her as a potential illustrator for a new edition of *Alice in Wonderland*, Nan had been both grateful and excited, confident her agent was batting for her.

The taxi dropped Eve at the door of the modest French brasserie that Susie Shepherd had picked for lunch. Susie was at the table, talking on her phone, when Eve joined her. The two women had been friends for years, ever since they had started in the same agency, although their paths had diverged. Eve had thrived on representing the interests of authors, whereas Susie had chosen to take the publishing path to be closer to those decisions. She now ran her own highly regarded and prestigious list. She was petite enough almost to pass as a child herself. But her Cleopatra bob, coloured the blue-black of a raven's wing, and her sharp dress sense lent her the necessary authority. Her black Tibetan terrier snoozed under the table by her Mulberry bag.

Susie stood as Eve arrived and they air-kissed without her pausing for breath in her conversation. She made a winding motion with her hand as if hurrying the speaker up, then indicated that Eve should look at the menu.

At last Susie extricated herself and hung up. 'So sorry. I had to talk to the bloody woman. All to do with licensing agreements for that picturebook series we publish, the Bobcats – you don't want to know.' She picked up her glass of water.

Actually Eve did want to know but understood that Susie was only demonstrating her own importance by dangling such a snippet of information. She had no intention of telling her more.

Before she had a chance to speak, Susie was off again. 'I haven't seen you for months. What's been happening?' She picked up the menu. 'Actually, let's order first. I've had such a morning, I'm famished. The jugged hare looks good, or the turbot, but . . . I think I'm going for the steak frites. What about you?'

Eve was relieved. She'd had lunch with Susie recently when they'd toyed with a lettuce leaf or two and she'd left the restaurant starving. She'd have what Susie was having and set herself up for the afternoon. 'It's good of you to give me lunch when half my clients are about to bugger off.'

'Forget it. I want to hear what's happened. Eve?' Susie indicated she should order first.

'Steak for me, please. Medium rare.' Eve was looking forward to this, wondering whether she dared a small glass of red. Then, remembering that Susie never drank, she decided against.

The waitress scribbled on her pad, then looked enquiringly at Susie, who was running her French-polished fingernail up and down the menu. Eventually she looked up and said, 'You know what? I think I'll have a tomato and mozzarella salad after all. The starter portion. Yup, that's it. I've been eating way too much recently.'

With a neat piece of one-upmanship, Susie had finessed Eve to emerge as the one with epic self-control, while Eve was left to face a meal she suddenly no longer really wanted.

Susie sailed on regardless, glass of sparkling water in hand. She leant forward confidentially. 'Now, tell me all about the Amy Fraser Agency. She's quite a number, isn't she?'

'Well, obviously I've never had to deal with her in the way you have.' Eve was deliberately circumspect. She knew that whatever she said would be taken and shared with the wider world of children's publishing. The one thing she had to keep in the forefront of her mind was the reason for this lunch. She wanted to leave it having persuaded Susie to contract Jim Palliser's four backlist titles now that there was TV interest in two of them. She would get even with Amy not by gossiping about her but by behaving better.

Susie talked on regardless. 'She came in to see me a couple of weeks ago. Thought I'd never get rid of her.'

'Well, she's got Rufus now, of course.' Eve just dropped the information casually, but it got her Susie's attention.

'No! She never said. How did that happen? You must be furious.'

'Not furious, more disappointed.' Much as she longed to join in the dismemberment of Amy, being seen to have a public falling-out with her was not in Eve's professional interests. Far better to play things down and let Amy hang herself. She gave a judiciously abbreviated account of what had happened.

Susie was unforgiving. 'You're well rid of her if you ask me. None of us can stand her, you know. She's hell to deal with, so demanding. I was going to warn you last year, when we had Mary Mackenzie's new book on offer from her, but you had so much on your plate.'

This was music to Eve's ears, although she disliked having driven home how badly she'd misjudged her ex-colleague. However, she was careful to remain neutral while she listened to Susie chatter on. Despite the talk, Susie's plate was completely clean and Eve was still eating when she finally got the chance to bring the conversation round to the real reason for the meeting. She refused to be shamed by her appetite, especially since she was enjoying the food now she'd got it, so she took her time, ignoring Susie's pointed glances at her watch.

By the time they left the restaurant, Eve was up to speed on all the latest industry news and gossip, essential to her job, and Susie had agreed to buy Jim's backlist. Eve had even persuaded her to take another look at Mary Mackenzie's novel for nine- to twelve-year-olds. So: one lunch down and a satisfactory result.

As Eve headed towards St Martin's Lane for her next

appointment, she was on cloud nine. Perhaps nothing was quite as bad as she'd thought. If the other publishers were like Susie, in the long run Amy might be less of a threat than she'd imagined. But right now she must continue to concentrate on salvaging the immediate damage to her client list and reputation.

Lunch had been so brief that she was left with over half an hour in hand. Killing time, she wandered along the road through a jam of taxis to the National Portrait Gallery. She had last been here many years earlier, when she had visited with Will. In London for a long, and as it turned out very wet weekend, they had taken shelter here during a sudden downpour. Now she walked through the entrance area and automatically took the escalator to the first floor to meander through the galleries. Gazing at the portrait of the Brontë sisters, she remembered how she and Will had once stood here together, hands clasped tight, her head on his shoulder. Those were golden days. What would have happened if he hadn't gone back to Martha? she wondered. How would their lives be different? Would they still be together today? But then the memory of her children stopped her. Nothing would make her turn back the clock and be without them. In fact she wouldn't turn back the clock at all, not even for the younger Terry. He wasn't really so bad now, just slow to readjust to the recent upheaval in his life. She could be too intolerant, too wrapped up in the business. But if that was what she felt about him, why couldn't she let the idea of Will go?

As one thought gave way to another, Eve became aware of someone else entering the room and standing a little way along from her. She glanced sideways for a second, at the exact moment he turned to look at her. A middle-aged man, quite handsome, in an open-necked shirt, untied striped scarf and dark cashmere coat. Then she looked again, realising to her astonishment that she recognised him.

Will!

Surprise registered on his face before a broad smile spread across it. Eve couldn't speak. All the breath was knocked out of her. Coincidences like this didn't happen. It was as if she'd conjured him up from nowhere. As she struggled to regain her composure, words continued to fail her.

'Eve? What are you doing here? You look terrific.' As he took a couple of steps towards her, holding out both arms as if to embrace her, she took a couple of quick steps backwards.

She was readjusting again to that weathered face, the slight stoop and the closely shaved head that had replaced the dark mane of before. But behind the glasses, the eyes were the same.

'Just wasting time before my next meeting.' She looked at her watch, pleased with herself for sounding suitably nonchalant. 'I should probably go.' But her legs were refusing to co-operate and she found herself rooted to the spot.

'I came to see the Freud exhibition, and then I remembered that we once came here together. Have you forgotten?' That smile again. 'Do you remember, the time we ran in out of the rain? Oh Evie! I haven't been able to stop thinking about you since last week.' The words burst out of him.

'I . . . no . . . I . . .' This couldn't be happening. They didn't like each other. They were virtually strangers now. And yet they weren't. She turned back to the portrait of the three sisters, who returned her gaze, inscrutable. Perhaps if she stared at them for long enough, Will would dematerialise or spontaneously combust. Anything.

Now he was standing inches away from her, side by side, looking straight ahead with her. In the neighbouring rooms were footsteps, voices. But for now, they were completely alone, with only the steady eyes of the sisters on them. Neither of them moved.

Then, 'I'm sorry.' He said it so quietly, she almost didn't hear.

'For taking your pillow?' Why did she say that? What a stupid thing. But she didn't look for his reaction, just kept staring forward, not knowing where this should be going, wondering how she should be reacting.

'For hurting you.' He sounded sincere. Perhaps he was. Perhaps his marriage had taught him about other people and tamed him.

Their hands brushed together. She started, then quickly side-stepped to the next picture, not even taking in its subject. Startled by the intensity of her response, she struggled to recover herself, used to taking control of a situation. 'Well, it's in the past now.' She surprised herself. That wasn't what she had meant to say at all. But Will hadn't finished.

'I haven't got an excuse for the way I behaved, apart from being too young to know better. I thought a quick, clean break was the right thing for both of us.' He was so matter-of-fact, as if he was talking about someone else. And perhaps he was. All that pain belonged to so long ago. Now that they were standing together, Eve was finding it hard to identify with the young woman she had been whom he had hurt so badly.

This time she didn't move away.

'How could you ever think leaving me for your ex-girlfriend was excusable?' But she found herself asking more in curiosity than in anger.

'I did love her,' he said quietly, as if this was justification enough for causing Eve such heartbreak. Then he added a little too quickly, 'But I loved you too.'

Before she could say anything, her BlackBerry buzzed for her attention. Thankful for the interruption, she rescued the phone from her bag. Terry.

One of chickens taken by fox. Chased it, couldn't catch. Luke rang. Will be home at weekend. Bringing girlfriend!

The message brought her up short. How was it that she and Terry could communicate so easily when they were apart? These days, when they were together, disagreement was never far away. The smallest behavioural tics had become sources of the greatest irritation. She didn't understand how they had arrived at this state of affairs.

'It's Terry,' she said, overbrightly. 'Luke, one of our twins, is bringing his new girlfriend for the weekend. Must be serious.'

'Mmph.' Will released a noise resembling a little laugh. 'I never imagined you with children.'

'You said,' she reminded him, brisk, irritated that he'd forgotten. 'Well, we've got four.' She couldn't keep the pride out of her voice.

'And married to Rose's brother! I'd never have imagined that either. Keeping it in the family.'

Immediately her hackles rose. There was something in his tone she didn't like. She or Terry might question their marriage, but she was damned if she would listen to Will, or anyone else, putting it down. 'You're hardly one to talk. Martha was your school sweetheart, I seem to remember. Sweet sixteen. At least I moved forward.'

This time he laughed properly: a deep chuckle that kept her rooted to the spot. 'Still the same old Eve, fighting like a tiger. And I did move forward in the end.'

There was an awkward pause. Embarrassed, she checked her watch. 'Christ! I really have got to go.' This time her legs obliged. Will accompanied her to the escalator, Eve unsure how they were going to leave things between them.

He didn't step on to the escalator with her. When she realised she was alone, she looked backwards to see him standing thoughtful at the top. Her insides did a little quickstep as he raised a hand in farewell.

'Can I call you?' he asked.

'Yes,' she found herself saying. 'Yes, do.' She could still feel the beat of her heart, the relief of getting away. And yet in among all that, there was regret too. She dismissed it abruptly. In the Ladies', she stared at her reflection, smoothed her skirt, and straightened her jacket before putting on her coat. Her mind was racing. What had just happened? Her life was complicated enough without adding Will into the mix. She calmed herself, knotted her scarf. He wouldn't call. His question was just a knee-jerk way of concluding their encounter. Of course he didn't mean it.

She checked her BlackBerry. She had ten minutes in which to get to her appointment with the MD of Flying Mango Books, ten minutes in which to focus on what she wanted to achieve from the meeting. That was what was important now. She readjusted the shoulder strap of her bag, tightened her grasp on the handle of her briefcase and made her way to the exit and out across the busy junction, dodging taxis, towards the Strand.

18

The knife slipped, slicing into the fleshy tip of Rose's finger. Her curse was drowned out by the voices of *The Pearl Fishers* crescendoing around her. Cradling her injured hand, she crossed to the tap and watched the blood run off into the rushing water. Wrapping a bit of kitchen towel around the cut, she went to the cupboard, where she found an Elastoplast. She hadn't much time. She was teaching her watercolour class at seven, and at Jess's insistence, Simon Connelly was due at five thirty. An hour should be more than enough for him to explain what he and Jess had dreamed up for Trevarrick.

She went back to slicing and quartering the cucumber, then put it in a bowl with sugar, salt and rice vinegar, hissing in pain as the vinegar seeped through the plaster into the cut. Then she did the same thing again with half a red onion and another bowl. She found the precision demanded by chopping, slicing and dicing therapeutic. At first there had seemed little point in cooking for one, but as the months went by, she had begun to enjoy the exercise. No longer having to cater for Daniel's likes and dislikes, she was free to experiment as she pleased. Not having his interference when she tried something new was in fact liberating, though she felt bad admitting that to herself. If he walked in this very minute, the first thing he would do would be to turn the music off.

She hummed along as she slid the swordfish steak into the plastic bag to marinade in squeezed lime, olive oil, and seasoning. There. When she returned exhausted from her class, everything would be ready. She liked to be on her mettle when she was teaching, even if these were enthusiastic adults who needed little more than encouragement, and food made her too sluggish.

At five thirty precisely, the doorbell rang. Simon was standing there, a bunch of white tulips in one hand, a briefcase in the other, and a drawings tube under his arm. She took the flowers, thanking him, and showed him into the kitchen, where they could most easily look at his plans.

'Tea? Or something stronger?' she asked, lowering the volume so they could hear themselves speak over the overture to *Rigoletto*.

'Tea would be perfect. Thanks.' He hung his coat and scarf over the back of a chair while she set about making a pot of Earl Grey and pulled out a tin of shortbread. As she moved around the kitchen, she was aware of him taking in his surroundings. He examined her paintings, considering each one as if they were classical works of art. Although she was used to friends and family looking at them, the scrutiny of a stranger made her feel too exposed.

'How are you?' He had moved over to the bookshelves, and was studying the photos of her family.

Disconcerted by his close interest, she hesitated, watching as he bent closer to Dan's business photo that she'd placed at the back with the one of them skiing. He stared at it without speaking.

'I'm fine,' she replied, not wanting to elaborate on the bewildering difficulties of being alone. 'It's been hard, but the family's been wonderful.' She immediately thought of Jess and Anna and how she must mend the bridges between them.

He came to the table, clearing his throat. 'I like your paintings. They're very evocative. Italy and Cornwall, I'm guessing.' As she brought over the tea, he took the papers from the tube and unrolled them, then rolled them in the opposite direction so they would lie flat.

'Thanks. That's right.' As he took his cup and saucer, he smiled, glancing at her for the first time. She was struck by how washed-out he looked. His face was thinner than she remembered, his skin grey with fatigue, shadows underlining red-rimmed eyes. She recognised in him a deep private sadness that echoed her own. Jess had mentioned the death of his father. Obviously that was taking its toll.

'So you've been helping Jess with plans for Trevarrick.' She came round the table to stand beside him to look at the drawings.

'Yes, well, both of them. Daniel took me down there to see the place last August.'

'I'd no idea he was thinking of renovating.' Nor did she remember his mentioning taking anyone to see the hotel, but perhaps it had been forgotten in the flurry of their getting ready to go to Italy. Everything surrounding that holiday had blurred and distorted in her mind.

'I don't know that he was really. I'd seen the photos of Trevarrick in the brochure and suggested a couple of improvements he might consider. He invited me to have a look.'

'Jess never said.' She was used to Dan taking off on short business trips if one of the hotels needed him, but was still surprised not to remember this one.

He must have noticed her puzzlement and tried to reassure her. 'I was only there for a few hours. We threw some ideas around together but no decisions were made. Jess only contacted me a few weeks ago about possibly taking things on a stage.' He moved the drawings so she could see them more easily. 'Look. She's asked me to take you through them.'

Nonetheless, Rose disliked the idea that she had been excluded from these talks. Jess had said nothing, probably thinking the time was all wrong, but both she and Daniel knew perfectly well how attached Rose was to her childhood home. Although she hadn't been directly involved in the business since they'd moved away to London, fifteen-odd years ago, she still cared deeply about what happened to the place.

'I hadn't appreciated that you'd gone quite so far,' she said, trying to translate the lines and measurements in front of her into a recognisable building, at the same time feeling as if the ground had been swept from under her feet.

'These are only rough. Nothing's been decided yet.'

'I realise that,' she said, rather more sharply than she'd intended. 'You'll need my go-ahead now Daniel's not here to give his.'

He raised his head from the drawings, leaving his finger on the point he was about to explain. 'Please don't be upset. I only came here because Jess asked me to. I think she meant all this as a surprise. A good one.'

'I'm sorry. That was very rude of me.' She put her hands on the table and leaned on them. 'But I'm afraid you'll have to explain what it all means.'

They stood so close their arms were almost touching. Next to hers, his hands on the plans were long-fingered, nails cut straight across. With a pang, she realised that his lemony aftershave reminded her of Daniel. She moved away from him. As he talked, fleshing out the description that Jess had given her in the café, providing the detail that made it real, excitement stirred in Rose's gut.

'To give you the best idea, I've brought this 3D image.' He opened his laptop to call up a stylised version of the back of the hotel she knew so well, but transformed. Under a clear sky stretched a blue pool, cabin-style changing rooms along one side, full-length glass doors completing an extension to the dining room. Retracted sideways, they brought the outside in, or vice versa, Rose was never sure which. Instead of the dark cosiness of before, the room was light and bright. On its right, the snug had been enlarged and given a glass roof and similar glass doors. On its left, the old bar remained untouched. Looking towards the sea, two palm trees were the only things that interrupted the otherwise all-too-familiar view down to the cliffs, across the wide sandy beach and along to the next headland.

'It looks like the South of France.'

'Pity I can't guarantee the sun.' He laughed.

'That's a disappointment.' As she laughed too, some of the awkwardness between them dissipated.

While she considered the drawings, letting Simon explain the finer detail, she couldn't stop the memories. As children, she and Terry had roamed that coastline, flying kites on the beach, hiding on the steep gorse-lined coast path, exploring the smugglers' caves despite their parents' warnings, taking out the family Wayfarer. They had raced down the hotel corridors, stolen food from the kitchen when the cook's back was turned, and been babysat by an array of young waitresses and barmen while their parents held court in the hotel bar or went out for the evening. These images were overlaid by those belonging to her and Daniel: long sunny summer walks, escaping her parents, who by then rarely left the building; nights in cold bedrooms, threadbare sheets and towels, the empty dining room and bar, the smell of damp, the sound of arguing, the few loyal guests. But how Daniel had loved the embarrassing shambles of her family life, compared to the rigorous Catholic confines of his own. He'd fallen in love with the countryside, the clifftop setting of Trevarrick and the long cliff path walks, branching off through deep woodland, hidden coves and river estuaries. His real affection for the place was what made him hurl himself headlong into the business of restoring and recreating the hotel after her parents' deaths.

Listening to Simon, Rose warmed to him, and was reminded again of Daniel, of his love for the place, of how hard he had worked on the original renovations, sometimes coming to bed after a fourteen-hour day. Nothing deflected his passion. Working together, they had achieved his vision, while Terry oversaw the costs and kept well clear of any of the physical involvement, agreeing that they should be equal partners given the amount of work Daniel was putting in. As they'd laboured, so Rose had grown to love the place again. In the months since Daniel's death, she'd forgotten just how much. And now she was being presented with an opportunity to take Trevarrick on to another level.

As Simon talked, she realised that selling the place was out of the question. Whatever the pressure put on her by Terry and Anna, she couldn't. More than that, being involved in the refurbishment, even at arm's length, would give her a project, something to occupy her mind. Perhaps that was why Jess had been so keen for her to see the plans. Not just so that she would have a home and a job, but in order to share something with her mother. How clever of Dan to have found an architect so sympathetic to the project, and how much cleverer of Jess to have thought to contact him again. The initial awkwardness between them had quickly vanished. Simon had a natural ease that she liked, a sense of humour too. He listened to her ideas and suggested compromises they might all accept without giving the impression of being either offended or patronising.

'*If*, and it's a big if,' she said, imagining the objections that would be raised by Anna and Terry. '*If* we were to go ahead, what sort of timescale are you thinking of?'

He rubbed his nose with a finger, thoughtful. 'Depends how much you want to upset the summer business. Normally this sort of renovation would be carried out in early spring or autumn, but we could probably get the dining room extension and snug completed by the end of June if I can get the right builders.'

'That quickly?' Rose hadn't imagined the whole thing taking off quite so fast.

'Well, as I say, you could wait until the season's over. It's up to you.' He hesitated. 'Of course, Daniel would have had the whole thing under way by now.'

She glanced at him, surprised by his sudden insensitivity. After his concern at the memorial, she had the impression that he was a more thoughtful man than that. In the background, the orchestra played on.

'No doubt,' she agreed crisply. 'But the situation's more complicated now. I have to consult with the rest of the family.'

'Of course. I'm sorry. I didn't mean . . .' A blush crept upwards over his face, making him look like a schoolboy who'd been caught flouting the rules. Flustered, he began rolling up the drawings.

'I know you didn't. Look,' she said, feeling sorry for him. He was only expressing his enthusiasm for the project. She could hardly blame him for that. 'I love the designs. You, Dan and Jess have obviously thought through every aspect of this between you. But I can't give you the go-ahead just like that. I wish I could.'

As he stretched an elastic band over the paper roll, it snapped and flew across the room. Neither of them went to retrieve it. 'I completely understand. Whenever you're ready.' Simon was focused on rerolling the paper.

'Can you leave those with me? I'd like to think it all over.'

'Of course.' He handed her the roll with a smile. 'If you need me to answer any questions, just call. I could come by and pick them up. In fact, I wonder whether . . .' He stopped, as the blush began to return to his cheeks. 'No, sorry. I shouldn't have said anything. Forget it.'

'Forget what?' She wanted Simon to leave, but not before he finished his sentence.

He shrugged on his coat and knotted his scarf, screwing up his face as if he wished he hadn't spoken.

'Please,' she entreated, more curious than ever.

'I've a couple of tickets to the Royal Opera House on Tuesday. Good ones,' he said, looking uncomfortable as he put on one glove then took it off again. 'A long-standing date that's been broken. I wondered . . .' He shook his head, his complexion fiery with embarrassment.

'Yes?' He couldn't be about to invite her to go with him, not on the strength of two short meetings, not when he knew how recently she'd been widowed.

'I'm sure you wouldn't. This is so presumptuous of me, and I know very last-minute, but I wondered whether you'd like to come with me? I don't know many people in London yet who I could ask. I just thought . . . Well, you obviously like opera . . .' He nodded towards the sound system and her CDs in the corner of the worktop. 'But I can see that it's a silly idea.' He flicked his hand as if he was waving it away.

But was it such a silly idea? They had already established that they had one thing in common: a love of Trevarrick. Hearing him talk about the place had excited her. She'd enjoyed the last hour of his company. Besides, what was there to stop her going to an opera with him? She'd admitted to Eve how much she wanted to be invited out again. He knew the rest of her family. Well, Jess anyway. Did that make it better? Or worse? However difficult she found it, she was going to have to get used to going out without Daniel. And the Royal Opera House. Who else would make her such an extravagant offer?

'I'd love to go with you.' The words were out before she'd realised.

'You would?' Her acceptance clearly surprised him as much as his question had surprised her.

'Why not? It's not as if my diary's packed with things to do these days. Yes,' she said firmly, dismissing her immediate regret at being so hasty. 'I would.'

Later that evening, home from her class, she phoned Eve. Having listened, outraged, to the whole Rufus and Amy scenario and then, quietly alarmed, to Eve's story of her latest encounter with Will, she saw a gap in the conversation. She dropped Simon's invitation straight into it. Eve's reaction was gratifying.

'You haven't said yes?' She sounded disbelieving but excited at the same time. 'He could be anyone. You know, the proverbial mad axe murderer . . . Anyone.'

'But he's not,' objected Rose, refusing to admit to any slight uneasiness. 'He's a perfectly nice man and a friend of Dan and Jess. And he loves Trevarrick. What more could I ask for? Besides, I feel sorry for him. He's obviously still grieving for his father, and he doesn't know many people here. We'll be company for one another.'

'Isn't that a bit over the top?' Eve still sounded doubtful. 'A father's hardly the same as a husband, but OK, you've got things in common. Go. Enjoy it. But I want every detail of what happens. What are you going to wear? Not black. Promise me.'

'I'm not promising anything of the sort.' Rose had been thinking of the black dress that Dan had liked her in. She would wear it for him. Sometimes Eve's imagination ran ahead of her. This wasn't a date, just two people keeping one another company . . . although she couldn't deny Simon was attractive. But he was at least ten years younger than her. Though that wasn't enough of a difference to make anything like that impossible or embarrassing. Amused, despite herself, she dragged her mind back to the conversation.

They hung up, having promised to meet up the following weekend. Rose ate in front of the TV, watching one of the *Frozen*

Planet DVDs. But she couldn't concentrate. The photography and commentary only provided a background for her thoughts. Apart from the anxiety about her own future, so much else was pre-occupying her. Eve gave the impression she didn't want to talk about Terry. But Rose worried about her brother, about them. His job had always defined him and the redundancy had clearly hit him hard. As much as she loved Eve, she was uneasy about her renewed contact with Will. There was an excitement in Eve's voice she hadn't heard for a long time that contradicted her protestations that they wouldn't meet again. Should Rose have stopped him from attending the memorial? But what would she have said? She had wanted to give everyone who had ever known Daniel the opportunity to be there, and judging from the condolences book, they had been. Refusing Will would only have been awkward and confrontational, neither of which she wanted.

And what about Jess and Anna? Their relationship depended on her decision over what happened to the business. But she had just decided to keep Trevarrick when the offer elicited by Terry from Madison Gadding was for all three hotels.

She could hear Daniel's voice saying, 'I don't want Adam having a share of the business, Rosie. That mustn't happen.'

She lifted the phone again, checking her watch as she did so. It was late, but Eve would still be up, Terry too. He had always been a night owl: a habit drummed into them as the children of Trevarrick, a hotel that when their parents ran it only came alive at night. That was when they put aside any problems, dressed up and emerged to play mine host. If she weren't 'resting', their mother would hold court behind the bar, the scent of Nina Ricci's L'Air du Temps undercut by cigarette smoke and gin. Meantime, their father, bluff in his tweeds, red-faced and never without a small cheap cigar, would prop up the corner of the bar, regaling their customers with bad jokes (where Terry got his sense of humour?). When they were too old for babysitters, Rose and Terry went ignored, having free run of the place until they were so tired they'd drop to sleep in an armchair in the old snug or under a table in a

181

camp they'd made. Sometimes they'd remain there all night, unless one of the staff found them and took them up to bed.

Terry answered immediately.

'It's Rose. I'm sorry to call again so late, but I think we should talk.'

'We should.' He wouldn't sound so relieved when she told him her decision, but for the first time since Daniel had died, she could see her way. Simon's visit had triggered something in her. At last she saw a simple method of resolving matters and taking the first step forward into her future. Hard as it was to accept, Daniel wasn't coming back.

'I know what I want to do.'

'You do?' Concern had crept into his voice. 'Well, I'm not exactly busy. I could come up to town whenever you like. The sooner the better, in fact.'

'Well then, how about tomorrow? I'm teaching till four, so come over late afternoon sometime.'

'I'll be there at five.'

For the first time in months, Rose went to bed feeling that at last, thanks to Simon, she was resuming some sort of control over her life. That was a lot to owe someone.

19

Terry looked terrible, rumpled, as if he hadn't slept for weeks. His shirt was untucked. A smear of something – his lunch? – decorated the left lapel of his jacket. No tie. Eve was obviously too concerned about her defecting authors and shoring up her business to have noticed that her husband was facing the world in such a state. The big sister in Rose reached out to pick at the stain. He snatched the jacket from her. 'Leave it, Rose. Please.'

Corrected, Rose took him through to the kitchen, where she'd laid out Simon's plans. She gestured towards the table. 'Have a look at these, while I make some coffee.'

'What are they?' he asked with almost total lack of interest. 'I thought we were going to talk about *your* decision.' The emphasis he put on 'your' spoke of the real resentment he felt at her owning two thirds of the business. He couldn't have expected Dan to leave his third split equally between the two of them, could he? The thought struck her for the first time.

However, unable to question Dan's will, Rose could only do her best by those he had left behind, making sure she was as fair as possible. 'I'll explain in a sec, but they're for Trevarrick.'

He frowned. 'You mean you've decided not to sell?'

'I've decided not to sell Trevarrick. When you look at the plans, I hope you'll see why.' She busied herself in the kitchen, getting out mugs, filling the kettle.

'I'm not interested in any plans.' He sounded quite adamant. 'I'm only interested in closing the deal with Madison Gadding as soon as possible.'

Rose was shocked by his vehemence. She stopped what she was doing and leaned against the counter, not understanding. 'But why? What's so important that can't wait? I see why Anna wants me to sell. She's found a property and thinks I'll release some money to her. But presumably you've got a pay-off, you'll find another job, and in the meantime, Eve's still earning. Things can't be that bad financially.' She crossed to the table. 'Look. The place will be transformed again.'

'I said I wasn't interested.' He slapped his hand on the table, making Rose recoil. Terry rarely stood up for himself against her. When it came to decisions, their relationship had always worked on the basis of her being the older, the wiser, the one in charge. She determined to stand her ground, despite disliking the turn the conversation had taken.

'What's your problem?' she challenged, 'I'm only asking you to look at some plans. I'm trying to explain my decision to you, hoping for your backing. Is asking you to listen too much to ask?'

'In this instance . . . yes.' He tugged sharply at his cuff, exposing one of the silver cufflinks inherited from their father, who in turn had inherited them from his.

'We must keep what we can in the family.' She must have been about sixteen when their father had said that to her. She had all but forgotten, but now the memory of them sitting in the otherwise empty bar together was suddenly quite clear. Her mother had gone upstairs for one of her lie-downs, leaving her father with a pile of paperwork. They were sitting by the window, with everything spread out in front of them, weighted down by her cup of coffee and his glass of whisky. Trying to get on top of their rocky finances, he'd confided in her. Her mother wanted them to move out and move on, but he couldn't see a future for them anywhere else. He was probably right. By then, they were rooted firmly in Cornwall and he wanted to spend his final years there. And now she was in a similar position. Trevarrick had meant too much to the two of them, and now to Jess as well.

'But you haven't even looked,' she protested. 'Sit down, let me get the coffee and I'll show you.' There must be a way of getting through to him.

With extremely bad grace, he did as she asked, but she noticed that he didn't even glance at the drawings. He steepled his hands in front of him and drummed the tips of his fingers against each other, staring at them as if there was nothing else in the room.

She brought the coffee over and put it down on the table. 'Biscuit?'

He shook his head, fingers still moving.

'Now,' she said firmly, starting again. 'What I wanted to show you is the way Jess and Simon – he's the architect that Dan used for the Arthur – are planning to make over the old place. I think his ideas are remarkable and completely in keeping with Trevarrick. They've made me realise how much I still love it. We can't let it go, and anyway,' she reached for her brother's hand, but he removed it to his lap, 'I need something to do with myself now, and this would be something to focus on.'

'You've got your teaching. You've got your painting.' He wouldn't look at her, but the muscles of his jaw were moving as he tried to control his temper. She recognised the signs.

'Yes, but they're not enough. I'm down to a couple of evenings and only two days a week at the college at the moment. The cut-backs mean I may have even less next term, and without Dan, I've got plenty of time on my hands.' How to explain the empty hours of nothingness in which time hung so heavy? Her private teaching was sporadic and her own painting was failing to provide the consolation she was used to finding there. Instead, days passed without her achieving anything. Sometimes she went out walking. She could cover miles of pavement or park, losing track of time, barely noticing the route she took. Sometimes she sat at home, lost in thought as time drifted past without her registering. 'At least let me show you,' she appealed.

He shook his head again, whistling out between his teeth. His silence invited her to start. As she got into her stride, she sensed him relax a little as he listened to what she had to say. He was reacting as she had, remembering how much they owed to the place. 'So you see,' she concluded, 'I want this to go ahead. Partly for our sake, our family's I mean, but for Daniel too. A kind of memorial, I suppose. Perhaps that sounds sentimental, but it's something I want to do.' That was one thing of which she was sure.

Terry said nothing, then gave a long, despairing sigh as he raked his fingers back and forth through his hair. 'I'm sorry,' he murmured. 'I can see why you want to do this, but I can't support you.'

'But why not? It'll make such an improvement.' Frustrated by his pig-headedness, Rose crossed to the window, wondering how she could persuade him. She stared out into the garden, dismal under a Tupperware sky. A grey squirrel hung upside down on the bird feeder, helping itself, its scrawny tail flicking as it filched the nuts. She banged on the glass to frighten it away. The animal looked up, beady-eyed, alarmed, then jumped to the ground and bounded up the garden.

'The truth is, I need my share of the money now.' He made a noise as if he was in pain. 'Or at least the promise of it.'

'But why?' Rose repeated, as she returned to the table.

He swung round in his chair to face her. 'I'm in trouble, Rose. Real trouble.'

To her surprise, he reached out and grasped her wrist, so tight it hurt.

'If I tell you, you've got to swear you won't tell Eve. She mustn't know.'

She wrenched her arm out of his grip, rubbing the red mark on her skin. The last thing she wanted was to get caught up in her brother and sister-in-law's quarrels, but she couldn't remember seeing Terry like this for years; not since he was a boy desperately pleading with her to lie for him over how the pair of china wally dogs over the fireplace in the bar got broken. They weren't valuable, but they had been handed down from their great-grandmother. Knowing how angry their father would be, she had hidden the football in the cloakroom and blamed the cat. Her childhood instinct to protect was re-emerging again, despite not wanting to keep another secret. Not telling him about Eve bumping into Will already felt like one betrayal too many. But he was her brother. She had to help him.

'Of course I won't if you don't want me to. What's happened?'

'I'm in deep shit.' He hung his head. If she didn't know him better, she'd have thought he was about to cry. 'I really am. I owe a lot of money.'

Only money. Thank God. She relaxed a little. 'Is that so urgent? You'll soon have another job and you'll be able to pay it back. Do you want me to tide you over?'

'I'm talking thousands of pounds. Thousands.' He didn't look up. His elbows were on the table, hands clasped round the back of his neck.

'But how? What have you done?' She felt real panic. Their parents had been cavalier about money and had died leaving nothing much more than the rundown hotel, but they had never, as far as she knew, run up any substantial debts. When they were in financial trouble, they didn't try to keep up appearances, just let the place disintegrate around them. Rose, Terry and Daniel were left to borrow what was needed to transform it.

'Gambling. I've got way out of my depth.'

She only just heard him.

'But you can't have run up that much.' He liked the occasional flutter on the horses. All right, perhaps a bit more than occasional. But not any more than the next man. 'You've only been out of work a couple of months.' Rose realised how Pollyanna-ish she was sounding.

Terry shook his head. 'It's been going on for longer than that. Much longer. Years, in fact. Do you think I could have a drink?'

Asking for a drink at this time of day meant it must be serious. Rose didn't argue, just took a tumbler into the sitting room and poured him a large Scotch. When she returned to the kitchen, Terry hadn't moved. She took ice cubes out of the freezer and added a couple out of habit, then filled a jug with tap water and put everything in front of him. At last he sat straight, added some water and took a sip. His expression told her there was much worse to come.

'Why do you think I was fired?' he asked quietly.

Had she missed part of the conversation when she was out of

the room? 'You weren't fired,' she said slowly. 'You were made redundant. That's what you told us.'

'No. That's the story the partners agreed I could put out. Oh God, it's such a mess.' He rolled his eyes to the ceiling. 'I couldn't tell any of you. You see, I'd had to borrow some money from them, and Colin, the other senior partner, found out before I had time to pay it back.'

'What do mean, he found out? What have you done?' Rose tried to sound calm despite her trepidation.

Terry held up a hand. 'Shh. Let me finish. I, er . . . I didn't ask them. I knew they'd want to know why I needed so much cash, so it seemed better to borrow and pay it back without them noticing. Except they did notice. Colin agreed that if I squared up immediately, before any damage was done, and then left the company, only Neville, our other partner, need know. They were very decent. The perks of a small company and an old friend. There was no redundancy.'

'You mean you stole from them?' But Terry would never steal unless absolutely desperate. If only Daniel were here. He would talk to him, see a way through this, maybe even trust him with a job. Who else would now?

'Not exactly. And it wasn't my fault,' he hastened to reassure her. 'Not really.'

'Whose fault was it then?'

'I'd had a bit of bad luck. Nothing that couldn't be put right. If Colin hadn't found out . . .' He didn't finish.

Rose remembered him hunched in front of the TV in Italy, not shifting until the horse racing was over, keeping a tally of the cricket scores and the football results on his phone. Eve had often complained about his Saturday afternoons spent engrossed in TV sports programmes. But Rose had never taken any of it very seriously. Wasn't that just what some men did?

'I'd maxed out my credit cards. Easily done.' Breezily said, as if the most natural thing in the world. 'I had to borrow the money just to pay them back and should have sorted it all out quickly

without anyone knowing, but then I had a string of losses . . .
A couple of them were dead certs, too. I don't know what happened.' He looked suddenly defeated. 'You don't want to know.'

Rose exploded. 'No, I don't. You bloody idiot, Terry. You
bloody, bloody idiot. Just tell me how much you owe.'

'Over two hundred grand.'

Rose felt the sum like a punch in the gut. She gasped.

'Well, maybe just a little less.' He brightened for the briefest of
moments before he went on. 'But the real problem . . .' he
swallowed as he clasped his hands tightly together, 'is that I've
taken a mortgage on the house without Eve knowing. She thinks
it's all paid off. Well, it was. But I had to find the money somewhere if I was going to pay off the firm and then two of my Visa
cards. I thought I was an expert at juggling debt. Turns out I'm
not. Now I'm about to default on the bloody mortgage and I'll be
in worse shit than ever.'

'And even if I find the money to help you, then what?' She
looked him straight in the eye, refusing to let him turn away.
'I'm not agreeing to the sale of all three hotels as a package to
Madison Gadding to fund your gambling habit. You need professional help.'

Terry looked pained. 'But a third of the profit from them is mine
by rights. You can't deny me that. Look, I didn't mean to get into
this mess, but once it started to go wrong . . . This is just a blip.
Once I've sorted it out, I'll be fine. I don't need to see anyone.
I don't need help. I can stop this tomorrow once I've straightened
everything out.'

'Tomorrow?' she shouted. 'Why not today? That's the talk of an
addict. Christ, Terry, can't you hear yourself? Therapy's for people
smart enough to realise they need help.' Furious, she wasn't going
to let him talk his way round her. 'A blip? How can you say that?
Why didn't you tell me before?'

'How could I? I can't talk to Eve and you've had so much on
your plate. I would have asked Daniel. If he'd been here, perhaps I
wouldn't have got in this mess.'

'You can't blame him.' Rose was outraged. Daniel would be as angry with him as she was, but he would do his best to be fair (as she was trying to be), and would stick to his guns (as she would too). 'I'm not going to sort out your problems by selling Trevarrick. Just not.' She ignored his despairing sigh. 'There has to be another way.'

Terry didn't stay for much longer. Once they'd finished their coffee, there wasn't much more to be said. His relief at having unburdened himself was obvious, although he was still determined not to confide in anyone else. 'I'm on top of it, Rose,' he insisted. 'I just needed you to understand why I need the money urgently.'

'I do. And I am going to think about the best way to help you. But there is one thing before I do anything,' Rose concluded. 'If you're going to get yourself out of this, you must tell Eve.'

Terry looked aghast. 'No,' he said firmly. 'I can't do that. You don't understand. I can't tell her the house is under threat. She'll kill me.'

'I wouldn't blame her, but you've got to be honest with each other,' said Rose, reminded of how Daniel had ultimately let her down. But would she really have wanted to know the truth if he had lived? Sometimes she thought the answer was yes; at others, no. This was hardly the same thing, though. 'However difficult it's going to be, Eve would want to know. In fact, she deserves to know, and I'm sure she'll be on your side. That's one condition. And I want you to get proper help. If you do those two things, I'll find a way to help you, with or without Madison Gadding.'

He pursed his lips, weighing up what might happen if he refused. Then he inclined his head slightly. 'I'll think about it. I will. Although I really don't want to involve her.'

'I know you don't,' sympathised Rose. 'But if you want my help . . .'

Eve was feeding the chickens. Five of them had followed her up the garden, flapping round the corner of the potting shed, waddling out from under bushes, fluttering down from the low wall that divided off the vegetable garden, clucking behind her. Her rescue hens. Their evident enjoyment of their new freedom after a half-life as battery hens was a pleasure. When she reached the run, they dashed in, fussing round the dish as she tossed in the pellets, dropping the leftovers from last night's supper on the ground. While they ate, their beaks tapping against the metal dish, she filled the drinker with water from the garden tap and put it in the centre of the run.

Terry was out. His note only said he'd gone to London, but she was praying that a job interview might have taken him from home. He had been so difficult over the last few weeks that she was pleased to have the place to herself for once. She had tried to be sympathetic, by not coming home too late, by cooking what she knew he liked, not complaining about the wall-to-wall sport on TV, telling him about what was going on at the agency, and had tried talking to him about his situation. But nothing jolted him out of this awful lethargy. He wasn't interested in what she had to say, or in talking. She imagined them living like this for the rest of their lives, and despaired.

Just as she was checking for eggs in the nesting boxes, her hand rummaging in the straw, her phone rang. With an egg in one hand, she didn't bother to check the caller identity, but she recognised Will's voice immediately.

'You said I could call. Bad time?'

'No, not at all.' She wiped the shit off her finger on to the chicken wire. Not finding another egg, she shut the lid of the box. Squeezing herself through, then hoicking the mesh gate past its sticking point, she checked the latch was secure. She didn't want to make it easy for the marauding local foxes. She retreated briefly to the warmth of the kitchen. The hens could wait to go into their nesting box until they'd finished talking.

'I'm hoping you'll have lunch with me,' he said. 'Call it unfinished business.'

Eve took in the kitchen, the pine table where nothing had been put away. The day's papers were spread across it, the jam pots had been left without their lids, the butter was lined with deep gashes where one of the cats had helped itself. The sink was piled high with dirty plates and a pan in which Terry had obviously made scrambled eggs. Damp tea towels were strewn over the worktop, interspersed with mugs of half-drunk tea and coffee, teaspoons laden with cold squeezed-out tea bags. He might at least tidy up after himself. That wasn't asking too much, was it?

Leaning against the bar of the Aga, Eve concentrated on Will and what he was saying.

'I'm off to Borneo. Been commissioned to do some photography on vanishing wildlife and the impact of the palm oil plantations. I thought we might get together before I go. Are you coming up to town at all?'

The pile of ironing sitting on the side seemed to be even higher than when she last looked. The fridge was emptier. The shoes by the back door were dirtier. But this wasn't entirely Terry's fault, she reminded herself. Usually they rubbed along together, sharing the chores. But the redundancy had knocked him for six, and she had been totally preoccupied with the agency.

'Say something, at least,' Will implored. 'Anything.'

She imagined the intimacy of a neatly laid restaurant table, the anticipation of good food, the company of someone who wasn't suffering from one of Terry's lugubrious moods, who wanted to be with her. But she knew that agreeing was quite wrong.

'I am,' she said, her heart wildly contradicting her head. 'I'll be up on Wednesday for a morning meeting.'

After settling on a restaurant, they hung up and Eve went back to shut up the chickens, her mind still on Will.

If she saw him, what harm? She tried to ignore the flutter that told her she was flirting with danger. All she was doing was agreeing to a lunch for old times' sake. Life was too short to hold a grudge for ever. They'd air their past, catch up a little more, then say goodbye. Her heart contracted a fraction. By the time she saw Rose, the lunch would be over and they would laugh about it together. Will would be out of the country and she wouldn't see him again. Terry would have a job, his mood would lift as his purpose was redefined and life would get back to normal. The years had changed them all. Nothing was what it once had been. A meeting with Will was hardly likely to be the seismic shift that she understood Rose feared. But to be on the safe side, perhaps she wouldn't tell her. Not yet, at least. And she certainly wasn't going to confess a thing to Terry.

May

20

The sand was left corrugated by the receding tide, pockets of water gleaming among the ridges and runnels. As Rose walked towards the sea, each footprint was quickly sucked away. She was back in Cornwall at last, and happy. The ghosts she had feared had kept their distance. She felt as at home as always. On either side of her the beach stretched away to the distant rocks, the tidemark a dark line on the flank of the cliff behind them. Children were racing after balls, carrying buckets, spades and shrimping nets, or flying neon-coloured kites with patient parents. Out to sea, a couple of hardy windsurfers tore back and forth. Behind her, families sat huddled by the cliffs or the beach wall, sheltered by garish plastic windbreaks, picking the sand out of their picnics. Everything was much the same as it had always been.

In the distance, a stick-like figure hopped awkwardly over the breaking waves, arms stiff at her sides, shoulders hunched. Anna. Rose clutched her daughter's discarded clothes and towel to her, feeling the wind's chill. The suggestion of swimming had been greeted with horror by the rest of the family at breakfast, but Anna was adamant. 'It'll be fun. Sun's shining. For old times' sake. Come on.'

But Jess had a million and one things to do in the hotel – 'Some of us have to work, you know' – Eve suddenly needed to go into Truro for some last-minute bits and pieces, the cousins had to erect their tents in the back field, Terry disappeared on a walk, and Adam took Dylan off for his morning nap.

Rose imagined Adam putting his hour's free time to good use by finishing the spalted beech bowl that he'd shown her. When Daniel was alive, she would never have spent so long in Adam's workshop, astonished by his small arsenal of tools, listening to him explain his craft, confused by the unfamiliar language of skew chisels and spindle gouges, cup chucks and spigots, being shown the various pieces of wood at different stages of preparation. Being there would have only invited disparaging comments from her husband. But as she traced the lines and patterns made by fungi in the wood, she had listened to Adam entranced. At last she could begin to under-stand what he was trying to achieve: gallery exhibitions, a future as a woodturner, a craftsman. She couldn't help reflecting how her own professional life as a painter had stalled for ever after she put it on hold when she had children. Private daubings for her own enjoyment were not the same as the exhibitions and recognition that she had once wanted.

In fact, Simon had said as much when they went to the Hockney exhibition together, admiring, discussing, dismissing. Afterwards, over coffee, he had asked her again about her own painting, and since then he had been encouraging her to take up her brushes. 'You owe it to yourself. You once wanted to exhibit; well, why not now? It's never too late.' She had just laughed, dismissive, but his words had struck a chord. Nor would he let the matter drop. As a result, she had begun to see the world with an artist's eye again, often imagining how she might translate it to canvas or paper – even this beach that she knew so well.

Since he had first taken her to the Opera House, they had met up several times, and each time they had become a little closer. She and Daniel had always preferred the easy enjoyment of a good film, a concert given by a band from their glory days, or just being together at home. Going to the theatre or the opera with Simon was a different kind of pleasure. In return, she had suggested a couple of exhibitions they then saw together. He was both interest-ing and interested. He didn't mind if she wanted to talk about Daniel over dinner or a drink, and listened attentively to what she had to say. Her kind, long-suffering friends had heard it all before, so she appreciated a new and sympathetic ear, surprised by how quickly they had become such good friends. Yes, Simon had entered her life just when she needed him. What was more, he had put some fun back into it. Only the other day, they'd stayed far too late in her local Italian, spaghetti and cheap plonk, as he regaled her with an account of his thwarted attempts to 'bag' a couple of Scottish Munros with a bunch of obsessive hill-walkers. She hadn't laughed like that since Dan . . .

A shriek made her look up, ready to run forward with the towel. But it was only a couple dipping their toes in the surf, squealing at the cold. All she could see of Anna was her head, bobbing above the water. Rose gazed up at the fragmented clouds, returning to her thoughts, this time about the day ahead.

Back at the hotel, the modest marquee was ready, the tables laid, the path across the lawn marked by tea lights in glass jars. Twenty-five years of marriage. One hundred guests to celebrate, all scattered around the local B&Bs and hotels. How Eve and Terry had survived this long she would never know. Children, dogged determination and their own peculiar kind of love for one another, she guessed. The party had been booked at Trevarrick a year ago, at Dan's suggestion. That generosity was so typical of him. If only he could have known what would happen. Without his death, Eve would never have met Will again, would never have embarked on this crazy whirlwind affair, about which Terry knew nothing. Rose only found out when Eve tripped up in conversation, eventually admitting that she'd been seeing him regularly since they'd once bumped into each other at the National Portrait Gallery. But here they all were, gathered to celebrate their long-lived marriage. Only Eve and Rose knew the truth. And Rose wished she didn't. Hearing both Eve's and Terry's confidences put her in an impossible position. Tempted as she sometimes was to spill the beans and get their problems in the open, she couldn't betray the trust of either.

At that moment, Anna rose from the water and stood still for a nanosecond, shaking her dripping hair back off her face, before she started to run towards her mother.

'Christ! That was freezing.' She grabbed the towel and started rubbing herself vigorously before wrapping it around her shoulders. 'But it was good. I can't believe Charlie and Tom didn't come down. Ten years ago, they wouldn't have thought twice. You should have come in.'

Rose laughed. 'In May? You're joking. Wild horses couldn't drag me in there.'

'You should be more adventurous, Mum. Nothing to lose.' Unembarrassed by being in public, Anna quickly stripped off her bikini and, taking her clothes from her mother, got dressed. 'Taking chances. That's what life's all about.'

As she rolled up the legs of her jeans, Rose watched her, momentarily envious of her firm young body, of her undimmed lust for life. Perhaps she was right. 'Is that what this garden centre's about?' she asked. 'Just a chance?'

They began their walk back up the beach together, arm in arm.

'No. This time I'm going to make a go of it. I want you to come and see how it's working out. It's so perfect. We're putting the outdoor plants in the vacant lot, and then indoors we've got the house plants, fresh flowers and eventually a café. I think Liz is going to move in upstairs with me. You remember her? We met in Morocco years ago.'

Rose had the haziest of memories of long hair, long skirts and the overwhelming scent of patchouli oil.

'I'll be living over the business! Mum, you won't believe it! I know what you and Dad think of me, but this is different.' She squeezed Rose's forearm to show that she accepted their judgement.

'Think' – still in the present tense, as if . . . Rose turned to look her daughter in the eye. 'Darling, we don't – didn't – well, *I* don't think badly. Never have. And nor did Dad. You and Jess are just so different.'

Anna's arm dropped to her side, then she bent down to pick up a stone, its smooth grey shape circled with a continuous white band. She examined it, weighing it in her hand. 'A traveller's stone. Look, the circle's unbroken. That means you'll come back here.' She put it in her mother's pocket.

'I hope so . . . But don't take that the wrong way,' Rose went on, running her thumb over the stone. 'I'm glad that selling the Canonford meant I could buy the property for you. I could never have sold all three hotels, especially not Trevarrick, but thank God Madison Gadding were happy to buy just the one. Now you and

Jess both have something of your own to work for and to remember Dad by. I think he would be pleased.'

Anna slipped her arm back where it had been, her other hand gathering her wet hair and sweeping it over her left shoulder. 'Would he really? I know I've been a bit flaky in the past. But this time will be different. I absolutely promise. Thank God Uncle Terry's so good on the numbers side of things. I couldn't have done it without his help.'

Rose smiled but said nothing, enjoying this rare physical closeness between them. At the same time, she couldn't help but think of her brother. His reaction to the news that she would agree to sell the London hotel had been ungracious if not sullen, but there was nothing he could do but accept it. He'd received more than enough to keep his creditors at bay, but she refused to realise any more cash for him until he confessed all to Eve, something he was still refusing to do. Didn't she understand? He didn't have a problem.

'Really,' Anna insisted. 'It will. Rick's so on it.'

Rose had met Anna's business partner several times before she agreed to support their plans. He was Anna's age, Australian and disconcertingly tattooed, but apparently sensible and clear-sighted about the centre and its possibilities. She had been struck by how close the two of them had become in such a short time, glad that Anna had someone on her side at last. She had been too much of a loner for too long. Rose was impressed with the seriousness with which they approached the garden centre and their determination to make it work. Perhaps Rick would be enough to make the difference between success and abandonment this time. She hoped so.

'Having him on board is genius,' Anna continued. 'We make a good team. Even though we did the same courses, I'm better on the landscaping side of things and he's got a much better business brain than me. And he's got the muscle, of course. But wait till you see the plants we're ordering and the way we're arranging the space. It's going to be brilliant. All we have to do is persuade Uncle Terry about the café. Such a great idea, but until he's done his flow charts, or whatever they are, he won't let us do anything remotely risky.' She sounded impatient.

'I know he won't.' Rose's smile was knowing. 'If there's a genius in any of this, it's me for suggesting he got involved.'

'You felt sorry for him, though. And he *is* your brother. But . . . OK, he's just what we need,' Anna conceded. 'Except he's such a miserable old sod these days – not the way I think of him at all. Do you remember how he'd read us stories every night on holiday?' A razor shell crunched under her foot.

Rose laughed. 'God, yes. Eve and I would sneak into the kitchen, open the wine and leave him to it. Nobody else would do.'

'But he was wicked at it, that's why. He acted out all the different characters, with all their different voices. The six of us were sprawled all over the bed, begging him for just one more chapter. And he always said yes.' Anna looked up towards the hotel, just visible on the clifftop, as she reminisced. 'Hard to imagine now.'

'We'd have to beg him to come down for supper. You were the worst. I remember you crying when I suggested Eve or I read instead. Dad knew better than to even try.' A silence fell between them, as those favourite family memories pressed in again. Sometimes Daniel would insist that he and Rose took the girls somewhere other than Trevarrick or Casa Rosa – 'Or they'll never know what the rest of the world looks like,' he'd say – but they were always happiest holidaying with their cousins in the two places they loved best.

Anna jumped over a dead jellyfish. 'And what about Auntie Eve, then? She's looking amazing, these days. Losing that weight really suits her. What's going on?'

'What do you mean?' Rose was immediately on the defensive. 'Nothing, as far as I know.'

'I thought she might be having an affair or something.' Anna stopped to put on her pink Converses, tucking in the laces rather than doing them up.

'Anna! Don't be ridiculous. What a thing to say on the day we're celebrating their silver wedding anniversary.'

'I was only joking. As if! I wonder if any more guests have arrived. Come on, let's get back and see what's happening.' Anna began to run towards the back of the beach. Rose, for once thankful for her daughter's gnat-like attention span, picked up her own pace, annoyed with herself that she had overreacted and almost given the game away. However, Eve's secret was still safe – for the moment.

They walked up the grassy path from the beach towards Trevarrick. The large country house was so much part of the local landscape with its weathered walls and grey slate roof. Built in the nineteen twenties, it had since been extended on one side to allow for a total of thirty rooms, some tiny bolt-holes, others luxurious suites, something for every taste, quirky but always comfortable and the majority of them looking towards the sea.

Jess was waiting for them, standing on the terrace, looking down over the beach towards the path. She looked smart, businesslike in her straight skirt and shirt, her hair pulled back into a neat ponytail. But beneath the pleasant exterior, Rose could sense tension. Something more than the arrangements for Eve and Terry's party was troubling her daughter.

'You've been so long, I thought you must have drowned.' Jess came towards them, stopping to pull a weed from one of the huge plant pots of pansies.

'Hoped, more like,' muttered Anna as she slid past her sister to hang her wet towel on the back line.

'Girls, girls,' protested Rose. 'Do you think we could have just one day without an argument? Is that too much to ask?'

'Don't blame me.' Jess turned away, rubbing her hands against the cold. 'There's still so much that needs doing. Including the flowers.'

Anna whipped round. 'I told you that I wasn't picking the cow parsley and stuff till the last minute. But if you're fussed, I'll do it now.'

'Whatever,' said Jess, turning her back to go into the hotel lounge. 'This seems pretty last-minute to me. Chef's going crazy because the lobsters haven't been delivered yet – the driver rang to say the van's had a puncture. They'll get here but it'll just mean a horrible rush for the kitchen.'

Rose stood between her warring daughters, wondering what she could do to help. She didn't want to add to Jess's evident stress.

'Oh, and by the way . . .' Jess tossed the words back over her shoulder as she went through the door, 'Simon is coming after all.'

'Did he phone?' Rose was taken by surprise as her heart lifted a little at the news. It would be good to have a disinterested friend here with no involvement in her family's domestic problems. She hadn't argued when Eve and Jess suggested he came, but a work commitment meant he'd had to refuse.

'Yeah. Said some client meeting had been cancelled. So he'll be at St Austell at about two.'

'I'll pick him up then,' Rose volunteered, eager for a task that would take her away from the pre-party tension.

'You sure? I could send the minibus.' But Rose could hear Jess wasn't keen on the idea.

'No, no. Dave's got enough on his plate tonight, ferrying people to and from their B and Bs. I'll go.'

A couple of hours later, Rose was in the Citroën, crawling behind a great green tractor almost as wide as the road. The drive towards the main Truro–St Austell road always gave her pleasure but never more so than at this time of year, when the hedgerows were so crowded with wild flowers. The daffodils were long over, the bluebells were on their way out but instead froths of cow parsley set off the red and white campions. In the distance she could see fields containing drifts of buttercups bruised with bluey patches of speedwell. But none of this could keep her mind from the object of her drive.

She tapped the steering wheel in time to Figaro's aria from *The Barber of Seville*, the second opera she and Simon had seen together. Simon. It was a long time since she had met someone with whom she had felt such an instant connection. Their separate situations had thrown them together: she newly widowed, needing support; he new to town, with few friends. He was impulsive, amusing, intelligent – qualities he shared with Daniel. Like Daniel, he was genuinely interested in her opinion without being afraid to offer one of his own. They enjoyed discovering the similarities in their tastes, often being entranced or left cold by the same paintings or pieces of music. They could talk about anything together – and did. She had begun to look forward to their outings.

Only the previous week he had taken her shopping, something Daniel would never have contemplated. They had been talking about Eve and Terry's imminent celebrations. 'Perhaps I could wear this,' she'd thought out loud, staring down at Daniel's favourite black dress, now on its fifth outing in as many weeks.

'No,' Simon had said, gentle but firm. 'You need something new, summery. I know! I'm going to take you shopping. I know just the place.'

Against her better judgement she had let herself be persuaded. He even anticipated her second thoughts by arranging to pick her up and take her there. Dreading the hell of a busy department store, Rose had been pleasantly surprised when they fetched up at a small shop off Westbourne Grove. 'I know the owner,' Simon explained as he swept her inside. On either side of the poky space were two rails so crammed with clothes Rose immediately felt panicked by the amount of choice. But when she suggested they went out for a coffee before they began, Simon had been adamant. 'Oh no you don't. We're not leaving until you're sorted out. I'll introduce you to Jan, who'll get you started, and then I'll go out and bring the coffee to you.'

Her escape tactics comprehensively thwarted, Rose had no choice but to give herself up to the two of them. In the changing room Jan sized her up as if she was a heifer going to market, then disappeared. Five minutes later she was back with an array of dresses, soon followed by Simon and the much-needed coffee. Then came the excruciating experience of the fashion parade. Rose had to hand it to Simon, he'd been brilliant: decisive, matter-of-fact and helpful. At first she emerged from the changing room in a sweat of self-consciousness, wishing she'd never got herself into this, but his businesslike approach to the matter in hand meant her embarrassment soon vanished. Lounging back on the red velour sofa, he was quick to give an opinion: 'No. Love the colour, but too short.' 'No. OK, but the neck's wrong.' 'No. Almost, but the colour's not quite right.' Each time, Jan had happily scurried off to find something else more suitable as the choice was fast narrowed down. Finally, when Rose emerged wearing a sophisticated but simple number in cerulean blue and green printed silk, he said: 'Yes. That's the one. Great shape and brings out the colour of your eyes. Perfect.' And he was right: it was.

As she pulled into the station car park, she saw him standing by the ticket office. In his suit, with his neat overnight case, he stood out among the holidaymakers, anoraks over their shorts and T-shirts, lugging overfilled cases into the waiting taxis. He resembled the eye of the storm, quite still while everything else was a whirl of activity around him.

She found a space by the platform wall, jumped out of the car and waved, shouting his name. He turned, his face immediately lit with a smile, and bent to pick up his case. At that moment, one of the seagulls perched on the station roof took to the air with a loud squawk. By the time Rose reached Simon, he was busy trying to wipe off the bird droppings that adorned the back of his jacket. Beside him, several schoolchildren were hunched in hysterics. She couldn't help smiling at this slight to his image.

'Isn't this meant to be lucky or something?' he asked, to the renewed sniggers of his audience.

'I hope so, for your sake.' Rose exchanged kisses with him. 'Give it to me. We can put it in the hotel laundry. Don't worry.'

'I don't want to be a pest.' Reaching the car, he folded himself into the passenger seat. 'Jess must have enough on her plate with the party and everything.'

'So much that a bit of bird shit isn't going to make the slightest bit of difference. Wait till you see the old place. Everything's just as Daniel planned it last year, and the place is crawling with Eve and Terry's friends. I haven't a clue who anyone is, so it's good you could come.' She reversed the car out and turned up the hill towards the road out of town.

'I feel a bit of an intruder, but I want to be here on Monday anyway to meet the contractor. We're already behind schedule. I'll have to crack the whip if we're to get the dining extension and the deck done before the school holidays. They'll start the pool and the snug in late September as we agreed.'

'Honestly, one more person won't make a difference. We know how much you love the place, and it's a glorious time of year. It'll be fun. Anna's already been swimming.' She circled the round-about above Asda, then put her foot down as they hit the dual carriageway. After a few minutes she said, 'I thought we might try to escape to St Ives tomorrow. It's one of my favourite places. I want to take you to the Tate and Barbara Hepworth's house.'

As she turned the car into the winding road that took them to Trevarrick, he turned from the window towards her. 'I'd like that.'

Back at the hotel, she showed Simon to his room and left him to unpack. The first person she bumped into as she went back downstairs was Terry.

'Sis, I need to talk to you urgently.' He grabbed her arm and pulled her through the French windows and across the terrace to an isolated table that was sheltered by the corner of the building. Out at sea, a couple of tankers moved slowly against the horizon, while closer to home several sailing boats skimmed the wrinkled sea.

Rose had been looking forward to this weekend for ages. The occasions when the family got together were few, and this year, for the first time, they had decided not to go to Italy. None of them could face it so soon after Dan's death. Instead, Casa Rosa was let for the summer. So this weekend was to be cherished. However, she had a nasty feeling that Terry was about to spoil the enjoyment. She fished her sunglasses out of her bag, stretched her legs out in front of her, feeling the sun on her skin, and waited.

'This isn't easy.' He shifted in his seat, screwing his eyes up against the sun.

She didn't imagine it was. The last time they'd spoken, he'd promised to find the nearest branch of Gamblers Anonymous and attend a meeting – for her sake, if no one else's. Of course, he'd made out the whole situation was under control. She'd trusted him then, but now she wondered whether he had kept his word.

'I . . . er . . . I need just a little bit more money. Just a little.' He stared out to sea.

'Why?' She was at her most chilly, regretting that she'd given in to Anna's impressive powers of persuasion and sold the Canonford before Terry had kept his side of the bargain. 'The sale gave you more than enough to straighten yourself out. What's happened?'

'I've been a complete idiot. I told Eve I'd put the money in a holding account for the children until we decide what to do with it. And I have,' he added hastily in response to his sister's glare. 'She's been so wrapped up in work that she didn't ask for details. But she will. At the time she was just glad to hear there'd be something for them. I'd kept two hundred K back and was about to square things when I was given a couple of tips . . .'

Rose stiffened.

'. . . but they didn't come home.' He waved his hand in the air as if that was the least of his worries. 'So I've had to default on another mortgage repayment, and the bank are on my tail. Rose, you've got to help me. You're the only person I can ask.'

A little of Rose had gone on hoping that Terry's insistence that he could easily quit was justified and that he would get himself out of financial disaster. She didn't want to admit the truth to herself. But she had been wrong. Her brother really was a gambler. An addict. He needed serious help. Not hers. She knew what they said about addicts. Leave them to reach rock bottom, wherever that was, and even then they must want to help themselves. However much she might want to believe in him, Terry still hadn't reached that point. All she could do was reinstate the conditions she had originally set, not even considering how to find more money for him until he at least kept his word and sought professional guidance.

'Have you done what you promised me you'd do?' She hated how schoolmistressy she sounded, but what else could she be?

'Not yet.' His knee jigged up and down so fast, she put out a hand to still it. He stared at her hand on his leg. 'I meant to, but I've had so much on my plate.'

'Really?' She removed her hand. 'Enough time to gamble, but not enough to try to quit or talk to Eve?'

'I think she may already have guessed. I left my Visa statements on the kitchen table and she must have seen them.'

'What did she say?' Rose couldn't imagine Eve keeping quiet about something like this.

'Nothing, yet.' He waved away an approaching waiter. 'But you don't understand.'

'I understand completely. Although I wish I didn't.' Rose got to her feet, impatient. 'I really believed you when we last talked about this. More fool me. So let me spell it out to you for the final time. I'm not going to release any more money, whether by selling the Arthur or making you a loan, until you tell Eve everything, and take some steps towards a cure. End of.'

He laughed, but it was the sound of a trapped animal. 'Cure! What are you talking about? This isn't an illness.'

'That's exactly what it is, Terry.' Rose was beside herself with rage and frustration. 'And until you stop thinking like that, you aren't going to get over it. Please tell Eve. Please.' Once Eve knew, they could at least put the mortgage repayments through her without giving Terry direct access to the money. Whatever Eve was planning to do with her life – and perhaps finding out Terry's secret would colour that – at least she could surely be relied upon to do the right thing until his gambling was under control.

Rose left her brother there, sitting staring out to sea. Instead she went in to find Simon, to see if he'd like a walk on the cliff path before they might be needed to help with any last-minute panics. What she needed was distraction from her family, and the sea air would clear her head.

21

Eve knew she was driving Jess mad by constantly checking that everything was going to plan. But she had to do something with her time while she waited for Rose's return. She had just left the pink-swagged marquee where Anna was beginning to arrange the armfuls of wild flowers she had picked into delicate centrepieces for each table. Eve's offer to help was met with a brisk dismissal. This was Anna's job, and only she could do it properly. The way she took her new career so seriously was a pleasure to see. Eve should be with her guests. But the thought of them, her and Terry's dear friends who had made time to come down here for the weekend, made her ashamed. Only she and Rose knew that this whole performance was a bloody sham. But the arrangements had been too far advanced for her to call a halt without hurting too many people. Suddenly she wanted the reassurance of her oldest friend.

'Remember me on Friday,' Will had said, as she had left his apartment earlier that week.

'Why then?' she queried, still heady from their lovemaking. 'I think of you all the time.'

'It's four months to the day since we met.' He pulled her close, and she felt him hard against her. He cupped her face in his hands and kissed her, his tongue nudging at her lips. Just his touch was enough to make her feel she was twenty again. When she was with him, nothing else mattered. When she wasn't, she thought about him all the time, wondering where he was, who he was with, what he was doing, when he'd next call. Everything conspired to make her want to stay with him, but however much she wanted to, she couldn't. She had to leave Terry. But not quite yet.

He ran his finger down the length of her nose, tapping the bump where she'd walked into a lamppost many moons ago. 'Don't go. Not just yet. I can think of plenty of things to amuse us this afternoon.'

'I'm sure you can,' she laughed, knowing those amusements would take place almost exclusively in the bedroom. 'I'm so, so tempted, but I've got to go home. Terry's expecting me back and I've got some work to do.'

'What? Reading? Can't it wait?' He kissed her again, pulling her with him towards the bedroom door. 'They're only children's books. They won't take you long.'

Momentarily incensed by this dismissal of her work, she extricated herself. Then she laughed. 'I've been putting them off for too long. You're a bad man, Will Jessop. A very bad man indeed.'

'But you like it. Don't try and tell me you don't.' He grinned and put his hand in the pocket of his cream linen jacket to pull out a distinctive blue box. Tiffany's – she recognised it at once. 'A little something to mark the best four months of the year so far. Well, that's my excuse. I was going to give it to you later, but if you insist on going . . .'

Her heart beating a tattoo, she undid the white satin ribbon and removed the lid, gasping as she saw the contents. Inside was a thin woven silver bangle. 'But I can't take this. It's far too generous.'

'Of course you can,' he said. 'Now stay with me.' He took the bangle and slipped it on to her wrist, where it sat glinting in the light.

'Will, I really can't. I must get this work done before we go away.' She noticed his pout at the 'we'. 'I've an author expecting to hear from me and I can't let her down. She's worried the book's not as good as it should be and I want to put her out of her misery, otherwise she'll spend the weekend worrying.'

'Bloody agency,' he muttered. 'Don't you want to spend time with me?'

She experienced that flash of irritation she got whenever he behaved like a spoilt child. 'Of course I do.' She sounded more tetchy than she meant to. 'But with Terry still out of work, I've got to do what I can. And I'm doing my best to find a replacement for Rufus.'

Now, standing in the garden of Trevarrick, Eve twisted the bangle around her wrist, pushing it back under her sleeve, where she kept it hidden. At first she had imagined only wearing it when she was alone with Will. But her caution vanished in the face of Terry's apparent indifference. As distracted as he was, he wouldn't notice if she appeared dressed in a silver suit of armour. Nothing she said or did impinged on his gloom. Was it just his lack of work and his consequent lack of a place in the world? Or could he possibly suspect her of having an affair? She had learned a lesson from what had happened between Dan and Rose, and had been so careful not to leave any clues. Nothing Terry had said or done had given her reason to think he knew. But she was aware of reaching a place where she would have to make a decision about her future. She couldn't continue the deception. Other people managed a double life, but not her. Where they might regard the necessary lying as a game, she couldn't bear the strain, the constant possibility of being found out. However, the irony of her position hadn't escaped her. Could she really do to Terry what Will had done to her all those years ago? Was she capable of inflicting so much pain on the dear father of her children, whom she had loved, did still love, but who no longer excited her? Being with Will had brought that last consideration home in no uncertain way.

As she stared out to the white horses racing across the surface of the sea, she felt an arm around her shoulder. She spun round. Rose.

'Penny for them.' Rose had a reliable sixth sense for when Eve needed to talk.

'Where have you been? I've been looking for you.'

'Showing Simon the sights, such as they are. That awful old sheepdog by the church wouldn't let us past, so we had to come the long way back.'

As she laughed, Eve was pleased to hear her sounding so relaxed. 'I'm glad he could come.'

'Mmm.' Rose bent to retie the laces of her trainer. 'It's so odd. I feel as if I've known him for years. I don't know what it is. He makes me feel anchored again, I suppose. It's a good feeling. But what did you want to talk about?'

Eve took a deep breath. She absolutely did want to talk about Rose and Simon. Their apparently platonic relationship intrigued her as much as it pleased her. But at this second, her own problems were pressing in on her. 'I don't think I can go through with this evening,' she confessed. 'I feel such a hypocrite.'

'Bit late for that now, isn't it?' Rose was matter-of-fact. 'Terry doesn't know, and as long as you're carrying on with Will, you should make sure it stays like that. You've got to keep up the charade until you decide what you're going to do. I'd far rather not have found out about Dan.'

Eve slipped her arm around her friend's waist. 'This is difficult for you, I know.'

They stood for a moment, twined together, then their arms dropped.

'Yes, it is.' Rose paused, snapping off a head of cow parsley and beginning to tear the flower heads into little pieces. 'I'm torn between the two of you. Of course I want you to do what makes you happy, but just not at the expense of my brother.'

'I know.' Eve looked back out to sea, flattening her skirt against the wind with her spare hand. 'I don't want to hurt him either. I do love him. I do. But these last weeks with Will . . . well, they've made me feel young again. I'd never have thought . . .' She saw Rose wince. 'I'm sorry, but it's true.'

That last conversation with Daniel in his study, when she'd tried to convince him to talk to Rose. Had he been feeling the same confusion of lust and regret that she had felt every day since going to Will's flat for the first time? Beside her, Rose stood with her arms crossed over her chest. How sad she looked, and how alone.

'But you know that's not real, don't you?' Rose shook her head. 'Perhaps you should take some time out. Leaving him because of a fling that makes you feel good about yourself – is that really what you want? And for Will?' Rose's voice was full of dislike. 'After what he did to you.'

Eve took Rose's arm, despite feeling her friend's resistance. 'I shouldn't have told you. I'm sorry. But if I didn't have you to talk to . . .' She left the sentence unfinished. 'Besides, sleeping with your first husband isn't really the same as having an affair, is it?'

'Ex,' Rose pointed out firmly. 'What's the difference? Of course it's the same thing. Look, I don't want you to break up your family when I know this is a phase Terry's going through and he'll be back to normal before we know where we are. He will. And then you'll regret all this.'

Rose sounded so certain that Eve felt bound to believe her. She had recognised the risks she was running when she agreed to meet Will for their first lunch after so long, but their affair had gathered a momentum that she had been powerless to stop. She hadn't planned to lose control of her emotions, but things had happened so fast that she hadn't realised how far she was falling. She couldn't turn the clock back now, whatever she or Rose wanted. She sighed. 'Perhaps you're right. I'm being selfish and I'm going to have to sort this out my own way, without hurting Terry or the kids. That's the last thing I want to do. Let's not talk about it again. It's too hard. We should get ready.'

'So you're not calling a halt to the proceedings, then?'

'No. This is Terry's night too. I'm going to forget about Will and have a good time. Tomorrow I'll begin to put things right.'

'I hope so.' But Rose didn't sound entirely convinced as they began the walk up the path towards the hotel. From the tennis courts came the pock, pock of a match in progress, occasionally accompanied by a yell of frustration or triumph. If she was honest, Eve wasn't entirely convinced either.

Eve was in the shower when Terry came up to their room. Wrapping herself in one of the hotel's fluffy white dressing gowns, she emerged pink and scented. At least she'd succeeded in scrubbing off the streaks of fake tan applied too hastily the previous day. She found her husband lying on the bed. His sturdy walking shoes were higgledy-piggledy on the sandy carpet.

'Good walk?' She picked up the shoes and lined them up in the wardrobe.

He opened his eyes, and gazed at her, propping himself on one elbow. 'Beautiful. You should have come. I took Sam and Minty with Pete and what's-her-name on the valley walk. They were bowled over – wild flowers everywhere, and skylarks over the field by the cliff path. Rose and Simon were sitting on the old bench up there – it was great to see her laughing again. He's good for her. We didn't stop because I was worried about the time. Pete had a bit of trouble climbing the road up from the Mill at the end, but we made it.' For the first time in ages, he sounded enthusiastic. Serious all of a sudden, he sat up and wiggled himself backwards until he was leaning against the mound of pillows and cushions, then patted the spot beside him. 'We need to talk.'

Immediately, she felt apprehensive. 'Can't it wait till after the party? We should be getting ready.' She tugged the towelling turban from her hair and rummaged in her case for her hairdryer. 'We mustn't be late. Rose and Jess will kill us.'

'No, it can't. Anyway, we've got a couple of hours.' He patted the bed a second time.

She had rarely heard him sound so decisive. And certainly not recently. But he sounded nervous too. Her guilt made her more sympathetic towards him than usual, so she sat down, lifting her legs and tucking her feet under the tan-and-chocolate-striped bed runner.

'Look at me.' Terry put his hands on her shoulders and turned her to face him, eye to eye. She felt the first intimations of alarm. He clasped her hands, holding them on her lap. 'This won't take long, but I just wanted to say sorry. I know I've been impossible for the last few months. This redundancy was a bugger to deal with.'

'I know that,' said Eve, squeezing his hand back, feeling supportive but guilty.

He hesitated, as if he was about to say something important, then clearly thought better of it. 'I, er . . .' He stopped, then screwed up his face with a slight shake of his head. 'I've got something for you. Twenty-five years is a hell of a long time, and I want you to know how much it's meant to me and how much *you* mean to me.'

215

All Eve's senses were on high alert. This wasn't Terry at all. Emotional outpourings were something they tended to avoid. Not his thing. But he hadn't finished.

'I know I haven't been much good at showing it recently.' He turned away to open his bedside drawer and pull out a small, neatly wrapped parcel, which he handed to her.

She hesitated, embarrassed by the memory of the inadequate silver birch sapling that she'd bought hastily the previous day and that was waiting for him downstairs. How on earth were they to get it home? She should have thought. She would get him something else. 'I was going to give you yours later.'

'That doesn't matter. Open this. If you don't like it, you can change it.' But she could tell he was pleased with his choice. It would be earrings. Always was. She didn't need a sixth sense to tell her that.

She peeled away the white and silver paper to reveal a box, identical to the one given her by Will only days earlier. Two Tiffany boxes in one week . . .

'A girl could get used to this.' She smiled at him, knowing he had no idea of the real meaning of her joke.

He'd already removed the white ribbon, so all she had to do was lift the lid. Taking as long as possible so the tension and pleasure built in equal measure, she peeled back the tissue paper. And there, lying on a white foam backing, was a thin woven bangle in silver, absolutely identical in every way to the one given to her by Will.

She gasped, as stunned by Terry's deviation from form as by the awful coincidence. Aware that he was waiting eagerly for her response, she looked up. 'It's lovely, Terry. Really lovely.' Genuinely touched, her eyes welled up with unexpected tears as she leaned forward to kiss him. They laughed, awkward, unsure which of them was most surprised by this unusual moment of intimacy. At that exact moment, she remembered the other bracelet, this one's identical twin, sitting by her wash bag on the shelf in the bathroom in plain sight.

'Steady on, old thing. It's only a bracelet. But I thought you deserved something a bit special for putting up with me for all these years.' A note of pride entered his voice. 'Twenty-five of them. And I know it hasn't always been easy.' He stopped, then realised she wasn't going to agree or disagree, so began again. 'And there's something else I've . . .'

But Eve wasn't listening any more. By now, she was sobbing – whether from gratitude or guilt she had no idea. Everything was muddling up in her mind. Giving something so generous was quite out of character for her ever-thrifty husband, the man who thought that, apart from the customary earrings, a decent Christmas present was a set of percale bed sheets or a replacement non-stick saucepan. Knowing how hard it was for him to say something so personal and appreciative made everything much worse. His words were an awful reminder of how her behaviour was threatening their marriage and how devastated he would be if he found out.

Terry inched towards the edge of the bed and stood up.

'Where are you going?' she gulped, still unable to control her tears.

'To get you a tissue.' He patted her shoulder and went towards the bathroom.

'No!'

He turned, surprised by her urgency. 'It's no trouble,' he reassured her.

'No, no, I'm fine.' She wiped her eyes with the back of her hand, to prove she didn't need anything, and sat up straight, her towel falling to her waist. Was that hope in his eyes as she yanked it up over her breasts and tucked the end in tightly. Come on. She wasn't *that* grateful! 'Honestly, I am. Come back here.'

But too late. He had disappeared through the door. She could hear him moving around, then . . . silence. Eve lay back on the bed, holding her breath, waiting. There was no escape. This was the moment she had feared, done everything she could to avoid – the moment of discovery. Now she understood even better what Daniel must have been feeling that day: dread, shame, guilt, despair, desire to do anything but face up to the reality of their situation. Whatever was said in the next few minutes could determine the course of their future together.

The loo flushed and she heard running water, followed by the sound of tissues being ripped from the dispenser for her. Any moment now. The door handle moved and the door opened. She lay back on the pillows, her eyes tight shut, waiting for him to speak, unable to think of any kind of convincing explanation. She felt the bed give as he sat down again.

'Here you are. Feeling better?'

What? She opened her eyes to see him holding out the tissues to her. She took them and blew her nose. 'I'm sorry.'

'What on earth for? Nothing I've given you has made you react like that before. I guess you must like it.' Smiling, he took his place beside her.

By some miracle, he'd failed to notice the other bracelet. Eve felt like crying with relief.

'Don't start again, old girl.' He patted her hand.

'Don't worry. I'm all right now.' She slipped the bangle on to her arm and laid her hand on his. 'There.' Then she kissed him lightly, disaster averted for the moment. 'Now, let's get ready. We mustn't be late. I'm first in the bathroom.'

'But you've only just finished in there.' She didn't even stop to acknowledge his protest. Her mind was on one thing only as she shut the door, locked it and grabbed Will's bracelet from behind the hairbrush that she'd forgotten she'd left there. She ran her finger around it before wrapping it in loo paper and stuffing it into one of the hotel sanitary towel bags. Terry would never look for it in there, not in a million years. She rammed it to the bottom of her wash bag, just to be doubly sure.

22

The Trevarrick library harked back to the days of Rose and Terry's father. One of his passions, before he was almost always too drunk to do much more than prop up the bar and throw what few hotel profits there were down his throat, was reading. He devoted one room in the hotel to his extraordinary collection of natural history, local interest and history books. On the walls not given over to packed bookshelves hung some of his collection of paintings by local artists, several of them famous now, capturing the local sea and landscapes. When Rose, Terry and Daniel had inherited and renovated Trevarrick, Rose had unpacked the others that he'd kept in storage and hung them around the hotel. These were paintings to be enjoyed, not hidden away in case they were stolen.

The first time Rose brought Daniel to Trevarrick, she had been beyond nervous about how he might react to her parents. She needn't have worried. His delight in this part of the south coast of Cornwall coloured his attitude to them. In his book, no one who lived here, as interested in what it had to offer as her father was (or at least had once been), could be as wilfully bad, as negligent as Rose had portrayed them. The first time he entered this room, his eyes had widened. He'd gone straight to the shelves on the left of the bay window. She could picture him standing there now, torn between the view across the garden to the sea, and her father's bird books.

'Look at this.' He'd pulled out Bonhote's *Birds of Britain and their Eggs*, one of her father's favourites. 'Nineteen thirty, and look at these illustrations.' He sat in the window seat, turning the plates with reverence. 'Fantastic.'

After that, she always knew where to find him when he had a

spare moment. He'd be holed up in the library, buried in one of the antique volumes. His love for Trevarrick was sealed in this room. When the three of them decided to make something of the hotel, this was the one room that, beyond essential repair and paintwork, hadn't really changed. The old spring-bound leather chairs were reupholstered so they were better for comfortable reading, the carpet replaced. But the shelves remained the same, and the collection had been a source of fascination to many a hotel guest since, but to Daniel most of all.

Whenever Rose wanted a quiet moment, she would come here too. As a child she'd hide away here when her father was pissed in the bar and her mother 'resting' upstairs. As an adult, she'd come to browse through the books, often finding Daniel following up something he had spotted on a walk, or recently heard about, or adding a new book of his own to the collection. She loved the books too, but her interest lay in the ones containing the botanic prints, always impressed by the devotion with which the painters recorded every detail.

Now she sat quietly in the chair by the window, remembering.

She jumped at the sound of the door handle turning. Groaning inwardly at having to engage with one of the guests before the party began, she was relieved to see Jess.

'Mum! You look gorgeous. New dress?'

'Don't sound so surprised! Simon helped me choose it. He's got a good eye, it turns out. What about yours?'

Jess's boldly flowered mid-calf dress that flared out from a wide belt cinched round her waist was perhaps less of a success.

'Do you like it?' Her daughter gave a twirl.

'Lovely.' Rose was careful. Her daughter was sensitive to anything that might be interpreted as a comment on the baby weight she'd had such trouble shifting.

'Yep. Found it in TK Maxx. Adam thinks I look like a herbaceous border, but I like it.' Jess threw herself into the chair nearest to Rose with a loud sigh. 'Thought I'd find you in here.'

Rose knew from experience how exhausting managing Trevarrick was. Everybody wanted a piece of you all the time, whether staff or guests or suppliers and tradesmen. Even being off-duty didn't deter the demands.

'Not many residents use this room any more.' Jess was thoughtful. 'In fact, I was wondering about getting rid of the books and turning it into a winter sitting room now we're opening up the snug with all that glass. I've seen some gorgeous wallpaper in—'

'You can't do that,' Rose interrupted, horrified. 'The library was put together by your father and your grandfather before that. There are some valuable books here.'

'Exactly. I wouldn't break up the collection, but try to sell it as a whole.'

'Sell what?' Anna stood in the open doorway. The look she'd chosen for the evening bordered on ethereal, and it suited her. Her hair was knotted on the crown of her head so that stray wisps curled around her face. Her long floaty green dress was held up by the thinnest of spaghetti straps and showed off her slight tan. On her feet were the most minimal of sandals, aquamarine varnish on her toenails. Yet again, Rose was struck by the differences between her daughters.

'I saw you coming in here and thought I'd ask if there was anything I could do now I've finished the flowers.' She floated across the room and took the window seat, leaning back on her arms, ankles crossed. 'They look great. You must go and see them, Mum.'

'Actually, everything's done, thanks.' Obviously pleased to be able to refuse the offer, Jess let her arms hang over the sides of the chair.

'That's all right then.' Anna waved at someone through the window. 'Millie,' she explained. 'In leather trousers! Are they part of the dress code? Anyway, sell what? What are you talking about?'

Jess shifted into a more comfy position. She sat sideways in the chair, her legs over the arm. 'Only these old books.' She waved a hand airily to indicate the shelves, just in case Anna was in any doubt.

Anna leaped to her feet at once. 'But you can't!'

'Not you too.' One of Jess's shoes fell to the floor, revealing a small hole in the toe of her tights. She lifted herself up and tugged at the bodice of her dress, which was beginning to gape at the buttons, pulling it straight. 'Anyway, since when were you so interested in what happened to this hotel? Only months ago you wanted Mum to sell it.'

'Not these! Look how wonderful some of them are.' Anna took a book from the shelf, eyes shining, reminding Rose of Daniel's enthusiasm. 'Look at this one. *Beautiful Flowers and How to Grow Them.*' She showed them the grey cloth binding with an art nouveau illustration of three irises, then opened it. 'Horace and Walter Wright. These illustrations are heavenly. You just can't get rid of them on a whim.'

'You'd forgotten all about them,' Jess objected, angry at being told what she could and couldn't do, shades of her father emerging. 'You'd forgotten because you don't care. It's out of sight, out of mind with you. You'll forget Dad before you know where you are.' There was a loaded pause as they all looked at each other, shocked by what she'd said. She rushed onwards as if that would make her words go away. 'And anyway, business comes first. If you're ever going to make a success of yours, you'd better learn that right now.'

'Jess, Jess. There's no need for any of that.' Rose was appalled to hear how heedlessly cruel one of her daughters could be to the other. Jess had the decency to look shamefaced. She heaved herself up and went over to Anna, attempting an affectionate hug, but Anna backed out of her embrace. Her eyes were bright with unshed tears.

'I'm really sorry. I'm so tired, I don't know what I'm saying. Just forget it. Please,' Jess begged. But however sincere her plea, it came too late.

'Forget it?' The hurt trembled in Anna's voice. 'How can I forget it when you say something like that? I'll never forget Dad, never. And at least I was with him when he died.' She ran from the room in a clatter of bangles.

Jess looked as if she'd been slapped. Rose didn't know whether to stay with her or go after Anna. There was enough animosity in the air already. Where had her daughters' extraordinary capacity for rubbing each other the wrong way come from? Usually, as now, it

222

appeared with impeccable timing. And yet mysteriously their relationship always repaired itself. As quickly as the rows started, the sisters would make up, able to obliterate the hurtful things they'd said that left Rose still smarting.

'I deserved that.' Jess took Anna's place on the window seat. 'And you're both right about the books. I know that too really. The hotel wouldn't be the same without the library. I'm getting ahead of myself, and I can't afford to do that at the moment . . .' She busied herself straightening the magazines on the low glass table so Rose couldn't see her expression.

'Perhaps just before the party isn't really the best moment to discuss it.' The last thing Rose wanted right then was more confidences. 'We can do that tomorrow. We should go and see what's happening.' But her attempt at encouragement fell flatter than a pancake. Jess didn't move.

Around them, the hotel was beginning to wake up for the evening: footsteps on the wooden floors, talking in the bar, laughter. Outside, one or two guests drifted across the lawn.

'Mum, there's something I've got to tell you. Not about Anna – I promise I'll make up with her. Promise. She'll understand when I explain.'

Rose doubted it would be that easy, if she knew anything about her other daughter. But she had been wrong before. She said nothing, just waited for Jess to say her piece.

'It's about Adam and me.' The tendency to blush that had embarrassed her so much as a child meant that Jess's chest and throat were suddenly flushed, her cheeks fiery.

Not their marriage too. Could this day possibly get any worse? Were there any members of their family left who hadn't fallen out with one another? Rose's longing for Daniel was suddenly so strong that it hurt. But she had to cope without relying on his leadership or his support. This was how it was to be. Whatever turmoil she was feeling inside, they needed her to appear calm, practical, straight-thinking.

'It's early days,' she said, groping for the right words. 'Marriage needs work, patience. You can't expect moonlight and roses all the way. The only way to get through a bad patch is to talk to each other.' That was hopelessly inadequate, but it was a start.

Jess raised her head, looking mystified. 'Marriage? What are you talking about?' A smile crept across her face. 'I'm not talking about that. I don't think I've ever been happier than I am with Adam. He's the perfect husband. Without him, all this . . . I couldn't. No, it's just . . .' She paused, twisting a bit of her skirt in her hands as she nerved herself to say whatever it was that was troubling her. 'It's just that I'm . . .' She shut her eyes as if Rose was about to exact some terrible punishment.

Rose waited, concentrating on picking at the cuticle of her thumbnail. Resignation, terminal illness, zero bookings, financial ruin – all manner of potential disasters ran through her head. Then . . .

'Pregnant.' There it was. The word fell into the gap between them.

The relief Rose felt was sweet. 'But that's wonderful news, isn't it? A brother or sister for Dylan.' She crossed the room to hug her daughter close. 'I thought you were about to tell me something terrible.'

Jess gave a wry laugh. 'It is wonderful, yes, but . . . just not right now. Not when I'm going to be needed here with all the building work and then we've got the relaunch next spring when the pool's done. And Adam's work is going so well. He's had interest from a couple of galleries in Plymouth and Birmingham. I really want this to go well for him at last, so I need to be able to support us in the meantime.'

Like so many important familial conversations, this one could have been had at a better time. The clock was ticking, and they both needed to be there for Eve and Terry's party as planned. But right now, Jess needed Rose too.

'There's never really a right moment for a baby,' she said, recalling Anna's birth, and her own subsequent decision to become a full-time mother. 'But it always works out in the end. What does Adam say?'

'Adam doesn't know.' The blush deepened.

'He doesn't know?' Rose repeated, shocked. 'But why haven't you told him?'

'I don't know.' Jess started moving the magazines around again. Anything rather than look Rose in the eye. 'I suppose telling him will make it real, and then I'd have to face up to what's happening. That sounds so silly. I know he'll be thrilled, of course. But it's not part of our plan. And I'm worried about how I'll cope with *two* little ones as well as running this place without having Dad to lean on.'

'But you've always got Terry and me, if all else fails.'

Jess laughed. 'Oh Mum! You know I'd always ask you, but . . .' She stopped her tidying at last. 'Well . . .'

'I know. It's not the same. But it isn't for any of us. We're going to have to muddle through to a new way of doing things.'

'Indeed.' Jess cleared her throat pointedly. 'Incidentally, I noticed that's what you've been doing . . .'

'Really? What do you mean?'

'Only you've been out with Simon quite a few times. But I think that's nice.' She qualified herself quickly.

'We're just good friends,' Rose insisted, suddenly embarrassed by trotting out the well-worn cliché. 'He's been an incredible support to me.'

'I know he has. But at least you're going out, trying new stuff. Anna and I don't mind at all.'

What did that mean? That they did? It certainly meant they'd been discussing her. But then what did she expect? Of course, whatever differences divided them, their concern for their old mother would always unite them. Well, there was no need for that. She wasn't intending on being a drain on them. Not in the least. Much more enjoyable for all of them that she had Simon rather than constantly having to nag at them to entertain her.

'Dad was never much interested in classical music or the theatre, so it's been nice to go with someone who loves them and knows something about them,' she justified herself. 'Besides, Simon's great fun and was a good friend of Dad's. We talk about him a lot.'

'I'm sure you do, and it's so good you can. I can see that.' Jess went over to the desk. 'You say Dad wasn't interested, but I meant to give you this.' She opened one of the drawers. 'I found it among the magazines. He must have left it the last time he came.' She took out a large thin book and handed it to her mother.

'What is it?' Rose took it curiously, hungry for another memento of Dan.

'The libretto for *Rigoletto*. Didn't you see that with Simon?'

'Yes, last month.' She remembered well the thrill of being in the Royal Opera House again. 'But this can't be Dad's.' Disbelieving, Rose opened the book at random.

There was a knock, and the maître d' put his head round the door. 'Sorry to interrupt, Jess. But we need to confirm where we're having the canapés and champagne. Do you want them on the terrace, now the wind's dropped?'

Jess looked at her watch. 'I'm so sorry. I lost track of the time. I should have come through to check with you ages ago. I'm coming now. You're all right with that, aren't you, Mum?'

'Of course, darling. Go and do whatever needs to be done. We'll talk more later, or tomorrow.'

Left alone, Rose concentrated on the libretto. Daniel and *Rigoletto*? That didn't make any sense. She had always been surprised that someone with his passion for rock music hadn't widened his taste to include more than just the jazz and blues he had embraced in his later years. He was interested in art and architecture, books and cinema, but he resisted what she regarded as some of the greatest music in the world. How often had she turned off a great concerto when she heard his key in the lock, or stopped a symphony at the end of a movement before he was due back. 'I don't know what you see in that classical nonsense. All that crashing and banging,' he'd joke, the man who still liked Led Zeppelin.

Yet in her hand was the libretto for one of the great operas, the nadir of musical form according to Dan. 'Musical pantomime,' he'd say. 'I just don't get it.' She flipped idly through the pages marked with pencilled annotations. She'd recognise that hasty scrawl anywhere, the way the tails of the g's and y's were cut off before the curl. This was his distinctive writing. The pencil (always a propelling pencil rather than a pen) was faint but the words were quite legible nonetheless, translating, commenting on the text.

Perhaps unknown to her he had had the Damascene moment she'd long hoped for. Maybe he had discovered the pleasure she took in the music and had been planning some kind of surprise for her. She smiled, imagining him reading these words that had probably seemed so alien to him. She ran a finger under a line: *è amor che agl'angeli più ne avvicina!* He'd translated it as 'love takes us towards heaven'. Doing that for her. That his notes ran out halfway through the third act must mean he hadn't got to the end. Distracted by something else? Or more likely he'd just given up.

She flicked back to the title page. There, she found an inked inscription, but this in a different, more feminine hand that used old-fashioned curlicues. Increasingly curious, she read the words, hoping for a clue to what had changed his mind. Someone had written:

Dear Dan, See this as the beginning of your classical education. We'll take the heathen out of you yet!

That nausea, last present during Dan's final days, rose in her throat again. He hadn't been reading it for her at all. After all their years together, someone else had succeeded in igniting his interest where she had failed. Furious, hurt, she slapped the libretto shut. As she did so, her eye caught a pencilled scribble on the inside flap. Before she could open the book again to read it, she had to sit down. The leather creaked as she lowered herself into her father's old swivel chair. Unsteady, the seat pitched slightly towards the desk, the spring squeaking from disuse.

Outside, the partygoers were beginning to gather, despite there being half an hour to go. Someone knocked on the window, but she didn't turn to see who it was. Over the growing buzz of voices, seagulls shrieked.

Rose closed her eyes, let her head fall forward, feeling the stretch in the back of her neck. Once she'd counted to five, she straightened herself up, resolved. She could cope with this. Whatever had happened was over. Whoever 'S' was didn't matter any more. She couldn't have Daniel now.

She opened the libretto again, turning to that opening message. Tearing her eyes away, she looked at the opposite page to see what was written there.

All it said was *S. ROH*. And a date – *2 April*. S. The blood rushed in her ears, blocking out the noise from outside, as the pieces of the puzzle moved towards their rightful places.

She fumbled urgently in her bag for her phone, almost dropping it in her hurry to access her diary. Swiping backwards to April, she found what she was looking for. There, on 2 April, she had noted her date with Simon. He had already booked the tickets, he'd said. Months earlier, to be sure of getting them. Again he had been 'let down' and invited her instead. This time to *Rigoletto* at the Royal Opera House. The excitement of being treated to seats in the grand tier, surrounded by the lamp-lit gold, cream and red of the auditorium, had made her feel like a child again. The background sounds of the orchestra tuning up, that thrilling sense of anticipation, the sweep of the crimson velvet curtain. Beside her the man who had helped her re-engage with the world, who had sympathised and supported, who had talked so knowledgeably about what Daniel had felt about this and that. Their friend. All those times when she'd wondered how he had understood Daniel so well, those times when he had seemed to speak with Daniel's voice.

She battled with her disbelief, her confusion, her anger. This couldn't be true. Not Daniel. Not her husband, the love of her life. At the same time, Simon's own sadness made a horrible sense. It hadn't been his father he was mourning, but Daniel. 'S' wasn't a woman. Inconceivable as it was, S could only stand for Simon.

There was another knock at the window. This time she turned, her vision misty. Jess was signalling at her. 'Are you coming? People are arriving early.' Automatically, she nodded and forced a smile. 'Give me one minute.'

She would need more than a minute to come to terms with this. But with what? She had just jumped to a conclusion from the slightest piece of evidence: a date; an initial. The coincidence was extraordinary, but sometimes coincidences were. This time she wouldn't hesitate, as she had with Daniel, but would follow her instinct immediately. She would talk calmly to Simon, voice her suspicions. Yes, that was what she'd do. If she was wrong, then they would laugh about it. If she wasn't . . .

But first she must find Eve.

23

Eve took a last look in the mirror, turning to see herself from behind. Not bad. Her dress was hip-hugging, but not as tightly as it would have been three months earlier. Her heels were high enough to show off her calf muscles but low enough to be able to walk without risk of breaking an ankle. The new haircut and colour that had cost a London fortune (almost £200! – she'd kept that from Terry) made such a difference, emphasising the planes of her face. Some things were worth the expense. What did Catherine Deneuve once say? After a certain age, a woman should choose between her bottom and her face. Something like that. But who in their right mind would want a large bum? Having lost weight, she looked better than she had for years. Everyone said so.

Terry had gone ahead, spruced up and looking forward to celebrating with their friends, though still obviously disconcerted by her reaction to his present. She couldn't help but think of the last time she'd seen Will. She couldn't remember when she'd last come so rewardingly and repeatedly. At her age too. She hadn't thought such a thing possible any more, that those days had long gone. Sex might not be everything. But it was still a hell of a lot. Yet with Terry, despite their amatory go-slow, she had so much else that they had built in their life together. Sometimes it was easy to forget that. What a bloody mess she was making of all this. She opened the minibar, took out a small bottle of white wine. A snifter for Dutch courage. She unscrewed the top, then hesitated, thinking better of it. A clear head might be advisable this evening. She screwed the top back on and slid the bottle into the fridge.

Refreshing her lipstick for the last time, smoothing her lips together, she left the room.

'Seen Rose anywhere?' Simon was standing at the bottom of the main oak staircase. He looked relaxed, shirt open at the collar.

She shook her head. 'No, I've been upstairs. She's probably over at the marquee by now.'

She watched him go outside, following her suggestion. He was a handsome man who must be at least ten years younger than Rose. Could something deeper than friendship be developing between them? She would never have thought Rose capable of looking at another man after Daniel, especially not so soon, but they had all been surprised by how swiftly she'd become close to Simon. How little one really knew about anyone else. We're a lot like icebergs, she reflected: plenty above the water but much, much more that was invisible, unknowable below.

Pleased with her observation, she went towards the hotel lounge, the room where they'd planned to have pre-dinner drinks if the weather let them down. The pale ochre walls were decorated with work by the local artists of whom Rose was so fond. The concept of a colour scheme to reflect the local landscape throughout the hotel had worked well. Cushions in various shades of blue and green set off the large sandy-coloured sofas and chairs. If it had been up to her, she'd have done away with the driftwood sculpture and the ship's clock, but her and Rose's taste often failed to coincide.

'Eve! Where have you been? I must talk to you.' Rose appeared through the terrace doors. Immediately Eve could see that something was wrong.

'But the party's about to start,' she objected, as a waitress with a tray of empty glasses made her way towards the terrace bar. Not long to go. She took a step after her.

'This won't take long. Quick. Come with me.'

Unable to ignore the urgency in her friend's voice, Eve followed her along the corridor to the library. This had better be good. As soon as the door was shut behind them, Rose picked up a book from the desk, opened it at the title page and thrust it at her. Mystified, Eve took it and listened as Rose detailed her suspicions. When she had finished, both women gazed at each other.

'Are you serious?' Eve was stunned by what she'd heard. The

coincidence, if that was what it was, was indeed extraordinary. But somewhere in the back of her mind, a dim and distant memory was stirring: Edinburgh days; she and Daniel at a party; an overheard snippet of conversation; a suggestion she didn't appreciate.

'I don't know what else to think. But it couldn't be true, could it? Daniel and Simon?' Rose shook her head as if trying to dislodge the idea, wanting Eve to agree. 'Of course, I know people found him attractive. But not like that.'

Eve guided her to the swivel chair, not knowing what to say.

Rose looked up at her, appealing. 'It must be true. What am I going to do?' The words came out as a whisper. 'This is like losing him all over again.'

Eve wanted to console her, to tell her she was mistaken, but she couldn't. Pandora's box had been opened. Almost as long as she'd known him, Daniel's sexuality had occasionally come up as a subject of speculation. That time in Edinburgh, when she'd overheard two men talking about him, certain he'd reciprocate their interest. She'd seen him since at parties, engaged in conversation, not afraid of eye contact, making the man or woman he was talking to feel like they were the only person in the room. He might accompany his words with a confidential wink, a touch on the arm, a warm smile drawing someone to him, making them feel privileged to be in his orbit. He both attracted and intrigued people. But she'd never thought more of it than that.

For the brief time they had been a couple, he'd never shown any sign of being sexually attracted to men. She'd have noticed, wouldn't she? But there had been rumours, chit-chat that she'd ignored. He'd laughed when talking about the goings-on at his Catholic all-boys boarding school, dismissed them as normal, an inevitable result of shutting a lot of pubescent boys away together, just part of what went on there, healthy experimentation, nothing more. Rose knew about that too. But there had also been a whispered-about closeness between him and one of the other male students in their year. Something was rumoured to have happened after Eve had gone off with Will. But that was pure speculation, nothing more. None of them really knew what he got up to in the wake of their affair, before he met Rose, least of all Eve. In public he flirted with everyone, male or female. Though the odd thing had been said, she'd never asked him. Didn't need to. Didn't believe it. Didn't care. If anything, the whispers about his sexuality only added to his charisma. But she did remember the way he'd go to those parties on his own, anonymous, presumably sleeping around – that was when the gossip had really started – until he met Rose.

Then a long-buried memory floated unbidden to the surface. Two men in the shadow of a doorway on the Royal Mile, standing close, their hands touching, kissing. She had been on the other side of the street, on her way home from a party with a gaggle of girls. One of the men had looked briefly in their direction but hadn't seen her. For a second, she thought he was Daniel. She soon forgot the incident, believing she had mistaken someone else for him. But perhaps she hadn't.

'Whatever he did, he loved you. I know he did.' Of that much she was certain.

'But you don't actually know, do you?' Rose sounded so world-weary. 'None of us knows what anyone else is really thinking or feeling, whatever they say. Not even the people you're closest to. How can you possibly know? Actions are meant to speak louder than words, but in fact they can be just as deceptive.'

How strange that Rose should echo her earlier thoughts so closely. There they were, two women with three marriages between them and to three very different men, each one of whom had surprised them in different ways. Eve had even made love to all of them, but knew them no better for that.

'Of course I don't. Except we could all see that he did. You mustn't doubt that.'

'Of course I'm doubting it.' Rose was almost shouting, made frantic by her discovery. 'He was having an affair with a man, for Christ's sake!'

'You don't know that.' Eve was cautious, trying to calm Rose despite her own unease. Feeling uncomfortably hot, she went to open the window a fraction.

'But I do. It explains so much of what's happened since. I must have been blind.' Rose slapped the libretto on to the desktop. 'I'm going to have to talk to Simon. I must know.'

'Not tonight?' Eve was instantly ashamed that her first thought was entirely selfish; not for Rose, but for the success of their party.

Rose gave her a sympathetic smile. 'Don't worry. I won't spoil things.'

'Are you two coming?' Terry spoke through the open window. 'People are beginning to arrive, and the first minibus is due in five minutes.'

'Eve, come and see the bar we've set up outside. Anna's flowers are fabulous.' Jess was right behind him, as if nothing had been wrong. 'I want to be sure you approve.'

'I'm sure I will.' Eve touched one of her aquamarine earrings. 'We'd lost track of the time. Coming?' She turned to Rose.

'I'll go upstairs for a moment and then I'll join you.' Rose picked up the libretto and moved towards the door.

'Oh Mum. You knew what time it started.' Jess hated it when her arrangements weren't observed to the letter. Flexibility was not a gift with which she'd been blessed. 'Don't be long.'

As Terry and Jess's attention transferred to something happening behind them, Rose and Eve hugged.

'We'll talk in the morning. I'm sure . . .' Eve whispered. But both of them knew that it couldn't be as straightforward as that.

The party was well under way. The lobster had arrived in time, and the simple but extravagant meal that began with asparagus and ended with raspberries (carrying the sort of carbon footprint that would outrage Terry, had he but known) was pronounced a huge success. The air was balmy, and any threat of rain had blown over. Fairy lights swung in the trees and tea lights illuminated the path between the hotel and the marquee, where the dancing had started. The cousins, led by Anna and Charlie, had been first on the floor, along with a couple of Eve and Terry's friends. Jess and Adam had soon joined them. Rose was glad to see the girls' differences patched up, although for the life of her she couldn't understand how they'd overcome them so speedily. It was easier not to ask. As the drink went down, inhibitions were cast aside, and the dance floor was now crowded with 'oldsters' (as Anna still would have them). Those old favourite songs had couples who clearly only danced once or twice a year still doing the same old moves they'd barely modified since their teens. Knees creaked as the braver among them twisted to a squat, occasionally having to be helped up by their partner. The noise of music and voices emerged from the marquee, growing more raucous by the minute.

Rose stood under a tree watching. Every conversation she'd had that evening had been a struggle. She could feel the sympathy for her – 'recently widowed in such tragic circumstances' – coming off people in waves. Eve and Terry had obviously done a thorough job briefing their friends to spare embarrassment. She did her best, but she felt the impatience of those she talked to, dying to get away to have fun with someone else. It was one of those parties where there was always someone more interesting standing behind her. But despite every effort, she couldn't be fun tonight. Not even under the influence. Never had she felt less like celebrating.

Not far from her was a rowdy bunch she didn't know; obviously good friends come outside for a smoke. They fell about laughing at a joke. The smell of the cigarettes filled the air. She stepped backwards into the shadows as she saw Simon come into the garden. He stopped for a moment by the open flap of the marquee, stretched his arms above his head and looked around him, nodding amiably at the smokers. A man without a care in the world. A man who had become her friend. Rose was suddenly choked with rage. Who the hell did he think he was, worming his way into their family, exploiting their trust at a time when they were so vulnerable? She had believed in him, opened up to him about Daniel, listened to his memories too. But how much had he left unsaid? If only he'd stuck to designing the hotels and stayed out of their lives. That should have been enough for him. What could he have been thinking when he first asked her to the opera? Had it really been the impulsive gesture he claimed? Or was being close to his family his way of staying close to Dan? Daniel – his lover? The thought made her sick to her stomach.

So far that evening she had managed to avoid Simon altogether by making sure she was always busy talking to someone whenever he came near. But the effort of making conversation was eventually too much for her. One more word about a 'simply marvellous' holiday, a teenager on a gap year or another 'absolutely adorable' grandchild and she'd scream. She'd had to leave the marquee.

Simon looked at his watch, brushed something from the thigh of his trousers, then began to walk towards the hotel. He passed close to where Rose was standing. She held her breath, pressing herself into the shadow of the tree. He stopped again, half turning towards the marquee as if hoping to see something, someone – her? She was only a few feet away from him.

The urge to jump out and physically attack him was almost irresistible. She longed to rip the fine linen shirt from his back, to punch him as hard as she could, hurting him for hurting her so badly. For hurting them. For not only Daniel's betrayal of her, but for his. Only the knowledge that she'd be ruining Eve and Terry's party stopped her. Besides, seeing their mother scrapping on the lawn was not the way she wanted the girls to find out. If they needed to find out at all.

Unable to see her, half hidden by the tree, Simon continued up the path, whistling under his breath. Everything about him was so well put together. She ached to disrupt that relaxed but considered style that she had thought she liked so much. She *had* liked it. Could she possibly have made a mistake? She simply couldn't imagine Daniel betraying her like this. But everything pointed that way.

She sank into a squat as the energy drained from her legs. Perhaps she should follow Simon to have it out now while everyone else was otherwise occupied. She had to know. The slightest uncertainty was torture. Twisting her wedding ring round her finger, she looked towards the marquee. Just inside, she glimpsed Jess and Adam dancing, their arms around each other, oblivious to the others around them. Jess's face was tipped up to his, saying something; Adam, with his head slightly on one side, was looking down at her, his customary thoughtful expression transformed with a smile, his hands resting comfortably on the curve of her spine. Eve came into view, laughing as Terry spun her under his arm in an improvised jive. They seemed to be getting along fine again. Perhaps Eve had seen sense. Perhaps Terry had confessed and they'd cleared the air. Let at least one of those be the case.

Around them, the other couples came together and separated, happy, laughing, touching, shouting and whispering. Couples. Something Rose wouldn't be part of again. She didn't want anyone else but the Daniel she had known. To think she had even slightly flirted with the idea of Simon. There were Anna and Charlie, jumping as if they were on the pogo sticks they had loved as children. Behind them, Millie, Tom, Luke and his new girl-friend. Again she longed to wind the clock back. But now every-thing was different. Ruined. She wasn't half of a well-loved couple, not one of the crowd, any more.

She straightened up. The night was getting chilly. She stepped out on to the illuminated path. Someone waved at her from the marquee. Terry. He shouted something, but his words were lost in Sister Sledge's 'We Are Family'. She waved back and started towards the hotel.

Maybe everyone else had known. Maybe they'd been laughing about her blind stupidity for years. How could she not have known? All those times Daniel was away on business, the times she had stayed at home while he met up with a friend or a business associate for drinks. What had he really been doing? He must have left clues, if only she had been alert to them. And then he came home to her, to their bed, as if nothing was wrong. But nothing *had* been wrong. Their sex life was as fulfilling as she had needed it to be. It had satisfied them both. So it had slowed up a bit in recent years, but wasn't that what happened to most married couples? Why should she have suspected anything? If only she'd never picked up his bloody phone by mistake, if she hadn't seen that text, then she wouldn't be going through this. But now she could imagine Simon sending his message on the spur of the moment, relaying his feelings as they occurred to him. That was how it would have been. How much easier it would be not to know. But now she had to.

There was only one person who could tell her the truth. She had trusted Simon with her most private feelings about Daniel's death. She had even confided in him how much she missed their Saturday-afternoon siestas, spent in bed with champagne and an old film. Her head throbbed with rage as she thought of everything she had told him. The least he could do was tell her all she wanted to know. As she neared the main building, she saw him through the window, sitting alone at the bar, nursing a glass of whisky.

She quickened her pace.

24

Eve was enjoying herself. The music was loud, the drink was flowing, people were having a good time. She hadn't wanted a staid standing-around drinks party, but something where her friends would feel able to let go. And that was what was happening. The tables, decorated with Anna's wild-flower posies, were littered with bottles, glasses and coffee cups. The meal had been extravagant and delicious but simple. As the evening progressed, the noise level had risen and she sensed things were going well.

She had deliberately kept a check on how much she drank so she could make sure everyone had a good time. As importantly, she didn't want to make a fool of herself in front of her few precious clients that they had invited. Not that she needed to worry. Laurie Murray, one of her longest-standing teen-lit authors, was sailing at least five sheets to the wind and coming into harbour beside her right then.

'Great party, Eve.' Laurie's eyelids were at half-mast, revealing the streaks of eye make-up congealed along the hollows. Similarly, her lipstick had bled into the tiny wrinkles around her mouth. For a wildly inappropriate moment, Eve was reminded of a cat's arse. She banished the thought, putting out a hand in support as Laurie lurched sideways.

'Glad you're having a good time.' Laurie had collapsed so that she was half sitting on one of the chairs. Eve sat beside her, amused to imagine what Laurie's adoring tribe of under-fifteen readers would think if they could see her now.

'We are.' Laurie waved a hand in the vague direction of her husband, who, wine glass in hand, looked faintly alarmed at his wife's progress. 'But Eve,' she said, leaning forward, looking intent, waving a finger under Eve's nose, 'there's something I've been meaning to say to you.'

'Really?' Eve tried to sound her most interested.

Laurie straightened herself on the chair. 'Now what have I done with my bag?' She grasped a fabric tie that led under her vast corseted behind to a bag of infinitesimal proportions, from where she retrieved a lipstick and small mirror. Eve waited nervously while her prized client attempted to cover up the wine stains on her lips. After she'd wiped a dab of red from one of her front teeth, Laurie started again. 'Now. Yes. I just want you to know how glad we are, and I know I speak for more than one of your authors, that you're coming through that bad patch. I, for one, have no intention of leaving the sinking ship. And I want you to know that.'

Eve couldn't help laughing as she grasped the other woman's hand. 'Thank you, Laurie. Though I'm not sure that I want to be thought of as a sinking ship.'

A look of embarrassment crossed Laurie's generous features as she realised what she'd said. She opened her mouth, but Eve stopped her.

'I'm as afloat as I ever was. All we need is one or two new crew members and we'll weather the storm.' This extended sailing metaphor finally defeated her.

Laurie lurched forward to give her a kiss on the cheek. 'Darling, you're quite wonderful. And that dress looks wonderful too. You'll have to tell me your secret. You must have lost pounds.'

'Well, there's something to be said for anxiety.' Eve extricated herself from her client's slightly sweaty embrace. 'We'll talk about it another time.'

But Laurie was there to stay. She leaned forward again, about to speak. Eve made an effort to look engaged, although her foot was tapping to the Beach Boys' 'California Dreaming'.

'Mum! At the risk of embarrassing us both, d'you fancy a dance?' Luke had come up behind them and was standing with his hand held out for her. He'd got rid of his jacket and tie and was looking, if she thought so herself, extremely fit. His hair was tied back high on his head in the topknot that she'd quite come round to. The scar

240

remaining from his cleft palate operation was barely noticeable thanks to his carefully trimmed designer stubble. And six feet one, too.

'We're talking, darling,' she pointed out as if he was six, while wanting desperately to take up his offer of rescue. If she knew Laurie, this conversation was likely to go round and around in circles.

'No, you go,' protested Laurie, standing uncertainly. 'I'll find Teddy.' With that, she set off across the floor, swerving past the dancers, to rejoin her other half.

Luke was already swaying to the Beach Boys, waiting for Eve to join in. 'What dinosaur put this playlist together? You must have been dancing to all this stuff when you were at uni.'

'We did,' Eve admitted, as, out of practice, she tried to get in some sort of groove, following Luke's example but not quite keeping up. Another drink would help. But no. 'And the playlist was down to Millie and Dad. It's meant to appeal to everyone, and look . . .' she cast around at the gyrating middle-aged couples and the few cooler members of the younger generation, 'it does the job.' Although, seeing her friends through his eyes, they all looked slightly tragic. But who cared? They were having a fun, and that was what mattered.

Luke raised his perfectly shaped eyebrows and gave the smile that she knew would break many a girl's heart before he'd done. They abandoned themselves to the dance. Five minutes later, her shoes had been thrown to the side and she was dancing in a circle with all four of her children as the music segued from one golden oldie to another. Everyone was on their feet. Whatever Luke said, Terry and Millie had done an excellent job. For as long as she was dancing, Eve didn't care what she looked like. Being on the dance floor with the others like this was fun. She stepped back and bumped into her bookkeeper, who was dancing on his own, eyes closed, while his wife was shaking it out with their foreign rights agent. Yes, you didn't have to be rip-roaring drunk to have a good time, Eve conceded, surprised at herself.

As the final chords of 'I will Survive' faded, Eve took herself to the side of the floor, leaving her children to do whatever choreographed group dance they had down for the next track. She found her shoes and tried to slip them on, but the straps cut into her puffy feet. Abandoning the struggle, she carried them over to the bar, joining a band of friends who had gathered there. Standing there, ignoring the nagging ache in her right knee, enjoying the congratulations and good will, she felt completely at home, surrounded by the people who were the warp and weft of her life. From university, to the school gate, to her and Terry's workplaces, there wasn't one person in the marquee who hadn't been involved in some part of their lives together.

The only person missing was Daniel. Dear Daniel. How he would have enjoyed all this. The whole thing had been his idea after all. Perhaps this was the sort of bash he would have preferred to the modest long winter weekend in Casa Rosa that he and Rose had hosted for the family when they'd hit their own silver anniversary. The celebratory family meal at Giovanni's had been delicious, but modest. She glanced around the marquee for Rose, suddenly aware that she hadn't been keeping an eye on her. Jess and Anna were on opposite sides of the dance floor. But there was no sign of their mother.

Whatever her friend was going through right now, Eve wanted to support her however she could. Rose must have left the steamy atmosphere of the marquee for some fresh air. Eve imagined her returning to her room, like an injured animal licking her wounds alone. What she must be feeling was unimaginable. To discover your husband was having an affair was one thing, but a homosexual affair . . . All those feelings of anger and betrayal must be compounded by self-doubt and inadequacy. Poor Rose.

'I'll be back in a minute.' Excusing herself, Eve negotiated her way outside through the tables and disordered chairs. The air felt pleasantly cool on her shoulders, the grass already damp underfoot as she walked back to the hotel. The lights beamed out of the lower rooms, while upstairs, curtains were tightly drawn. She couldn't see anyone in the bar or the dining room. Instead she ran upstairs and along the corridor to Rose's room. She put her ear to the door. Ridiculous. What did she expect to hear? She knocked gently.

'Rose?' she said as loudly as she dared. 'Rose? It's me, Eve. Are you all right?'

Nothing.

She tapped again. 'Rose?'

Still silence. Rose must be in bed. She couldn't blame her. She'd have offered her a Diazepam if only she'd thought. Eve headed back to the party. At the top of the stairs, by the large oil painting of St Ives harbour, she hesitated. Everyone had admired her sandals. Those who hadn't weren't going to now. Why not change into something more comfortable for dancing? She backtracked past Rose's room, stopping for a second outside it again, then hurried on to her own and Terry's.

Opening the door, she chucked her sandals on the bed. She resisted the temptation to throw herself alongside them, and bent to pull out her oldest pair that she'd brought along just in case. The glitter had all but faded from them (a bit like their owner, she reflected), but she had restuck a couple of sequins that had been hanging on by their last threads and . . . they would do. As she slipped them on, her feet giving up thanks as she did, she heard her BlackBerry. The phone lay where she'd left it with her make-up in the bathroom. Who would be calling her this late? Everyone knew it was the day of their party. She checked the caller ID and almost dropped the phone – Will. Suppose Terry had picked it up. She thought she had covered every base, making sure Will understood that he wasn't ever to call her on this number except in a real emergency. But she shouldn't have given it to him at all. Was the fact that she had significant, a sign that her subconscious was working overtime? Deep down did she want Terry to find out? If he did, everything would be in the open and . . . then what? She couldn't bear to think about the turmoil and hurt the discovery would cause. But Terry wasn't here. He was downstairs enjoying himself.

'Hello.' She whispered the word as if there was a danger of being overheard.

'How's it going, babe?'

How she hated Will calling her that, as if she was a woman half her age. He meant to flatter her, but in fact the word made her feel like Grandma Moses and him sound like a superannuated Lothario.

'I had a feeling you'd be there.' His voice was full of longing.

'What are you doing calling me now? It's complete chance that I was up here. You know the party's tonight.' Then, worried that she'd sounded too sharp, she added, 'We said we'd talk tomorrow, that I'd call you when I could get away.'

His breathing was in her ear as if the phone was pressed up close to his mouth. Her stomach cartwheeled. She sat on the lid of the loo, shutting her eyes and stretching her legs out in front of her, flexing her feet.

'I couldn't wait.' His pleasure at having reached her was obvious. 'Simple as that. Just wanted to hear your voice.'

She opened her eyes, only to notice the varicose vein that trailed across her shinbone like a knotted blue worm. She pressed at it with her free hand to make it disappear, but it sprang back, resistant. She bent her knees so she couldn't see it any longer.

'But darling, you can't call me when I'm with Terry. That's one of our rules.'

'Rules are for breaking, Evie. Otherwise why have them?'

She heard the chink of ice cubes in his drink and pictured him stretched out on his soft black leather sofa, navy-blue (only) silk-socked feet on one end, his head propped against a cushion at the other, raising his glass. The murmur of music was just audible in the background.

'Anyway, I couldn't resist trying. And now I'm glad I did.'

She could feel herself melting under his attention. But she couldn't talk to him. Not now. She glanced at Terry's bracelet gleaming on her wrist, at his toothbrush next to hers.

'I've been thinking of all the things we could have been doing if you were here instead.' His voice reminded her of warm dark treacle. He gave a little groan that all but did for her.

If only she *could* be with him. Some of the things they had done together only days earlier swam into her mind, making her giddy with longing as she remembered the more intimate detail. She had surprised even herself with a flexibility she didn't know she still possessed, and she couldn't help wondering what other positions he had tucked away in his repertoire. At the same time, she knew where she belonged right now. With her family.

'This isn't right, Will.' Yes, she must be firm. 'I can't talk to you now.'

'When can we talk then? I need you here, with me. You belong here.'

Eve peered at herself in the mirror. Instead of the young woman she had once been, the young woman that Will brought out in her, a middle-aged woman stared back. However flirtatious and girlie she felt inside, the outside was never going to change – only age more. She put an elbow on the grey marble counter, knocking her SP20 super-restorative day cream to the floor, and rested her forehead on her fist. This was utter madness, but . . .

'I'll call you tomorrow and we'll fix something then. Promise.' She knew she'd keep that promise, however difficult it would be to find a moment on her own. She couldn't resist him. 'I must go. They'll be wondering where I am.'

'I guess I'll have to be satisfied with that then.' But there was a smile in his voice. She had pacified him. Until the next time.

They said their goodbyes and she sat staring at her BlackBerry, the bringer of good news and bad. She had got herself in far too deep. Whatever she decided to do would hurt one of them: Terry or Will. Choosing between them was impossible.

She got up and ran the tap, to hold a cold flannel to her cheeks, then to the back of her neck. Having repaired the resulting damage to her make-up, she stowed her phone in the pocket of her suitcase, somewhere Terry would never look, with the ringtone off. If she underestimated her husband and he did find it, at least there was no text trail for him to follow. She had made sure of that by only contacting Will through her office email or phone. The BlackBerry was only for emergencies – she thought she'd made that plain.

Locking the door, she stood for a second, head held high,

shoulders back and down, stomach in, back straight. Deep breath. Right. She was ready to face the fray.

Back in the marquee, she rejoined her friends at the bar. If anything, the music was louder than before, the dancing more frenzied. Someone pressed another glass into her hand. An ex-colleague of Terry's engaged her in a paralysingly dull exchange about the benefits of train travel to Cornwall. Behind her, two of her friends were discussing a third at the tops of their voices.

'Her husband doesn't suspect a thing,' yelled one of them.

Eve froze, horrified. How had they found out?

'When's she going to tell him?' said the second, struggling to make herself heard. 'Surely he'll guess? You can't keep something like that secret.'

There was a rushing in Eve's ears as the cold hand of panic gripped her in a stranglehold.

'When they get to the airport. Not till then.'

What? She glanced over her shoulder. Annie, an old family friend, overflowing from a tight purple satin sheath that might have graced the wardrobe of *Strictly*, was shaking her head as her companion, comparatively dowdy in a patterned dress Eve recognised from a mail-order catalogue, caught Eve looking in their direction.

'Eve,' she shrieked. 'We were wondering where you'd got to. I was just telling Jenny that Susie's planning a surprise holiday for Pete. They're going when he's finished this terrible child abuse case he's involved with.'

'Isn't it marvellous? I'd be bound to be found out if I tried anything like that on Charles. He's far too quick,' said Annie, her bosom shaking like a milk blancmange as she laughed.

'Really?' Eve said weakly as the final chords of Coldplay drew to a close. The dance floor thinned out as a slow number Eve didn't recognise took over. 'How lovely.' She turned back to the conversation.

'Space on your dance card?' Terry was at her elbow. She raised her spritzer to her lips. She could see the danger signals: the flushed cheeks, the pinkish rims to his eyes, the wine-stained lips. For all his disapproval of her 'inappropriate' drinking, Terry knew how to enjoy himself when the time was right. Earlier, she had spotted him dancing with one of their neighbours, a young blonde woman who'd lived alone with her young son since her husband went off with the local hairdresser. Drink might make him flirtatious but Terry was a one-woman man. Of that she was confident. Just as confident as Rose had been in Daniel, it occurred to her. But he was waiting.

'I do seem to be free,' she said, taking his hand and following his lead. To begin with they danced separately, and out of synch. A sense of rhythm was not one of the blessings gifted to Terry at birth, though his enthusiasm made up for it. She caught sight of Charlie saying something to Anna, who nodded towards them and giggled. Now that they were one of only five or six couples left on the dance floor, but the only one not in a clinch, Eve began to feel self-conscious. As if reading her thoughts, Terry reached for her and pulled her into his embrace. She shut her eyes and tried not to think of Will.

'What a party.' The smell of red wine on his breath made her turn her head away. 'You've done it all brilliantly, darling.'

She was about to explain how Jess was really the guiding force when he tightened his grip.

'We need to talk.' The urgency in his voice made her pull back to look at him. His earnest expression gave her a sense of foreboding. Their young blonde neighbour. Could the bracelet have been more of a farewell than a celebration? Had she completely misjudged him? Could he be going to pip her to the post and announce he was leaving her? Being so wrapped up in her own affair had made her ignore what must have been going on under her nose. She felt oddly panicky despite knowing how ridiculous the idea was. Guilt was making her imagine things.

'Not now, though?' She gestured at the party around them. 'We've got the rest of the weekend.'

But the drink had given him courage. She could see it in his eyes. He had chosen his moment and he was determined to have it.

'Come into the garden, somewhere quiet – just for a minute.' He took her hand and guided her out of the marquee.

'Terry! What are you doing? We can't leave the party now.'

'It won't take long, and anyway no one will notice. This way.' He led her through the bushes towards the secluded stone folly on the opposite side of the hotel. A mini Graeco-Roman temple, built many years ago on a whim of his grandfather, its fluted pillars and domed roof coupled with the palm trees now silhouettes at its side giving the impression of being somewhere in the Mediterranean. Away from the more formal garden, the ground was rockier, with clumps of thrift and little white daisies pushing up where they could. In the distance, Eve could hear the crash of the waves on the rocks. High tide.

'We haven't been here for a long time.' The single spotlight outside dimly illuminated the interior. Terry was brushing the seat with his hand. Then, with a flourish, he gestured that she should sit down.

Wishing she was wearing something warmer, she took her seat, and waited for him to begin.

25

By the time Rose reached the bar, Simon was ensconced in a corner, in one of the large armchairs angled towards the window. From there he had a view of the marquee, but also, beyond the clifftop, of the inky darkness over the sea, sporadically lit by the moon. She could just see the top of his head, heard the sound of his glass hitting the glass tabletop, the page of a magazine turning. He was alone, apart from the barman, who had taken a stool behind the bar and was absorbed in a well-thumbed paperback.

Nervous but determined, buoyed up by her rage, she cleared her throat.

Startled, Simon peered around the wing of his chair. His face lit up when he registered who was there.

'Rose! I'd given up trying to talk to you. You've been so busy. If I were paranoid, I'd say you'd been deliberately avoiding me.' He laughed easily, confident that couldn't be the case. 'The dress looks great, especially with those shoes. Are they new?' He didn't wait for her reply. 'Can I get you a drink?' He lifted a finger to hail a non-existent waiter, then realised and lowered it.

'I'll get my own, thanks.'

She didn't miss his look of bewilderment at the animosity in her voice.

'Have I done something? I think you should tell me if I have.' But not really believing that whatever it was could be anything serious, he half returned his attention to his reading.

She didn't grace him with a reply. Now that the moment of confrontation had arrived, she was experiencing a sudden loss of nerve. Asking for the truth would make her conclusions real. And just suppose she had got it all completely wrong. The hope, however faint, that she might have paralysed her. If that was the case, her new and, until now, precious friendship with Simon would be ruined for ever. But if he was responsible for her last terrible days with Daniel, then she owed it to herself. *Miss. Love. Come back.*

Her silence unnerved him. 'Rose. For God's sake, what's wrong?' He threw down the magazine and twisted his body so he leaned round over the arm of the chair, expecting her to answer.

But Rose didn't reply as she walked over and sat down to face him, her back to the window. Her mouth was dry. She ran her tongue round her teeth and swallowed, as she prepared to speak. She saw him in a new light now – this impeccable, handsome younger man who had drawn Daniel into his orbit. Daniel had always been easily flattered by the interest of someone younger, someone good-looking, particularly if they had the added bonus of being urbane and intelligent. Simon leaned towards her, his brow furrowed as he tried to work out the reason for this sudden unprovoked hostility.

She waited, wishing the nausea would leave her, as the barman brought over her Perrier and carefully orientated a place mat so the illustration of the hotel faced the right way. He seemed to take an age to get it precisely right. Then at last he left them. Simon raised an eyebrow, inviting an explanation.

'How could you?' She was surprised to hear the toughness in her voice as her resolve returned.

A look of puzzlement crossed his face. 'How could I what?' he asked. He clearly hadn't a clue what she was talking about. 'Rose, what's this all about? Put me out of my misery, please. What am I meant to have done?' He gave the small smile that until now had bonded them.

But there was something in that smile that she saw now for the first time: a reliable winning charm that infuriated her. Any remaining reserve vanished as everything that she wanted to say clamoured to be let out.

'First of all,' she began, doing her best to keep her voice level, 'I want you to explain why you've abused the trust of our family. What kind of a person does something like that?' She heard her voice catch. Praying he hadn't noticed, she bit the inside of her lip until the pain focused her. 'You disgust me. I can hardly bear to sit here with you.'

'What are you talking about?' He stretched both hands out in appeal, his frown deepening. 'I still don't understand. I thought we were friends.'

'So did I, and that's what hurts.' If he thought that pretending ignorance – if that was what he *was* doing – was the way to convince her, she would show him how very wrong he was.

This time he said nothing. He looked to the ceiling before crossing his legs. He tilted his foot and examined his shoe, which gleamed under the light. Rose waited. He shifted in his seat, uncomfortable under her fierce inspection, then raised his face to look at her. His head to one side, his eyes finally met hers. She could see only bafflement there. Either she had made a terrible mistake, or he must be supremely confident in the safety of his secret. She needed to be more direct.

'I know, Simon.' She refused to look away, and was rewarded by the sudden unease that crossed his face. Her hands were clasped so tightly together they hurt. 'I know,' she repeated, twisting her wedding ring round her finger.

'Know what?' He drained his whisky and uncrossed his legs as if he was going to get up and walk away. Then he hesitated. His expression changed again, as disbelief then alarm were superseded by self-confidence. That look said she couldn't possibly have found out. Not possibly.

Rose read each emotion, each thought, as clearly as if he'd spoken them.

'I still haven't a bloody clue what you're talking about,' he protested, but less insistently than before.

That reaction was enough to spur her on. She was fighting him for her marriage and needed the truth, however much it hurt.

'I know about you and Daniel.' Her voice was little more than a whisper, but the effect of her words was instantaneous.

He jerked backwards. His face paled to the colour of parchment. He swallowed, darting his eyes round the room, looking anywhere but at her. But he wasn't beaten yet. He recovered himself quickly. '*What* about us? You're talking in riddles, Rose.' He sounded self-assured, even aggressive, as he challenged her to confront him, to accuse him out loud, to say the unimaginable. But Rose wasn't going back down now.

'Did you love him?' she asked, dreading the answer.

He stood up abruptly, knocking the drinks table with his leg, and went to the window. His reflection stared back at them both from the darkness beyond, gaunt and frightened. 'That's a preposterous question.' But his voice was tired. The game was up.

'Did you love him?' she repeated. 'You might as well tell me, Simon. You see, I found the libretto. He'd written in it. I've worked it all out. You gave me Daniel's ticket to the opera, didn't you?'

He nodded his head, just once, capitulating at last. 'Yes,' he said. 'Yes. If you must know. I did.'

Rose's pulse was beating like a jackhammer. She took a sip of water.

'Did he love you?' How asking that question hurt. But it was the one to which she most needed an answer. Without that knowledge, she couldn't go on.

This time, he turned to her. 'I think I need another drink for this. You?'

She nodded her assent, grateful for a moment to prepare herself for his reply. Having reached this point, a strange calm had settled over her. Simon crossed to the bar, ordered from the barman, then returned and sat down with two whiskies. He slid one across to her, keeping his gaze down. This time, whether from shame or anger, he couldn't meet her eye.

'Well, did he?' she insisted. 'Love you, I mean.'

At last he raised his head, but his eyes had a faraway look in them, as if he was remembering another time. Rose was shocked by the sadness and longing that she saw there. He shook his head, refocusing his gaze on her. For a moment, he pressed his lips together as if he wasn't going to speak. Then he thought better.

'No,' he said, briefly closing his eyes as if in pain. 'No, I don't think he did.'

Rose's thoughts were racing. So everything she had most feared was true. Daniel had had an affair. But with Simon. With a man. She still didn't know whether that made it better or worse, but at least she didn't have to live any longer in the aching ignorance of his lover's identity. Simon really *was* 'S'. And perhaps he was telling the truth. Perhaps Daniel really hadn't loved him. She wanted to believe that more than anything. Nothing she had found had proved otherwise. Whatever she felt, with her new knowledge came an unexpected sense of relief as everything about her terrible last days with Daniel fell into place for the first time. Of course he hadn't confessed to her. Now she understood a little better what had happened between them. He must have been terrified of her reaction. Ashamed too, perhaps. Other than her shock and disbelief, he would have foreseen her anger, the crucifying self-doubt and the pain he would inflict. But if Daniel hadn't reciprocated Simon's feelings, then perhaps he had never stopped loving her. Perhaps that was what he meant when he'd said 'It's not what you think': words she had puzzled over since.

'I think you'd better tell me everything, don't you?' The anger she'd felt before knotted in her throat, tight and controlled. To think she had liked this man, trusted him, had even entertained ideas of there being more to their relationship one day than mere friendship. The thought made her skin crawl.

'I don't know where to start.' He sounded utterly defeated, so broken that, for a brief moment, Rose almost pitied him. But any sympathy left her as quickly as it had come.

'At the beginning, I think. Let's start with where you met.'

'Must we do this now?' He gestured towards the party that was in full swing outside. Various partygoers entered and exited the marquee. The group of smokers she'd watched had begun dancing on the grass. The fairy lights bobbed in the trees.

'Yes,' she said firmly. However much she'd prefer to be out there with her family, getting this over was way more important to her right now. 'We won't be seeing each other again after tonight.'

He shook his head, took a sip of his whisky, then a deep breath, and began. 'It was through Michael Heston, owner of the Court-house Hotel in Edinburgh. He's an old friend of mine. I'd re-designed the hotel for him when he bought it. He introduced me to Daniel at the opening, knowing he was looking for an architect to renovate the Arthur. We met to discuss his ideas and I went to see the place for myself. We had a lot in common. But you don't need to know all that . . .' He broke off.

Perhaps she didn't, but if she was to understand Daniel and their marriage then she had to. Without that understanding, she wouldn't be able to move on. She took one of the cushions from behind her and hugged it to her stomach. 'I do,' she said.

'Then you need to know that I was married too. Some years ago.'

She failed to hide her gasp of surprise.

'Only briefly,' he qualified, looking away from her as he went on, talking quickly as if to get it over with. 'Jackie and I met at school, stayed together and married partway through my degree. Looking back, I knew deep down that I was gay but was too scared to acknowledge it. My family, especially my father, would have been horrified. He was a small-minded bigot, a local bank manager and upstanding pillar of the community where I grew up: a big fish in a small local pond where everything functioned as it should. Nothing out of the ordinary tolerated, unless behind tightly drawn curtains and locked doors.' He gave a wry smile. 'And as it turned out, I was right. I believed that I loved Jackie. I really did. But subconsciously, I suppose I must have been hoping that by marry-ing her, she would somehow save me from myself. And of course she couldn't. That was a terrible thing to do to anyone.' He lifted his glass to his lips and swallowed. 'After only a couple of years, I couldn't pretend any longer. I met someone – a man who . . .' He stopped. 'Again, the detail's not important. But I couldn't deny who I really was any more. The whole story came out. Jackie and I divorced. You can imagine how the local gossips loved it, as well as the public humiliation and shame felt by my father.'

'Did you have any children?' Rose asked, absorbed in his story despite herself, almost forgetting the reason for his telling it.

He gave a short laugh. 'No. Thank God. That would have made everything even worse. Hurting her like that was bad enough. Her family, too. Predictably, my father disowned me, and my mother, who was devoted to him, followed suit. They had to, to save face. At least that's how they saw it. However much she loved me, her marriage to him came first. I understand that better now than I did then.' He paused, giving them both time to remember Daniel. 'My brother tried to keep the channels of communication open, but it was quickly made plain to him that he would receive the same treatment if he persevered. He's a weak man, who still lived there and was part of the same community. He didn't want any trouble. So that was that.'

'But haven't you tried to talk to them?' Rose was incredulous, unable to understand how a family could turn its back on one of its members. Surely the whole point of a family was to support one another. The parents had to be the ones who set the example. The unresolved argument between Daniel and Jess flashed into her mind.

'At the beginning I did,' he explained, eager for her understanding now he saw he had her interest. 'But if nothing else, my father was a stubborn man who never went back on anything he said. Letters to my mother were returned unopened. Christmas cards too. If I called, they hung up the phone. Eventually I gave up and moved to Edinburgh. I never saw him again.'

Rose wondered at the lack of affection in the way he referred to them as 'mother' and 'father', remembering the grief she'd witnessed at Daniel's memorial. How much of that had been for his father and his past, and how much for Daniel?

'He died,' said Simon. 'An old friend from home contacted me in January. My family couldn't even bring themselves to tell me. That's how bad things are. When I called, my brother told me they'd had the funeral without me. I wasn't welcome. So there's no going back for me. Not even now.'

'And Daniel?' Her voice hardened. 'What has any of this got to do with him?'

'Ah, Daniel.' Simon's shoulders dropped. 'I don't know what to say to you, Rose. We met. We got on. Perhaps he recognised something of himself in me. I don't know. We had a lot in common. A married man denying his bisexuality.'

She tried to protest. 'Bisexual? That's impossible. I would have known . . .' But would you? cried a doubting voice inside her. The fact is, you didn't.

He talked over her. 'It wouldn't be the first time, let's face it.'

'I guess you'd know,' she snapped back. Cheap shot.

He considered her. 'We had shared interests. We . . .' He stopped, seeing that hearing about what they had shared would only hurt Rose more. 'In exchange for him introducing me to all that jazz he loved so much, I tried to introduce him to opera.' He gave the same wry laugh as before, but this time it was threaded with sadness. 'He tried, but he didn't really get it.'

She couldn't bear the affection she heard there.

'Did you have . . . sex?' The question burst out of her. But it was what she was thinking. She didn't want the answer, but she had to know if it would help her to come closer to understanding the man she had loved for almost thirty-five years.

The question hung in the air as they heard a footstep on the wood floor.

'Can I get you anything else?' The barman had chosen that moment to arrive at Rose's side, unannounced. He appeared not to have heard any of their conversation.

They declined together. He turned back to the bar, disgruntled, unnecessarily plumping up cushions, wiping the odd table, straightening chairs. When eventually he had retreated out of earshot, Simon spoke. 'He loved *you*, Rose.' He sounded broken. 'That's the truth. Whatever happened between us isn't relevant. Not any more.'

She so wanted to believe him, to agree that none of this mattered, that her memories could remain intact and unspoilt. But how could that possibly be?

'And what about *me*?' she asked, angry again. 'What about Jess and Trevarrick? Why wasn't Daniel enough for you? What were you hoping to gain from us?'

He gave a resigned sigh, long past defending himself. 'I don't know. Perhaps I was jealous. From where I stood, Dan had everything – a charmed life, if you like. Perhaps what stopped us from having the partnership that I longed for was you and his family. Of course I'd already met Jess when we came down here . . .'

'Of course.' How she hated him for having intruded into their lives, entwining himself irrevocably with them.

'When he died, Jess's invitation to work up some designs for Trevarrick was a godsend to me. It gave me a way of staying close to him that I hadn't looked for. I don't expect you to understand.' Their eyes met at last, hers hostile, his full of regret. After a second, he looked away. 'I hadn't bargained on meeting you. I thought I would just be working with Jess. Then it would be over. But she asked me to visit you and I was curious. When I came round that night, you were so sympathetic to the designs. I liked you. Simple as that. I'd heard so much about you, but of course I would never have initiated meeting you in a million years. I asked you to take Dan's ticket on the spur of the moment. There was something that made me want to look after you.' He saw her pull a face at the idea. 'Or at least give you some support when you were having such a tough time. Perhaps I thought Daniel would have wanted me to. I don't know. Perhaps I wanted to make up in some small way for the damage I might have inflicted on your marriage. I didn't expect to see you more than a couple of times, but then we got on so well . . .' He stopped, waiting for her.

'You mean you felt sorry for me?' So that was it. Pity, and a connection to the man he had loved.

He looked towards the darkness again. 'No. You didn't ask for that. At first, being with you made me feel close to Dan again, but then everything changed. I realised we had more in common than just him. This place, for example. Our enjoyment of great music. The meals that took so long because there was so much we wanted to say. You were alone and so was I. We had fun, didn't we? And we've helped each other through such a difficult, dark time. I hated myself for not being honest with you. But what would I have said? I *am* sorry. I really am. I wish you hadn't found out.'

'Why? So you could get away with your grubby little secret? I'd have been left forever wondering what I'd done or hadn't done to make Daniel have an affair, wondering who she was. I assumed it was a woman, of course.' However much of what he said was true, she couldn't forgive.

'No, that's not why. Because Dan would never have wanted you to know. If I hadn't encouraged him, he would never have let anything like this happen. It had been too long.'

'Then why the hell did you?' she yelled. 'Why?' She felt her control begin to slip, although she resisted the impulse to reach out and slap him. Physical violence was never the answer. She raised her hand to signal to the barman, who had begun to come in their direction, that everything was all right. They didn't need him.

'Because I'd never met anyone like him. Because I knew he was tempted and I wanted to be the one who seduced him.'

'You make me sick.' She was disgusted by his self-justification. Then she remembered what he had just said. 'And what do you mean, it had been too long? Too long since what?'

'Since he'd slept with a man . . .'

Rose stared at him, aghast. Simon wasn't the first. Was that what he meant? Could that be true? It couldn't be. She felt as if she was sinking beneath a fast-flowing current that was carrying her away from everything she had known.

'Are you all right?' The words came from far away, but she felt the touch of his hand on her shoulder. That was enough to propel her towards the surface, flinching at the unwanted contact. 'Don't touch me,' she whispered. 'Just get out of here . . .'

'But that was years ago, when he was a student . . . He hadn't . . .' Simon spoke urgently, realising what he had done, anxious to impress on her the truth.

But Rose had heard enough. 'I'm not interested, Simon. You've said plenty. Please, go . . . and don't come back here again.'

'But the renovations, the hotel . . . I'm needed here,' he protested strongly, but he looked lost and frightened.

'Not any more. I'll speak to Jess. I don't know, perhaps we'll bring someone else in on the job, or we can use one of your partners if we have to. You can think of something to tell him.'

'You'll tell her?' His eyes widened.

'I don't know what I'm going to do.' She swigged the rest of the whisky. It caught the back of her throat, making her cough. 'But right now, I'm going to my room. Just make sure you've gone by the time I'm down tomorrow morning.' As she crossed the room, she turned to take a last look at him. He sat, staring out at the night, clasping his glass, a crushed and disappointed man. 'I'll make your excuses.'

26

The stone bench was chilly. Eve leaned against the back wall of the folly, rubbing her hands together, her feet cold in her sandals. Having brought her here so purposefully, Terry was struggling to find whatever it was that he wanted to say. He remained leaning against one of the pillars, staring out towards the path cut by the moon across the sea.

Finally he broke the silence. 'I proposed to you here.' He sounded wistful. 'Do you remember?'

'Of course I do.' How could he imagine that she would have forgotten? Had they grown so far apart?

'Long time ago.'

She said nothing, seeing how hard this was for him. Better to leave him to build up to whatever he had to say. She shivered. More than twenty-five years ago, he had inveigled her here on the pretence of looking for Doggle, the ancient hotel tabby cat who been missing for a day. She'd had no idea that the folly even existed. Back then, under the care of Terry's parents, the original mock temple had been all but forgotten. Completely overgrown, the domed roof leaked, and inside, the stone seat had been broken and weeds grew up between the cracks in the tiled floor. Even so, it had still breathed romance. She had followed him inside, calling out the cat's name, startled to discover a tartan rug spread on the floor, wild flowers in milk bottles arranged on the remains of the broken seat, a bottle of champagne in a cooler beside a huge bowl of strawberries and a jug of cream, bowls and spoons. He stood proudly beside his handiwork as she took it all in. Only later did she learn how Rose had encouraged him – partners in crime for once. But then, sinking to one knee, sticking to the script that he had written for himself, he'd asked her to marry him. And, touched by his thoughtfulness, the care he had taken, excited to have found a man she loved after thinking she never would again, with whom she shared so much, and whose sister was her closest friend, she had accepted. They had married almost a year later. For better, for worse.

'Terry . . .' She stopped. For a wild moment she was tempted to confess to her affair with Will, clear the air. But she checked herself in time. There was no point in saying anything until she had made up her mind where her future lay. Otherwise she would hurt him unnecessarily. 'Perhaps we should go back.'

'No, no.' Her suggestion seemed to galvanise him. 'I've got to tell you something. Rose says I must.'

'Rose?' He'd confided in his sister first, and yet Rose had said nothing. Eve bristled, uncomfortable at the thought that there might be secrets between the two of them. If anything, Dan's death had brought her and Rose closer together than ever. She had told her friend everything, and she thought Rose had reciprocated by confiding in her about her growing friendship with Simon.

'I had to ask her to help me with the money,' he said, as if that explained everything.

'What money?' She rubbed at the goose bumps prickling on her arms.

'You've seen my credit card bills . . . you must have wondered.'

'No.' She was mystified as to where this could be leading.

'But I stupidly left them on the kitchen table a few weeks ago. You tidied them up.' A note of impatience had entered his voice, as if she was being deliberately obtuse. 'I've been waiting for you to say something.'

She shook her head. 'I didn't look at them. I wouldn't.' Actually, she would, but she must have tidied them away without thinking.

'But you've been so distant,' he said, perplexed. 'I thought that must be why. You must have guessed.'

'Terry, I honestly don't know what you're talking about. Just say whatever you've got to say and let's get back. We really should.'

'This is even harder than I thought it would be.' He leaned his head back against the pillar.

'If you can tell Rose, you can tell me,' she encouraged.

He turned to face her, his arms folded across his chest, his left heel kicked back against the stone. His face was in shadow but she could sense the tension there.

'I've got myself into a bit of trouble.' He hesitated before diving in, the words coming in such a rush that Eve had to struggle to make sense of them. He lost her near the beginning when he started explaining how his betting had become something much more serious. At first, she didn't understand why this deserved quite such a momentous presentation. He'd bet on the horses for years and never got into any serious trouble. He was too cautious or tight-fisted for that. Sometimes a flutter or two too many, the odd loss, but nothing more. And the losses had never been anything that couldn't be quickly absorbed. But then he wasn't talking horses any more but other sports, all of which were being played all over the world at all times of the day and night. How easy it was to place a bet without her realising. How he started small but then things escalated. A couple of credit cards she didn't know about. A mortgage. The sums of money he was quoting spun around her head, not computing. At last he drew to a close. 'So,' he concluded, his voice dropping to an ashamed murmur, 'I ended up owing two hundred K.'

There was a silence as she took it in.

'But that's almost quarter of a million,' she said incredulously, as if he must have made a mistake. The night air felt even cooler. She rubbed her arms vigorously as she recalled the modest earnings of the agency that month, the minimal salary she would have to draw, the absence of his income, and at last the implications began to hit home. 'Terry, you can't have. How the hell are you going to pay that sort of money back?'

'That's the point. Telling you is the start. I was going to earlier on in the bedroom, but I didn't know how to start, and then, what with your reaction to the bracelet, I couldn't.'

'But you could now, in the middle of the party?' Hysteria edged into her voice. 'For God's sake, Terry. What were you thinking?' But she knew that he had only done what she had done so often,

262

had a glass or two for Dutch courage. He had screwed up his nerve until he couldn't wait any longer.

'It's not ideal, I know.' He carried on across her splutter of protest. 'But I'm telling you because I love you, and because I want you to know the truth. I just couldn't tell you before.'

'But the money . . .' She couldn't bring herself to repeat the amount. 'Where will we find it? Our house?'

'We,' he echoed, looking away from her towards the sound of the sea. 'That's one of the things I love about you, Evie. We've always shared everything, haven't we?'

She peered at him through the darkness, wondering how their perceptions of their relationship could be so different.

'But not this time,' he went on. 'I'm getting out of this on my own. Well, with a little help from Rose. I was wrong about Madison Gadding. It turned out they were still interested in the hotels individually. So she's already helped me once by agreeing to sell the Canonford. That's why she did it. Thank God. I took some of the money we had earmarked for the kids.' His face was hidden but she could hear his shame. 'But I will pay it back.'

'Damn right you will. You took the kids' money?' Eve couldn't believe what she was hearing? 'And Rose knew all along?' That was the greatest hurt of all. Not that he had kept his secret from her. She could understand that. And the money would be paid back somehow, she would make sure of that. But Rose!

'She's my sister,' he said, as if it was unreasonable of Eve to expect Rose's loyalty in the circumstances. 'I had to tell someone.'

And you couldn't tell me? But the words remained unsaid as Eve reeled, realising what this could mean to them.

Footsteps and laughter were coming in the direction of the folly.

'Shit!' Terry muttered under his breath, before stepping out into the shadows.

A girl screamed, then giggled as she recognised him. 'Uncle Terry! My God, you scared me.'

'Sorry, Dad. We didn't think anyone would be here.'

Anna and Charlie. They must be on the hunt for somewhere to have a discreet spliff. Tough. Eve tipped her head back against the uneven wall of the folly, the flaking plaster catching at her hair. She raised a hand in protection. What a bloody mess her marriage was. Their individual lives had jolted on to parallel tracks, with neither of them really noticing what was happening. As each one had become more involved in their own interests, they had lost sight of what the other was doing. She would never have envisaged them becoming so separate, she reflected sadly. She heard Terry trip over something and swear. Then he appeared again, silhouetted against the furthest pillar.

'They've gone,' he said, taking off his right shoe and rubbing his big toe. 'I don't know which of them is worse, the way they lead each other on.'

'Anna's the oldest,' she said, defensive of her boy.

'But Charlie's old enough to know what he's doing,' Terry said firmly, slipping his foot back, then joining her on the bench. He didn't notice when she shifted away from him. 'So now you know. Rose'll be so pleased.'

'Why? What's it got to do with her?' Eve couldn't help her quite unreasonable jealousy that he'd taken Rose into his confidence first. After all, she was guilty of the same crime, confiding in Rose about Will, expecting her silence. Except, she thought, that was different.

'I would have told Daniel,' Terry explained, apparently aware for once of the swirling undercurrents. 'But I had to talk to someone. The agency seems to have kept you busier than ever recently . . . I've hardly seen you.'

That was true. When she wasn't actually working, there'd been those afternoons and evenings explained away by meetings with imaginary would-be clients or publishers when in fact she'd been spending them with Will. Grateful for the cover of darkness, she felt herself blush. Using that time to see Will meant that she'd had to spend more hours on her work at home. Nothing would stop her commitment to her clients.

'And Rose is family. We own the business together,' Terry went on. 'She agreed to sell the Canonford so that I could cover my debts and so that we could have help financially. But then I put some – well, most of the money I took on a couple of sure-fire winners that weren't placed. So I'm in trouble again.'

'I don't believe it. You haven't even learned your lesson. And what about Daniel?' she protested, unable to believe what she was hearing, suspecting that even now, he wasn't telling her the whole truth. 'He built up the business, those hotels are his.' Someone had to speak up for him. The other two seemed to have forgotten the work, the passion that Daniel had put into those places.

'He's dead, Eve,' Terry pointed out bluntly. 'Rose and I don't want the hotels. We never did. Just Trevarrick. And you know what? He'd be pleased to be helping us out of a spot.'

'How can you call this a spot?' she exploded. 'How are we going to find that kind of money? He'd be absolutely horrified. How could you have let yourself get into this mess?'

And how could they? Again the words remained unsaid.

His shoulders slumped, arms hanging loose by his sides. 'I'm ashamed. I am. But can't you understand?' he pleaded, looking towards her. 'Rose thought you would.'

Eve clenched her jaw tight as he went on.

'I had the money and the time, and the excitement made everything else disappear. I could forget I didn't have a job, that I was letting you all down. I've promised Rose that I'll get professional help, even though I don't need it. I can stop without that.' He reached out for her, but she stood up, ignoring his hand.

'But you didn't have the money, did you? What happened to your redundancy payment?'

Terry looked at the ground and didn't reply. Then, in a small voice: 'I was fired.'

'What?' Eve sat down again, forgetting the cold as she listened to him explain the truth of his situation, unable to believe what she was hearing. How could she not have noticed what was happening? Only too easily, said that small inner voice. You had the agency, Will. You weren't interested. As Terry finished, she stood up to face him.

'And our house? That's everything we own – our history, our family. How could you risk it like that?' The idea of losing the roof over their heads was terrifying. And the agency? How would this affect it? Would she have to consider selling up? But in this economic climate, who would buy? A couple of clients had already changed their mind about joining Amy, to her ex-colleague's public fury. But this could destroy her. 'How do I know it won't happen again? How can I trust you now?' Eve's head was spinning. First Rose's discovery about Daniel, and now this. How much they'd misjudged or misunderstood the men they'd married so many years ago. She stood up and took a step towards the garden, then turned back to look at him, bent over, a picture of despair.

'I thought you'd understand.'

She only just caught what he said. In the distance, the waves still broke on the rocks and the music in the marquee wafted in their direction. An owl hooted.

'I couldn't have got through the last twenty-five years without you. I need you to help me get through this.' He wrung his hands together. 'I need Rose to sell the Arthur. But she won't. With my share of the proceeds, I could put things back on track. With your help.'

'You should have told me before . . .' Eve didn't move. Her instinct told her to go to him, to reassure him, to help him, but something prevented her.

Will.

This was the crisis point. Terry had just handed her a cast-iron reason to leave him. He had put everything they had on the line. Everything. But was that so different from what she had been doing?

'Telling me in the middle of our party. How could you?' She had a sudden urge to run away as far as she could, away from both her husbands for a brand-new, problem-free start. But that would solve nothing.

She stormed out of the folly, hearing him say something but not catching the words. She was too angry to stop and listen to any more of his excuses. Her immediate job was to appear as if nothing had happened. None of her family, none of her clients or friends must suspect anything was wrong. Tomorrow she and Terry would talk again. Then they would be sober and she would make him take her through everything that had happened, exactly what was owed and how he planned to repay it. She would change their joint bank accounts, so that only she had access to them. Nobody, but nobody, was going to take her home or her livelihood away from her.

Terry followed one or two steps behind, saying nothing as they approached the marquee. One or two of the tea lights on the path had burned out, but the party was still going strong.

He'd been right: no one had noticed their absence. Within moments, they were reabsorbed into the throng. A hard core of dancers had formed and were dancing more frenetically than ever, the younger generation at their centre, the older diehards at the perimeter. Jackets had been hooked over chair backs, bags and shoes were scattered by the tables. The more faint-hearted had retired to sit down or to stand by the bar. Even in the subtle lighting, faces were slick with sweat, the hairdos that had arrived so carefully styled were in disarray, shirts were untucked, ties loosened.

Eve needed a drink. Within seconds, a glass of wine was in her hand and she threw herself back into the proceedings as best she could. As quickly, she lost Terry, who was snatched up by someone needing a dance partner. Perhaps being told he was leaving her would have been easier. At least the decision wouldn't be her responsibility. As she turned to talk to Helen Martin, a dumpy, be-whiskered older woman who was one of the most successful illustrators Eve had on her books, she caught sight of Jess, unmistakable in her sunflower dress, detaching herself from Adam's knee and coming in her direction.

'I'll be back in a minute, Helen,' she excused herself.

'Is there anything more you need, Aunt Eve? Adam's going back to the babysitter, but I'd like to go with him, if I could.'

Eve became aware of waitresses beginning to clear the tables of the party detritus. 'Oh, but it's not time to stop yet, is it?' she asked, rather hoping the answer might be yes. Their guests would go to bed or back to their B&Bs and she could sleep on what needed to be said to Terry.

'You can go on for as long as you like,' Jess smiled, knowing how her aunt could party till the small hours in the right company. 'But some of us have got to work tomorrow. If they clear the worst now, the rest can be done first thing in the morning. They won't get in the way. You might have to turn the music down, though. Just for those who've gone to bed already.'

Being treated like a rebellious teenager by her niece was ridiculous but kind of flattering at the same time. 'Don't worry, Jess. I'll make sure they behave. They'll park their Zimmers in an orderly way.'

'I'm sorry.' Jess grinned at her. 'But you know what I mean.' She looked around the marquee. 'I haven't seen Mum for ages, so I guess she must have gone.'

'She must,' agreed Eve, remembering how much she wanted to hear Rose's side of her involvement in Terry's story, not to mention what she was going to do about Simon. What an unholy mess they were in. 'You go, and I'll make sure no damage is done.'

'Thanks.' Jess kissed both her cheeks as she wished her good night. Eve watched the pair of them leave the marquee, arms tight round each other, Jess's head leaning into Adam's shoulder. Adam gave Jess everything she needed. If only Daniel could have seen that.

'Shall we?' Johnny Sheringham was standing beside her, ruddy-faced but beaming. His bow tie had twisted almost in a right angle and was resisting its owner's attempts to straighten it. He and his wife had been their neighbours in Cambridge for as long as she could remember. Pam was in a care home in the final stages of dementia – at sixty-three. How much more unfair life could be.

'Yes,' she said, taking his proffered hand as if they were about to dance a gavotte. 'I'd love to.' If he could shelve his problems for an evening, she could certainly shelve hers, or pretend to. Life was short. There was nothing she could do now but enjoy herself and make a start on sorting things out in the morning, when she'd had time to absorb thoroughly what Terry had told her, find out exactly what their financial position was, and think through what needed to be done.

27

'Yes, I'm absolutely certain that I want us to sell the damn place,' Rose declared in answer to Eve's question. 'For a start, I want to help the two of you out of this mess my brother has got you into, and second, I don't want anything to do with somewhere that meant so much to Daniel and Simon and nothing whatsoever to me. I can't bear to think of them canoodling together over their plans.' Her face was set, warning Eve not to say any more.

They were in the hotel lounge, looking out at the thick sea fret that had blown in from offshore: one of those unpredictable turns of Cornish weather. The marquee was still there, its shape just visible through the mist. Most of the guests had left the previous day, and Eve and Terry had waved goodbye to the stragglers that morning, putting on such a good show that no one would have guessed they were barely speaking. There had been little chance for them to have anything other than snatched exchanges. Terry remained contrite but monosyllabic, eager that no one should get wind of what had happened. The longer conversation Eve was resolved they would have had to wait. After lunch, he had gone upstairs for a much-needed lie-down. Denied a walk by the weather, the two women had opted for the comfort of the great indoors and a cream tea.

Eve poured them both a second cup. They were curled on either end of the large central sofa, in the midst of a thorough post-mortem on the weekend. Eve had spent a second hung-over morning in succession nursing her anger with Terry and her irritation that Rose hadn't told her about his gambling. When she said as much, Rose was short. 'If someone – whoever it is – asks me to keep a secret, I do,' she'd bitten back. 'That's why I haven't said anything to Terry about Will. Cuts both ways.' Eve could do nothing but accept her point. So their friendship lurched forward, ruffled but still intact.

'I don't expect it was quite like that,' Eve ventured now, wondering despite herself what it *had* been like between Simon and Daniel. Not something she could speculate over with Rose, however. 'I can't imagine how difficult it must be for you, especially when you and Simon have become such friends.'

'I can't even think about that, and I certainly don't want the Arthur. Truly. Daniel was the hotelier, not me, not Terry.' Rose punched the faded blue cushion to emphasise her point. 'Now you can take charge, clear Terry's debts, begin to sort him out. And selling the place means I can help the girls with some of the rest. The garden centre's taking off more slowly than expected, despite Rick's steadying influence . . . but it's early days. And Jess and Adam could always do with some extra cash.'

'You're being incredibly generous.' Eve put the pot down, thinking that that sounded like a lot of responsibility heaped on Rose's shoulders. How would she cope?

'Not really. Daniel's left me comfortably enough off, and I don't need the hassle of the business. I don't want to run the hotels in any capacity. Keeping Trevarrick's enough for me. Besides, seeing Adam's work and listening to him talk about it has inspired me. I'm going to take my painting seriously again, before it's too late. Simon went on and on about it, and Adam's given me that final nudge. In fact, he's asked me to come and stay down here in a few months to help out. During my spare time, I'll have the ideal opportunity.'

'When did that happen?'

'This morning, after breakfast. Jess's pregnant and worried about how she's going to cope, so they want me to come and help. She told him yesterday and this is his solution. I'm looking forward to it.'

'But that's wonderful news.' Eve shunted herself across the sofa to hug Rose. They held each other close for a moment. Over Rose's shoulder, Eve gazed at a picture of St Michael's Mount, its silhouette small against a dramatic cloud-filled sky. On the table beneath it, the day's papers had been neatly folded. She gave Rose an extra squeeze before detaching herself and moving back to where she'd been sitting. 'They must be over the moon. I wish mine would get on and produce something. I'm quite jealous.'

'But Jess is worried sick about how she's going to manage.' Rose sounded suddenly anxious. 'There's no Dan to turn to and of course Simon's not going to be here in charge of the builders.'

'You told her?' Eve couldn't hide her astonishment.

'I had to. How could I explain away his disappearance otherwise? More importantly, I think I owe the girls the truth. There's been enough lying in this family.'

Eve understood that Rose meant her as well.

Simon had gone without saying goodbye to either of them. He had left an envelope in the cubbyhole for Rose's room. She was with Eve when she picked it up, but had slipped it into her bag unopened. 'Whatever he's got to say can wait,' she'd said, that closed look coming over her face again.

'And? How did she take it?' Eve couldn't imagine how hard it must have been for Rose to break the news of Daniel's betrayal not only of her, but of the family, something that had been so important to both of them. Until those final weeks of his life, Jess had been so close to her father. She must have been devastated. Eve wondered whether Rose had done the right thing in her haste to have everything in the open. In her shoes, she would certainly have been more circumspect.

Rose pulled a face. 'He'd left her a note saying he'd gone away on unexpected business, but I had to tell her the truth. I lay awake all night agonising about whether or not the girls should know. But you know what? They're adults, and if they were to find out somehow from someone else, that would be much, much worse. It's better they know and we can deal with it together. If I didn't tell them, then I'd have been complicit in Dan's betrayal of us. That's what it was, after all, and there's been enough of that.'

Eve found it impossible to imagine taking such a decision. Wouldn't it have been better to leave things to fate, trusting that the girls wouldn't find out? Wasn't ignorance bliss?

'She was utterly distraught, of course. She refused to believe it at first. Why would she? But once I told her everything Simon said, showed her the libretto, she started remembering little signs that she didn't recognise at the time when they were here together. That was hard to hear.'

Eve gave her an inquisitive look.

'Oh, you know, the odd shared joke and sidelong look, that sort of thing.' Rose screwed up her nose. 'I can't bear to think of it. But at least we've got a reason for Dan being so particularly bad-tempered during those last months. He must have been fighting his demons.' She noticed Eve's startled expression. 'Too psycho-speak for you? Jess and I wondered if the stress of having a secret relationship . . .' She gave up in the face of Eve's obvious scepticism. 'But if she believes that, then at least she can stop blaming herself for his death. And that at least would be a good thing to come out of this.' Rose took a scone and sliced it in half. 'Want a bit?'

Eve shook her head. 'OK. I accept all that. Everything that was going on would stress anyone out. And what about Anna?'

'I haven't seen her. She beetled back to London with Charlie first thing yesterday. Didn't he say? Nothing like a free lift. I dread to think what state they were in after the party. I don't think they even went to bed. But apparently Rick needed her at work in the afternoon. I'll talk to her when I'm back in London.'

'And you?'

'I don't know.'

Eve could see tears welling in Rose's eyes.

'I've learned so much about Dan in the last eight months. I thought I knew him through and through, but turns out he wasn't the person I thought he was at all. Except . . . at the same time, he was. He was a great dad to the girls. OK, he had a short fuse and could be bloody stubborn, but they're hardly crimes. And he was a great husband to me. What do I feel?' She gave a huge sigh. 'I don't know any more. Exhausted. Betrayed. Angry. Confused. Forgiving. Disappointed. All those things. More than anything, I'm furious with him for not being here to talk about it, and explain. That's what I want most of all.'

Eve reached out a hand to her. Rose took it. They sat there for a few minutes in silence. There was nothing Eve could say. Eventually Rose swung her legs off the sofa and sat up straight. The effort it took for her to smile was plain. 'I'll probably come back here in three or four months' time. I'm thinking of selling the London house and getting a flat so I keep a toehold there. Jess and Adam's suggestion has decided me, and anyway, I'm rattling around that old place on my own.'

Eve studied her friend, impressed by her apparent composure. 'Don't rush into anything. It's still early days.'

'The funny thing is,' Rose continued, as if she'd read Eve's mind, 'knowing the truth is better than agonising about who *she* was. I've wondered about her for months and sometimes, however hard I tried to get her out of my mind, I thought the fact that I would never know would drive me mad. Even though *she* turned out to be Simon, it's like a weight's been taken away. Can you understand that?'

Eve reached for her cup, shaking her head. How could Rose be so calm and rational? Where were the rage and the pain of Saturday? If she were in her position, she would be shouting and screaming, infuriated and devastated by the betrayal of both men.

'Look.' Rose tried again. 'I don't want to discuss it with Simon. And I probably never will. I can't discuss it with Dan. So I've got to accept that there was a part of him I didn't know about. We do all have our secret compartments that we don't let everyone see. Simon said he wasn't the first, that Dan had slept with another man – or maybe even men – in Edinburgh. But I don't want to think about that. I can't. Not yet, anyway.'

To Eve's relief, their conversation was brought to a sudden halt by the sound of the door opening. They turned to find two couples who had evidently braved the weather coming in to order tea. Bedraggled and damp but chatting cheerfully, they brought with them the smell of the outside. Jess was right behind them, directing

273

the hotel porter, who was hefting an armful of logs. Whatever was going on inside, she put on a good professional show, though her red-rimmed eyes betrayed how upset she was.

'I know it's the middle of May, but we need a fire in here to cheer the place up. You were lucky the weather held till this morning,' she said to Eve, as she waited for the fire to be laid to her satisfaction. 'Where's Terry?'

'Gone for a nap . . .' Eve paused as a thought struck her. 'I hope.' She and Rose exchanged a look, missed by Jess. He wouldn't have snuck off to place a bet, would he? Not after all that had been said. He wouldn't dare.

'Good for him. I wouldn't mind one myself, except I've got to work. But all that's going to change soon.' She began to stroke Rose's hair. 'Isn't it, Mum?'

'What? When I come to be your dogsbody?' Rose looked up at Jess, smiling. 'I can hardly wait. By the way, did you speak to the builders, or shall I?'

Jess's expression hardened. 'I told them there would be a new project manager coming on board. There's stuff they can get on with. I also had a call from him: Roger Fanshaw. He's coming down on Thursday and we'll take it from there.' Her expression brightened as she looked at her aunt. 'What about you, Eve? Couldn't you come down for a proper holiday, now Mum's going to be here?'

'I'm not sure what my plans are at the moment.' Eve noticed Rose give her a quick sidelong glance. 'I've got a lot on my plate and I'm not sure how things are going to pan out.'

'But I thought you said the agency was back on track now May's got her feet under the desk.'

'She has made a massive difference, that's true. It's so wonderful having someone who wants to do her job well, but who's ambitious for something else – her own writing. She's not trying to compete with me in the way Amy did. But I've *got* to find someone to replace Rufus. His going leaves quite a hole and I'm still having to work at convincing people that it's not a sign that the agency's adrift.'

But both Eve and Rose knew it wasn't the agency that was providing Eve's biggest headache. Nor was it likely to be the biggest catalyst for change. Some secrets were too dangerous to be shared.

July

28

Rose was facing the usual Saturday-night TV toss-up between an interminable search for a musical superstar, a pointless game-show or the repeat of a tired old detective drama. None of them appealed, but any one of them would pass the time equally well. Mindless entertainment was better than none because it required no effort and stopped her thinking. How Daniel would have disapproved. 'Why don't you go and paint something?' he would suggest. Anything rather than wasting valuable time. Jess's old bedroom, with its north-facing window, made a great studio. The easel was up, her paints were sorted into colour boxes, her smock hung on the door. Clearing out what was left of her daughter's childhood detritus had given her something to do for a day or two, but in fact Rose had yet to lift a paintbrush since she came back from Cornwall. She had spent the subsequent weeks in a ghastly kind of paralysis, unable to muster the energy to do much more than wander from sofa to chair to kitchen to bed, every step an effort, tortured by the questions she was desperate but unable to ask Daniel.

She had put her marriage under a microscope, twisting and turning it every which way, trying to make sense of what it had been, of who Daniel had really been and of her own responsibility for what had happened. But without his contribution, she would never be clear about what they had really had together. The idea of living without knowing was making her utterly miserable.

She picked up the TV guide, convinced she could find something better to watch if she tried harder. She ignored the tear that dropped on to the paper, smudging across the Sky film channels: old films, films she'd seen, films she didn't want to see. Another tear joined the first. She wiped her eyes, resigned to these unpredictable bursts of crying, triggered by anything as trivial as her frustration with the TV programming schedules. That morning, dropping a book and losing her place had been enough to set her off. But what did it matter, as long as there was no one else there to see?

Only six o'clock. Every day took twice as long as it ever had when Dan was alive. On her own, with nothing in particular to look forward to, the hours dragged by. She had friends she could phone, but they were married, with weekends packed full of social commitments to which, now she was on her own, she was rarely invited. The flurry of sympathy and support had inevitably died away as time passed, and they had returned to their own lives, confident they had done their bit and relieved to get back to normal. Despite everything, she did miss Simon, or at least the things that they'd done together. Getting used to being on her own was a long old haul. She had read enough and talked to enough people to know that she had to be patient. But boy, was it easier said than done.

As she washed up the grill pan, tears ran unchecked over her cheeks. Brokenly humming 'Abide With Me' didn't help. Earlier that afternoon, walking round Hampstead Heath had taken her mind off Daniel for a welcome couple of hours. But alone again, her thoughts homed right back to him, and to Simon. She reached for the tissues by the toaster, just one of the boxes she'd placed at strategic points around the house. She blew her nose, then dried the pan, wiping her hands on her jeans. Without thinking, she picked up one of the photos that she'd recently dug out of an old album. These and memories were all she had left of Dan. But did either of them represent the truth? She had no way of knowing. Here, they had been caught laughing together just after Eve and Terry's Labrador puppy had taken a surprise bite out of seven-year-old Anna's doughnut. She stared into Daniel's eyes, trying to read into them something that would explain what she now knew about him. But for all they shone with laughter, they remained unfathomable.

'What was going on in your head?' she whispered. 'Why didn't you tell me, and why aren't you here to bloody well sort this all out? I don't know what to think any more.'

As she replaced the photo, the doorbell rang. She wasn't expecting anyone. Through the spy hole she saw Anna, pushing her hair off her face. She'd obviously come straight from work in her uniform of green polo shirt and mud-spattered jeans.

'Have you been crying again?' Anna asked, the moment they separated from their embrace. She peered at Rose's face, clearly not going to be content until she got the truth.

'I'm fine now you're here.' Rose waited till Anna had undone her muddy Doc Martens and left them by the door, then took her hand and pulled her into the living room. 'Now, to what do I owe this honour?'

'Nothing really.' Anna threw herself down in the nearest chair. 'Just wanted to see how you're doing.'

Since she had told Anna about Simon and Daniel, her daughter had been more supportive of her than Rose would ever have expected. Over the weeks, Anna's initial shock became outrage and anger at her father's betrayal of them. Eventually those feelings were being replaced by a genuine sadness for her father, sympathy for him having to live a lie. She and Jess had been brought together by their concern for Rose and how she was faring. She had spent long evenings with Rose airing their feelings, going round in circles as they tried to make some sort of sense of what had happened.

But this time Rose sensed that there was something else. Anna was so transparent. She was keeping something back, but Rose bet it wouldn't be there for long. She could wait.

'Tea?' She stood by the fireplace, straightening the candles and propping up the single invitation that sat there, to Eve and Terry's twenty-fifth. On second thoughts, she took it and dropped it in the bin. In the mirror, she barely recognised her reflection – a weary-looking old woman stared back. She rubbed her cheeks to bring some colour to them.

'Love one. I'll get them.' Anna jumped to her feet and left Rose fiddling while she went to make the tea. Returning silently in her socks, she put the tray down on that day's unopened newspaper, then came up behind her mother and hugged her tight. Their reflections gazed back at them, emphasising their similarities – the tip-tilted nose, the defined bone structure, the boyishness – and their differences – Anna outdoorsy, tanned and healthy, Rose pale and tired.

'Mum, we know what's going on and we're worried about you.' Typically, she went straight to the point.

'What? You and Jess?' Rose was pleased to hear they had kept the peace. If the shared knowledge of Dan's betrayal had caused a truce, then it was a small consolation that at least something good had come from it.

'Of course. I do still think she can be beyond difficult, but Dad and Simon . . .' She let their names fill the silence. 'Well, how could we not talk about that and about you?' She squeezed Rose and kissed her cheek.

'And what did you conclude?' Rose was on the verge of tears again. She tore a tissue from the nearby box and blew her nose.

Anna squeezed her again and passed her a second tissue. 'Well, I'm afraid, that somehow we've all got to find a way of moving on. You can't hide yourself away like this for ever.'

Ah, the easy acceptance of youth. But Rose couldn't help smiling. 'Why don't you say exactly what you mean, darling?' She sat down and took her mug. *Keep Calm and Drink Tea*, advised the caption.

'OK, well perhaps that was a bit blunt. But you know what I mean.' Anna leaned forward and scrutinised her face close-up.

'You make it sound so easy.' The hot tea burned the roof of Rose's mouth. She returned the mug to the tray.

'But you know I'm right really, don't you?' Anna insisted, sitting opposite her. 'What's done's done. We can't bring Dad back. And even if he did have a fling with Simon, what's the betting that's all it was? A stupid mid-life crisis moment that meant nothing. Plenty of middle-aged men have affairs to prove to themselves they've still got it. So his was with a man? We've got to make ourselves believe it doesn't matter. I know it's impossibly hard, but we've got to try, otherwise we'll go under. Even St Jess is on her way to believing that. We've got to take our anger, put it in one circle of a figure eight, then cut the join and let it float away from us.'

Rose gave a watery smile. That therapist again, no doubt.

'And you've got to as well.'

'But it does matter,' Rose protested. The fact that Daniel had chosen a man instead of her mattered dreadfully, although she wasn't exactly sure why. In some ways it should have made it easier. 'I can't have been the wife he wanted, can I? Perhaps he could have been happy with someone else all along.' She couldn't bring herself to say 'another man'.

'Mum, come on.' Anna's no-nonsense approach was nothing if not bracing. 'If he'd wanted that, he'd have left you a long time ago. Don't think like that. You'll go mad. Try to remember him for what he was to us. A bloody difficult old bugger at times . . .' Her hand flew to her mouth. 'Wrong word! But he was Dad. And how awful it must have been for him not to be able to come clean with us. Don't punish yourself. There's no point.'

'That's so easy to say.' Rose envied her daughter's robust attitude to life, which had been so effectively fostered by those stints in therapy. If only she could muster the same resilience. But perhaps with the girls' support, and with Eve's . . . who knew what super-human effort she might be capable of? And what would Daniel want her to do? She thought she knew the answer.

'Have you heard from Simon?'

'He wrote me a letter, you know.' She could recite every miserable word by heart, but the same three stuck at the front of her mind – *he loved you*. For some reason, she hadn't thrown it away but kept it tucked into the incriminating *Rigoletto* libretto that she'd brought home and kept on the top shelf of the bookcase. 'But not since.'

'Quite odd, his friendship with you,' Anna observed, thoughtful. 'But then I suppose you have got loads in common – apart from Dad, I mean.' Her hand shot to her mouth again. 'God, sorry. I don't seem to be able to say quite the right thing.'

She looked so appalled with herself that Rose had to sympathise. 'But we do, or rather we did,' she conceded. 'I enjoyed his being around. He made me feel safe, not so alone. Good timing, I guess.'

'Jess misses him at Trevarrick. She says Roger's nothing like as good – even though he must be referring back to Simon. Unless he's removed himself from the job completely.'

What was this? Surely they didn't want her to let Jess reinstate him? That wasn't going to happen. However much she loved Trevarrick and wanted the renovations to go ahead as planned, she could never accept Simon's presence there again. 'Well, she'll have to manage, I'm afraid.'

'OK. Keep your wig on.' Anna patted the air in a calming gesture. 'I just thought I'd warn you. But I did come to talk to you about something else as well.'

'I had a feeling.' Rose hazarded a guess that they were about to change the subject back to Anna. Her daughter was obviously building herself up to saying something momentous. And here it came.

'I slept with Rick.' Now Anna's eyes were welling up, and Rose passed her a tissue. 'I shouldn't have.'

'Oh Anna, why not?' Touched that Anna wanted to confide in her, Rose couldn't see a problem. Rick seemed a perfectly nice guy, and it was time Anna had someone in her life at last. Then a thought struck her. 'You're not pregnant, are you?'

'Mum! For God's sake. At the grand old age of thirty-one, I have got the hang of contraception. Nooo,' she wailed, impatient with Rose for not catching on. 'It's because we work together.'

'So?' Rose still didn't understand. 'Dad and I worked at Trevarrick together at the beginning. Why's that a problem? We had some great times.' She had remembered as many of them as she could since his death.

'That was different.' Anna's impatience showed. 'You were married. Rick and I aren't. If we fall out, how's that going to affect the business? It could mean disaster.'

Rose was mystified. 'Why should you fall out? If you like each other . . .'

'It was one night, that's all.' Anna spelled it out slowly for her. 'And he's got a girlfriend.'

'Oh.' Rose wasn't sure what to say next.

'We had a couple of drinks to celebrate finishing a big land-scaping job. Liz was away, so I asked him back to the flat and, well . . . you know . . . Oh God. If only I could undo everything.'

'Then talk to him,' Rose suggested warily. 'Tell him you want to go back to the way things were. That you don't want it to affect the business.'

Anna curled herself up in the chair. 'But I like him, Mum. I don't really want to go backwards. And if I talk to him, then he might agree. That's what I'm frightened of.' She punched the arm of the chair with a fist. 'I really don't know the best thing to do.'

'Then do nothing,' advised Rose, wishing she could provide a solution, but falling back on that tried-and-tested course of action. 'Do nothing until you do know, and perhaps by then he'll know too.'

Anna didn't stay for long. All her life she had hopped from one thing to the next with the speed of a demented butterfly. Voicing the problem had been enough for her. That, and checking in on Rose. Then it was time to go home for a bath and whatever the evening held in store.

'I hope you're going to like this.' Terry stirred the ingredients of a casserole on the hob with a metal spoon.

Eve just stopped herself in time from suggesting he use a wooden one that wouldn't mark the dish. At least he was cooking. Far better than the ready-meal she would have brought home in a last-minute rush.

'Sure I will. Smells heavenly.' But her attention was more fully on the editorial notes that she was making for an author. They had a meeting the following morning, and she wanted to be completely ready with her advice. That, after all, was what would be expected of her. Some authors required more of her input than others, and Erica Johnson was particularly demanding. Not that Eve minded. She loved the editorial involvement, helping shape the work, ready to sell.

'Have you nearly finished that?' He sounded impatient. A repeated bone of contention was that she liked to work at the kitchen table when they had a perfectly good desk in the living room. But the desk was too small. She liked to be able to spread her work out. Terry thought work shouldn't encroach on the kitchen.

'One more chapter.' She wished he wouldn't complain. They both knew how important her work was to their financial future at the moment. 'Then I'm done.'

There was the pop of a cork, then Terry was standing beside her. 'Glass of wine for the worker. A cheeky little Verdicchio. You'll like it.' He touched her shoulder, his thumb briefly on the back of her neck, before returning to the cooking.

Just as she took a sip, her BlackBerry rang. Terry tutted as she took the call, but she couldn't ignore it despite his accusing stare. Fortunately it wasn't a client needing reassurance, but Anna. After the initial pleasantries, she came to the point.

'I've been round to Mum's and I'm really worried about her. Jess is too. She's obviously not eating much and looks like a ghost.'

Eve had worried that Rose was coping badly. The fact that she hadn't returned Eve's last couple of calls was a bad sign. She let Anna go on.

'When I got there, she'd been crying again. Nothing we do seems to work. I tried to talk to her about Dad. But it's soooo difficult. I'm doing my best to support her by trying to show I can handle it, but inside I still feel so muddled. One minute I'm furious with him, the next I feel sorry for him. I mean, how awful for him not to be able to be true to himself. Jess is the same. And then I tried to take Mum's mind off the whole thing by asking her for some advice, but it was hopeless. Auntie Eve! You're her best friend. Couldn't you go and see her? I know she'd love that.'

Eve prevaricated. She wasn't sure she could leave Terry on his own. Not that she wanted to take the role of prison warder, but there seemed no alternative at the moment, however much she longed to get away to London.

When she hung up, Terry was ladling up the fish curry. Something had prevented her from telling him about Simon and Daniel. She didn't want him to change his view of Daniel, a man for whom he'd always had such admiration. He wouldn't understand. But she knew Rose would insist on his knowing sooner or later, once the rest of their lives had been sorted out. She relayed the conversation without going into unnecessary detail. 'Do you think we should go and stay with her for a few days?'

He pulled out his chair and sat opposite her, leaving on the Domestic Goddess apron that Millie had given him for Christmas. 'We could. But why don't you go without me? I'll just be in the way.' He stalled her objection. 'I'll be all right here on my own. Promise.'

Was this a clever plan to give himself space to gamble again? He wouldn't, would he? Not after being so determined to find a counsellor and a local Gamblers Anonymous. Since his confession, he'd been dead set on proving to her that he meant what he said. He could get the better of his addiction. Hating herself for distrusting him, she put a forkful of curry into her mouth. Immediately she reached for her glass of water.

'Not bad, is it?' he asked proudly. 'Perhaps a bit too much chilli.'

A bit! The top of her head had practically blown off. 'Mm-hm,' she agreed, swallowing. 'I still think we should go together.'

He tucked in enthusiastically. 'You'll do a much better job of cheering her up on your own. I think it's a good idea. And I promise I won't slip backwards. I know that's what's worrying you.'

'Won't you?' She shouldn't ask but couldn't help herself. She didn't want to be the one responsible for any relapse, not now they were on the road to putting his debts behind them. Thank God for Daniel and the hotels. Without them . . . well, it didn't bear thinking about.

He stopped eating and looked at her. 'Absolutely not. You're going to have to learn to trust me, otherwise it's hopeless. I can't have you watching over me every hour of the day and night. I have to do this myself.'

He was right. However difficult she found it, she couldn't babysit him for ever. Her initial anger on learning what he'd done had been channelled into a ferocious determination to get their fortunes back to square one as soon as she could. If that meant temporarily forfeiting her London assignations with Will, then she was prepared to wait for as long as she had to. Fortunately he had been travelling, so hadn't been pressing to see her. She couldn't abandon Terry when he was at his lowest ebb, just couldn't. Seeing him like that had brought out all her loyalty and support for him. She had surprised herself as much as him. Having reached the nadir, he really did seem to be doing all he could to clean up his act. He wanted to save his marriage, believing the distance between them had grown thanks only to his addiction. He had no idea of Will's involvement.

In fact, Eve could think of nothing she would like more than seeing Rose. If she could do anything to help her or cheer her up, she would. Being in London wouldn't be wasted because she could double up and make some overdue work appointments too. In fact, she had a couple of projects that would benefit from her talking them up in person. The office would be safe in May's hands, and besides, Eve would be only a call away. And then of course there was Will . . .

29

Will was late. Eve held her wrist as far away as she could, twisting it as she tried to make out the time on her fashionable but minuscule watch. Even with her reading glasses, she still could barely see the numbers. She moved her arm irritably, trying to catch the light. She had been waiting for twenty minutes and her mood was thunderous.

As she groped in her bag for her BlackBerry to check her emails, the bristle of her hairbrush pierced down behind her middle nail. She cursed under her breath and squeezed the tip of her finger until the pain wore off.

They hadn't seen each other for weeks, and yet he couldn't be bothered to get himself here on time. What did that say for their relationship? But it was typical of him. First time round, this had happened time and again. Once she had thrown a glass of water over him when he appeared, protesting that he'd had to watch the end of some Wimbledon match when she knew one of the players he named had been knocked out of the tournament the previous day. After that, he had mended his ways – to a degree. But time had helped them both forget.

This time she extricated her phone successfully and called up his number. She heard his recorded voice apologising for not being able to get to the phone and inviting her to leave a message. Why? What the hell was he doing? They'd made this arrangement days ago. Her last words to him had been 'Don't be late.' He'd just laughed.

She flicked over to her postbox. Her emails mounted up with the speed of a Tetris game if she didn't deal with them whenever she could. This was one of those opportunities, she reminded herself, trying to take the positive from the situation. One from Rufus, asking to see her. She flagged it to attend to later, intrigued but not wanting to fire off a reply without some thought. Others from clients and a couple of publishers whose queries could be quickly answered. One from Terry. He had promised to email after every Gamblers Anon meeting.

I still feel like a bit of an amateur beside some of the others. But I've been and I've kept my word and not placed a single bet. Don't worry. Enjoy yourself.

Terry had continued to encourage her to visit Rose. He was genuinely concerned for his sister's prolonged grief over Daniel's death and believed Eve could help her. Of course he had no idea that Will might be an added temptation in the equation. She had told Rose she was meeting Will for coffee, just coffee, for God's sake. Rose had been icy in her response, despite this brief interlude taking nothing away from the long, lazy evenings and the couple of outings the two of them had planned. Eve had also persuaded herself that she and Terry needed a few days apart to take stock. She needed distance to weigh up what was important to her now.

She sat back and sipped her coffee. Around her, the café was filling up. She had arranged to meet him in the morning because she wanted to get back to Rose. Guilt at going out to meet Will warred with her longing to see him again. The longing had won. She'd even left the house early and bought the gun-smoke linen dress especially for the occasion. And he still wasn't here.

As she returned her attention to her BlackBerry, it rang – too loudly for the two primped and suited women on the next table, who glared and muttered to each other. They no doubt still depended on their landlines and enjoyed the freedom of a mobile-free existence. Despite their annoyance at the interruption, Eve answered, whispering as a concession to them. 'Hello.'

'Eve! Don't hang up, please. It's Simon.' She almost dropped the phone.

'Why the hell are you phoning me?' she hissed, turning her back on her neighbours, whose hostility was quite open now.

'I've got to talk to you.' His urgency kept her listening when she knew she should hang up. 'Let me explain. Please.'

'Explain what?' She kept the phone to her ear.

'About Daniel. You're the only person who'll understand. I know you knew everything about him. He told me.'

'That's not true.' Then, all at once, she knew. She hadn't made a mistake. Dan had been one of the two men on the Royal Mile all those years ago after all. He had seen her, and said nothing. That kiss. Two men standing so close, in the shadows. She'd seen them but hadn't wanted it to be him, hadn't wanted the rumours she'd heard to be true. Back then, a little sexual experimentation was far more shocking that it would be now. He would have worried that her knowing would change his relationship with her and their friends. So rather than mention it, admitting or denying, he'd decided it was better for him to say nothing. With luck, she would convince herself she was mistaken. Exactly as she had, thus burying the secret deep. Why would she have thought anything when he hooked up with Rose so soon afterwards, so obviously devoted to her from day one? But by doing that, he had based their continuing friendship on a conspiracy of silence that she had failed to recognise until this minute. He couldn't even admit the truth to her when he'd had that very last chance. How naive she had been.

'I need your help to see Rose again.' Still urgent, but pleading too.

'Why would she want to see you after what's happened?' She was shocked by his nerve.

'Because I can help her through this. We can help each other.'

His arrogance silenced her for a second. As she tried to find an appropriate put-down, she was distracted by a commotion on the other side of the table. Will had pulled out the opposite chair and was sitting down, dropping a shopping bag, mouthing apologies, passing a crimson rose across the table – an embarrassingly showy gesture of conciliation. All this to the now intrigued glares from the neighbouring table.

'I've got to go,' she muttered, acknowledging Will's presence with a smile, before returning her attention to the call. 'I'm sorry.'

'Then I'll call you tomorrow so we can talk. Same time?'

'No! Don't do that.' The last thing she wanted was to be pestered until she gave in. Instead, she'd take control. 'I'll meet you upstairs in the Patisserie Francine in Covent Garden at ten tomorrow morning. I've got a meeting in Bloomsbury at eleven thirty.'

She hung up, already half regretting the arrangement. Before she had time to think further, the rose was being pressed into her hand as Will leaned across to kiss her. He smelled as if he'd just emerged from the shower, damp and fresh. His face was smooth, newly shaved. He'd changed his cologne to something more floral than before. She wasn't sure that she liked it. Feeling a thorn prick her finger, she pulled her hand back, letting it tear through her skin. The rose fell between them on to the table.

'Great start,' he said, as if it was her fault, then passed her a paper napkin.

She pressed it on the cut to absorb the beads of blood, then picked up the rose and stuck it in her long water glass to admire the velvety claret-coloured petals that unfurled from the even darker centre. 'It's beautiful.'

'To make up for keeping you waiting. You haven't been here long?' That smile again.

'Is over half an hour long in your book? It is in mine.'

Her snippiness obviously surprised him. He wrinkled his nose in boyish appeal. 'Come on, darling. Don't be like that. I couldn't help it. Unavoidably delayed.' He reached across the table for her hand. But before she had time to take it, his cuff caught the glass holding the rose and sent it flying towards the floor, at the same time splashing water all over the leg of one of the women at the next table.

While their incandescent neighbour was mopped up and placated with a piece of chocolate torte, Eve's thoughts returned to Simon. Meeting him would give her a chance to tell him what she thought of him. She would hear what he had to say and then dispense with him fairly but firmly, however convincing his self-justification. That was the very least she could do for Rose. She had seen for herself how important his friendship had been to her. He had given her the sort of kindness and company that even Eve, her closest friend, could never have provided. That was another reason why finding out the truth had to be so hard. Rose had lost both him and Daniel now. However, Eve knew what she had to do. And to tell the truth, she quite relished the idea of involving herself – just a bit.

Eventually she had Will to herself again. His earlier good humour was teetering on the edge of extinction, most of it having been used to sort out the shenanigans on the next table.

'What kept you?' She couldn't stop herself asking.

'Oh, you know,' he said vaguely. 'Wasn't watching the time. I've got a lot on at the moment, before I head off to Africa the week after next.'

Eve had forgotten he was off again, this time to the Okavango delta, in his tireless quest for photographically obliging wildlife. But she was unhappy with his excuse. 'Doing what?' she asked, noting the flicker of irritation in his eyes.

'For heaven's sake, Evie.' He always called her that when he was making up to her. 'We're not married any more. This and that, OK? Anyway, what does it matter? We're here together now.'

In fact, no, it wasn't OK at all. Their time together was precious and she hated wasting it. There was something different about him that she couldn't quite put her finger on. Perhaps it was just the new scent, the new grey-and-red-checked shirt that he wore like a jacket over the dark T-shirt, or her own predisposition for suspicion. Despite all that, she forced herself to concentrate on the little time they had left. Within minutes they were back on an even keel, the chaos of his arrival forgotten, and she had a hundred per cent of his stomach-melting attention.

'You're looking better than ever,' he said, once again reaching for her hand, this time successfully avoiding everything on the table. 'And you're wearing the bangle. That means a lot to me.'

Eve glanced down at the bracelet Terry had given her and said nothing. Instead she gave what she hoped was a smile that smouldered, at the same time remembering the bangle Will had given her still wrapped up in the sanitary towel bag buried among her wash things. She would never be able to ask him if she could change it. Too complicated. Too many ramifications. Another secret. She swiftly changed tack, reminding him of the time he'd given her a silver Russian wedding ring that she'd thrown at him in a temper. It had rolled away into a drain in the gutter outside their flat. Their efforts with a number of unbent wire coat-hangers had met with nothing but failure. They laughed, reminded of their shared past. Neither of them mentioned their future but it was there, as large as any elephant in the room. Eventually he asked the question she'd been hoping to avoid.

'Have you told Terry yet? About us?' His eyes were so intent on her, she felt like a butterfly pinned to a board. To avoid them, she bent to return her BlackBerry to her bag.

'No, I couldn't. Not yet.'

As she faced him again, she saw that flare of irritation, gone as quickly as it came.

'I haven't been able to. He's got too much on his plate.' She couldn't confess how torn she was between the two of them. Will or Terry. Terry or Will. Will wasn't interested. Nor would he be interested in Terry's problems and how it was Eve's immediate duty to support him, whatever her final decision. He didn't want her problems, just solutions for them both. And he wanted her. But ever since the anniversary party, she couldn't ignore the two most pressing issues, of Terry and the agency – she remembered Rufus's email and wondered briefly what he could want with her. Walking away from her marriage was much more tricky than she'd imagined.

'Evie, you promised weeks ago.' He was full of reproach. 'What's the point otherwise?'

'I know I did, but things have got in the way.' How feeble she sounded, as vague as he had been earlier, but sharing Terry's problems with Will would be a disloyalty too far.

While Will ordered two more coffees, Eve was horribly aware that this precious meeting was going all wrong. When they were brought to the table, she played with her spoon in the cappuccino foam, delaying drinking it for as long as possible, desperate to prolong their time together and to smooth things over.

'I can tell you're still pissed off with me for being late, but

I'll make it up to you.' He scratched his temple as he thought, obviously struggling to come up with something. Then his expression lit up. 'I know. I'm going to Bath next Wednesday to see one of the photographers coming to Africa. I'll be finished after lunch. Why don't you meet me and we could stay over and make a night of it?'

She didn't have to think twice. If she couldn't explain to Rose, then she would tell her and Terry that she was visiting an author. And what was one night? Nothing. It might even help her make up her mind. Yes, the deciding factor. 'I'd love to,' she said, and leaned across the table to kiss him.

The Patisserie Francine was busy, with most of the customers sitting at tables on the street. The July morning was already hot, presaging the first day of a predicted heat wave. Eve didn't want to make the meeting with Simon any more pleasant than it need be, so she chose a table inside, at the back, where the smell of coffee was strong. She ordered herself a cappuccino, then attended to her emails. Before she'd left, she and Rose had discussed how to reply to the one from Rufus. Accordingly, she sent him a message to suggest they meet while she was in London. Whatever his intentions, neutral territory suited her best. This was one of those times when she wished she had an office in town. Without one, she was restricted to meetings in other people's offices or in restaurants and cafés. However, she told herself firmly, things could be a lot worse. Still angry and hurt by his defection, she kept the message brief. He probably had no idea how much damage he and Amy had inflicted on the agency at a time when she needed the business to be operating as well as it could. Lost in thought, she stared into the middle distance, beyond the counter piled with baskets of croissants, scones and home-made biscuits.

She didn't have to wait long before Simon was threading his way through the tables towards her. He sat down, pulling up the neatly creased knees of his chinos as he did so, and ordering a latte from an assiduous waitress who'd scurried after him. 'Anything more for you?'

Eve shook her head, refusing to give an inch. She wasn't going to make this easy for him. He looked nervous, adjusting his rolled-up shirtsleeves, glancing around the other customers until eventually focusing on her.

'Thank you for agreeing to meet me. I know it can't be easy.'

Eve thought of Rose, whom she'd left reading the paper. She had thought it better not to mention she was meeting Simon. This was something she had to do for Rose's sake. Or that was what she told herself. But now they were face to face, she realised their meeting was a mistake. This was between the two of them. Despite his invitation, she shouldn't be involving herself.

'Just say whatever you've got to say,' she said. 'Rose doesn't know I'm here.'

He looked taken aback by her aggression, but replied immediately. 'I'm hoping you'll persuade her to see me.' They waited as the waitress put down his coffee. He emptied a sachet of brown sugar into it and stirred, then offered the bowl to her as an afterthought.

She raised her hand in refusal.

'Simon, I can't. There's nothing to be gained from it. Get that into your head. Rose is her own woman. If she's decided she doesn't want anything to do with you, then that's the way it'll be.'

'I want to help her. I told her Daniel didn't love me, and I meant it. He never intended her to find out about us.'

'You amaze me.' She was unable to stop the sarcasm in her voice

'This is so difficult.' His voice caught, but he recovered himself. 'You do know Dan was bisexual. He told me you knew.'

She tried not to show any emotion at all as he went on.

'But he'd been completely faithful to Rose – completely – until we met. I was immediately attracted to him, you see. Perhaps he wanted one last throw of the dice, just to find out about himself. Who knows? We laughed at the same things, enjoyed—'

'Spare me the detail,' Eve interrupted sharply. 'OK, Dan was bisexual, and I can just about accept that, after years of marriage, he was flattered by the attention of a younger man, but what I don't get is what the hell you thought you were doing befriending his wife. How could you do that?'

'Everything all right here?' The waitress was at her side, and Eve realised that eyes had been raised from papers and laptops and were staring at them.

'I'm sorry. Yes, we're fine. Perhaps the bill.' Eve wasn't going to give him any more time than necessary. The waitress having returned to the counter, she sat back in her chair staring at him. What she saw was a younger man desperate for her approval. But she resisted sympathy. Resting her arms on the table, she leaned forward for his explanation. 'Well?'

'I didn't plan anything. Far from it. I explained that to her. Jess involved me with Trevarrick, then asked me to show the plans to Rose. I could hardly refuse.'

Eve bit back that in her opinion, that was exactly what he could have done.

'When we met, I liked her. I felt as if I knew her from everything Dan had told me about her. I hadn't intended to ask her to the opera, but I did. We were both lonely and helped each other through what was a difficult time. I felt I owed her something . . .' He stopped to drink his coffee.

'And now?'

'And now . . . I know she's hurting, but I'm sure I can help her understand what Dan was going through and how much their marriage meant to him. He talked about her and the girls so often. So I'm asking you to persuade her to meet me. I want to make things better if I can, and I'd like you to give her this.' He took an envelope from his briefcase and passed it to her.

She held it between finger and thumb as if it was about to explode, then turned it in circles, focusing on the neat but ex-aggerated curls of the letters. 'Make things better,' she repeated, not believing what she was hearing. 'You're one of the reasons things are as bad as they are. Why can't you post it?'

'Because if you give it to her, and explain, there's a chance she'll read it.' With his elbows on the table, he joined his hands as in prayer and at last looked straight at her. 'Please.'

He looked so earnest, so anxious, so repentant that her resolution to hold firm wavered, then dissolved.

'All right,' she replied, regretting it even as she spoke. 'I don't expect it will do any good. She'll probably bin it anyway. But I'll see what I can do.'

30

The too aptly titled *Leaving* had perhaps not been the best DVD they could have chosen. Rose had watched uncomfortably as Kristin Scott Thomas left her well-to-do husband and children for a life of blistering passion with a cash-strapped builder that went on to end in tragedy. All she could think of was her brother, alone at home while Eve, sitting beside her glued to the screen, continued her affair. They had talked about nothing else but Eve's dilemma since Eve had got back the previous day.

'He's a jerk.' Rose's opinion of Will hadn't changed since he'd left Eve in the first place. 'I wish you wouldn't. Terry really doesn't deserve this.'

Eve just looked away and said, 'I know. But the sex. It's so good. I can't—'

Rose put her hands over her ears. She didn't want to hear any more. There was little hope of anything she could say influencing Eve, but at least she'd said what she thought and had stood up for her brother. They might not be as close as they once were, but she couldn't help feeling as protective of him over this as she had over childish things. She'd hoped she'd be able to drum some sense into Eve during her visit, but so far it hadn't happened.

Eve was in her dressing gown, stretched out on the sofa. A wide blue headband kept her hair off her face, which was covered in some regenerative anti-ageing muck. Between them were a couple of mugs of camomile-and-spearmint tea. She was looking at an old colour supplement when her phone rang.

'Will! Hi!' She let the magazine drop to her lap.

Rose noticed how her voice had become slightly breathy, un-hinged even. But despite her irritation, she was also startled by the unexpected longing she felt herself. To love and be loved. Didn't everybody deserve that? Even Eve with Will – if that was what they both felt for one another. Even if she never experienced those feelings again, at least she'd found them with Daniel. Eve had turned away from her, but she could hear every word.

'I wasn't expecting to hear from you . . . Yes, I'm fine . . . Can't chat, I'm with Rose. Yes, I'll see you then . . .' She giggled like a love-struck teenager. 'Well, if you put it like that . . . I can think of a few things we haven't tried too . . .'

Rose's heart skipped a beat. Before she could overhear any more, she left the room. The desire in Eve's voice spoke volumes. But how could she do this to Terry? Why couldn't she see what a mistake she was making? Despite only having seen Will at the memorial, that once had been enough for Rose. He was still the same charming, raffish type, but there was something untrustworthy about him. If Eve wouldn't listen, then she would have to find out for herself. And Rose would be sure to be around to catch the pieces.

'Rose! What are you doing?'

Eve's voice shattered her thoughts, and she returned to the living room. 'Just thought I'd give you a bit of privacy.'

'That was Will.' Eve's face was flushed and smiling.

'No! I'd never have guessed. What did he have to say for himself?' She asked without being at all sure that she really wanted to know. She sat back in her favourite chair, the one she'd re-covered in the clay and sweet pea stripe.

'The thing is . . .' Eve rolled on to her side to face her, her expression hard to read under her thick white mask, 'he's asked me to go to Bath with him on Wednesday. Just for a night,' she added hurriedly.

Her diplomatic skills finally exhausted, Rose snapped. 'For Christ's sake, Eve. You can't carry on with this. Look at you! You've been like a cat on hot bricks ever since you got here.'

Despite the white mask, Eve looked abashed. 'But Rose, he—'

'I know what he makes you feel. I know about the great sex. Or enough about it. You've told me a thousand times. But you have to sort this out once and for all. It's not just about you. Think about

Terry and the kids. What they'll say. What they'll do.' All Rose's maternal instincts were at the fore. As far as she was concerned, family came first, however difficult or trying they might be. 'Terry's your husband.'

Eve stuck out her chin, defiant. 'But I've already said I'll go. I haven't had a chance to talk to Will properly, what with everything else that's been going on. We only had coffee yesterday, and there's so much we need to discuss.'

For the first time, Rose saw the real possibility that Eve might leave Terry for Will, as inconceivable to her as it was. But the more she voiced her disapproval of them meeting, the more Eve stuck to her guns. Perhaps she should change her tack. 'It's been great having you here, you know.'

Eve beamed.

'I'll miss you. Talking to you has really helped me and I do feel calmer, but to be honest, the subject of you and Will is beginning to drive me round the bend. If you really want to go to Bath, then go. Have one last fling. Say goodbye. No harm done.'

The gratitude at being given permission to go shone from Eve's eyes. 'I still say sex with an ex doesn't count.'

Rose kicked off her shoes before curling her legs underneath her. 'I know that's what you think, but to me, it's all the same. Either way, go if you must, but if I were you, I'd end it there. Enough said.'

With the understanding that the subject was closed, Rose picked up a summer exhibition catalogue and helped herself to one of the truffles Eve had brought with her.

'There's something else.' Eve's clear reluctance to say whatever it was made Rose look at her in alarm. 'I did something today you're not going to like. But . . . I did it for you.' She sounded unsure. 'I think.'

'And?' Rose stopped flicking the pages and waited.

Eve had curled herself into a ball, arms around her knees. Only her geisha-like face remained exposed. 'Well, the thing is . . . Simon asked me to meet him.' She pressed on, ignoring Rose's intake of breath. 'I did, and he asked me to ask you to meet him. I think you should hear him out. There.' She rolled on to her back again, clearly anticipating Rose's outraged reaction.

But Rose didn't feel outrage, just an intense weariness that crept into every limb, making them so heavy. 'I thought the idea was that we supported each other. Seeing Simon doesn't seem to me to be doing that. I thought I'd made it absolutely plain to everyone who needs to know.' The catalogue slipped to the floor with a thump.

Eve started and sat up abruptly to face her again. 'I thought I'd help by seeing him off.' The mask was beginning to crack around her mouth.

'And did you?' Eve's nosiness had taken her one step too far this time, but Rose didn't have any energy left for anger.

'Well, no. Not exactly.'

'Then you'd better tell me what happened.' The thought of them meeting gave Rose the oddest feeling, not so much one of betrayal but of loss. Although she hadn't known him long, Simon's friendship had definitely been instrumental in helping her through her loneliness. Her attachment to him had been deeper even than she realised.

'I kept it short.' As if that made it better. 'But I did feel sorry for him. There was something about him that I can't explain. He wants to see you.'

'I hope you told him that there was no way on earth that was going to happen.' Rose picked up the catalogue and went to put it with the others on the bookshelf.

'I did, of course.' Eve leaned back on her hands, arms straight, shoulders hunched by her ears, as if she was about to propel herself across the room after Rose. 'But he gave me something for you.'

'For God's sake!' Rose's impatience with Eve made her crack again. 'And you took it?'

'Honestly, Rose, if you'd seen him, you'd understand. He wants to put things right between you.'

'If that weren't so sick, I'd laugh.' Rose leaned against the mantelpiece, looking down at Eve, unable to believe she'd been so easily taken in. 'He was my husband's lover. How do you think that makes me feel? Have you no imagination?' And yet she had to acknowledge that as well as her feelings of betrayal and revulsion, the smallest part of her missed Simon, his conversation and companionship, their long talks about Daniel and the release afforded her by the music they'd listened to together, the music he chose, his growing interest in the thing she loved most passionately: art. All they had in common had made their short-lived friendship strong. Anna was right.

'I'm really, really sorry. I thought I was doing the right thing.' Eve crossed the room to hug her. 'I only wanted to help.' Rose twisted her face away a moment too late. For a second they were stuck together. Then the left side of her face peeled away part-coated with Eve's mask. They couldn't help smiling as she wiped at it. 'But I might as well give you this anyway. I said I would.' Eve pulled the envelope from her dressing gown pocket.

Rose took it. 'I know you meant well. It doesn't matter.' She stared at the writing with its familiar curls and swirls, about to tear the envelope in half, then thought better of it. Instead she folded it and tucked it into the pocket of her jeans.

'Aren't you going to open it?' Eve's sense of drama predictably got the better of her.

'Not now.' Rose patted her pocket, aware of how much she was disappointing her friend. 'Perhaps not at all. Shall we talk about something else? I don't want to think about him any more.' She passed Eve the box of truffles.

But when she reached her bedroom twenty minutes later, having arranged to meet Eve after her meeting with Rufus ('A breakfast meeting. He'll hate that. And shopping will take you out of yourself'), she had second thoughts. She sat on her bed and stared at the envelope Eve had given her. The writing of her name reminded her of the inscription in the libretto. She glanced at the photo of Daniel that she kept by her bedside, taken by her at the Casa Rosa two years earlier. He was sitting at the terrace table, playing patience. The girls were out of shot, rescuing the burning fish from the barbecue. He smiled back at her, confident, loving, a family man. A man with a secret he couldn't tell. But whatever he'd done, he had loved her. She knew that in her heart. What would he want her to do now?

She took a biro from the bedside table, slid it into the envelope, then hesitated before ripping it open. The paper tore unevenly before she pulled out a letter. As she unfolded it, something fell to the floor. She let it lie there while she read what Simon had written, her stomach churning.

Dearest Rose,

I've explained everything the best way I know how. I can't tell you how sorry I am for what's happened. Perhaps I should have been honest with you from the start – but how could I have been? What I said to you at Trevarrick was true, and I believe you know that deep down. I was never really under the illusion that Daniel would leave you. I loved him. He desired me – briefly. That's all. I know how difficult this is for you, but believe me, neither of us intended to hurt you.

But your friendship meant much to me, and I believe it was important to you too. Despite everything, I hope we might be friends again. This may be too soon, but perhaps time will heal the wounds we've caused and you'll have a change of heart.

I have two tickets for a concert at Kings Place – Brahms. Bought for you. Here's one of them. I'll be sitting in the other seat. I hope you'll join me. But it's up to you, of course.

Simon

She bent to pick up the ticket, turning it in her fingers. The date was a month away. She felt nothing. Moving like a robot, her brain numb, she slipped the letter and the ticket back in their envelope and put them in the drawer. There was no question of her joining him, but she would decide how to reply, if at all, later.

She went to the bathroom, took a sleeping pill from the packet she'd been about to throw away, and returned to the bedroom. She took off her jeans, and without bothering to remove anything else, slid under her duvet, shut her eyes and waited for welcome oblivion to claim her.

Another day, another restaurant, another potentially awkward encounter. But Eve was ready. She had been sure to arrive fifteen minutes early to make sure she was in her seat. She wanted Rufus on the back foot from the start. In the Ladies' she made sure she was looking her best and most businesslike. Her suit was expensively tailored, her blouse ironed within an inch of its life and her heels appropriately high. She'd brought her briefcase even though there was nothing in it relevant to Rufus. As she was shown to the table, she was furious to find him *in situ*, coffee and toast already in front of him. Then she allowed herself a moment of amusement. He knew her too well.

Crossing the room, she took in his appearance: hair on end, trademark odd socks and worn old trainers. Amy clearly hadn't got her claws into him as thoroughly as Eve had anticipated. She couldn't imagine her erstwhile colleague happy at being seen with someone so scruffy, however eccentrically or endearingly youthful others might find him.

He looked up as she arrived. 'Eve. Long time. This looks good.' He poured them both coffee from the pot already brought to the table. 'Something to eat?'

She tightened her lips. A fully fledged blowout was not on her agenda. 'I'm sorry, Rufus. I've had to schedule an unexpected meeting, so I'll have to keep it brief.'

He smiled. 'I thought you might say that.'

'What did you expect, after you've practically single-handedly sabotaged my agency? A warm handshake and a glass of champagne? I don't think so.' She pulled out her chair and sat opposite him, wrinkling her nose at the sharp undernote of sweat that overrode his aftershave. What was Amy thinking? She had never struck Eve as a woman who would let any husband of hers be anything other than perfectly turned out. Husband-to-be, she corrected herself.

'Does it have to be like this between us?' He leaned back, appraising her.

'I think the short answer to that is probably yes,' she said, beginning to enjoy herself. 'I shall do all I can for your backlist, of course, in the most professional way possible, but I think our friendship is over. Don't you?'

'Not quite. I've missed your blistering backchat no end.' He took a piece of toast and scraped on some butter.

'Well you should have thought of that before taking off with my assistant.' She stirred her coffee, quite calm.

'That's why I wanted to see you.' He sipped his.

'Not to ask me to be matron-of-honour, I hope.' She allowed herself a grim smile at the thought.

His laugh turned into a cough as coffee splattered from his mouth over his toast. He wiped himself down with a napkin. 'Oh God, I'm so sorry. But you couldn't be further from the mark, for once.'

'Perhaps you'd better tell me, then.' All of a sudden, Eve had an inkling that she might like what Rufus was about to say.

'I'm wondering whether you might consider taking me back on your books.' His boyish face beamed in expectation of her reaction as he reached for his coffee.

She stared at him, silenced for once, as he licked off the cappuccino moustache on his upper lip. Eve thought carefully, aware that this might be some kind of Amy-led scheme. But she had no idea what Amy could want from her now. In any event, agreeing to represent her future husband would bring ramifications of a not entirely pleasant kind. 'Rufus, if this is because you and Amy have had an argument, the answer's no. Besides, I'm sorry, but I think her being your wife is going to make our relationship, *if* I were to take you back, extremely difficult. Too difficult probably. No, it won't work.'

'But you don't understand,' he protested, putting his cup down.

'Explain it to me then.' Yes, she was definitely enjoying this. Let him work for what he wanted. She looked pointedly at her watch.

'Amy and I, well . . . it hasn't exactly worked out.' He dabbed at the coffee on his plate. Anything rather than look at Eve.

'Which? Your professional relationship or the personal one? I can imagine she might not be experienced enough for the first, though of course I couldn't speak for the second.' This was getting better and better.

'You know perfectly well what I mean.' His features creased into a puckish grin that disappeared as quickly as it came. 'It's over. I know that's quick, even for me, but she was so livid when I refused to invest in her company. I thought it was too soon, and would bind our interests too closely, but she didn't see it that way. She said some terrible things. She made me realise that I was being roped in to some weird desire she has to outdo you. She's so impatient for her own success. That's what she really loves – not me.' The voice of a disappointed child got to Eve. But business first.

'So *if* I agree to represent you again, you're saying that Amy will have nothing to do with our agreement or whatever deals I set up for you?'

'Nothing.' He shook his head, miserable. 'I know how bad it will look for her agency to have her first big client returning to its original fold, but I have to do this for my own sake. For my books. If you'll have me.'

An author could be relied upon to put their career before almost anything else. Rufus as much as anyone. His aberration with Amy was over and he'd seen sense before it was too late. Eve was tempted to play him along for a little longer, getting her own back for the damage he'd caused. But she couldn't leave him hanging when her answer was bursting from her. 'In that case, of course I'll represent you again. I'd like nothing more.'

As she stood up, he followed suit and they hugged awkwardly across the table. Eve was unable to hide her delight. If you're patient, what goes around sure does come around, she reflected. Amy's loss would be her gain. And once she had announced Rufus's return, there were one or two others who doubtless would want to follow him. She could image Amy's frustration and disappointment. Eve's day couldn't have started better. She couldn't wait to tell Rose, and then when they'd done with shopping, she had lunch with the editorial director of Perfin Books, who was, without question, one of the biggest gossips in the business. All she had to do was entrust to him the secret of Rufus's change of heart. By the end of the afternoon, most of the world of children's publishing would have heard. How very satisfying that would be.

31

Two days later, Rose walked out of the Tate into the sunshine. Although she'd come to a temporary halt with her own painting, she still found inspiration and pleasure in the work of other artists. The Munch exhibition had been eye-opening and, to her relief, with *The Scream* nowhere to be seen. That howling skull was a little too close to her own feelings for comfort. Since Daniel's death, she had felt like hanging on to her head and letting rip more times than she cared to count.

Eve had said goodbye four hours ago. She would be on the train to Bath by now. To her surprise, given the circumstances, Rose already missed her, even though her sister-in-law had brought more problems with her than she had made disappear. She had descended on her almost a week ago, bowed down under a bunch of lilies, her case, a couple of bottles of wine and a box of hand-made truffles. She had brought a frenzy of plans for occupying Rose, but they had rather fallen apart under the pressure of business meetings and the failure of her resistance to Will, impervious to Rose's disapproval. The promised action-packed time of distraction had taken a back seat to Eve's own dramas. But what had Rose expected?

In fact, the visit had cheered her no end. She hadn't needed the consolation of the cinema or theatre. Eve's belief in the healing power of retail therapy didn't work for her either, even though she was happy to trail along as adviser and even bag carrier. Just having someone at home to talk to had been fun. She wasn't even angry about Eve seeing Simon. Her irrepressible love of meddling was to be half expected. In fact, it had been clever of Simon to think of her. For once, instead of acting on impulse, he'd thought through what he was doing.

Having tried to hide how excited she was at the prospect of her night away with Will, Eve had failed so miserably that the two women had spent several awkward moments during their last couple of days together in which neither had known quite what to say. Their friendship had been stretched to breaking point over the inconclusive Will/Terry debate. Nonetheless, having Eve around was preferable to the yawning emptiness of the house that was waiting for her now.

As Rose passed the beds of silver birches on her way towards the Millennium Bridge, her friend remained foremost in her mind. Although family ties dictated that Rose side with her brother, she was sympathetic to Eve. Terry couldn't have been the easiest of husbands, and right now he must be one of the worst. She could hardly blame Eve for grabbing a bit of excitement when it came her way. Attention and great sex – a seductive combination. She wondered for the nth time what Terry would say if he knew. Would he really be surprised, given that he too was so caught up in his own problems? Rose was guilty of not phoning him recently in case she said something that would give Eve away, although she knew he needed her support. But the sale of the Arthur was going through, and Terry knew that the money would soon be realised to clear the remaining debt. Beyond that, he had a hard struggle ahead. But at least he had finally admitted that his gambling had got way out of control and that he needed help. That must be surely half the battle. That, and taking the steps to stop himself.

As she reached the bridge, she heard her ringtone. Glad to talk to someone, she dug her phone out of her bag, delighted to find her younger daughter on the line.

'Jess! How are you?'

'We're all fine. Dylan's talking all the time now; just constant chatter. I can't wait for you come down and see him again.'

Rose was looking forward to that too, being part of a family. But Jess sounded rushed. Phoning during the working day meant there was a purpose to the call. Rose waited.

'I've had awful morning sickness but it's getting better now. Adam's been great, though he's using every spare moment he can to finish the bowls for the Plymouth exhibition. Mum, we need you!'

This was music to Rose's ears. 'I'll be down in a couple of months or so, but I've got to give the classes I've committed to and tie up a few loose ends.'

'You should think about doing something like that when you get here,' Jess suggested. 'I want you to have your own things going on too.'

And so did Rose. Although she relished her role as grandmother, and was looking forward to helping out when needed, she wanted her independence too. 'I'll think about what I might do,' she said. 'But first I need to find somewhere to live. I can't stay in the hotel for ever. Incidentally, how's the building going?'

'That's really why I'm calling.' A deep breath travelled down the line.

Rose readied herself for the worst. She had stopped just as she reached the beginning of the bridge's span. As she looked at the familiar landmarks on either side of the Thames, she realised how much she was looking forward to this new start Jess was offering her. She would find herself a cottage near Trevarrick, and have a studio flat to return to in London when she wanted. She could not abandon all this completely.

'Mum, it's dreadful. Roger, the project manager, doesn't get it at all. It was bad enough during the first stage of the work, when he was unfamiliar with what was happening, but now he keeps trying to change the plans. I know work's not starting until the end of October, but he's suggesting we change the orientation of the swimming pool and use different tiling, something much lighter than the slate, that's much more expensive. He doesn't think the glass we've chosen for the snug is the best for the job. Apparently there's some German-manufactured glass that's better. Look . . .'

She hesitated, and in that second, Rose knew exactly what she was about to be asked.

'We need Simon to see it through. We really do. I can hardly bear to suggest it, but Trevarrick matters so much to me now. It's everything Dad left behind—'

'Not quite everything,' Rose butted in.

'You know what I mean. But Simon's the only architect I've met who really gets the place. I don't want him here either, but we do need him, just until the work's finished the way Dad would have wanted it. You won't have to have anything to do with him. I'll keep contact to the bare minimum, don't worry about that, but he does understand what we both want and what Dad would have wanted too.'

Rose stood stock still, unable to believe her ears.

'I know it's hard,' Jess went on. 'And I never thought I'd be asking you this. But he wouldn't need to be here all the time. Just a couple of visits or so to oversee things again.'

'That's out of the question,' said Rose, feeling her blood pumping. 'I'm amazed you've even asked me. I know you and Anna think we should try to move on, but I thought you were with me on this.'

'Oh Mum, I am.' Jess's sympathy was audible. 'You know how upset and furious I've been with Dad, and I would never do anything to hurt you, but I need this to be done properly. And face it, so do you. You loved the original plans too.'

For a moment, Rose was back in her kitchen, going over them for the first time with Simon, listening to him talk so enthusiastically and knowledgeably, forging a new friendship, sharing a vision for the future of Trevarrick. 'Yes, I did,' she conceded. 'But things have changed.'

'No they haven't. Not really.'

'How can you say that?'

A young woman pushing a Rolls-Royce of a buggy slowed down as she heard Rose's raised voice. Rose forced a smile to show everything was all right, waving her free hand to indicate a problem that would be easily resolved. The woman shrugged her shoulders, reciprocated the smile and walked on.

'I can say that because I want to remember Dad as he was.' Jess sounded absolutely sure of what she was saying. 'I haven't been able to stop thinking about him. Don't think I haven't. I've talked and talked to Adam so much about what's happened, and he's made me look at things differently. I was devastated at first, but he's right. We can't undo the past, but I don't want to be constantly wondering whether our family life wasn't what it seemed. It was what it was. I really believe Dad loved us all, even if he did have a bit of an odd way of showing it sometimes. That temper!' She gave a little laugh. 'And he loved you. I know he did.' She hesitated over what she was going to say next. 'I don't understand his friendship with Simon. I don't even want to think about it, but we should try to remember him the way we can, not torture ourselves with what might or should have been.'

'It was more than a friendship.' Rose started walking again, keeping to the right, looking downriver to Tower Bridge. Where had her daughter found this new maturity? She guessed they had Adam to thank.

'But Mum, it doesn't matter what it was now. Don't you see that? Dad's dead.'

'I know that.' She spoke sharply. 'I think about him every day.'

'Of course you do. But we can't live in the past. Do you know what Adam said? Of course you don't. Well, he said, "The best thing to do with the past is to take what you want from it to make your future and leave the rest behind." He thinks you'll never lose by doing that. Think about it, Mum. All I'm doing is asking you to reconsider. Please.'

'Perhaps we should talk again when I'm not walking outside.' Those wretched tears were threatening yet again, and a crocodile of gabbling schoolboys were making it conveniently hard to hear. Rose said a brisk goodbye and tucked her phone back in her bag as she continued towards St Paul's.

An hour later, she was at home. Throughout her journey she had thought of nothing but what Jess and indeed Anna had said. Perhaps they were both right. Perhaps she should take their lead, let go and move forward. But how was that possible? How could she ever get her mind round what had happened? Yet Adam's advice to Jess still rang in her ears: 'The best thing to do with the past is to take what you want from it to make your future.' If she was to have a future at all, perhaps she should listen.

She made herself a mug of tea, then went upstairs to her bedroom. She opened her wardrobe and took out the dress Simon

313

had helped her buy, unworn since the party. Holding it in front of herself as she stood by the mirror, she saw again how spot-on his choice had been for her. What a successful day that had been: shopping, then lunch and laughter. Returning the dress to its place, she sighed, then opened her bedside drawer and took out Simon's envelope. She sat on the edge of her bed and stared at his writing for a long time.

Will had been in Bath all day, so Eve travelled down on her own. A bit of her was relieved to get away from Rose for twenty-four hours. The drip-drip of badly disguised disapproval was beginning to get her down. She knew exactly what she was putting at risk and who she might be hurting. If she wanted a guilt trip, she was more than capable of sorting one out for herself without her sister-in-law breathing down her neck. Rose was only looking out for her brother, but that irked Eve, given that her own relationship with Rose was much closer than Rose's with Terry. As adults, the two siblings had increasingly little in common. In fact, sometimes Eve thought she was the glue that kept them together. So it was rich that Rose had come out on Terry's side.

Terry. Whenever she had thought of him in the last few days, she had been rocked by sadness and regret. Once she had helped him through his current problems, and completed sorting out their finances, she would be free to leave the marriage. The sale of the Arthur was going through as planned, and with Rufus's unpredicted return to the fold, her own business prospects had improved. Terry had to stay on the straight and narrow. Knowing how much depended on it, he was doing his best. She admired him for that. But the more she tried to picture a life without her husband, the harder it became. There seemed so many obstacles in the way of a life without him. Despite his faults, he loved her and would do anything for her. Many women weren't as lucky with their husbands. And she could hardly claim to be fault-free. He put up with a lot.

The financial crisis his gambling had provoked had driven home to Eve how much her family meant to her and how unbearable it would be to leave the nest in which she had invested so much time and love. They had brought up the children there; Millie had even been born in their bedroom, and the place was imbued with family history. She wouldn't find that anywhere else. Nor would she find anyone, least of all Will, who would share her interest in her children's lives. As far as she could tell, he found it hard enough to muster enough attention for his own kids. That was something she couldn't understand about him.

She, not Terry, would have to be the one to leave. Their mutual friends were bound to take sides. And the children? Would they suffer? Even though adults now, their parents splitting up was bound to affect them in some way or other, especially Millie, the baby of them all. Would *they* take sides? Especially when they knew who she'd left their father for. How would they be able to celebrate individual achievements as a family without things being awkward between them? Millie's graduation, for instance. Marriages. Grand-children. For a fleeting moment, she pictured Rose carrying Dylan up to bed, his arms around her neck, his soft cheek pressed against hers, Daniel proudly looking up after them. She envied her that. Christmas wouldn't be the same without their long-established family rituals. And the summer? Would she ever be able to visit Casa Rosa again? And of course Terry – she would miss all the little things that irritated, amused or made her love him, all the things they had in common. Her mind kept racing with lists of the losses and possibilities that were in her gift. And Terry would even get custody of the chickens!

But equally, when she was with Will, she couldn't imagine a future without him. He understood her, flattered her, made her feel all things were possible, that life could be exciting and unpredict-able. He made her feel like a different woman. Terry may have once done the same – it was hard to remember – but those feelings had been buried a long time ago in the mundane routine and the stresses involved in trying to have it all. Was that what she was doing again now? She wasn't so sure that she liked this different woman Will had unearthed, whose overriding concerns were shallow and selfish.

But the way she felt when she was with him was incomparable. She couldn't let that go.

She walked from the station to the hotel, an elegant Georgian building. She put her bag on the pavement under the iron and glass porch and stood for a second gazing up at the honey-coloured stone and the multi-paned sash windows. One night with Will, without any of the pressures of her everyday life. Twenty-four hours of un-interrupted pleasure and room service. Perhaps they'd emerge for dinner in the evening, and a stroll around the town. If it really was going to be their last meeting, better make it a memorable one. She shut her eyes in the most pleasurable anticipation, only to open them to the clearing of a throat.

'Can I help you?' A uniformed doorman was half bent over her case.

'Yes, thank you. I'm just checking in.' Her stomach fluttered with excitement.

They went in together and straight to the reception desk. Will had expected to arrive about half an hour before her, unless his meeting overran.

After glancing at her computer, the receptionist looked up with a warm smile. 'In fact Mr Jessop hasn't checked in yet. Would you like to go ahead to the room?'

Minutes later, Eve was sitting on the edge of a four-poster bed swagged in the palest of blue and grey. The almost matching toile wallpaper featured plump cherubs surrounded by garlands of flowers. She was flattered that Will hadn't skimped on the expense. In Terry's hands, they would have occupied the most modest of rooms. Once, he had even economised by choosing the one with-out an en suite. In the middle of those nights, Eve could be found trailing along the chilly corridors in search of a loo, wrapped in a thin faded kimono provided expressly for the purpose.

She lay back, feeling the give of the mattress, letting herself relax, smelling the clean white bedlinen. Then she sat up swiftly. Will might be late, but that gave her time to get ready for him. She unpacked her bag, stashing it away in the bottom of the wardrobe, hanging up the dress she'd brought for the evening – just in case

316

they ventured out of the room – putting her new satin and lace underwear in a drawer. Then she undressed, putting on one of the thick white towelling robes before taking her sponge bag into the bathroom. Examining herself closely in the mirror, she took her tweezers and plucked out a rogue hair from her chin, sure that it hadn't been there when she last looked. Just another of the pleasures that came with hormonal change, designed as reminders of time passing. Other than that, with a little minor titivating, she looked as good as she was ever going to. Lastly, she unwrapped the loo paper from the bracelet Will had given her and used it to wrap Terry's. Then she slipped Will's gift on to her wrist. Satisfied, she returned to the bedroom, pulled back the sheets and slid between them, careful not to disturb her hair or make-up. That would happen later.

After five minutes, when Will still hadn't appeared, she got out and padded over the shag-pile carpet to retrieve her bag. Having resolved not to spend any moment of her time in Bath on her BlackBerry – she had allowed herself twenty-four hours to be devoted exclusively to pleasure, not work – she took out her Kindle and found her place in the thriller she had started on the train. Back in bed, she lay reading, time flicking past in big red numbers on the bedside clock. But aware that Will might arrive at any moment, she couldn't concentrate. The plot had too many twists and turns for her to follow. At any other time she'd have been gripped by its complexities, but not today.

After another ten minutes, she got up and made herself a cup of coffee. Instead of bog-standard instant, there was a tin of freshly ground Colombian and a cafetière. By the time she'd finished, the supposedly seductive scent of her perfume was lost under the haze of coffee that filled the room. After a debate with herself about where to drink it, she climbed back into bed, aware that she had already spoiled the inviting newness of the sheets. She picked up her Kindle to try again, this time immersing herself more success-fully.

When the coffee was finished, she got up and forced open the paint-stuck window with a bash of her fist to get rid of the smell.

317

Instantly, the unmistakable aroma of frying onions wafted up from somewhere below. Their room must be directly above a kitchen vent. She slammed shut the window immediately, but too late. The atmosphere had transformed from boudoir to bistro in a stroke. She rubbed her bruised hand. Perhaps it was as well Will was delayed. There was time for the room to return to normal if she upped to arctic for a little while the aircon that she'd spotted too late.

Feeling suddenly and inexplicably nervous, she opened the minibar. A bottle of white wine winked at her. What harm? She poured herself a large glass and took it back to bed with her. Besides, the sun was inching towards the yardarm. Picking up her thriller, she scrolled back a few pages to reread what she had just read and already forgotten, forcing her way back into the plot despite herself. Eventually she lay back against the down-soft pillows and sighed, closing her eyes as she looked forward to Will's imminent arrival. However long his meeting overran, he must be due to get away soon.

When she next opened her eyes, she found she had rolled half on to her side. The white pillow was peachy with rubbed-off foundation and powder. A little pool of dribble had accumulated under her right cheek, soaking attractively into the pillow. Momentarily dazed by sleep, Eve couldn't remember where she was. Then reality struck home. She sat up, noticing first the empty wine glass, then the clock. The numbers were quite clear: 18:30. Now 18:31. She rubbed her eyes, remembering too late the mascara she'd lashed on in preparation for her role as femme fatale. There must be some mistake. She picked up the clock and shook it, pressed the buttons. No mistake: 18:32; 18:33. Will's meeting must have finished ages ago. Something must have happened to him.

She picked up the phone and dialled reception. 'Have any messages been left for room twenty-five.'

There was a silence as the woman looked. Everything would be clear in a second.

'No, I'm afraid not. Nothing.'

'Are you sure?' She swung her legs out of bed, despite the temptation to bury herself between the sheets.

'Absolutely. I've double-checked.'

As she put the phone done, Eve had an overwhelming and extremely unwelcome sense of déjà vu. Refusing to consider it, she abandoned the sleep-tossed bed and went to the mirror by the door. A gorgon looked back at her. The combination of sleep and products had stood her hair on end. Her right cheek was creased where she'd lain on the crumpled pillow. Her smudged mascara had given her panda eyes above cheekbones that perhaps, now she looked at them in this light, were after all a bit too gaunt for a woman her age. Tears began to well in her eyes. Don't do this, she reprimanded herself. You are not nineteen. All the same, she snatched a handful of tissues from the box. After blowing her nose and repairing the damage so that she looked presentable again, she poured herself another glass of wine.

She'd been in the room for over two hours. No one, not even Will, could be this late. Could he have had an accident of some sort? How would she find him in a city she didn't know? Unless he was lying injured in hospital somewhere. She didn't even know where his meeting had been. In desperation, she cast away her resolution for a virtually tech-free couple of days, found her Black-Berry and switched it on.

As soon as it came to life, she saw she had a number of emails waiting for her. She scrolled down them and found one, just one, from Will. Sent at three fifteen, when she had already been on the train from Paddington, phone off, her mind exclusively on the excitements of the twenty-four hours ahead of her. With trepidation and incipient anger, she opened it.

Evie babe, SO sorry but not going to be able to make Bath after all. Meeting cancelled and something came up last minute in London that I have to attend to. I'll make it up to you.

She stared at the words in disbelief, then read them again. And then again, as all the stuffing leaked out of her. He wasn't coming. She had travelled all the way here for nothing. He'd known she was catching the three o'clock train and had sent the email after she was on board – and that was all he could say. He was too busy even to bother to phone the hotel to speak to her. As she lay back against the pillow for a final time to let the impact of what had happened sink in, she couldn't avoid the memory of another pillow. Even though it was over twenty-five years ago, she could envisage it exactly, complete with its special anti-allergy pillowcase, jammed into the back window ledge of Will's car next to his dog-eared set of *National Geographic*s. The bastard!

She sat up, filled with a rage unlike anything she had felt before. How dare he treat her like this? If he thought she was going to roll over and accept it, he could think again. If their relationship was going to work at all, a few things needed to be said. And there was no time like right now, while she was boiling with fury. She called up his number and waited. She didn't need time to think what she was going to say, if he answered at all. If he didn't, she would make sure they saw each other the next day to have it out. He wouldn't get away with this. The ringing tone went on and on. Just as she was about to give up, he answered.

'Where the hell are you?' She didn't give him a chance to speak, proud that she kept her voice under control. Low, firm but extremely forceful.

'Bill, sweetie. It's your phone.' The voice she heard was distant; the phone was obviously being held out to Will. But there was no question that it belonged to a woman: a young, softly spoken woman who might be Welsh. Eve stared straight ahead of her, motionless. She didn't need to hear any more. She didn't need an explanation. Whatever he said would be a pack of self-justifying crap. She cut off the call before Will reached the phone.

She didn't know how long she sat staring into the distance, replaying the story of their recent relationship. Of course she had been married and he was single, free to do whatever he wanted, but she had never imagined that he was capable of repeating history in such a callous and humiliating way. Did he imagine she'd never find out he was seeing someone else? Or perhaps that was why he let the other woman answer the phone. He wanted her to know and was too cowardly to tell her. He had let her jeopardise her marriage with no reason. All right, that was her fault. She had allowed herself to be put in that position, had welcomed it even, but in the wrong-headed belief that what they had rediscovered between them would be worth it. This time there was no going back for either of them. Her anger was directed at herself for having been so gullible, believing that he was a different person when he hadn't changed at all. She stared at the BlackBerry in her hand. Slowly she called up Rose's number and lifted the phone to her ear.

Rose heard Eve out without interrupting. Eventually she ran out of things to say, aware that she was going round in circles. More than anything, she was grateful to Rose for not saying 'I told you so', for not even sounding as if that was what she thought. When Rose eventually spoke, she was clear, confident that her advice was what Eve needed to hear.

'Come back to London, Eve. You can stay the night here. I'll wait up for you. And then tomorrow, you know what you need to do.'

'What?' asked Eve, although she knew the answer.

'Go home,' Rose said. 'Go home.'

July – One Year Later

32

The Stansted departure lounge was heaving with people. Eve was fuming. Her children having long ago left school, she'd forgotten the hell of school holiday travel, when every family in the land criss-crossed the world in search of the sun and a stress-free fortnight. People crowded the cafés, caroused in the bars, browsed in the shops, queued at the money exchanges, wandered aimlessly. Everyone was shouting at everyone else. Excitement or stress, it didn't matter. Here and there a child cried or endured a bollocking for running off as tempers frayed under the pressure.

She gazed across the sea of bodies to find a pair of seats. Nothing. She should have known better than to leave the flight arrangements to Terry. But pressure of work meant that she had leaped at his offer to make them, despite the fiasco of their last journey to Italy. She could endure all this, she told herself, if they could relax once they got to Casa Rosa.

Amid the seated masses, a tattooed, shaven-headed man with a can of lager got to his feet. Such an unflattering look, she reflected, particularly with his T-shirt stretched tight over that beer gut and a swastika above his right ear. 'Terry,' she hissed. 'Over there. You take it. And watch out for Anna. I'll be back in a sec.'

Terry obliged, negotiating his way over legs, bags and children, and sank down on to the seat, their hand luggage at his feet. He pulled out the distinctive pink pages of the *Financial Times*, a certain escape for him. He was used to travelling with Eve and was resigned to what she was about to do.

In WHSmith, Eve homed in on the children's section of the bookshelves. The books were in some chaos already, but that was what she had come for: to restore order . . . and to promote her authors. An agent never sleeps. Glancing over her shoulder to make sure the shop assistants were busy elsewhere, she moved quickly, shunting the stock along the shelves so there was room for her to display her authors' books face-out. All's fair when it comes to sales, she told herself, as she moved Rufus's latest book from the shelf to the table, successfully hiding a pile belonging to another agent's author. Having completed her task, one author after another, also noting which of them weren't there at all, she walked as swiftly as she could to the other branch, where she repeated the process. Job done, she returned to Terry to find the seat beside him empty. She took a tissue and dabbed at a coffee stain before sitting down, perching on the edge in case her skirt got marked.

While he read the paper, apparently unperturbed by the chaos of their surroundings, she concentrated on keeping calm, breathing deeply. She wasn't afraid of flying. What she loathed was the whole experience of budget travel, of being herded cattle-like into a container only to fight for neighbouring non-reclining seats with minimal leg-room, paying over the odds for any kind of refreshment, and most likely being kicked in the back by an overexcited child or deafened by the baby crying in front – and all with no respite for at least two hours. While no one could blame the child or the baby, it was a bit too up-close and intimate for her.

By the time their flight was finally called, she had lulled herself into a state of mind where she was feeling a certain warmth towards her fellow human beings. After all, she kept reminding herself, they were the ones who bought her authors' books and kept her in business. And what were they doing but having a holiday, enjoying themselves, just as she was? Who was she to be so Scrooge-like in her quite unreasonable condemnation of them?

She did her best to preserve this new-found sense of goodwill to all men as she and Terry stood squashed between Hilary's Heavenly Hens, a raucous party of six generously endowed women on the wrong side of thirty (that was being generous) in pink sparkly tops and antennae, and a rowdy family with three young children who refused to stay put in the queue. Eve saw her continuing good humour as a test of character that she was determined to pass. She channelled her thoughts to other things. There was still no sign of

Anna and her friend. But there was nothing Eve could do. Either they would turn up or they wouldn't. There was no point getting exercised about it.

Inching forward, Eve shrank back as the steward making random checks on the weight of hand luggage paused beside her. She held her breath, lifting her case quite cheerily as if it wasn't pulling her arm out of its socket. He hovered there for a moment. She smiled at him, but thought better of making a comment that might provoke him. He glared in return, then pounced on one of Hilary's Hens. Eve and Terry shuffled past the poor woman as she was forced to unpack her suitcase, having to share out half the contents between her friends.

On the plane, they sat with an empty seat between them. Eve arranged her jacket and bag over it proprietorially, hoping they could keep the extra space for themselves. She focused on her Kindle, determined not to catch the eye of any of the other passengers. If they wanted the seat, let them dare to disturb her and ask. So far, so good.

Just as the plane was settling down and their row of three seats seemed secured, there was a flurry of activity at the door and in burst a final couple, who were swiftly directed down the aisle by the crew. Eve looked up at the disturbance to see Anna at last, hair flying, followed by a tight-T-shirted young man with his hair pulled back in a ponytail.

'Auntie Eve!' Anna stopped beside her. 'How incredibly lucky. Could you move in one?' As Eve obliged, sorry to lose the extra space but delighted her niece was there, Anna touched the man's hand. 'You'll be OK, Rick?'

So this was Rick! Rose had said he was coming. Although shouldn't one of them be looking after the garden centre? Wasn't July a busy time for them? According to Terry, the business was beginning to pick up nicely, but Eve supposed Anna must know best.

Rick's smile lit up his face, contradicting the conclusions Eve had already drawn from the dark ponytail, silver nose- and earrings, the complex coloured tattoo on his arm. 'No worries,' he said with a strong Australian twang. 'I'll seeya at Pisa.'

'That's Rick,' Anna explained unnecessarily, as he found himself a seat further back. 'I'll introduce you when we land. I'm sure you'll like him.' She polished a large orange Perspex ring on the hem of her see-through shirt.

'I'm sure I will,' said Eve, not entirely sure at all. 'What happened?'

'We overslept.' Anna tugged the seat belt from under her and clicked it across her stomach. 'Thank God we made it. I'm exhausted. Sorry, Auntie Eve, but I desperately need to destress.' She shook her hair out, then began to scrape it back so she could clip it up with a barrette stuck about with pinky-red crystals, before flinging herself back in her seat and closing her eyes, giving a melodramatic groan. They stayed shut during the safety routine, despite the pointed glares from a Tangoed hostess with a bleached topknot and tight shirt, and eventually Anna sank into a sound sleep. Eve returned to her Kindle and the remaining part of the first of two young-adult submissions that had been delivered the day she left the office. She didn't want them or their authors to be sitting waiting for her return and this was as good a moment as any other to get on with them. Beside her Terry slept too, head against the side of the plane, mouth open, the occasional snore fluttering forth.

Rose walked back from the pool to the house. Her towel was slung around her neck, her body warm in the sun. She rubbed her hair dry with one hand as she passed the table under the walnut tree, gazing at the old farmhouse bathed in the Tuscan summer light. While the rest of her life might have weathered a sea change, Casa Rosa had remained steadfast: the warm shades of the solid stone building, the shallow pantiled roof, the small brown-shuttered windows and heavy wooden doors. Nothing had changed since their last visit, almost two years ago. After Daniel's death, she had let the place to holidaymakers. Terry had volunteered to come over to meet the lettings agent for her and attend to a couple of maintenance problems that needed resolving. Thank God for Marco, their indefatigable odd-job man, who had kept the place so well in her absence.

Nonetheless, every minute of every hour contained a reminder of Daniel. All the little jobs that he would have done on arrival had demanded her attention: hanging out the hammocks; checking the pH levels of the pool; making sure the septic tank hadn't overflowed; repairing the outside chairs where the sun had melted the glue; looking for evidence of mice and spiders; replacing dead plants; seeing if the plumbing leaked; going through the mail that had welcomed her on the doormat; checking for breakages made by the previous tenants.

She stopped by the pots of miniature roses arranged at the feet of the pergola, neatly deadheading them with a few careful flicks of her thumb. Then she went to the geraniums, picking up her secateurs from where they lay on the low stone wall, and snipped the dead heads from them too, carrying the cuttings to the compost heap. With every movement she felt the sun drying her off, until it began to burn her unprotected skin. She draped the towel over her shoulders and upper arms. Before going indoors, she cut some stems of orange and purple bougainvillea and carried them in with her.

She opened the dresser cupboard and took out two small ceramic vases, filling them with water and arranging the bougainvillea before taking them to where Eve and Terry would be sleeping. This time she was putting the two of them in Jess's room. She didn't want to repeat the arrangements of their last visit. Besides, Jess and her family would be much more comfortable in the privacy and space of the old stables.

Satisfied that everything was ready for them – soap, shampoo and shower gel by the bath, towels folded on the rail, bed neatly made, hangers in closet, shutters closed – she went to her and Daniel's . . . no, she corrected herself, just her bedroom and turned on the shower.

When she'd first arrived, she had considered swapping bedrooms with Anna, not wanting the memories that she might find in hers. But to her surprise, the room had welcomed her, cocooning her within its four walls. Daniel's holiday clothes still hung in the locked half of the wardrobe. But they didn't upset her, despite knowing that she would have to get rid of them before the end of the summer. The bag that he had bought her long ago in the market by the Medici chapel was slung over the back of a chair. The picture of a Madonna and child hung over the bed, watching over her. She and Daniel had chosen her together in a junk shop they had found down a Sienese back street. The blue of her robe blazed out from the flaked gold leaf of the background. As she looked down at her child, her expression was one of the most loving Rose had seen. Rose understood completely that maternal devotion that refused to be derailed. Her last few nights in here had been undisturbed. It had taken two years, but at last she felt at peace.

She showered quickly, then grabbed a pair of white shorts and got dressed before slipping her feet into her flip-flops. She let her hair dry naturally. With the slight glow already lent to her by the sun, she needed no more than a brush of mascara and a slick of lipgloss and she was ready. She stopped by Anna's room. Every-thing was ready for them. She stroked flat a wrinkle in Anna's top sheet, pulled to the shutter with a loose hinge. The knotted mosquito net over the bed swayed in the breeze. As she left the room, Rose caught sight of herself in the wardrobe mirror. What a difference time could make to someone, both inside and out. She looked well again, still slim, her skin with that gloss a holiday could give. She had come a long way since Daniel's death.

In the kitchen, she fiddled around, putting things away. The familiar routines were always soothing. Humming a snatch of 'Amazing Grace', she was piling oranges, lemons and apples in the bowl on the table when she heard a shout. She spun round, orange in hand, to find Dylan in full Spiderman get-up behind her.

'Dylan!' She put down the fruit and squatted to hug him. She felt his hot breath on her face, obviously fresh from a tuna sandwich, as he wriggled with pleasure in her embrace. She looked up to find Jess behind him, sweaty from the heat, with little Daniela sitting on her hip, all smiles. Bringing up the rear was

Adam, unflustered as ever, carrying his and Dylan's backpacks. At their ankles, next door's ginger cat had made its entrance, purring a noisy welcome. Immediately Dylan transferred his affections from Rose, reaching out a sticky hand to grab its fur.

'You're earlier than I expected. No, Dylan, not a good idea.' Rose tried to take his hand as he attempted to grab the cat's tail, but he snatched it away.

'I got the times wrong. We left at some ungodly hour from Gatwick, which means we're completely shattered.' Jess collapsed into one of the chairs. 'Can I smell coffee?'

'You can indeed. I was just making some.' Rose reached for more cups from the dresser. 'I've put you in the stables. Hope that's all right?'

'I'll take our stuff round there,' suggested Adam. 'Come on, Dylan. Leave the cat. Let's you and me explore.' He waited a second. 'Now!' he added firmly. 'We might even go for a swim.'

Dylan emerged from under the table and ran after his father down the corridor, shouting for him to wait. Rose looked after them, amused, recognising that the peace she'd been enjoying was now well and truly over.

'This all feels a bit funny.' Jess shifted the baby on to her knee and gave her a teaspoon from the drawer.

'I know,' said Rose, her reasons for being an advance party justified. 'But every day it gets easier.' She had taken the decision to come ahead of everyone else so she could adjust to being back, before finding the strength to help her daughters when they arrived.

'I shouldn't really have left Trevarrick,' Jess said suddenly. 'I've got so much to do there. We shouldn't have come.'

'Yes you should,' Rose said calmly, stroking Dani's cheek. 'It's time we got back to normal, and that includes having our annual holiday together. Dad would have wanted that.'

Jess was about to say something when they were interrupted by the sound of a horn.

'That must be the others. I didn't think they'd be here so soon.' Rose put her arm around Jess and together they went to the front door to greet them.

331

By the time Terry pulled up under the oak beside the other cars, Rose and Jess were at the door to greet them. Eve and Anna were first out. Rose hugged Anna, then Eve as if she wasn't going to let her go. 'Good journey?'

'Everything went according to plan. Unlike last time.' Eve wished she could bite back her last sentence, which would remind them all of too much. Instead she went for a deft change of subject. 'Where do you want us?'

Rose and Terry exchanged a smile as they kissed each other hello. Their hug lasted for longer than usual too. As they separated, Eve thought how much better Terry seemed with that look of permanent anxiety eradicated. However, his wardrobe could do with a bit of a makeover. When had that T-shirt got in there? First revealed when he removed his zip-fronted jumper in the car, it showed two hands busting apart a thick chain above the slogan *Man of Steel*. Never had a T-shirt been less appropriate.

'I've put you in Jess's room,' said Rose. 'The four of them are better off in the stables. I'm so glad you're all here.' The words obviously came from the heart, making Eve wonder what had been going on before their arrival.

'Anna!' Rose put her arm around her daughter's shoulder. 'Why don't you show Rick your room, then we'll think about lunch. There's no hurry.'

Terry was hefting Eve's case out of the boot of the car with a grimace of pain. Rick moved to help him, lifting it with ease. 'Let me, mate. Where to?'

Anna squeezed his Japanese-dragon-themed bicep. 'This way.' She led him into the house.

Eve watched, unable to help the flash of envy at their youth. Why spoil all that natural beauty with tattoos and piercings? She didn't get it. She turned back to the car to help Terry, who was still unloading the last couple of bags.

'A BMW,' she explained to Rose, as if the car needed an introduction. 'This year's been so tough, but we've made it through and I think we're going to weather the storm. So I treated us.'

'You treated you, you mean.' Terry gave her an indulgent smile.

Rose looked at her quizzically. Eve knew what she was thinking. She could have equally well have been referring to the agency or her marriage. But now was not the moment to go there. She gave Rose what she hoped was an enigmatic smile, followed Terry inside and together they went upstairs.

Terry was unpacked and changed before she had even begun to hang up her things that were now spread all over the bed. He grabbed a towel from the bathroom shelf. 'I'm off for a swim. Can't wait. Shall I see you down there?'

She took a couple of hangers from the wardrobe. 'I'll finish off up here, then I'll go and find Rose. Maybe I'll have one after lunch.'

There was nothing quite so unprepossessing as a sun-deprived Englishman in a pair of swimming shorts and sandals, she thought fondly as he left the room. Hurrah for spray tans. She glanced at her arm, glad to see there were no streaks. She twisted it so she could see her elbow. Damn! Not quite as good as she thought. Oh well, a few days here should sort that out. As she hung up her dresses, she couldn't help but reflect on how much the two of them had gone through since their last visit. She was so proud of the way Terry had tackled his gambling. He had had a couple of relapses, but nothing too financially damaging, and he had confessed shamefaced immediately. His resolve and the support of Gamblers Anonymous had got him through. He had been determined to prove to her that he was as good as his word. Will had made her decision to stay with Terry easy in the end, but despite what had happened between them, she didn't regret their brief liaison one bit. It had taught her what was and wasn't important to her.

As she laid out the jewellery she'd brought on the chest of drawers, she mused on how she and Terry had almost come full circle. Or had they? Initially badly bruised by the cards life had dealt them, they had retreated into the comfortable confines of their marriage. The familiarity with what lay within it, however imperfect, made life so much easier than grappling with what was outside. They had so much that she couldn't give up, and she had settled for that. But sometimes she still couldn't help wondering whether that was enough. Terry never seemed to question their relationship. Unlike hers, his parents had stayed together to the end, and he took it for granted that he and she would too. As far as he was concerned, this wasn't something that needed to be discussed. She, on the other hand, couldn't help teasing out the good and bad aspects of their marriage. She would sit staring out of the window of her office, wondering about the alternatives, even if they weren't remotely realistic. But that was how she was. She couldn't envisage a relationship with Terry that wasn't full of possibility but that also contained the frustration, compromise and indecision that went with their long marriage. The two of them might have regained some sort of equilibrium, and yet, and yet . . . she couldn't help but question whether it was possible to have a relationship where none of those things existed. Was that *so* bad?

She checked her BlackBerry. Her emails consisted of the usual battery of problems and queries that she would deal with that afternoon in a quiet moment. More interestingly, there was an invitation to lunch from Nick Plowright, the charismatic MD of Touchlight Films. They had met a couple of weeks ago at an awards dinner. Recently over from the States, he'd said he didn't know London well, asked what she would recommend at the theatre. A musical? He loved them. So did she. They had hit it off immediately. What could she do but offer to accompany him? It would have been rude not to. After all, it could be classed as networking, and networking was one of the things that kept her in business. You never knew what might come up. And here he was suggesting lunch. She would go. Nothing would happen between them. Or would it? She wouldn't be human if she didn't occasionally think 'What if?'

She flicked off her phone, put her clothes away, tidied up the bathroom and readied herself for the sun. Glancing in the mirror, her cherried sundress did all it could for her cleavage, which was now glistening with suntan oil. Her toe- and fingernails gleamed in complementary shades of sherberty peach. Even she had to admit she looked pretty damn good for a woman of her age. She was looking forward to the next few days.

33

Everything was almost ready to take outside – plates and knives and forks on the tray, salad, more cheese, fruit – when Eve came into the kitchen.

'Terry's gone straight to the pool – factor thirty-fived up. I thought I'd see what's happening in here.'

'You mean you want a glass of chilled white!' Rose knew Eve too well.

'Well . . . Oh, twist my arm.' Eve smiled and went to the fridge door like a homing pigeon. 'Actually, I'm being much better now. If Terry can give up the gambling . . .' She smacked her hand on the table. 'Touch wood, anyway. I thought I might compromise a bit on my alcohol intake. But this is holiday . . . so it doesn't count.' She found the bottle, took out a couple of glasses and poured the two of them a drink. 'Cheers.' As she raised hers to her lips, there was the sound of footsteps on the terrace outside. A shadow crossed the doorway and a figure stood silhouetted there.

'Hello, Eve. Good journey?'

Eve turned towards the voice, then stood apparently paralysed. 'Simon!' She gripped the back of the nearest chair and put her glass on the table. 'What are you doing here?' She looked round to Rose for an explanation.

If Rose had wanted his entry to have an effect, she couldn't have handled it better. 'We decided at the last minute . . .'

He came into the room to put a white and green plastic Co-op bag on the table. 'I think I got everything you wanted, but my Italian's worse than non-existent.'

'I'm sure it'll be fine. I can always improvise if need be.' She poured him a glass of wine. In the distance they could hear Terry

336

splashing up and down the pool, oblivious to the drama going on up at the house.

Eve hadn't moved for a full minute before she pulled out a chair and sat down. 'But I don't understand.'

Rose glanced at Simon and they exchanged a smile. 'I only invited him a few days ago. Bit of a spur-of-the-moment thing.'

'I think I'll go and put up the hammocks,' he said. 'I said I would and you two have obviously got lots to talk about.'

Eve's eyes followed him as he went into the utility room and emerged with a hammer and the hammocks, obviously quite at home.

'You know where they go?' asked Rose, brushing a fly from the bag of shopping.

'Between the olive trees? Where Dan was lying in that photo you showed me?' He went to the door and pointed towards the spot.

'Of course, I'd forgotten.' Rose remembered the photos they'd pored over the previous evening. Her family's past. She was aware of Eve watching them beadily.

As he left the house, Eve's breath exploded out of her. 'Well! I knew you were friends again, but I never expected him to be here. Why didn't you say?'

'I'm sorry. I should have told you he was coming. I did tell the girls, but you didn't pick up when I tried and it was such a rush. And to be honest, I knew what you'd say.' The truth was, she hadn't really wanted to have the conversation at all. 'I was in London a few days ago on my way here. We often go to a concert and have supper. You know that . . .'

Eve gave her a look, encouraging her to go on.

'I really like my evenings with him. They're so relaxing after life with the family in Cornwall. He's fun to be with, he appreciates me and . . . well, it's great being able to go out with a man who isn't interested in me, well, in *that* way. Makes everything so straight-forward.' She ignored Eve's disbelieving grunt.

She and Simon had been in her tiny one-bed flat, at the table in the corner of the living room. Rose had moved in only a matter of months ago and there was a distinct whiff of new paint in the air that not even her cooking and a couple of scented candles would disguise. In a corner was a stack of pictures waiting to be hung; the ones she hadn't taken to her Cornish cottage. Simon had spent the last half-hour advising her on the art of hidden storage. He had seen several possibilities where she saw none. Suddenly the potential of her rather poky London bolt-hole was looking better. While he talked, she had put the finishing touches to their supper, then brought it to the table. They began to discuss their separate plans for the summer. As she talked about hers for visiting Casa Rosa, the whole venture seemed too much to bear.

'I can't go.' She'd said the words quite firmly, her mind made up.

'Go where?' Simon was picking the meat out of a mussel with a fork.

'Italy. I thought enough time had passed and that I was brave enough to face it, but I'm not.'

He looked up from his plate as if she was stark staring mad. As well he might, since she'd just told him the whole family were depending on her being there when they arrived. Between them they had decided to revive the old holiday tradition for one more year, and then they would decide what to do with the place.

'What's happened? I thought you wanted to go back.' His brow furrowed as he tried to follow her train of thought. He leaned over to pour a glass of the red wine he'd brought with him.

'I did. I do. But it's too much. I must have some time to myself there before they come. I want to get used to everything first so I can help Jess and Anna when they arrive. But I don't think I can bear it. I'm sure they'll all understand. Perhaps we could do it next year.'

Simon put down his fork and took her hand. As he looked straight at her, she was touched by the concern in his eyes. 'Listen to me,' he said. 'The longer you leave it, the worse it will be. Remember how you dreaded going back to Trevarrick? And yet it's worked out so well there for you. You've got the cottage, you're

338

close to the grandchildren and you'll soon have the shop. It'll be the same with Casa Rosa. You've got to face the fear and go, or you never will. Besides, the others are expecting you. Aren't all the tickets booked?'

'Oh God, I know they are.' As she slumped in her seat and took a sip of her wine, an idea struck her. 'You wouldn't . . .' She stopped, then continued tentatively. 'You wouldn't come with me, would you?'

'Me?' He'd looked flabbergasted. 'What would they say?'

'Yes, you,' she said, warming to the idea by the minute. 'Just for a few days. And we'll get over whatever they say. They've grudgingly accepted the idea that we see each other again anyway, even though it's taken time. I'd love you to see the place and I could face it with you – if that doesn't sound too crazed.'

'I'm not sure.' He had hesitated, weighing up the implications of her suggestion.

'Please.' The more she thought about it, she more she realised that having someone with her who cared about her would make all the difference. Not that her daughters didn't, but they would have their own demons to battle with first and she wanted to support them, not lean on them. And so it had been decided.

When she'd finished explaining, Rose was surprised to find herself wrapped in one of Eve's bear hugs. When she was finally let go, Eve was beaming. 'I'd have come with you if you'd said. But I can see that him being here sort of makes this easier for you. I can't say I exactly get what's going on, but I'm trying, and if it's what you want – then great. How did the girls take it?'

'Not quite as well as I'd hoped.' Rose remembered Jess's reaction with a sinking sensation. 'I should have thought it through, I know.'

'You've invited Simon!' Jess had erupted down the phone. 'He's not family. Why him? Of all people.'

Rose didn't answer immediately. Then, 'I know it's difficult for you to understand, but whether you like it or not, Simon's been a rock to me.' She heard the tsk and ignored it. 'What was it you said to me? Something about taking what you want from the past for the future. That's all I'm trying to do.'

'God, Mum! I was talking about hiring him back on the job, not bringing him on our family holiday. The first one since Dad died. Isn't that a little bit insensitive?' In the background, Rose could hear Dani banging something on the table.

'I don't think so. Not after all this time. We have to do things differently now. And I think Dad would be happy with the way things are. Although he didn't mean me to meet Simon, now that we have, he'd rather we got on than not. I'm sure of that. Isn't that enough for you?'

Jess was only half listening to her; she sounded as if she was giving Dani a bottle. The banging stopped immediately. If only Jess could be so easily pacified.

'Well, it should be,' Rose went on, not giving Jess a chance to say any more. 'He's a good man, even if he has come into our lives in rather an unconventional way. Please try for my sake, if nothing else.'

Jess's attention was back with her. 'Unconventional? That's one way of putting it. It's just so difficult . . .' The rest of the sentence was lost as Dani started crying. In the end, they'd had to cut the conversation short. They hadn't tried again before leaving.

'Of course it's difficult for her,' explained Rose to Eve. 'But having anyone new here would be difficult whoever they were. She'll come round,' she added confidently, despite the fact that everything was telling her it might not be that simple. Perhaps she should talk to Adam. But no, that wouldn't be fair on him. They could only wait and hope.

'Well I certainly hope so.' Eve took the tray and headed for the door. 'Or it's going to be a difficult few days.'

Rose consoled herself with the fact that Anna had been more accepting. As time had gone by, her older daughter had slowly come round to what had happened. 'It's kind of weird that my mum's friends with my dad's gay lover, but at the same time it's kind of cool, I guess.' She held up her ring so the light flashed through it. 'Jess won't like him coming, though,' she warned.

'Jess hates change,' said Rose, considering each word before she spoke. 'It will be unbearable without Daniel at first. But Simon will prop me up—'

'You don't need to say any more,' Anna interrupted. 'I just want you to be happy. And Jess does too, except she wants you to be happy with someone she approves of. With someone you're having sex with, I suppose.'

'Anna, please!'

'Oh come on, Mum! You're the one who wanted everything in the open. I'm only being honest.'

That was true: Rose had wanted there to be no secrets between them and had told them so. If she hadn't shared Daniel's secret, perhaps things would have been easier, but she could never have lived with the lie. Deceiving her children was out of the question. To her, that was so wrong now that they were old enough to try to understand their father. Far better to be working things through together. Dan would have wanted that too, she was certain. Time. That was all that was needed. Everything would work out.

'What's up?' Terry walked into the kitchen fresh from the pool, a towel around his waist, hair on end. He looked over his shoulder. 'We met down at the pool.' Simon, just behind him, had obviously followed his example of cooling down after his exertions with the hammocks.

The physical contrast between the two of them was marked: Terry clearly hadn't seen the inside of a gym since he was at secondary school, and put beside Simon's, his face was undistinguished.

'How was your swim?' Eve asked, getting out a choice of drinks for lunch from the fridge.

'Every bit as good as I remember it. I've missed being here.' Terry picked a piece of salami from a plate and put it in his mouth. 'Delicious.'

The sound of the phone in Terry's other hand interrupted them. He checked the caller ID and shook his head. 'Bloody Flying Mango Books. I told them quite clearly I was on holiday. Hang on a minute.' He stepped back outside to have the conversation in private.

Rose looked surprised. 'But Terry doesn't work on holiday. That's never happened before.'

'That's because he's never worked for me before,' Eve said proudly. 'You know the Rutherford Agency never sleeps, even when on holiday. He's about to find that out the hard way.'

'At least he's working again.' Rose picked up the jug of iced water, taking it out to the table, Eve beside her carrying the bottle of wine and some apple juice.

'And enjoying it,' added Eve. 'Next to hiring May, hiring him has been one of the best decisions I've made for the agency. He's brilliant with the money and the contracts, especially all that small print. I trust him completely. The two of them deal with all the back-room stuff between them, which means I can concentrate on what I love doing best. I've signed up two new authors this year, and I think I'm about to pull off a film deal for one of them, which is really exciting. And it's great for us to have something in common again apart from the children.'

'So things are OK between you?' Rose hadn't dared broach the question before.

'They're fine.' Eve leaped to reassure her. Whatever happened in her life, she had resolved to be more circumspect about confiding in Rose. She had put her in an unforgivably difficult position when she was seeing Will and didn't want to repeat that. 'The grass may be a bit dried up on this side of the fence, but there are enough green patches to keep us going.'

Rose couldn't help laughing at the image. 'So you've given up looking over to the other side?'

'Well, a girl has to look from time to time,' Eve protested with a smile.

'What's so funny?' Jess came from the stables holding Dylan's hand. Adam was behind her, carrying Dani, showing her the flowers on the terrace, picking off a bit of bougainvillea for her.

'Nothing, darling. Come and sit down. We've got everything, I think. Simon's got the bread.'

Exactly on cue, Simon arrived at the table with a loaf of olive bread in his hand. Rose pulled out one of the chairs. 'Dylan, come and sit by me.' The little boy ran over and tried to clamber on to her knee until Rose swung him on to his seat.

Eve noted the forced jollity in Rose's voice, and the imperceptible clenching of Jess's jaw at the mention of Simon's name. She hoped no one else noticed, least of all him. If he did, he said nothing, just began to help everyone to food and drink, joining in the conversation but never dominating it. He was doing his best.

Anna and Rick didn't appear until the rest of them were well into the meal. When they emerged from the house, holding hands, it was quite plain to everyone what had delayed them. Both were fresh from the shower, both glowing with pleasure. Anna was wearing a skimpy black bikini, a sarong tied loosely around her waist, while Rick was in shorts, stripped to the waist. Eve heard Rose gasp. His honed and toned body was a walking work of art. The coloured tattoos on his right arm spread to the top of his chest. Those on his left cut off halfway up his bicep. Running down his side was a series of Chinese characters. Round his navel wound another dragon. They couldn't see his back, but they could imagine. As they walked to the table, Eve's eyes were on the studs in his nipples. She heard Rose's second intake of breath.

'Anna!' she whispered. 'What have you done?'

Anna stood by the table, hands on hips. 'Don't you like it? I had it done months ago.' Around her waist and past her pierced navel, where a pink stone twinkled in the sunlight, twined a tattooed garland of coloured flowers and two dragonflies.

'Why would you do that?' asked Jess. 'What'll it look like when you're ninety?'

Anna looked as if she was about to snap back when Eve realised it was up to her to smooth the waters. Rose seemed to have lost the power of speech, while the others at the table kept their heads down as they ate.

Eve cleared her throat. 'It's rather beautiful. In its way.' Everyone turned to look at her, surprised by her reaction. 'Sit down, do,' she said faintly. 'Have some lunch.' She noticed Rick's steadying hand on Anna's arm before they sat at the opposite end of the table to Jess.

Beside Simon.

Battle lines were drawn.

34

After clearing the lunch things, everyone dispersed to amuse themselves at different ends of the house and garden, leaving Rose and Eve to take their coffee alone on the terrace. Eve had given in to the heat and had abandoned her sundress for a swimsuit and a brilliantly patterned sarong. They lay in the two recliners in the shade of the house, swaddled by the late afternoon heat, the air full of the buzz of insects and the shrill song of the cicadas. In the distance, the occasional shout and the sound of hammering signified that the siesta was over and work had resumed on the villa along the valley.

'That was awful.' Rose looked at Eve as she spoke, anxious to see her reaction. She was disappointed. Eve was lying flat on her recliner, eyes shut, her face immobile. If she didn't know otherwise, Rose would have assumed she was asleep. 'Lunch, I mean.'

'Oh, it wasn't that bad.' Eve spoke as if her mind was somewhere else altogether.

'How can you say that? At least be honest. I know what you're thinking. I shouldn't have asked him.' That she should have accepted Simon's offer to make an early exit was all she had thought about since Jess had made plain her dislike of him being there. Rose's selfishness at wanting him to stay to support her was going to blight their long-awaited holiday.

Eve's eyes opened and she propped herself up on one elbow, half turned towards Rose. She pursed her lips before reaching for her coffee. 'Actually, I wasn't thinking that, but since you said it . . .' She left the sentence unfinished, her meaning plain.

'Everyone was on their best behaviour. Which is a good thing.' Rose hastily pre-empted Eve's next comment. 'But it was all so bloody awkward. I could kill the girls. They might at least make more of an effort.' She pictured Simon, who had tried so hard to behave normally, an impossible ask given Jess's brisk, non-committal answers to his increasingly self-conscious questions. His face, open and willing at the start, had gradually closed down as he was shut out of the conversation. Anna and Rick had been no help at all. They were entirely wrapped up in one another. If the rest of the table had gone up in smoke they wouldn't have paid any attention. 'Did you notice how quiet he was?'

'Not really. But you know what Jess is like.' Eve lay back down again with a sigh of contentment. 'It's bound to be awkward to begin with. She'll get used to him being here.'

'Thank God for the kids, at least they provided plenty of distraction.' Rose had no idea when Dylan had developed such a violent dislike of tomatoes. While he spat the offending fruit all over the table, little Dani had been content with whatever was given to her. She sat in her baby chair beaming, gnawing at pieces of cucumber and cheese clasped in her chubby fists.

'I'm quite envious,' said Eve wistfully. 'You're such a hands-on granny. That's the trouble with having boys. When their girlfriends have babies, they'll all gravitate home to their mothers, not to me.'

'How do you know that?' protested Rose. 'They'll love you. Anyway, what about Millie?'

Eve turned her head, shading her eyes with her hand. 'She's a boyfriend-free zone at the moment, still hanging out in a great gang of mates. They hunt in packs these days. No sign of any boyfriend action at all.' She paused. 'At least, she's not telling me about it. Bit like Anna used to be.'

'Having longed for her to have a boyfriend, now I almost wish she hadn't.' But Rose didn't mean it really; she just wished they'd tone it down a bit. The rest of them didn't need to be repeatedly reminded of the excitements that might have vanished from their own longer-term relationships. In fact, she was delighted and relieved that Anna had found someone who had got her measure and could deal with it. Then she remembered. 'And those tattoos! How could she ruin her body like that? She'll regret it when she's older, and the skin's gone.' She angled her own arm upwards and studied the loosening flesh with distaste, pushing at it with a finger.

'They're only young. Live and let live, that's what I say.' Eve rolled on to her back again to lie beached, knees bent, eyes shut, her chest rising and falling as she took several long, contented breaths.

Rose was all of a sudden rocked with longing for Daniel. Every time she thought she had adjusted to his loss, the intensity of these rare but overwhelming waves of emotion took her by surprise. She wanted nothing more than for him to be here with her on the terrace, discussing their two daughters in the way they used to. Nobody knew Jess and Anna in the way they did, or shared the feelings that they had for them. How could they? Their frustrations with them would be forever underpinned by a bedrock of shared parental love. She sat up abruptly, blinking the tears away. 'I can't sit here any more. Have you finished your coffee?'

Eve groaned. 'Mmm. Why?' She wiggled herself into the recliner as if she was bedding herself in for the duration. She straightened one leg and rotated her ankle.

'I thought we might go for a walk.' Rose was already on her feet, collecting together the coffee cups, absolutely certain of what she needed to do.

'Now? Are you crazy? It's way too hot.' Alert to the change in Rose's voice, Eve opened one eye to see what she was doing, then shut it again.

'It's cooler than it was,' Rose insisted. 'Besides, I think it's time to go back there.'

'Where? You've lost me.' This time Eve raised her head and looked at Rose, obviously puzzled.

'I want to go back to where Dan died. I haven't been able to so far, but I need to go now. Will you come with me?'

Eve sat up immediately, swinging her legs round. 'Of course I will. If you're sure that's what you want to do. But don't you want to go with the girls?'

'I don't want to force them into going there until they're ready. They'll ask when they are.' The girls were already dealing with being back at Casa Rosa in their very different ways. Anna was apparently oblivious to the undercurrents, while Jess was being reminded of too much. 'I could have gone with Simon. I know he wants to see where Dan died, but I can't share that with him. Not yet. I need to be by myself, but I need someone with me. Does that make any sense?' She stared in the direction from which Anna had come running on that terrible September day. She could almost see her coming towards her again.

'I'll be one second. Just let me get my shoes.' Eve hoisted herself to her feet and disappeared inside, leaving Rose to pace anxiously around the terrace until she remembered the coffee cups and took them inside. As she washed them up, knowing that one second in Eve's world meant at least five minutes, Simon and Adam walked in.

'We're going into town. That OK with you?' Simon was looking more relaxed again. He'd put on a loose shirt over his shorts and flip-flops, and his smile had returned.

'We're going to get some wood to mend the roof of the shelter by the pool,' added Adam, his shambolic holiday T-shirt and shorts such a contrast with Simon's careful appearance. 'There's not much point putting everything away if they're just going to get rained on in the winter.'

'Yes, but you don't have to do that now, do you?' asked Rose, surprised that Adam was offering to do precisely the sort of work he'd refused to do for Daniel.

'No time like the present.' He was decisive, mind made up. 'Jess has got the kids. She suggested I did it and Simon's offered to help. We'll only be half an hour or so.'

Simon's relief at being accepted by one of the party was palpable. His laid-back appearance hadn't deceived Rose, and she was glad Adam was sensitive enough to have picked up on it. 'Well, that's fantastic then. Thanks. Eve and I are going for a walk. We'll see you when you get back.'

By the time they'd left the kitchen and she'd lined up the cups on the draining board, Eve was waiting for her on the terrace, having exchanged the sarong for a loose lilac shirt dress, a wide-brimmed straw hat and plimsolls.

'However many outfits have you brought? That's the third one in almost as many hours.' Rose smiled, looking down at the shorts she had worn almost every day.

'One for every occasion.' Eve was undaunted by criticism of her carefully considered wardrobe. 'Let's go. If you're sure you want to do this.'

'I'm sure.' It was as if something was drawing Rose back down that track to where they had found Dan. The time had come.

Just as they reached the edge of the garden, she stopped. 'One minute.' She ran quickly back up the stones of the path to where she'd left her secateurs that morning. She picked them up and walked over to the flower bed, where she clipped off a stem from a white rose bush. She and Dan had chosen the plant together, one among several they had driven down here one long-ago spring. They had left the girls at a school sports camp to be brought by Eve and Terry with their cousins a week later, while they had driven leisurely through France, stopping for a couple of nights on the way. Their old banger was weighted down by a rocking chair and a couple of rugs on the roof rack, while the back seat and the boot were laden with plants, pictures and general stuff they thought they might need. They had stayed in small local *auberges*, neither of the names of which she could remember now. But she remembered the fun they'd had, drinking local wine from the barrel, eating omelettes and *truites bleus*, strolling arm in arm through narrow medieval streets, collapsing on to lumpy sagging mattresses where they lay curled around each other. How they had worried that the plants might not survive the trip, but survive they had, and this mass of scented white flowers was a constant reminder of that brief but magical interlude.

She carried the flower to where Eve was waiting. 'Winchester Cathedral, Dan's favourite rose,' she explained, touching the mass of white petals before holding it up for Eve to smell its honey-sweet fragrance.

The walk seemed to take an age. Nothing like the panicked race from the house that they had made the last time. They exchanged one or two observations about the blaze of poppies along the

349

roadside, the other wild flowers, or the unrecognised cry of a bird, but both of them felt the weighty significance of what they were doing. As they rounded the final corner before the spot where Dan fell, Rose felt unaccountably nervous. She slowed her pace, feeling her heart thumping against her ribs, grateful that Eve had the sensitivity to hang back. She looked around her. There was nothing to indicate the tragedy that had happened here, that had altered the course of all their lives. But what had she expected? That the grass on the verge would still be flattened where Daniel had fallen, leaving the imprint of his body there for ever? That the stones on the track would still be stained with her blood where she had scraped her knee as she knelt to hold him? By her foot a couple of large black beetles trundled across the track. There was no natural memorial here for Dan. The world went on without him, unmoved by his death.

She knelt where she'd knelt before. Or was it where she'd knelt? She couldn't remember exactly. There was nothing to signal the precise spot. As she bowed her head, she could feel the stones pressing sharply into her knees again. She leaned forward and laid the rose on the side of the road where nothing could run it over, as close as she could remember to where they'd found Dan's body. She was dimly aware of Eve's sniffs in the background.

'I'll never forget you, Dan,' she said, too quietly for Eve to hear. 'You still mean the world to me and always will. Simon's helped me to understand.' The tears ran down her face unchecked. As she remembered her husband, she experienced a sense of profound peace that lulled her towards an even greater acceptance of what had happened to them.

After a minute or two, she felt a hand on her shoulder. 'Here,' said Eve and thrust a tissue into her hand. 'I had a feeling we might need these.' She blew her nose as she stepped back, leaving Rose alone with her thoughts. But Rose wasn't thinking. She was with Daniel again, feeling his strength and support. That was all she needed.

Eventually she rocked back so the soles of her feet took her weight. Once she was standing, the two women hugged, alone together on the track as if nothing could separate them. But eventually they stepped apart, laughing at themselves. Rose rubbed at the indents on her knees from the stones. 'They say that what hurts you makes you stronger. You know what? I think I am a stronger person now. Dan wouldn't want me to put up with this nonsense from Jess. When we get home, I'm going to talk to her.'

Eve looked sceptical but said nothing.

'OK, but I'm going to try. And I'm so, so glad I've come here at last. Thank you. I couldn't have done it with anyone else.'

'I wish I could say it was a pleasure.' Eve looked away, back to where Dan had lain, her eyes brimming with tears again. 'But you know what I mean.'

'I do.' Rose gave her a weak smile and squeezed her arm. 'Let's go back. Now I know I can come here with the girls, and I can even bring Simon here too.'

'Do you really want to do that? Isn't it too private?'

'No. Not any more. I want him to see. I want him to understand by being here what Dan and I had together. I want him to respect that, and I think he does. At the same time, he's told me so much about Dan that I didn't know. He was a much more complicated and conflicted man than I realised. I wish we could have talked about what he was feeling, and especially about what he felt about Simon, but he was ashamed, frightened of what might happen.'

'Perhaps you wouldn't have understood anyway.' The suggestion sounded tentative.

'You're right, of course.' Rose couldn't keep the regret out of her voice. 'I probably wouldn't. It's taken me months to begin process- ing all that's happened. Poor Dan.' She gave a long, heartfelt sigh.

They walked the rest of the way in silence, arm in arm. Rose thought about her husband, wondering not for the first time what he'd make of her friendship with Simon. He might be shocked, horrified that she had found out the truth about him, but then perhaps he'd be relieved and glad it was in the open at last. She believed he would be pleased that the two of them had found such a strong connection, bound together by their love of him.

As they neared the garden, they could hear Dylan shouting excitedly somewhere in the direction of the pool. Up at the house, the sounds of Dani's shrieks travelled towards them, until one of her parents obviously caved in to her bedtime demands and she quietened down.

'Between the devil and the deep blue sea,' laughed Rose, jogged out of her introspection by her demanding grandchildren. 'Which way to turn?'

They stood, uncertain which direction to go in. Then Eve took the initiative. 'I think we deserve a small drink. It's almost six thirty. Prosecco?'

'Under the walnut tree?'

Eve nodded.

'Let's do it. The kids will be asleep soon. Then we can think about supper.'

As they turned towards the house, there was a loud splash as someone dived into the pool. A blissful moment of silence followed: the peace that Rose had spent the past few days enjoying with Simon. Then, a second splash. Suddenly a woman's scream shattered the balmy summer afternoon.

'Jess!' Rose wheeled round and ran towards the pool with Eve in hot pursuit, everything else forgotten. As they breasted the slope, they could see the drama being resolved at the pool's edge. Anna was in the water, passing up a drenched Dylan to Rick, who was crouching on the edge. Beside them a frightened-looking Jess stood waiting to wrest her son from their arms. On the ground beside her were his blue armbands and her phone.

Rose ran up to them, relieved to find them all in one piece. 'Whatever's happened?'

No one spoke as Jess hugged Dylan to her, so tightly he began to fight against her hold. Anna was the one who replied, at her most casual. 'Oh, Dylan just fell in the pool.'

'I was swimmin',' the little boy said, his dark eyes big in his face, his hair plastered to his head, water running down his body. 'Again! Again!' He wriggled to be let down.

'I think not,' said Anna, bending over and twisting her hair to wring the water out of it.

'Dylan, you must never do that again. Never. Do you hear me?'

Jess ignored the rest of them, fear and guilt making her shout at her son, who stared at her, stunned, not understanding why he deserved her fury. 'You must never go near the edge without your armbands. We've told you over and over again.'

The little boy's chin quivered, his brow furrowed and his mouth opened wide to let out a great wail of distress. He stretched his arms out to Rose as she reached for him. After all, it was hardly his fault that his mother's eye had left the ball. 'Shhh. Shhh. Let's put them on so it doesn't happen again. Then you can go for a swim. Look, what's this?' Rose pointed at a green octopus on the plastic arm-band as she squatted down to pick up the first one and shunt it on to his arm.

'Octopoo.' He began to giggle, stabbing it with his finger.

Beside them Jess was enveloping Anna in a bear hug as the words tumbled from her mouth in her rush to make amends. 'I know it was all my fault. If I hadn't been on the phone . . . He could have drowned. Thank God you were here. I'll never be able to thank you enough. Not ever.'

'Forget it,' said Anna, sheepish despite her usual love of the limelight. 'I'm glad I was here too.' She extricated herself from her sister's embrace and went back to her lounger, where she stretched herself out beside Rick.

'Bloody phone. Bloody Trevarrick,' said Jess, kneeling down by Rose. 'I'm sorry, Dylan. Mummy just got a nasty fright.' She kissed his forehead and let him climb on to her lap for a cuddle. 'Chef's just resigned,' she explained to Rose over her son's head. 'I was about to put on his armbands when Mark called to tell me. I looked away for one second. Literally just one. I didn't even realise he'd fallen in. I thought the splash was one of the others. I've told him so many times not to go near the edge. Anna saved his life.'

'Thank God you were so quick off the mark, darling.' Rose looked over at Anna. But her daughter wasn't listening. She had moved on to Rick's lounger and was squished up beside him, his arm round her, his hand tucked into the back of her bikini bottom while she kissed him.

'Gawd. Young love. Get a room, you two,' called Eve, dispersing the tension immediately as the others laughed, relieved that some-one had the balls to say what they were all thinking. Eve was sitting on the edge of the pool, her shoes off, her legs dangling in the water. Her kicks sent ripples across the still surface towards the shadow at the other side. 'Think I might have a swim.' She undid her buttons to reveal her swimsuit, tossed the dress away from the edge and lowered herself in. 'Come on, Dylan. Let's see what you can do.'

Rose released the boy, who ran over, the armbands making his arms stick out from his side like a mini Michelin man, and jumped in beside her.

'Sorree.' Anna extricated herself from Rick's embrace and came over to her sister. Rick sat up, grinning amiably as he watched the four of them, then raised himself from the lounger and dived in to swim towards Eve. 'Come on, Dylan. Swim between us. Kick those legs. Let's see if you can do it.'

With her son safely distracted, Jess sat down with a thump. 'Oh God, I'm a hopeless mother.' She hung her head, then picked up her phone and put it in the shade under her lounger.

Rose was about to contradict her, but Anna was there first, squatting down beside her. 'No you're not. That's the last thing you are.' She stretched upwards to kiss her sister's cheek. 'You've got two gorgeous children and you're the best mother in the world to them. Anyone could make a mistake like that. Anyone.'

Had Rose died and gone to heaven? Anna was thinking about someone other than herself at last.

'I'm glad I was here to save my little old nephew.' Anna looked over at Dylan's splashy but determined efforts to bridge the gap between Rick and Eve, and smiled. 'I expect you'll return the favour one day. Now, if anyone's going to be a hopeless mother, it'll be me.'

Jess raised her head, quick as a whippet. 'You're not saying . . .'

Anna threw her head back and laughed. 'God, no. You must be joking. No need to start gathering the hand-me-downs yet. But you never know. One day . . .'

Rose's first thought was for that flowered tattoo, stretching out of shape as Anna's stomach swelled. Slightly ashamed of her reaction, she yanked herself back to the here and now. The girls were smiling and chattering together. They didn't need her. With peace restored, she decided to go inside and make a start on supper.

35

It was way past Dylan's bedtime, so it wasn't long after the swimming lesson was over that Jess headed back to the house. Eve was right behind her, the idea of a glass of chilled Prosecco having reasserted itself in the forefront of her brain. With her dress over her arm, she carried some of the detritus that had been left by the pool. She followed Jess into the kitchen and loaded a couple of mugs and three glasses into the dishwasher. Rose was washing a lettuce in the sink.

'I'll be back to help in a minute,' Eve volunteered. But before anything else, a shower beckoned.

'No rush.' Rose shook the leaves and put them into the salad spinner. 'Simon's offered to cook tonight. I don't think anything's going to happen for an hour or so. I'm going up to change when I've done this.'

'But Mum, I was going to make that fruit tart thing Dad liked so much.' Jess was holding Dylan tightly to her. He was wrapped in one of the coloured beach towels so only his face was visible.

'Couldn't you make it tomorrow instead? I've a feeling Simon's got everything organised.' She wound the handle of the spinner until its whirring filled the room.

Eve could hear the effort it cost Rose to keep her voice light and reasonable while fighting her exasperation with her daughter's resistance to Simon's presence. Jess had clearly decided to award herself the role of Daniel's flame-keeper, as if the rest of them had forgotten him. As if. She remembered the single white rose marking the spot.

'Fine,' came the tight little response. 'I'll take Dylan to bed.'

'Why don't you ask him?' added Rose. But Jess had left the room, leaving her mother speaking to an empty space. Rose flung

356

her hands in the air. 'This holiday *is* going to work. I haven't a clue how, but it will.' She took the leaves from the spinner, bagged them in plastic and put them in the fridge. 'There. Shower and then a drink. Think we might need it.'

Eve wasn't going to argue.

In their room, Terry was hunched over his laptop. He'd already turned the small table by the window into an office. Pieces of paper covered in numerical scribbles lay spread out by the computer. He'd emptied the rest of the contents of his briefcase on to the bed: pens, paperclips, a calculator, his phone and a pack of chewing gum. Eve cleared a space for herself and lounged there, checking her emails. The only addition to her backlog was one lengthy email from May updating her on everything that had been going on at the agency that day. As a result of her assistant's efficiency, there was nothing imperative to attend to. Most publishers and clients had learned how reliable and knowledgeable May was, and knew to direct their queries to her unless they could only be dealt with by Eve. Instead she powered up her iPad and opened the word game she was playing with one of her five regular but unknown cyber opponents. Terry took absolutely no notice.

'You haven't been here all afternoon?' she asked after a couple of minutes. She dragged the word EPHAS into place. She had no idea what it meant, but the app accepted it and awarded her a gratifying fifty-three points. Good enough.

He tutted at the interruption, but twisted round in his chair to reply. 'What was left of it. Yes, I've been trying to sort out these e book royalties with May. Flying Mango have sent us two cheques, which as far as I can see are for completely the wrong amount. Their contracts people must be monkeys, and getting hold of them has been almost impossible, never mind getting them to see sense.' Distracted, he ran his hand through his hair.

Eve registered the few silvery strands above his ears for the first time. So even he was beginning to show signs of getting on at last. 'Can't it wait till we get home? We're only here for a week.' She wasn't at all sure that she liked being on holiday with someone so bound up in their office work – even if it was her office. She preferred Terry sprawled in the hammock, enjoying what rural Tuscany had to offer. The part of the workaholic was hers, not his although she couldn't deny how pleased and relieved she was that he took his role at the Rutherford Agency so seriously.

'No, it can't.' He closed the laptop and picked up a pencil. 'If I don't sort it out now, no one else will until I get back home, and then I'll have to rush it. In my old office, there were other people who could cover for me while I was away. Not any more. But once this is sorted, that should be it.' He bent back to his task.

How many company accountants could be found at work in baggy shorts and a T-shirt with a slogan reading *Grumpy Old Git*? In fact, now that he'd ditched his previous work uniform of suit and tie, his growing collection of sloganned T-shirts definitely needed culling. She might do that when they got home and his attention was elsewhere. And perhaps she might lose those heavy leather walking sandals with Velcro fastenings at the same time. She dragged her eyes from his feet and hopped off the bed to go into the bathroom. When she'd first suggested that Terry help out at the agency, she'd felt bound to double-check the accounts regularly. She was ashamed of harbouring suspicions when he promised her faithfully that he'd done with gambling. His marriage to her meant everything. But she had to be certain. Not a penny had been misplaced. He'd been true to his word. Her own gamble of giving him the job had paid off, and given him back his self-respect.

She turned the tap and held out her hand to test the temperature of the water. Ice-cold needles rained on her arm. Dan had always insisted on the bathrooms in his homes and hotels having the best power showers available, but a cold shower was far too spartan for Eve, even during a baking Italian evening. She turned up the heat, donned the pink frilly shower cap provided by Rose, peeled off her swimsuit, and stepped in.

As she stood there, she looked down at her body. Despite the ravages of childbirth and time, she was much more comfortable with it since her affair with Will and, of course, her Pilates sessions – a new fad of hers. Yes, she'd put a bit of weight back on, and yes, her stomach did have a bit of a wobble if nudged, but the simple solution was not to nudge it. Looking downwards wasn't the most tantalising of sights, but at least she could still see her toes. She did look after herself, bar the odd weakness here and there, and still made the most of what she had to work with. Even if Terry took her for granted, she was not going to subside quietly into a morass of middle age.

Her body cream (or crème, to be strictly accurate) smelled of nectarine, peach and honey. Good enough to eat. Or at least lick, she reflected with a sad smile, as she slathered it on. She was now convinced that she and Terry would never revisit that level of intimacy they'd once had, although there had been a bit of an upswing in their lovemaking of late. Nothing too outré, but a definite improvement. Some of the ideas Will had shared with her were proving more than useful. Wrapped in a cotton bathrobe, she set about her face with vigour, cleansing, toning, moisturising and making up in the most subtle but effective way.

Back in the bedroom, Terry was packing away his stuff. 'You've been ages,' he commented. Not a complaint, merely an observation.

'Lots to do,' was her answer as she picked out the cherry dress from her wardrobe and prepared to go downstairs, leaving him to get ready on his own.

In the kitchen, Simon had taken charge. He was chopping onions when she came in. Rose was going through one of the kitchen drawers. 'I'm sure the garlic crusher's in here somewhere. Didn't you put it away when you tidied up last night?'

'Have you tried the dishwasher?' Simon looked up from his task, his face glowing where the sun had caught it. 'Or maybe I did put it in the other drawer. I can't remember.'

Rose laughed. 'You're hopeless.' She opened the drawer above.

How comfortable they seemed, like partners who'd been together for years. Eve felt quite excluded. A piece of piano music that she didn't recognise rose and fell around them.

'Can I do anything?' she asked.

'Pour us all a drink, why don't you?' said Rose. 'You know where it is. Is your room OK, by the way? Do you need anything?'

'It's perfect in every way, as you well know.' Eve busied herself with bottle and glasses. 'What are you making?'

'My version of chicken cacciatore.' Simon stopped what he was doing, blinking away a few oniony tears. 'It's too hot to cook anything complicated.' As if demonstrating the point, he took the tea towel tucked into his waistband and wiped his face before setting off again.

'Can I have one, Eve?' Jess came through the door and flung herself down on a chair. 'It's been such a long day. Dani went out like a light and Anna's reading Dylan a story. She's a saint.'

Eve obliged, passing the glass across the table, wondering when Jess would stop behaving as if Simon wasn't in the room. The tension between them was noticeable immediately and transmitted itself to the others.

'Do you remember how Dad would go mad when we used his special filleting knife?' Jess looked towards the knife in Simon's hand.

He stopped chopping for a moment, then carried on as if she hadn't spoken, the regular sound of the blade hitting wood accompanying their conversation.

'I don't think we need to preserve the knife in aspic, do you?' said Rose a little too sharply. She took the garlic crusher from the drawer and put it on the table with a clatter. 'It's not as if he ever used it much himself. Your father was far from being a cook.' Dan's half-hearted attempts in the kitchen were the subject of many a family joke.

'But he wasn't serious,' qualified Eve for Simon's benefit. 'He'd go mad over all sorts of silly things.' She laughed. 'Remember that time when we were up late and he went out to have a pee in the garden and the lawn sprinklers went on and completely soaked him?' She was pleased to see Rose and Jess both crack a smile at the memory.

'And the time he mended that deckchair?' Jess was laughing now. 'The moment he sat in it, the whole thing collapsed. I'll never forget his face. He was so cross it had broken again.'

Although he was concentrating on what he was doing, Eve

360

noticed a faint smile cross Simon's face. He must have his own memories of Daniel: a different Daniel that he couldn't share with them. Perhaps he could with Rose. Was that part of what bound them together? He went to the fridge and pulled out two chickens. As he began to divide and bone them with deft, confident movements, Eve caught Jess watching him, apparently impressed by his dexterity. Then she obviously remembered herself.

'I must call Mark and see what they're doing about replacing Chef. He's given a week's notice and we're doing a big wedding next weekend. It's a nightmare.'

Adam had come unnoticed into the room, tiptoeing up behind Jess and placing his hands over her eyes so she jumped a mile. 'Leave Mark to handle it, Jessie. Isn't that why you hired him as your deputy?'

She touched one of his hands and gazed up at him lovingly. 'I know. But I can't help wanting to know. Dad wouldn't have left it to someone else to sort out. He always said that if you want a job doing well, you should do it yourself.'

'But you're not your dad,' Adam said quietly and firmly, his thumbs massaging the back of her shoulders. 'You're a different boss and they all like and respect you for that.'

'Well said, Adam.' Rose passed him a bottle of Peroni. He would never be a fizzy white wine man. 'Enjoy your week and sort it out when you get back.'

'Mark always seemed extremely capable to me,' offered Simon, immediately looking as if he regretted opening his mouth.

Jess turned on him. 'What the hell would you know?'

There was complete stillness in the room as the others waited for his response and what that would provoke. Even Adam's influence didn't always calm Jess's belligerent streak. But Simon drew himself up and looked her square in the face. 'I've spent a fair amount of time with him during the build, so I got to know him quite well. He has a good deal of respect for you.' He went back to his work, leaving the others hearing his unspoken *though right now, I can't for the life of me see why.*

'Simon's right.' Adam was holding her shoulders quite tight, the

361

Peroni untouched on the table. Jess's head twisted round to look at him in surprise. 'Leave him to it. Talk to him in the morning, if you must. Calling him at night looks as if you don't trust him and that you're panicking. Concentrate on your family now.'

The wind left her sails as quickly as it had inflated them. 'I guess you're right. I'm sorry.' She put her phone down. 'What's Anna doing? Reading Dylan all the books we brought?'

'Could you help me lay the table?' Eve stepped in briskly, passing Jess the handful of knives and forks she'd been gathering from the table drawer. Time to rescue the mood of the evening. 'Let's eat under the walnut tree.'

Jess took them and went outside, Eve following with the tray of plates that Rose had already organised. Here she was again, in the role of peacemaker. Perhaps the United Nations could find a role for her! She waited until they got far enough away from the house to be able to speak without being overheard. 'Jess, listen to me. You've got to relax or you're going to spoil everyone's holiday, including your own.' She could tell by the set of Jess's shoulders that her words hadn't been well received. Jess banged down the knives and forks and began setting them out round the table.

'But why has Mum brought Simon here? Casa Rosa is hers and Dad's place. He doesn't belong here.' Another knife was slammed into position.

'Is that for you to say? Your mum's alone . . .'

For a moment she thought Jess was going to object, but her niece obviously thought better of it and lapsed into a loaded silence.

'Yes, I know she's got you and the family. But you've got to let her lead her life the way she chooses. You can't control everything. That's what Daniel used to do.' Eve paused as she remembered. 'You're like him in so many ways, you know.'

Jess pulled out a chair and sat down, picking at a knot in the wood of the table. 'Now I feel awful.'

'Don't. Rose understands that you've got a lot to deal with too. But if having Simon here helps her, then let it be. Please. We all have someone else. Without him, she's alone.'

'I didn't think I'd mind. He's been so good over Trevarrick, and of course I'm happy that he's designing the shop there for Adam and Mum. That's a genius idea and will be great for both of them. Imagine Mum as a shop girl!' Jess smiled. 'But him actually being here . . .' She couldn't finish; her voice caught.

Eve put down the last of the plates beside her niece and stopped to stroke her hair as if she was a child again. 'It'll work out if everyone makes the effort. It can't be easy for him either.'

They didn't move from where they were. Eve kept up the slow, rhythmic movement of her hand, having no idea what was going through Jess's head but hoping she'd said enough. She understood how difficult it must be for Jess to accept that her father had had a gay lover, let alone that this charming, urbane and occasionally impetuous man had become her mother's close friend. Nothing had prepared any of them for that. What she had said was the only thing that made sense. However, she knew only too well that sometimes it needed time for sense to percolate through into their children's brains. Sometimes it never percolated at all, because they knew better. And sometimes, admittedly, they were right. But not this time. As the minutes ticked by, she felt Jess begin to relax. Then: 'You're such a wise old bird.' Jess reached up for her hand, brought it to her mouth and kissed it.

'Less of the old, thanks.' Eve snapped at Jess's arm and laughed. 'Let's get the glasses.' The moment had passed.

By the time they got back, the rich smell of onions, tomatoes and garlic was filling the kitchen. Terry and Anna had joined the others and were organising themselves drinks to take on to the terrace. Simon was busy preparing a large salad. Rose leaned against the table, noticeably tensing when Eve and Jess returned. The movements were slight: a rise of the shoulders, an intake of breath and a narrowing of the eyes. But Eve noticed them all. She went to the cupboard and began to get the glasses they needed, arranging them on a tray.

'Can I help?' asked Jess, going over to Simon.

Everybody carried on doing what they were doing, but Rose's head lifted a fraction, while Anna and Terry exchanged a brief look. Nervous, they all waited for Simon's response.

'Are you any good with rice?' he asked, glancing up, as if nothing was out of the ordinary. 'I can never get it quite right.'

Eve doubted that was true. No one who could joint a chicken with such dexterity could be a beginner with anything as basic as rice. Rose's smile confirmed her suspicions. Well, good for him, playing the game. He wanted this to work as much as everybody else.

'I'm the same,' Jess said. 'But I'll have a go.' She turned and winked at Eve.

It was as if the whole of Casa Rosa breathed a collective sigh of relief. Rose changed the music to one of Ella Fitzgerald's songbooks. As 'It don't Mean a Thing' bluesed out of the speakers, Anna and Terry took their drinks to the terrace, laughing. Adam followed them out with the baby alarm in one hand.

'Am I too late to help?' Rick appeared, his hair slicked back from the shower, wearing loose board shorts and a short-sleeved shirt that hid most of his tattoos. He was really quite handsome once they were tucked out of sight, although Eve couldn't come round to the piercings.

'It's all under control, thanks,' said Jess as she poured the rice into the weighing scales. 'You and Anna can do the washing-up afterwards.'

Eve pushed a glass into his hand. 'Anna's on the terrace with Terry and Adam. 'Why don't you help yourself and join them?'

'It's a deal,' he said.

Rose smiled at Eve and raised her glass as she followed him out. Eve picked up the tray. Who knew? Perhaps Jess was right. Perhaps things were under control after all.

36

By the time Rose had parked the car in one of the outlying car parks and walked up the hill to the old town of Lucignano, the heat was punishing. Despite what had been meant to be an early start, she, Eve, Simon and Terry had arrived far later than she had meant them to. They had risen late, taken their time over breakfast and waited while Simon had his early-morning swim: a reminder of Daniel's regular exercise routine, as Eve had rather tactlessly pointed out, drawing a wounded look from Jess. Eventually they'd set off, leaving the others by the pool, with Adam making noises about mending the shelter until he was persuaded to wait until Simon got back to help him.

Arriving at the Porta San Giusto, the four of them pushed on between the two cafés on either side of the gateway and walked through the ancient boundary wall.

'This is spectacular.' Simon was the first one to speak as the four of them paused in the shade inside the circular medieval town. To their left, the narrow via Roma bent away from them, its modest buildings, built for the poorer classes, contrasting with those in the via Matteotti that led off to their right, curving down the hill. Here the street was wide and light, the grand houses, now worn with time, built for the nobility. Between them stood a string of stalls that made up the regular Thursday food market, noisy with people and chatter.

Rose smiled at him. She'd anticipated how much he'd like the place. She always felt a funny sense of possessive pride when she brought friends here, almost as if she was responsible for the town's shuttered buildings, the cobbled streets, the hustle and bustle of the weekly market. She was already looking forward to taking them into its heart, to the gothic church of San Francesco and the neighbouring Palazzo Pretorio with its modest museum.

Shaded by white awnings, the market stalls were laden with local produce. They wandered down the street, Eve and Terry walking ahead while Simon and Rose lingered to look at the boxes of fat shiny aubergines, big beefy tomatoes, courgettes with their trumpet flowers, large red radishes, lettuces, potatoes, brilliant peppers, big pots of basil. They passed stalls laden with wheels of local cheese, others with eggs, olives, bread and more. While Simon lagged at a fruit stall, buying peaches, nectarines and strawberries, Rose watched Eve and Terry, who had already found the small café on the left of the street and dived into its dim interior. How much better they seemed to be getting on of late. Eve had spared Rose the intimate detail about how they'd recovered from the trials of the last year, but it was enough for her to see them relaxed in each other's company again.

Other people's marriages were impossible to fathom. What brought people together, what kept them together and what tore them apart: how could one ever understand the chemistry of attraction? However well Rose thought she understood what made another couple tick, whether they were dear friends of hers and Daniel's or those closer to home – Eve and Terry, Jess and Adam, her own parents – there was always something kept hidden from outsiders. As indeed there had been in her own marriage. No one could ever know everything that went on in the head of their partner. Could they? No one should ever take anything for granted. Or had she been particularly obtuse during her own marriage? Sometimes she thought she must have been. But then as she had relived so much of it since Daniel's death, she was convinced he had given her no clues. Despite everything else, though, he had loved her. She was sure of that now.

'The others have gone for a coffee,' she told Simon as he emerged from the scrum of people surrounding the fruit stall clutching three bulging brown paper bags. 'Shall we join them?'

'I'd rather explore. Unless you want to.' He waited for a stray dog, its teats engorged with milk, to cross his path, then joined

Rose and put his purchases into the carrier bag that she held open. 'Let me carry that.' He took it from her.

Nothing pleased Rose more than the prospect of meandering through the concentric streets, climbing up and down the linking stairways, peering into hidden gardens, encountering the street life: children playing, little old ladies in black sitting outside their front doors, groups of men gathered gossiping under the shade of trees in the small square. 'I'll tell them what we're doing and we can meet at the gate in an hour.'

The rest of the morning disappeared quickly as the two of them explored the tiny town, visiting the modest museum and neighbouring church, ending up in the bar to the right of the gate where they drank *espressi*, taking in their surroundings, observing an argument among a group of card players, and waiting for the other two, who were not far behind.

They arrived back at Casa Rosa in good time for lunch. Jess had fed the children, who were already adapting to an Italian lifestyle and were tucked up for their siesta. Simon gave her the loaf of foccacia they'd picked up from the bakery. 'Couldn't resist this.'

Jess thanked him and put the flat rosemary-flavoured bread on the worktop before carrying on arranging the cheese on a plate. Rose held her breath. She thought the previous evening had gone too smoothly to be true. Her daughter looked up. Her gaze flicked between Simon and Rose, as if making up her mind about something, then she spoke. 'I thought we could have a tomato salad. It's a family staple out here. Would you like to make it?'

'Sure.' Simon grabbed an apron from the hook on the back of the door, and went to the knife block, carefully avoiding Daniel's filleting knife. 'Or what about a bread salad? I could use up the bread from yesterday.'

'*Panzanella?*' Jess's face lightened. 'Great idea.' She reached for the tin of olive oil on its tile and passed it to him. 'You know where the onions and garlic are, don't you? And I think there's a cucumber in the fridge.'

He nodded and set about his task, humming as he put the kettle on and prepared to skin some tomatoes.

Food. One of the great levellers. Rose had never expected the two of them to find a common ground so quickly, but find it they seemed to have. If the kitchen was where they could find harmony, she certainly wouldn't complain. She suspected that she had Eve to thank for brokering the peace, but she wasn't going to ask; just accept it for what it was for as long as it lasted. Terry had taken himself off to grapple with whatever financial anxiety was still bothering him. He had tried to explain to them the problem he was trying to solve while they had been having coffee at Lucignano, but she had lost track of the detail. It was definitely better that he sorted it out on his own. Eve had gone upstairs to change for a swim.

With nothing else to do, Rose drifted towards the pool, where Anna and Rick were soaking up the sun. They lay motionless on adjacent loungers, islands in a sea of coffee cups, glasses, suntan cream, books and flip-flops. They looked asleep, their hands touching to bridge the gap between them. She studied them, unexpectedly almost converted to the tattoo winding around her daughter's torso. Beside the dragons and other indeterminate shapes on Rick's arms and chest, Anna's flowers seemed modest and even decorative.

She felt an arm around her shoulder. 'How can you resist?' Eve had changed into her swimsuit and was leading her to the edge. The water, blue and almost motionless apart from one or two struggling insects that had skimmed too close to the surface, was irresistibly inviting in the heat.

Rose swiftly stripped off her shorts and T-shirt to reveal her swimsuit. 'Last one in's a wuss!'

The splash from their synchronised jumps elicited startled shouts of objection from Anna and Rick, who sat up at once as they were showered with water. Rick picked up a beach ball and, tossing it into the air, leaped in too. Anna was right behind him, her long hair flying. Once they surfaced, he swam with strong strokes to the ball and flipped it up and over to Rose. Within minutes the four of them had begun a fast and furious game of water volleyball, screaming and shouting with laughter. They only stopped when

Simon eventually came to stand on the edge of the pool to tell them that lunch was ready.

They clambered out, dried themselves and wandered up to the walnut tree, where the others were waiting. Food was passed around, drink distributed; a couple of insistent wasps were flicked away. The baby monitor that Jess had put on the table remained silent.

The atmosphere round the table seemed markedly more relaxed than it had been so far. Rose hoped she wasn't imagining the improvement simply because that was what she longed for. Without the children to distract, the conversation turned around what they might do once the day had cooled off a little.

'Well I'm doing absolutely nothing,' announced Eve, as she loaded her fork with Simon's *panzanella*. 'I'm going to take a siesta under a fan, then, when it's a bit cooler, I'm doing a bit of pool work. Anyone got any better suggestions?'

'The kids'll be up soon,' said Adam, tapping the top of the baby alarm. 'But Simon and I thought we might at least make a start on the shelter by the pool. Then it'll be done.' He was obviously dying to get stuck into the task.

'If no one wants me, I thought I might take my paints and start a new canvas,' said Rose. 'If I'm going to have anything to sell at Trevarrick, I'd better get painting.'

'You'll never do enough to fill a shop,' laughed Anna. 'Aren't you being a bit overambitious?'

'Not at all. You haven't heard the latest. Adam's putting in some of his work and we're going to run our online business from there too. But we're going to be taking work by other people as well. Did I tell you that?'

Anna shook her head.

'They'll all be local, though,' Rose explained. 'That's the criterion. Have you seen Jemma Dowling's jewellery, for instance? Or Ali Kent's driftwood sculptures? Fantastic stuff. Those are the kinds of things we'll be selling too. All carefully selected by us, of course!' She grinned at Adam, who nodded his head in support.

The shop had been Simon's idea. He had, of course, been the one who had consistently encouraged her to take up her painting

369

again. Once she had settled at Trevarrick, she couldn't resist the temptation and began to put her spare time to good use. She soon rediscovered how therapeutic she found the work. When he saw her Cornish landscapes and still lifes stacked up in her room at Trevarrick, he had been excited. 'You can't hide these away,' he'd protested. 'I'm sure people staying here would love them, for a start. They'd make very classy souvenirs.' He hadn't said anything more, but had obviously been brooding on the subject when a day or so later he sprang his idea on her. 'What about the stable on the other side of the road from Trevarrick?' he suggested. 'It doesn't look as if anyone's used it for years, and it would be the perfect location for a hotel shop.'

Flattered by his faith in her but certain Jess would hate the idea of any more building work, she had laughed at the thought. Life at Trevarrick was only just getting back to normal after the disruption of the pool building and then the relaunch of the hotel. The last thing Rose wanted was to be the cause of any more upheaval. More than that, the sale of the London house had gone through and she was about to move from the hotel into her cottage. She had plenty on her plate to be going on with. However, without thinking, she had mentioned Simon's idea as a joke at supper with Adam and Jess one night. Jess had laughed the idea off as Rose had, but Adam took it more seriously.

'You know, there might be something in that.' He scratched his beard as he spoke, thoughtful. 'I'd love some of my bowls and plates to be sold at the hotel. They are local craftsmanship after all. I won't stop the exhibition work,' he reassured a suddenly anxious-looking Jess. 'But this could be something that would work for both of us, and we could help other local artists too – give them a new outlet.'

By the end of the evening, he had convinced both of them that that was what should happen. Jess's agreement was only on condition that Simon would be responsible for the design of the conversion. Whatever else she might have felt about him, she trusted him to come up with something that would fit exactly into the idiom of Trevarrick.

'If it all goes according to plan, we'll be opening at the end of the summer holidays.' Rose raised her eyebrows inquisitively at Simon, who responded with a confirming nod. 'So I might as well add to our stock when I've got the chance.' The additional truth was that she couldn't imagine a finer way to spend the late afternoon than by losing herself alone in the landscape. She wouldn't return up the hill to her old favourite spot, where the memories would crowd in too fast. Instead, she would walk in a new direction and see what she could find.

'Actually, Mum, there's something I'd like to do with you, if you wouldn't mind.' Jess spoke up. 'Before I do anything else, I'd really like to go to where Dad died. Once I've done that, I think I'll feel better about being here again. I don't know why, but it feels right. I'd like you to be there, though.'

Simon got up and started to clear the plates. Eve rose to help him.

'I'd like that too,' added Anna, before she turned to Rick. 'You wouldn't mind, would you?'

Rick draped his arm round her shoulder. 'Not a bit. You do what you've gotta do. If he's up for it, I'll give Dylan another swimming lesson. Without those bands this time. And then I promised him we'd go look for dinosaurs in the olive grove.' He made a face, as if to ask *Why?*

The others laughed.

'In that case, why don't I have the gorgeous Dani,' offered Eve. 'Then Adam and Jess are free to do what they want. I'd love that.' She disappeared in the direction of the house with the serving plates.

'Well that's settled then. Let's wait till it's a bit cooler, then of course I'll go with you.' Rose was quietly delighted. Her painting could wait. She hadn't expected their two daughters to ask to visit the spot so soon, if at all. But to go with them so that the three of them could remember Daniel together, for however long they wanted, would perhaps bring her daughters some of the acceptance they still needed to find. She reached for her glass and, smiling, raised it.

'To Daniel. Wherever you are. We all still miss you, darling.'

There was a moment of silence before the others at the table followed suit, echoing her toast. 'To Dad.' ' To Daniel.'

Rose looked over at Simon. He was staring at the table, apparently lost in thought. He twisted the thin chain he wore around his wrist, then, as if aware of her gaze, he raised his head and they exchanged a supportive smile.

The sharp ringtone of a mobile interrupted the moment. Terry stood up as if he'd been shot.

'Not Mango Books again! For God's sake.' He felt in his back pocket and pulled out his phone, but it was silent. He sat down again with a sigh of relief. Anna and Rick were busy looking under the towels they'd dropped on the ground. Rose glanced around for her own phone before she remembered she'd left it inside. Then she spotted the culprit. Eve had left her BlackBerry on the floor by her chair. Rose picked it up to take to the house for her, but Eve was already on her way back to the table, carrying a bowl of fruit and a pile of small plates. Rose glanced at the caller ID and stopped still. She just managed to prevent her jaw from dropping as her assumptions about Eve and Terry were abruptly tossed into the air all over again. As she double-checked to make sure she wasn't mistaken, Eve briskly took the phone from her hand. 'I told you the Rutherford Agency never sleeps, didn't I?'

Beside her, Terry gave an exaggerated groan as he put his arms behind his head and stretched out his legs. 'You're not joking.'

'Sorry, darling. I should have left it inside,' said Eve. She looked to see who it was. Her eyes widened and she quite definitely reddened a little, even if Rose was the only one who noticed, before flicking the phone to silent and switching it off. 'It's no one who matters. They can wait.' She passed Terry the fruit bowl and kissed his cheek. He looked as startled by her unexpected show of affection as the rest of the table, but grunted contentedly and raised his hand to her face.

Rose had no doubt now about the identity of the caller. She had thought that perhaps a work contact of Eve's shared the same name. Will was a common enough name, after all. But Eve's reaction had confirmed her initial reaction.

'Fruit?' Eve passed the bowl. Rose caught her eye over the pile of nectarines and peaches and gave the smallest shake of her head to convey her disbelief at what she had just seen.

Eve answered with a confident smile. 'They shouldn't have called,' she said by way of explanation. 'But it's nothing to worry about.'

Rose gave her a look as she reached for a peach. She wished she could be as certain.

Acknowledgments

As always, I want to thank my terrific and tireless agent and friend, Clare Alexander. My novels wouldn't happen at all without her.

Huge thanks are also due to:

My eagle-eyed editor Kate Mills, as well as Susan Lamb and their formidable publishing team – with a special shout-out for Jemima Forrester, Gaby Young and Louisa MacPherson.

Lizy Buchan for being at the end of the phone, always with sage advice about writing, life, and everything else.

Julie Sharman for listening (a lot) and reading and being brave enough to say what she thought.

Sue James and Tessa Hilton for their unstinting support, and Gaby Huddart for an idea she gave me on a train that turned into much more.

Sue Fletcher, Nick Stuart, Martin Neild and Tessa Kerwood for some glorious Italian days.

Sally O'Sullivan and Aisling Foster who spent our all-too-brief holiday trying to come up with the perfect title.

Rebel Rebel, one of the best florists in town – www.rebelrebel.co.uk

And most of all, my long-suffering husband Robin who puts up with more than he should have to, and our three sons, Matt, Nick and Spike.

Facebook facebook.com/FannyBlakeBooks
Twitter @FannyBlake1